At various times, four young ladies attended Miss Gordon's Seminary in Bath. All of them had a wish for the future, and they each discovered that wishes don't always come true in the way one expects!

Harriet Ogbrook wanted position, and her launch into Society brought her a fateful introduction to an earl.

Lucinda Winterton wanted the one thing her life had been lacking—someone to love her, and she never gave up hope that one day love *would* come her way.

Elfreda Pride had a loving family but dreamed of bringing her deceased father's dream to fruition. If only she had the money to do so....

Athena Delaney hoped for stability, having known both the dizzying heights of extravagant wealth and the depths of grinding poverty. Yet it was her fate to be charmed by a man who was everything she wanted to escape.

Four women, four dreams, four loves.

handing back the list. "I shall look forward to

Regency England: 1811-1820

*"It was the best of times,
it was the worst of times...."*

As George III languished in madness, the pampered and profligate Prince of Wales led the land in revelry and the elegant Beau Brummel set the style. Across the Channel, Napoleon continued to plot against the English until his final exile to St. Helena. Across the Atlantic, America renewed hostilities with an old adversary, declaring war on Britain in 1812. At home, Society glittered, love matches abounded and poets such as Lord Byron flourished. It was a time of heroes and villains, a time of unrelenting charm and gaiety, when entire fortunes were won or lost on a turn of the dice and reputation was all. A dazzling period that left its mark on two continents and whose very name became a byword for elegance and romance.

REGENCY QUARTET

BY
JANET GRACE
ELIZABETH LOWTHER
GWYNETH MOORE
GAIL MALLIN

Harlequin Books

TORONTO • NEW YORK • LONDON
AMSTERDAM • PARIS • SYDNEY • HAMBURG
STOCKHOLM • ATHENS • TOKYO • MILAN
MADRID • WARSAW • BUDAPEST • AUCKLAND

Published June 1993

ISBN 0-373-31200-8

REGENCY QUARTET

FROZEN HEARTS
Copyright © Janet Grace
A SINGULAR ELOPEMENT
Copyright © Elizabeth Lowther
PRIDE HOUSE
Copyright © Gwyneth Moore,
THE ECCENTRIC MISS DELANEY
Copyright © Gail Mallin

CONTENTS

Frozen Hearts

Janet Grace

CHAPTER ONE

THE GATEPOSTS WERE VAST and wide, of smooth pale stone. Topping each, some fabulous creature that Harriet could not identify gazed down at the carriage, blank-eyed. Either side of the drive was a neat stone lodge, and barring it were huge wrought-iron gates.

Their coachman had blown a long blast on his horn as they rounded the curve in the road, and already, while the horses stamped restlessly, sensing home, the lodgekeeper was hurrying out, snatching his cap from his head, all smiles, hauling open the great gates.

Harriet's heart was pounding with emotions that almost left her breathless, uncertainties and fears, excitement and delight, a surge of pride, but all surrounded in a haze of disbelief. Was *she* this girl, sitting, paused, beside her wide-eyed maid, at the entrance to what her guidebook had described as "one of the finest houses of the county"? Could *she* really be Harriet, Lady Trenarth, third Countess of Trevereux, at the gates of Trevereux Abbey?

The door of the carriage swung open, and she started, jerked from her thoughts. The man who was now her husband stood looking up at her.

"I am sorry. I did not mean to startle you." He was smiling, but at sight of her stiff face his smile faded, and he continued, grimly polite. "I would like you to meet Mr. and Mrs. Becket. John keeps the gate for me." He paused. "For us," he amended, a touch im-

patiently, then moved back from the doorway to allow the Beckets to make their greetings.

They were full of smiles, "my lady"'s and bobbing
curtsys, their curiosity overt in their eyes. Tongue-tied
with a sudden embarrassment, Harriet hardly knew
what to say. She felt her reaction to be stiff and inadequate, and she withdrew back into her seat, watching with angry doubt and envy her husband's easy talk
with these people. At last the horses jibbed impatiently, he laughed and raised a hand in farewell, and,
closing Harriet's carriage door with barely a glance
within, he returned to his own coach, and the entire
cavalcade moved off down the drive to Trevereux Abbey.

"I WISH YOU to be happy here."

Maximilian Trenarth, the third Earl of Trevereux,
turned reluctantly from where he had been gazing out
of the window, deeply contented to have returned to
the home he loved, and looked across the small drawing-room at his wife.

Even after the weeks of their honeymoon her stiff
responses rebuffed him, and he found himself ad-
dressing her formally, as Lady Trenarth. He still, in his
mind, thought of his wife as Miss Ogbrook, the heiress he had so diligently courted.

So necessarily courted.

Yet despite his urgent need for her fortune, to save
the estates, even to save the Abbey itself, he had
thought at first that he had been that luckiest of men,
one who could find love with the woman that duty to
his inheritance demanded he should marry. At first he
had been certain she cared. But now? She had accepted his offer. He could say no more than that.

He frowned as he looked at her. She sat, apparently composed, a small, slight figure watching him
from wide grey eyes.

Lord Trenarth had long regarded himself, and been regarded, as a most desirable young man. Tall, slim and strong, with dark hair and amused dark eyes, an excellent seat on a horse and a fashionable taste in clothes, he had, all his twenty-eight years, been dogged by eligible females casting their hearts at his feet, and he had enjoyed several liaisons with pert little beauties from the London opera houses and theatres. It had never occurred to him that, having made his choice, and found to his surprise that this small, wide-eyed sparrow of a girl was capturing his heart, she should remain inexplicably immune to his charm.

The night before the wedding he had made the mistake of confiding something of his feelings to a close, but inebriated friend.

"Of course the rich Miss Ogbrook cares for you, Max," the friend had informed him earnestly. He had poked a wavering finger at Max's waistcoat buttons. "Only consider the facts. *She* is the daughter of a rich cit. *You* are an earl. Hey, presto! You are the answer to all her dreams. Stands to reason. Mousy little piece, ain't she, though? Oops, mustn't say that now! Not the done thing. Not of a man's fiancée. No, indeed. Never mind—there's a fat fortune!'

He had hiccupped away, leaving Lord Trenarth hurt and angry, proudly hiding his hopes of more than a marriage of convenience.

His frown deepened at the memories.

"I hope you will be happy here as Lady Trenarth," he began again, a touch impatiently, for she had not responded. "There is too much to show you today. After the journey no doubt you are tired. Tomorrow, if you wish it, I will take you over the house and the gardens."

He moved towards her, where she sat by the fire. The October afternoon was cold.

"Thank you, my lord." She regarded him coolly, all her emotions hidden, frustrating him. "I trust I shall soon learn my way about and conduct everything to your satisfaction." Then, more tartly, rebuffing him, "But please, don't unduly concern yourself on my behalf."

"Of course I concern myself!" He allowed a spurt of irritation through his usual guarded politeness. "You are my wife. This is my home. Our home." He glared at her set face in irritation, then articulated grimly, "I merely wanted us to be happy here, for God's sake!"

"Thank you, my lord." She paused. He watched her twist her handkerchief between her fingers, become aware of what she was doing, frown, and fold it away. "I will do my best."

He stifled an angry sigh. Sometimes he felt as if a sheet of glass stood between them, as if nothing he said could touch her. Other women he could have shaken, shouted at, argued with, pulled into his arms and kissed, losing misunderstandings in passion. But those had been other, turbulent relationships, now put aside. This was his wife, and he felt he did not know her at all.

He was ashamed to find himself relieved when Cornwell the butler glided apologetically into the room.

"You asked to be told when Mr. Hicks arrived, my lord. He is waiting in the office now."

"Thank you, Cornwell. I shall be with him directly." Lord Trenarth turned back to his wife. "Mr. Hicks is my agent for the estates here. I have to see him now. I trust you will be comfortable here?"

"Yes, of course," Harriet replied. "Please, don't keep Mr. Hicks waiting."

She turned back towards the fire. As Lord Trenarth left he was unhappily certain that they parted
with mutual relief.

Harriet thought she had been left alone, and was
startled when a quiet voice at her shoulder asked, "Is
there anything you require, your ladyship?"

For a moment Harriet experienced again the panic
that had overtaken her as she had been welcomed by
all the staff of Trevereux Abbey. Unlike her father's
servants, they did not line up silently, knowing their
place and keeping their distance. These were a staff
half of whom had known "his lordship" from a boy,
who regarded themselves as part of the family, and
who were held by her husband in great affection. She
had felt very much the outsider, despite the protestations of welcome. She had not felt like the lady of the
house.

"I will take a tray of tea, if you please, Cornwell,"
she said, conscious that she was issuing her first order, and not quite meeting his eye. "With some cake."

"Certainly, my lady."

He bowed and glided out.

Harriet let out a long sigh. She leaned back in her
chair, and let her eyes drift around the room.

The white-painted panelling was restful. One wall
was almost covered by framed watercolours painted by
the family: views of the park, of pet dogs long since
deceased, of brothers or sisters. Her husband had told
her who they were when they first came in, but she had
forgotten. The long sash windows had green brocade
curtains, faded now on the folds, and the carpet was
worn where others of the family had stretched their
feet towards the blaze. It was known as the small
drawing-room, she remembered; a family room, cosy
and informal. And she realised again with a small
shock that now she was one of the family.

Slowly she smiled.

It was only later, though, when she had pleaded exhaustion after the journey, and had escaped dinner with her husband by requesting her meal on a tray in her room, that at last she felt she could relax.

Harriet leant on the sill of the open bedroom window and stared out, relishing the sharp cold of the air against her face, savouring the unaccustomed country smells, so different from the familiar soot of London. The early dusk was fast closing over the sloping lawns, the cedar trees, the lake and the parkland beyond. A few late birds winged through the gloom and into the shelter of the trees.

Behind her Susan, her maid, was chattering on as she unpacked the mound of trunks, valises, and bandboxes that Mr. Ogbrook had deemed essential for his only child on her honeymoon.

"And just think," Susan was saying, "that Mrs. Wellow, the housekeeper, said that this bedroom has always belonged to the Countesses of Trevereux, every one. Always. This very room! Fancy!" She paused and sat back on her heels, gazing about her in wonderment, as if expecting trails of such past glories still to be hanging ghostly about the furniture. Harriet laughed, and turned to face her, closing the window.

"You make it sound as if they were in here with their ruffs, or even wimples! There have only been three Countesses of Trevereux!"

"And you are the third!" Susan's face was filled with simple pride.

"Yes," Harriet echoed slowly. "I am the third."

And suddenly her doubts were swept aside by a fierce burst of satisfaction.

I achieved it, she thought.

After all they said, I did it.

I married an earl.

CHAPTER TWO

LYING IN THE GREAT four-poster bed that night, thinking of the other women who had been brought as wives to Trevereux Abbey, to lie, and to love and to give birth, here where she lay, Harriet waited. Maybe tonight, her first night in his home, he would come to her.

She had long ago dismissed Susan, and lay now against the pillows, watching the moving shadows cast by the single candle burning on the table beside her, across the flowers and folds of the bed curtains, up under the great canopy that stretched above her. The great bedposts cast long pillars of black, stretching into the darkness that cloaked the corners of the room. When at last she heard his footsteps on the landing, the quiet words spoken to his valet before the door to his room was closed, followed by the long silence, then she knew that he would not come. She blew out the candle, and lay staring into the blackness.

All her doubts rushed back. She thought about what she had done.

She had known for a long time that she must marry an earl. Ever since her first year at Miss Gordon's exclusive Bath seminary, when she was thirteen years old.

Her father had chosen it for her after Mama had died, hoping that she would make the sort of well-connected friends who would best help her through a London season and on to the marriage her fortune

deserved. Hoping she would gain the polish a rich cit's
daughter needed to move up in the world. It had been
a lonely time, that first year, for a shy and much-loved
only child, a time made bitter by the spiteful taunting
of sharp-eyed, sharp-tongued Maria Vintner.

"Ogbrook, hogbrook! Washed the pig dirt off your
skirts yet? You'll never learn to act the lady! I don't
know why Miss Gordon took you in at this school.
What is your papa?" She would lean forward, feigning interest. "Is he a knight? Is he an earl?" Then,
laughing at Harriet's flushed face fighting back the
tears, she would answer her own questions. "A shop-
keeper in a grubby apron, more like!"

Then the wonderful day when Lady Jane Wallespie, tall and beautiful, leaving soon for her London
début, had rounded on Maria.

"Leave the poor child alone, Maria. It is you who
sound straight from the pigsties, with your ugly jeers."
She had turned then and smiled at Harriet. "You wait.
I dare say Miss Ogbrook will put us all in the shade
one day when she marries an earl!" And she had
strolled away with her friends, already half gone from
the rest of them into the sophisticated adult world.

"She'll need all her father's shop-soiled gold to buy
an earl," Maria had muttered, "for she has no looks
to catch one." But she had muttered it quietly. Lady
Jane Wallespie was a goddess to the younger girls.

Soon afterwards Maria had left the seminary, and
Harriet had gone on to make friends. But she had
never forgotten. And although she never spoke of it
except in jest, irrationally, deep inside, she knew that
she needed to show the Marias of this world. Even to
show herself. She needed to marry an earl.

Her London Season had hardened Harriet's secret
determination. Her vast fortune, and the dowager
Lady DeMoyne, whom her father had paid extravagantly to sponsor her, had ensured that Harriet was

received everywhere. But to be received was not to be accepted, and Harriet had grown accustomed to hearing herself referred to as "that heiress, y'know, the rich cit's daughter," and known that bets had been laid as to who would walk away with the rich cit's fortune.

"It sickens me to hear them speak so," Harriet fumed to Lady DeMoyne, returning from a crowded musical evening which had featured a scraping string quartet, and a shrill Italian soprano, both largely ignored by the gossiping audience. "Not for myself, I am used to such casual spite, but for my father. He is a good and caring man. I am *not* ashamed of him, and I refuse to be made so."

The dowager shrugged, shifting her massive bulk against the velvet squabs as the coach jolted over the cobbles. Harriet felt rather than saw the surge of movement in the darkness.

"It is nothing. New money is always despised, but it will buy the goods all the same. Invited everywhere, accepted at Almack's, and a Court presentation next week. No one asks for more. And if you are angry at the chatter of fools—" she gave a fat chuckle "—it gives a sparkle to your eyes and a sharpness to your answers that has done you no harm that I can see. Sir Richard Hart, Lord Clayden, and Viscount Ellerby were fairly jostling for your company tonight."

Harriet frowned and shook her head.

"They jostled for my fortune, not my company," she said.

"Everyone here has something to sell," the dowager responded tartly. "Looks, connections, titles, or riches. You have riches. Sell them, like everybody else."

So Harriet had hardened her resolve, and was to be seen everywhere, her small slight figure defiantly straight against the gossip, her conversation scrupulously polite, and her wide grey eyes regarding those she danced with with a disconcerting directness, putting the less brazen fortune-hunters to shame. And she had despised them all, brazen or not. Not one could touch her heart.

One night, she could still remember it with burning clarity, she had seen a man who had made her catch her breath. She could still not say exactly why, except that he was tall, with very dark hair, and dark eyes beneath straight black brows, and he had looked about him coolly, as if he was unimpressed by the parading crush of Lady Buckler's ball. All that evening she had remained aware of his presence, despite the stream of hopefuls coming to lead her to the dance floor. She had known exactly when he retired to the card tables, and reserved jealous pangs for the girl he had escorted to the late supper. And then, when the night was almost over, he had approached Harriet's dowager chaperon.

"Why, Max, you wicked man, I have not seen you for an age." Lady DeMoyne rapped him on the arm with her fan, the ivory struts clacking together. "Where have you been?"

"Lady DeMoyne." He was smiling as he bowed neatly over her hand. "I have been kept out of Town on family business. And I see I have missed the arrival of the newest and brightest faces this Season. Make amends now, and introduce me to your protégée."

He turned then, with a small bow, and smiled at Harriet. She felt her heart thudding, and a flush creep up her cheeks, but she managed to hold out her gloved hand very properly to the newcomer, after the dowager leaned towards her and said, "My dear, allow me to introduce Lord Trenarth, the Earl of Trevereux."

"Miss Ogbrook. Ah, this set is just finishing. Would you care to join me for the next dance?"

She shot an anxious look of enquiry at her chaperon, for young Walter Mellet had sworn he would be
back to claim her, but Lady DeMoyne gave a sharp
nod of approval. Mellet was a younger son of no con-
sequence. Lord Trenarth was an earl. With her hand
resting lightly on his arm, stealing shy glances up at his
face, filled with wonderment at this sudden turmoil of
her emotions, Harriet walked out to take her place on
the dance floor.

So it had begun. The happiest days of Harriet's life,
when waking each day brought new hopes of seeing
him. To her wondering disbelief, over the weeks that
followed, increasingly frequently he would be there, at
soirées, at dances, joining their party at the opera. The
chaperoning dowager had smiled benignly, and people began to talk.

Harriet knew that she was too small, and that her
hair remained an obstinate mousy brown. She would
never be a beauty. She accused her father of paternal
fondness when he told her she had fine grey eyes and
a mischievous smile, both of which could break hearts.
She was certain men had only ever admired her for her
fortune.

Yet now... now she almost believed that this man
loved her for herself. He had none of the ingratiating
airs of the fortune-hunters who beset her. His quiet
teasing and his shrewd conversation, catching her unawares with laughter, the crisp dark curl of his hair
against the immaculate white of his cravat, the crin-
kle at the corner of his eyes when he smiled at
her... she was dazzled with delight. And he was an
earl! It was like living in a fairy tale.

Looking back, filled with shame at how naïve she
had been, she knew it had all been too good to be true.

The memory of how she had discovered the truth
could still cause Harriet to blush, and hot tears to well
into her eyes, no matter how angrily she blinked. They

ran now unheeded, down her cheeks, wetting her ears
and her hair and the lavender-scented linen of the pil-
lowcase, as she still gazed blindly into the blackness of
her room.

It had been at some dreadful crush, too hot almost
to breathe, when an arrogant young man with a cravat as tall as a Grecian pillar, and shirt-points like
dray-horses' blinkers, had stepped heavily back on to
the flounce of her dress, and ripped it half way.

Her companion had turned to deliver a blistering
put-down, but she had quickly laid a hand on his arm.

"Truly, my lord. It is not important. I can mend it
in a trice." She smiled up at him, flushed and bright-
eyed, and the comment had withered on Lord Trenarth's lips. He had smiled back down at her.

"Are you accomplished, then, as well as beautiful,
Miss Ogbrook?"

"I declare, you are easily satisfied, my lord, if you
deem a woman accomplished who can merely sew a
seam!"

"Well . . ." He paused as if pondering the matter, a
smile teasing the corners of his mouth. "I do demand
laughing grey eyes, hair soft as silk *and* an irresistible
smile as well, you must understand."

His dark eyes were laughing at her.

"Those are not generally considered to be accom-
plishments, Lord Trenarth. Would you not also demand fluency in French and Italian, familiarity with
the major authors, a fine sketch-book filled with
landscapes and likenesses, and a talented perform-
ance on the pianoforte to accompany a strong soprano voice?"

"It always surprises me how very different are the
talents a man *does* appreciate in a woman, compared
to those the female kind feels he ought to appreciate!
But you terrify me, Miss Ogbrook. Are *you* such a
prodigy of multiple talents?"

"No, my lord. I have to disappoint you. I am proficient in but two of those areas, and I shall leave you to ponder which while I mend my dress."

She left the Earl of Trevereux regarding the unfortunate sprig of fashion who had done the damage as if he were somewhat lower than an earthworm, and made her way upstairs. Seated among the abandoned shawls and pelisses, stitching busily with the needle and thread kept in her reticle for just such emergencies, she overheard some other girls enter the adjoining room.

Harriet had an honest nature, and a dislike of eavesdropping. She was about to make her presence known. But the first words she heard left her stunned. White with shock, she was trapped, and had to hear.

"Isn't it *awful* seeing poor Max reduced to chasing after that drab little Ogbrook girl? The Earl of Trevereux forced to toady to a vulgar cit's daughter. Driven to where he must betray his heart, and sacrifice lifelong happiness for a despicable fortune."

"My mama says that at least he has the courage and sense of duty to do what is necessary to save Trevereux Abbey. He has already sold off his father's racing stables, and the town house, but it was not enough. She says it may be unfortunate now, but his grandchildren will thank him."

"Only if they never meet their great-grandparents!"

"Come now, Isabel. At least she doesn't make a great parade of her riches. And she is the wealthiest catch of the Season."

"Well, I think she's a pathetic dab of a thing. To think of her taking the place of Charlotte as the Countess of Trevereux—it is beyond bearing. Charlotte told me—" here the voice was lowered conspiratorially, "—that Max almost broke down in the anguish of telling her that their understanding could come to nothing. He was broken-hearted, but reso-

lute in his duty, and what could she do? To see him so
noble and so stricken. She was forced to accept it
gracefully, and now poor Charlotte is left abandoned. I pity her from the bottom of my heart."

"You make too much of it, Isabel. I knew of no
understanding."

"No, indeed, I do not exaggerate, for Charlotte told
me herself. It was a secret arrangement between the
families, and luckily so, or how could she have stood
the humiliation?"

"I can almost find it in me to pity Miss Ogbrook if
what you say is true."

"Miss Ogbrook? Oh, pooh, Lizzie. Don't be so
charitable."

"To be courted by a man whose heart is given elsewhere, and then merely for her money? To know that
any promises of affection or admiration must be no
more than expediencies. Yes, I pity her."

"Nonsense. Such arrangements happen all the time.
And a girl of such vulgar breeding cannot have the
sensibilities you would expect from one of us. She is
only a common little title-hunter. Why, she will get
precisely what she wants. Leave your shawl here with
mine, or we shall never find them again."

When they had gone Harriet found she could not
move. It was as if she had frozen, needle poised over
the damaged hem. Then like a jerking marionette she
tacked the tear, broke the thread and neatly stored it
away again in her silk and gauze reticule. She walked
back down into the throng with exaggerated care, told
her chapèron that she suffered from a sudden megrim, and, without a word of farewell to the Earl of
Trevereux, departed for home.

She cancelled all engagements for a week, bedev-
illed by headaches and lethargy, numbed with the hurt
of those echoing words that circled endlessly inside her
head. She could not bring herself to confess to Lady

DeMoyne the folly of her dreams and the pain as they
had shattered. She buried the pain deep within herself.

One morning she awoke dry-eyed and pronounced
herself better. Pinning one of the white roses he had
sent round for her onto her sash, and furiously tearing the others apart as she flung them away, she made
her choice.

If she could not marry the Earl of Trevereux for
love, why, then, she would marry him for convenience. She could despise him as a fortune-hunter. Despise him for abandoning the girl he loved just for the
sake of wealth. But she would marry him. After all,
hadn't she vowed she would do it? He needed a fortune. If not hers, he would hunt for some other. She
wanted a title. His would do very well. She would hold
up her head, be glad of her frozen heart, and show
them all that vulgar Miss Ogbrook could marry an
earl. She convinced herself she did not care.

The marriage took place at the end of the summer,
at St. George's, Hanover Square. Mr. Ogbrook paid
for every splendour, while anxiously asking if she was
certain she would be happy. His daughter was reaching social heights he had not dreamed possible when
he had first taken her to the seminary in Bath, and he
worried at her cold determination.

"I had hoped you would find happiness," he ventured tentatively, for he felt he hardly knew this cool,
polished young lady.

"But I have, Papa! How could you think otherwise? I am going to marry an earl. A peer of the realm.
What more could any girl wish for? I shall be the
Countess of Trevereux. All my dreams come true! Be
happy for me."

Her father sighed, and stifled his misgivings, not
knowing what more to say. Besides, he liked the young
man who had asked for his daughter's hand. Far from

being the affected fop Mr. Ogbrook had dreaded, he seemed a fair and level-headed young man. Perhaps, he told his daughter, it would all work out for the best.

The honeymoon tour of the Lakes had passed in a whirl of bumping carriages, obsequious innkeepers, boat-trips, walks, and dramatic views of brooding cloud-swirled mountains reflected in still dark waters. Of endless discussion of the scenery, and none of themselves.

And, buried as a deep unhealing wound beneath these memories, was the memory of the first night when he had come to her. Despite the preparations of Lady DeMoyne, she had waited rigid with fear. How could she relax with this man, knowing that each of them was merely playing a part? He was affecting love for her; she was desperate for him to perceive in her no more than civilised indifference.

He had been tender with her. But afterwards she had wept silently, desperate with the shock, the pain and the indignity, and most of all with the heart-rending certainty that he was wishing her to be someone else. That in his heart he yearned for the girl he truly loved, a girl called Charlotte. He had lain beside her, stroking her hair, and told her he would not distress her again until they knew each other better, till she was ready. But his face had been set and grim when he'd left, and he had not come to her room again.

They were held apart by the cool courtesy that Harriet dared not let lapse, and she wondered now if he ever would.

It was just as well, she told herself, that she secretly despised him.

It was a long time before she slept.

CHAPTER THREE

"HARRIET! I WAS NOT expecting you down so soon. Would you care for some coffee?"

The Earl of Trevereux was at the far end of the great rosewood dining table, near the long window, sitting sideways, one elbow on the table, one leg nonchalantly crossed up on to the other to provide a rest for the *Morning Post.* One hand held a page of the paper poised, the other cradled a cup of coffee. Before him on the table a large silver tray on clawed feet supported a matching silver coffee-pot. He smiled at her, surprised and pleased, and swung round, pushing the newspaper aside, and standing to pull back a chair for her.

Harriet ventured a smile back at him, relieved to see him so relaxed. She had been uncertain what was expected of her on this first morning, and had chivvied Susan to hurry through her dressing, loath to appear unwilling to fill her role. She had never been invited to any of the great stately homes, but had heard tales of terrifying formality and strictest protocol, where to break a rule of etiquette was to forfeit all chance of further invitations. She had been afraid, not knowing what was customary at Trevereux Abbey. But not, it would seem, terrifying formality.

"Thank you, sir. I have already disposed of an excellent trayful of toast and hot chocolate up in my room..." Harriet paused.

She had been about to refuse, but suddenly it seemed easier to accept the coffee, and have some reason to sit with him. Without the schedule that had been imposed upon them by the visits and excursions of the honeymoon, Harriet was at a loss as to how she should fill her time, or occupy his.

" . . . but yes, I would like coffee."

In response to the earl's tug on the bell-pull, Cornwell the butler came silently in.

"Would your ladyship wish your proper place prepared at the table?" he enquired, reproach in his voice, making to pull back the chair at the far end of the great table. "I would have made it ready, but his lordship has customarily breakfasted alone."

Harriet regarded his expressionless face down the expanse of dark polished wood and flushed uncertainly. Was she only imagining his disapproval that she should have ventured down to the dining-room? Should she sail majestically down the room with cries of, "But of course I expect my place to be prepared, Cornwell. See to it!" Did she dare?

"Don't be a fool, Cornwell," her husband remarked mildly. "Lady Trenarth will sit here beside me, where I can at least have the pleasure of distinguishing who she is. You will please lay a place here every morning, in case she should wish to join me. For now we just require fresh coffee for two."

"As you wish, my lord."

The butler bowed stiffly and withdrew.

It was a tiny incident, and her husband paid it no more attention, but it revived all Harriet's uncertainties. The day seemed to stretch before her filled with hidden pitfalls for one who had no idea what was expected of Lady Trenarth, Countess of Trevereux. She listened while he read from an article in the *Morning Post* discussing the fierce repression of renewed Luddite riots in Nottingham.

"I am sorry for such men," she said defiantly, hoping perhaps to anger or shock him, "forced either to break the law while they break the machinery, or to let their families starve."

She was perversely annoyed when he agreed.

"You are right. The pace of change in the textile industries can be desperately hard on those men whose skills are no longer required. The law must be upheld, but, as you say, with understanding of the plight of those who suffer. But I shall not let political argument spoil this morning. You must see your new home."

He stood up and stretched, smiling down at her. He was plainly happy this morning, and Harriet was finding it hard to hold back against his good humour. She looked away from him, this man who had forced himself to marry her for her money.

"Fetch a bonnet and shawl," he said, as she finished her coffee, "and I will show you the Abbey itself while the sun is still shining. There are some ugly clouds gathering."

They went out of the heavy oak main door, across the gravel still scored by yesterday's carriage wheels, through formal gardens in the old style, then across lawns at the side of the house. Here the house walls were not brick, but stone, weathered and lichened, with small deep-set windows.

Abruptly, at the turn of a corner, incongruous and Gothic, the wall of the house became the wall of the towering Abbey ruin. Harriet stopped, and stood staring.

The great end wall of the nave still survived, pointing accusingly heavenwards, broken only by the gaping doorway, and the vast circular window. Bare of all trace of glass, the window now drew its colour from the cloud-massed sky beyond. Jackdaws circled round the broken stones that topped the wall, their harsh

chacking calls punctuating the warm stillness of the
morning.

"The Abbey was founded here in 1253," the earl
said. He stood, hands thrust into the pockets of his
buckskin breeches, head back, gazing up at the birds.
Harriet stood back a little, watching the set of his
shoulders, the line of his throat, disturbed by him, resentful of his confident ease. "It was a busy and
thriving community for three hundred years. You will
see some of their rooms. Much of the living quarters—dormitories, refectory, wash-house and dairy—
were incorporated into the early house, this stone
wing. Even the cloisters, and the undercroft, which
has long been our best wine cellar. Henry the Eighth
wreaked all the dire destruction upon the Church, of
course, and upon the Benedictine monks who had
lived here, then kindly donated the remaining land and
buildings to my grateful forebear for loyal services
rendered. Not a tale in which I find I take great pride."

He took her arm, his hand warm through the thin
muslin of her sleeve.

"Come inside."

He led the way up a couple of wide, moss-crusted
stone steps, and through the huge doorway. No trace
of the roof remained. Although the far wall still stood,
it had been more extensively damaged than the front,
and much of one side-wall had gone, almost to ground
level in places. But the other side was complete, part
of the present house, and topped with roofing, with
ornate lead gutters, and down-pipes that flowed out to
the floor of the church. Sweetbriar had rooted in the
worn stones, with honeysuckle and the white fluff of
old man's beard. Brambles were beginning to invade
the grassy floor, their leaves the dark red of autumn.

The couple were standing in the centre of the ancient building. Harriet gazed around her, awed and
entranced by the majesty that still clung to the stones

in their ruinous decay. The air was so still now that it seemed to hold its breath, the clouds darkening overhead. Lord Trenarth turned to face Harriet.

"So, what do you think of our Abbey?" When she paused he continued lightly, "My cousin hates it. She calls it a monstrous Gothic horror, and swears it is the very place where phantom monks will parade at midnight, chanting ghastly dirges as they swing the ghostly incense! She will not walk here alone, even in broad daylight."

"Oh, no!" Harriet spoke with an unexpected passion, for the place had moved her strangely, as if the mute memories of the gaunt stones were filled with poignant beauty. His flippant tones infuriated her. "How can she fear such a place? Can you not see? It is beautiful! Old bones long ago picked clean and forgotten by the men of greed and ambition: given back to the seasons, to the sun and wind, moss and lichen, flowers and birds. A silent celebration of the men who built it."

She flushed and halted, embarrassed by her own outburst, angry that she had betrayed any emotion before him. He was watching her intently, startled, and she looked away, but abruptly he took her unwilling hands in his.

"You are right," he said. "And you have expressed my own feelings better than I could myself. I have loved coming here ever since I was a child." He paused, then laughed, giving her a sideways look. "If only to escape the attentions of my foolish cousin!"

He turned and pointed to the highest point of the front wall, above the ruined window.

"When I was twelve I climbed up and sat astride there."

She drew in a quick breath of horror, and turned on him.

"You could not! What folly! It is so dangerous! So high! The stones are crumbling. You might have been killed!"

He laughed aloud at her then.

"All twelve-year-old boys do things that are horribly dangerous. My friend the gamekeeper's son came with me. Our sons will be just the same. And I dare say I shall tan them afterwards just as my father tanned me."

He had spoken casually, but, flushing in angry confusion, Harriet turned away, and he paused, frowning.

It was just then that the first great drops of rain fell, a welcome distraction. Even as they turned to go in, the clouds resolved their indecision and dropped a deluge over the countryside.

Grabbing her hand, Lord Trenarth pulled Harriet after him in a headlong rush, not back the way they had come, but towards the wall of the house, and a small archway she had not noticed. Dodging wildly between the brambles, he dived into the shelter of the arch, pulling Harriet roughly after him. His arm was about her as they both stood, panting and laughing, turning to look back at the wall of water that hissed down beyond them.

"Oh, no! My bonnet! It will be ruined!"

"Take it off. It is dripping wet."

He neatly tipped up her chin with his free hand, and pulled at the green silk ribbons that held it, loosing them, and slipping the bonnet off. The sodden brim sagged sadly in his hand. Harriet laughed a little breathlessly.

"I will have to throw it away."

"I will buy you another," he said, dropping the offending creation to the ground, and pulling his handkerchief from his waistcoat pocket. Harriet could feel the warmth of his arm through the clinging damp of

her dress where he still held her, pulled a little against
him. With the handkerchief he gently wiped the rain-
drops from her face. Instinctively she closed her eyes.

Her face turned up to his, her lips parted, her breath
still ragged from running, acutely aware of her body
beneath the clinging muslin, her breasts rising and
falling; she knew that she would feel his lips upon
hers. The brief moments that she waited seemed an
eternity.

Then his hand was behind her head, bringing her to
him, and the touch of his lips was firm, warm, gently
insistent. For a brief instant delight surged, washing
over her. Then, at the stirrings of her own response,
she panicked, terrified of the emotions they aroused.
She flinched sharply away, and immediately he loosed
his hold upon her.

"There, I have made you wet again," was all he
said, wiping his own face impatiently with his hand,
and giving her the handkerchief. "Come and get
changed or you will become chilled."

He turned away from her, into the dark recess behind them, and opened a small arched door of great
age, which gave immediately on to a short downward
flight of steps and then a long stone-flagged passage.
Light reached them only dimly from the far end.

"I was going to show you all of this," he said over
his shoulder, striding ahead, forcing her almost to run
to keep up. "It is part of the old monastery. But it
must wait."

And through a warren of corridors that left her utterly bemused he led her back eventually to a part of
the house she recognised from the previous day, and
at last to her own bedroom.

"I will leave you to change," he said, and walked
briskly away down the corridor, without looking back.

Harriet could still feel the stroke of his hand as he
wiped her face, the touch of his lips. Scowling, her

hand pressed against her mouth, she watched till he rounded the corner, then slowly opened the door to her room.

Later, when she was dry and changed, she ventured downstairs again, only to be informed by the expressionless Cornwell that his lordship had been called out by his agent, Hicks, and was uncertain when he would return.

"A fire has been lit in the small drawing-room, my lady," he concluded.

"Thank you, Cornwell."

Harriet frowned. She had no wish to sit solitary and dull. Taking a corridor at random, she set off to explore her new home.

But in almost every room was a maid or footman intent upon the grates, or the dusting, sweeping, or polishing, even rehanging freshly washed curtains. Her interruption would cause a glance of horrified surprise, followed by a wooden-faced withdrawal from the room, despite Harriet's anxious protestations that she had no wish to interrupt their work. Eventually defeated by the disruption her progress caused, she retired, dismal and lonely, to the small drawing-room. Taking up the *Morning Post,* she set herself to scan the pages, perversely determined to be able to hold intelligent conversations with her husband, whatever else the limitations of their relationship.

It was not long before she was interrupted. Mrs. Wellow the housekeeper presented herself, and stood stiffly before Harriet, eyes fixed on the wall beyond Harriet's left shoulder.

"I am sorry, my lady. I would have come earlier, but you were busy with his lordship. You will want to discuss arrangements for the day."

Harriet stared at this poker-faced, starched-aproned lady in growing horror. What arrangements, she wondered, did one discuss? Having progressed straight from school to her first Season to marriage, and never having been allowed by a fond father to consider household management, Harriet could find no answer in her frantic thoughts. Yet still Mrs. Wellow waited.

"I don't believe there is anything I wish to discuss today," she managed at last, with what she hoped would pass as unconcern. "Please proceed with all your normal duties."

The stiff face before her seemed to set a little more grimly.

"Very good, your ladyship," said Mrs. Wellow.

Anxious to make amends, Harriet blurted out, "I was pleased to see so much cleaning..." Her voice tailed off, as she waved a hand vaguely towards the rooms she had explored.

Mrs. Wellow gave a curt nod.

"Will that be all, your ladyship?"

"Yes, thank you, Mrs. Wellow."

Harriet watched the retreating bombazined figure with something like despair, a feeling increased when immediately afterwards another large lady presented herself, clutching a list in neat copperplate handwriting.

"Mrs. Ganby, the cook, your ladyship. If you would care to approve the menus for the day?"

Harriet obediently took the list, but although she studied the intended dishes—roast capons, goose pie, pickled salmon, a round of cold spiced beef, a dish of wild mushrooms, fresh greens, boiled potatoes, a ham, a brace of pigeons and a woodcock, glazed carrots, and, eventually, custard pudding, apple tarts, jellies and a syllabub—she could think of nothing to add, no intelligent comment to make.

"That sounds wonderful, Mrs. Ganby," she said, handing back the list. "I shall look forward to it."

At least the cook looked gratified, but she queried,
"There's nothing your ladyship would wish to add?"
and seemed disappointed when Harriet could think of
nothing.

"Very good, your ladyship," she replied gloomily,
and withdrew.

These encounters set the tone of Harriet's first few
days as lady of the house. Unsure of her duties and
responsibilities, with no one to ask, she was lonely and
unhappy, and hid the fact behind a stiff, determined
face. She dreaded her morning encounters with Mrs.
Ganby and Mrs. Wellow.

Her husband was frequently out of the house on
estate business of which she knew nothing. In fair-
ness, he was scrupulous in setting aside some time each
day to be with her, showing her the house, discussing
the portraits in the long gallery, walking in the gardens. But she felt uncomfortable, resentful, certain she
was an unwelcome intrusion in his busy days, that her
talk of exotic Lord Byron's newly published poem *The
Corsair* was of less interest to him than the state of the
cottages at Longborn, or the yield of wheat from Ten-
Acre Field. They seemed sometimes like two strangers, stranded at some distant inn while their coach
horses were changed, searching for polite nothings to
fill an enforced half hour together.

The only other interruption to her days were the
visits of her new neighbours. A stream of them came,
leaving cards, or stopping for a precise half hour.
Cornwell always showed them into the Chinese Room,
and there Harriet would join them, to rack her mind
for conversation, while suffering the gimlet scrutinies
of a suspicious county Society. Her certainty that they
came to criticise made her shy, and overformal. They
left her profoundly uncertain of how she had survived each ordeal, and increasingly determined not to
care.

There was only Susan to talk to, and she brought no comfort. Susan too was finding rural life difficult. She was homesick for the familiar London bustle, and she told Harriet so at tedious length.

In the lonely darkness of those long nights Harriet often wondered why she had ever wished to marry an earl, had ever thought that to be a countess would be a dream come true.

CHAPTER FOUR

"Now that you have had a little time to adjust to your new home," Lord Trenarth remarked one evening, his hand hovering over the chessboard that lay on the baize-covered card table between them, "you may wish to offer some form of entertainment to our neighbours?"

His voice ended in a mild query, as he decided his move. Giving a last wary contemplation of Harriet's pieces, he shifted a knight forward.

On the evenings they spent alone together the earl had been teaching Harriet how to play chess. Somewhat to his surprise she had proved an astute pupil. She had now beaten him on three occasions, and he was obliged to give his game a great deal of concentration. It was with a mixture of amusement and irritation that he watched her poring over the pieces, the glint of battle in her eye, relishing her ability to challenge him. There were times when he wanted to shake from her face her satisfied smile when she succeeded in outwitting him, yet her skill and her pluck held him in admiration.

"It is expected that we should entertain?"

She was chewing her lip, her concentration upon the carved ivory pieces, unconscious of the shawl slipping down to expose her shoulder, and the curl of hair that had escaped its ribbon and lay against her cheek.

"Why, yes, I should say so. But it is by no means essential. The decision is yours."

Harriet sat back from the table and looked at him. She wished she understood him better. At times his twenty-eight years seemed a generation away from her eighteen. When he looked at her sternly her heart beat faster in resentful apprehension. When he smiled at her, he threw her into an angry confusion. But often she could read nothing of his thoughts at all, this man who had only wanted her money. She never had understood him, she realised. Had he not fooled her into thinking he cared, when all the time his circumstances forced him into a marriage of convenience? At least he would never know how much her heart had once been touched. Now, of course, she had ceased to care.

He was watching her now, his dark eyes slightly hooded, the candles casting a moving golden glow over his skin, while the black of his hair was full of shadows. He tugged loose the cravat under his chin, and stretched back in his chair, lacing his fingers behind his head.

"I did not intend to cast you into utter confusion."

Harriet flushed, glancing across at him. A vision had been conjured in her mind of the succession of hawk-eyed visitors who had called, and of herself endeavouring to act as hostess to all of them at once, plus any others her husband should see fit to invite. The prospect frankly terrified her, though she would have died rather than let him know it.

It seemed he read something of this in her face, however, for he sat forward abruptly.

"My dear Harriet. Forget I mentioned it. There is no need whatsoever for us to entertain just yet. People are forgiving of new-married couples."

"No, my lord," she burst out, stung. "Of course we must do something. You are right. It will be expected of us. I was merely wondering what would be appropriate. Do you think a dinner, with an informal dance afterwards?"

"Certainly, if that is what you would like."

"I am afraid I will have to trouble you for a list of those we should invite."

"It will be no trouble at all."

Harriet lost the game of chess that night. She had been stung into suggesting they hold the dance, determined that no one, her husband least of all, should have cause to suggest that the cit's daughter was inadequate in her role as Countess of Trevereux.

With Max's help she sent out a hundred invitations, thirty of which included an invitation for dinner. From his recommendations Mrs. Ganby organised the menus. Mrs. Wellow informed Harriet of what would need to be done in the house, and Harriet duly agreed. Mrs. Wellow organised it.

Apart from writing the invitations Harriet took no part in the preparations at all. She felt unneeded, her presence no more than an interruption in the bustle. She had found a half-completed piece of embroidery on a frame in one of the bedrooms, and began setting despondent stitches in it to fill her time, thinking frustrated and resentful thoughts. What, she wondered despairingly, did countesses do?

The dance took place on a raw November night, when the clouds that had spat miserable drizzle all day cleared away, to allow a sharp frost with a crackle of ice on the puddles. Fires blazed in every room, and the brightness of candles within cast swathes of light out across the gravel to welcome the arrivals.

Anxious to live up to the occasion, Harriet had agonised over her wardrobe. Gifts that her father deemed suitable for a countess hung from every rail, overwhelming her with their various splendours. Eventually she chose a ballgown of rich cream satin, with a glistening silver gauze over-tunic, and scallops of tiny seed-pearls embroidered above the hem. It would, she thought, have passed the dowager Lady

DeMoyne's critical eye. She had been going to wear her pearls with it, but gave in to Susan's wistful plea that she wear the diamond necklace and pendant earrings that had been one of her father's wedding gifts.

As soon as the guests began to arrive she felt she was overdressed. Despite her husband's smiles and compliments, she felt too glitteringly fine beside his cream-coloured breeches with the plain silver buckles, and his dark blue jacket of best superfine. The other ladies, strident in their confident greetings, wore plainer muslins and silks, and looked sideways at her finery. Harriet tilted her chin a little higher as she held out her hand in welcome.

The dinner passed in something of a haze, Harriet barely knowing what she said to those who sat by her. Then there were more arrivals to be greeted, and a progression through to the Long Blue Room for dancing, the numbers being too small to merit opening up the great ballroom.

She walked boldly out on to the floor to lead off the dancing with her husband. She managed a confident smile in answer to his questioning look. But a cry behind her of, "Charlotte! As beautiful as ever! I have not seen you in an age!" and the quick, instinctive glance that her husband gave, sent her wooden-faced through her steps. Her brain might insist that a thousand girls were named Charlotte. Her heart thudded a persistent warning that this would be the one who mattered.

There were duty dances to follow, the earl leading formidable ladies onto the floor, while Harriet suffered the attentions of their husbands, a succession, it seemed, of heavy jowls and red noses beneath sprouting grey eyebrows, tightly stretched waistcoat buttons above heavy feet. Beside her their wives seemed all to peer down at her from thin horsy faces.

"Running a great place like this must keep you busy, Lady Trenarth," she heard time and again, and Harriet would wonder guiltily what it was that she was not doing, as she nodded earnestly and replied, "Yes, indeed, sir, there is so much to be done."

As she danced she heard a snatch of murmured comment.

"A pity she felt the need to trick herself out so fine."

"Well, what can you expect?"

"And the poor child hardly opens her mouth."

"Poor Max, tied to a vulgar mouse!"

Followed by shushings, and giggles.

She might have married her earl, she thought bitterly, but, for the rich cit's daughter, nothing had changed.

It was a relief when she was led back to her seat, and seemed, for a brief moment, to be left alone. For some reason, her eyes sought out her husband. It took a moment to spot him through the throng, bending his head a little to catch something said by a seated girl. The girl gave her head a little toss, making her dark curls bounce, and Max laughed. Then her view was blocked by a tall lady in a strident yellow gown, and Harriet was left irrationally angry, very glad that she did not care what her husband did.

"Don't let these people daunt you!" said a quiet voice beside her.

She swung round. A vast young man was pulling a chair up beside her. He was broad-shouldered, long-legged; the chair vanished beneath him as he sat, and she wondered for its safety. He had fair hair, blue eyes, a bluff, open expression with a teasing smile, and something of a soldierly air.

"If you show dismay they will only sharpen their claws the more. Chin up, and outstare them, as haughty as you please."

Harriet glared at him, an icy retort on her lips. Then she shrugged, and smiled ruefully. His face was kind.

"Oh, dear. Was it so very obvious? You are quite right, of course. But sometimes the imperious glare has a way of wavering."

He laughed. "I am Miles Frampton. We were introduced, but I suspect your eyes had glazed over by then. I have been a friend of Max's since we were boys. It is good to be able to wish him happy, and with such good reason. Please, come and meet my mother and sister. They are not a bit formidable."

Nor were they. Mrs. Frampton was a comfortable woman with a warm smile, her daughter Elizabeth six months younger than Harriet. As she talked, for the first time Harriet felt there might be someone in the locality with whom she could be friends.

She danced with Miles, then again with her husband, who smiled beside her, the accomplished host, politely attentive. Sometimes she suspected she read encouragement and sympathy in his glances at her, and she smiled back a brittle smile, determined he should think her perfectly at her ease. As the music finished another young man appeared before them.

"Max, Max, won't do. To spend the evening dancing with your wife! You will become staid and dull. Besides, you must give us poor commoners who cannot catch an heiress some chance of fun. Run away and dance with my sister. You know she yearns for a sight of you. Lady Trenarth, leave this man who is merely a husband, and dance with me!"

Harriet sensed her husband's irritation, though his response was entirely affable. She was not herself sure that she liked this man, who flashed her a winning boyish grin. But Lord Trenarth stepped back, and so she smiled brightly, took his hand, and allowed herself to be led back into the dance.

"I can understand why Max tries to keep you to himself," the young man said, squeezing her hand as they met and turned with the music. "Anyone would do so. There is something about your eyes... And your smile... why—it is enchanting!"

Harriet raised an eyebrow, but she felt a flush run up her cheeks.

"Are you always so full of compliments for other men's wives, sir?"

Her voice was sharp.

"That depends, of course, upon whether they deserve them, Lady Trenarth." The steps of the dance moved them apart, but he kept his eyes fixed intently upon her face, until they were close enough to speak again. "Just look around you. Half the ladies here are other men's wives, and, well..."

He paused, with an expressive grimace, and Harriet was betrayed into a giggle. He was a personable man, tall and slim, with brown hair and oddly pale hazel eyes.

"You see," he said, watching her laugh, "enchanting!"

"I have to confess, sir," Harriet said, "that I do not remember your name."

"To think that our introduction could have passed you by without notice. I am utterly mortified. Whereas your name, Lady Trenarth, Harriet, is engraved upon my heart!"

"It must have been a very hasty engraving job, sir, and I suspect the space is cramped by many another name," she responded tartly. "But do you have no name of your own?"

"Coningsby. Austin Coningsby." He laid a hand on his heart, and bowed. "Eternally at your service, Lady Trenarth."

"You mentioned a sister. Which is she?"

"Why, she is dancing with Lord Trenarth, of course. There, across the room in the other set. Max, with my dear sister Charlotte."

As the movement of the dance took them apart once again, Harriet stared across the room. Her attention caught by Austin Coningsby's impudent flirting, she had not noticed who Max had joined when he left her. But there could be no mistake. It was the same girl. The girl he had been listening to so attentively earlier.

The stab of jealous anger caught Harriet by surprise. And the twisting ache of hurt. She was suddenly quite certain that this was the Charlotte who had caused her such pain, the girl her husband loved.

She had glossy dark brown hair, which tumbled in artful curls down her back, and bright brown eyes. She was standing very close to Lord Trenarth, head back, laughing up into his face, and he was smiling. It looked as if they shared some secret joke.

Harriet felt very cold. A nudge from the lady on her right was a jolting reminder of her place in the dance, and she forced bright smiles and flippant answers as once again she listened to Austin Coningsby's banter, but her attention was on Austin's sister, as she and Lord Trenarth danced past.

"Oh, Max," she heard Charlotte say, "you must have missed me. It has been so long..." and then they were out of earshot.

Harriet was flushed as the dance ended, her thoughts whirling and furious. Did everyone in the room know about Max and Charlotte Coningsby? If the talk had spread about Town, the story must certainly be common knowledge here. Was everybody watching her sideways with that mix of spite and false sympathy beloved of gossips, eager to see her response? Was Austin Coningsby merely amusing himself at her expense? Knowing she would need comfort apart from her husband? Or hoping to witness her public humiliation and distress as Max and Charlotte danced together before half the county?

Well, she tossed her head, eyes bright and angry, cheek colour high. No one here was going to believe she was distressed. No one would even know she cared. She didn't care. She managed a laugh, breathless, and leaned a little on to Austin Coningsby's arm. He looked down at her appreciatively.

"You are overheated, Lady Trenarth. This I cannot allow. Come. Together we shall track down the elusive lemonade, I shall boldly slay it for you, and bring it as a trophy upon a silver salver."

"You are absurd, sir," Harriet returned gaily, and she made herself laugh, looking boldly into his face, and playfully squeezing his arm. "But your offer sounds very tempting."

Lord Trenarth, standing alone, watching her from across the room, suddenly looked very grim indeed.

By the time supper was done, and guests were beginning to depart, relief and exhaustion were overwhelming Harriet. The Coningsbys were amongst the last to leave. Harriet watched with a fixed smile as Charlotte impulsively kissed Max's cheek as she thanked him for the evening. In return Harriet offered Austin a hand to press to his lips, and a provocative smile in response to his flirtatious promises of early return. She did not look at her husband.

By the time everywhere was clear, after Harriet had helped a girl who had come running back in for a mislaid reticule, Max had vanished. She frowned. She had, perversely, wanted to wish him goodnight, and hear his verdict on the evening.

"His lordship is in his study, my lady," Cornwell informed her, in response to her query.

She had only once before been in his study. It was a small room, with a large oak desk filled with pigeonholes of papers, leather-covered armchairs, and bookshelves filled untidily with a variety of volumes, from novels to treatises upon methods of agriculture. It smelled of woodsmoke, and leather, and Max's old dog, Champion, who spent most of his life now stretched before the fire. The dog raised his head as the door opened.

"Harriet! I thought you had gone up to bed."

"No, my lord."

He was sitting by the fire, glass in hand, an open brandy bottle on the table beside him. He did not bother to move. She walked over and stood looking down at him, careful to keep just out of reach. He was watching her from under drooping lids that held a sudden hint of menace.

"May I have a drink?" she asked.

He made as if to refuse, then shrugged.

"If you wish," he said, and reached a glass from a small cupboard.

The brandy was fiery, and made her gasp, but it warmed her. She perched on the chair opposite him. There were so many things she wanted to confront him with angrily. So many things she knew she could never say. And always the knowledge that she had known about Charlotte. She had still made the choice to marry him. She had wanted an earl. She stared at him, brooding.

"Did you enjoy the evening, my lord?"

Was it better to say something rather than nothing?

"For pity's sake, call me Max. Everyone else does. You are supposed to sound like a wife, not a butler."

Harriet flushed.

"I am sorry my manners do not please you, sir," she retorted. She spoke angrily, remembering who else called him Max with such possessive ease. She gulped at the brandy crossly, swallowing fast, her eyes smarting.

Max regarded her with exasperation. He was angry, and his pride was badly dented.

He had determined that she should come to him willingly. He would not be a husband who brutally forced himself upon his wife. Yet, after all his care and patience to make amends for her fear and misery on that first night of marriage, to befriend her, to give her time, to allow what he hoped would be a lasting affection to grow, he had been forced to watch the cheap tricks of Austin Coningsby receive her blushes and smiles. He had been startled by the sharpness of his hurt and jealousy.

The brandy was giving a brightness to her eye. He noticed with a shock that her glass was empty.

"I would like some more, please..." she paused, then "...Max."

Max stood up. He knew that he should not be plying an eighteen-year-old girl with brandy, even if the girl did happen to be his utterly infuriating wife. She looked so fragile with her finery awry, sleek curls of brown hair creeping down onto her shoulders, dress slipping a little to expose the firm roundness of her breast. Her lips were parted as she watched him. He picked up the bottle, and looked at her sideways, then set it down again.

"I can't do it, Harriet," he said, bluntly. "You would be drunk."

"That is insulting!"

She stood up, cheeks flushed, frowning up at him in indignation.

"But true!"

She glared, searching her mind for a retort, and he was suddenly surprised by tenderness. She was so very young.

"Harriet!" He put his hands on her naked shoulders and paused, stroking the smooth skin at the nape of her neck. Slowly, he pulled her towards him.

A vision of Charlotte reaching up to kiss him leapt into Harriet's mind, and she felt a surge of nausea. Angrily she pulled away from him, head down, tears burning in her eyes.

"For God's sake, Harriet, what is the matter with you? Am I so repulsive? Others have not thought so."

He grabbed her then, and pulled her roughly against him. His hand deep in her hair, he forced her head back and kissed her hard, his lips crushing down on hers. She fought against him furiously, beating her hands against his chest, and he could taste the salt from her tears. In disgust, whether at her or himself he was unsure, he abruptly let her go. She reeled back, gasping for breath.

"You were ready enough to respond to Austin Coningsby and his flattery," Max said bitterly. He paused to steady his ragged breathing. "I am forced to wonder why you agreed to marry me at all, when it is plain you hold me in such aversion. Perhaps it would have been better for us both if you had not."

"But that would not have been so *convenient* for you, would it, sir?" she burst out, reckless with misery and confusion. "You were in need of a fortune, were you not? A nice fat fortune from a rich cit with which to save your Abbey. Why do you complain? You have the money. You cannot pretend that had you been free to marry for *love* you would now be married to me." The tears were running down her cheeks now, and she rubbed the back of her hand through them angrily.

"Did you never think you were marrying for love?" Lord Trenarth asked, quietly.

Harriet was very aware of the effect of the brandy now. She knew she should not say the things she was going to say. So she said them anyway.

"When I realised," she said harshly, "that the man I loved did not return my love, then I decided to marry for a title. That is all." She shrugged, turning away to hide another welling of tears. "You wanted my money, I wanted your title. You see? Isn't it convenient? We both have precisely what we wanted."

"So it would seem," Lord Trenarth replied, regarding her very grimly. "Our only problem now is in learning how to live with that fact."

CHAPTER FIVE

TWO DAYS AFTER the dance, lonely, almost desperate, Harriet made an impulsive decision that changed the tenor of her life at Trevereux Abbey.

As usual, she sat after breakfast in the small drawing-room to receive Mrs. Wellow. She still dreaded these encounters, reminders of her own inadequacies. On this morning she stared desolately at the housekeeper's impassive face, and thought—why not? And again—why not? Nothing could make her life much emptier.

"Please, Mrs. Wellow, sit down. There is something I wanted to say."

Mrs. Wellow looked dubious, but lowered herself carefully onto the edge of a chair.

"Yes, your ladyship?"

Harriet was clasping her hands tight together in her lap, and staring down at them. She glanced at the housekeeper's face. Her eyes were heavy with a mixture of unhappiness and defiance.

"I wish to ask for your help, Mrs. Wellow."

The housekeeper looked intently at her mistress then, her attention caught. She had trodden very carefully with this new lady of the house, not knowing what would be expected of her, anxious for her job, determined to support his lordship.

"Yes, your ladyship?"

"Mrs. Wellow. I will be quite frank with you. There is nothing else I can do." She paused and drew a deep breath, then hurried on. "I am sure you will have realised by now that when you come to me each morning I have no idea what to say to you. I have never run a house like Trevereux Abbey. Never even stayed in one. I have never run any house at all. I know nothing of what is expected of me." She drew another shaking breath, but her voice was steady when she continued. "So, that is why I am asking for your help, Mrs. Wellow. I have no one else to turn to. If I had, I doubt if any would know better than you. Please, will you teach me? Will you teach me all the household duties of the Countess of Trevereux?"

The housekeeper was staring at her, a flush mounting her cheeks, and with increased despair Harriet concluded that, angered and insulted, Mrs. Wellow would now utterly despise her.

"Oh, your ladyship!" that lady burst out. "Oh, to think! There we were, thinking it would be our ways you were critical of...you so young and fresh from Town...and then that you didn't care to be bothered. But never mind that now. That's done with. Of course I will show you, my dear, of course."

Her round face was suddenly wreathed in smiles as the importance of her task dawned upon her.

"Why, there is so much to show you, so much that needs to be done! This house has been without a mistress for so long...and a master, well...you know how men are! ... however good, he can't seem to understand the half of it. Yes, indeed, m'lady. Why, I *wish* you had spoken earlier. No matter! We can start at once!"

Abruptly adopted as Mrs. Wellow's especial charge, and taken under her ample wing, Harriet found that her life was transformed. Full of bustle and gossip, the housekeeper took her through storerooms and cupboards, laundries and linen presses, wash-houses, dairies, cellars, and pantries. She counted sheets,

blankets, pillows and quilts, examined mountains of
table linen, heard mutters over the inadequacies of the
sewing-room, and the quality of the calico for the
maids' uniforms. Doors were flung wide on medicine
cupboards, and gaps in their supplies tutted over.

In the kitchens Mrs. Ganby proudly displayed her
work, done despite the awful inadequacies of the open
fireplace with its creaking machinery of spits and
smoke-jacks, and the huge brick bread ovens. She
spoke wistfully of modern ranges, and new plumb-
ing.

Outside Mr. McKay the head gardener took Harriet and Mrs. Wellow through the great walled gardens, showing off the winter vegetables, the raised
heated beds, the huge glasshouses, and all the dor-
mant promise for next summer in the fruit trees
against every wall. Beyond again was the home farm,
with the hens, ducks, geese and milking cows, and
stores of grain. Beyond that, the park with its wild
game. All were sources of the vast quantities of pro-
visions carried in daily to the kitchens to pass Mrs.
Ganby's beady-eyed inspection.

Harriet was dazed but excited by these whirlwind
tours. Suddenly the business of this great house, which
had seemed to run with an oiled, silent smoothness
beyond human intervention, began to make sense. The
people who ran it began to have faces and names, not
just uses and uniforms.

Harriet began to make decisions, with Mrs. Wellow's help, on what should be done. There was money
now to spend, after all, as there hadn't been for many
a long year. They schemed happily together. The sewing-room was moved from the dark and cheerless attic where it had always been to a light and airy
bedroom with a fireplace, and a new girl taken on to
assist old Nanny Gabb now she was too old to manage alone. Materials were bought for new servants'

uniforms, and new linen chosen for the best beds, the
old to be turned sides to middle and used in the servants' wing. Recipes were unearthed for medicines,
and Harriet tried her own hand at making some,
laughing over the foul-smelling messes of goose-grease
she sealed into pots.

Mrs. Wellow was in her element, busy and important. Harriet was trying her hand at everything, and
the staff loved her for it. She looked forward to Mrs.
Wellow's morning visit. She felt she had a role to fill.
More, she felt she had a friend.

There was another improvement, too, in Harriet's
life. Miles Frampton had returned to Town, but his
mother and sister had become regular callers. Sensing
Harriet's uncertainties, Mrs. Frampton decided they
would all pay their social calls together. It was a com-
monplace now for the villagers along the crisp frosted
lanes to see the smart Frampton carriage bouncing
over the ruts, the three ladies gossiping and laughing
within. Visits were no longer an ordeal in such cheerful company, and Harriet sensed that she was steadily
gaining acceptance. She even felt she made a few
friends in the neighbourhood.

Another regular caller, of whose welcome Harriet
was less sure, was Austin Coningsby. Sometimes he
came with his sister, Charlotte, but often he was alone.
Outwardly polite, he would sit in the Chinese Room,
twirling his beaver hat between his fingers, teasing
Harriet over the tedious obligations of social visiting
that necessitated these frequent calls at Trevereux Abbey. When they were alone together, sipping the tea
that Cornwell had delivered on its silver tray, his face
filled with hidden disapproval, then Coningsby's voice
and eyes were full of innuendoes and subtle flatteries.
He could surprise or shock her into giggles and
blushes. She was guiltily pleased by his hints of her

attractions, made to feel she was a daring woman of the world.

If he was at home, Max would join Harriet when visitors called. She noticed that he tended to be increasingly available when the visitor's name was Coningsby, and she glowered, certain she knew why. She watched Charlotte's face grow animated when he entered the room, and barely noticed how abstracted was Max's response. She was too busy in lively chatter with Austin, laughing a great deal, proving how little she cared where Max's heart lay.

It was Austin who, shocked that she could not drive herself about, strode round to the stables and bullied the men there until they had brought out and swept down an old pony trap, and harnessed up a fat-bellied cob. After that he regularly took Harriet driving on the tracks through the park and the neighbouring farmland, and she learned fast, wrapped up against chill winds and drizzling rain, her cheeks whipped red and her eyes sparkling as they sped along.

Max watched with apparent indifference, his face closed, his dark eyes expressionless. He and Harriet lived a life apart, conducting themselves with scrupulous politeness when they met over meals or before visitors, going their separate ways between. Of the driving lessons, he had coolly pronounced himself pleased that she had found some way to occupy her time. Smarting at his indifference, Harriet turned yet more to the comfort of Austin's easy, flattering company.

By mid-December Harriet was driving well enough to venture out without supervision. With Susan perched beside her she explored all the lanes round about, and often made her way down into Trevereux village. It was Mrs. Wellow who suggested that she should begin visiting their tenants in the cottages they passed.

"The old ladyship, his lordship's mother, she always made a point of visiting in the winter, especially the old people and those with young children. Just to make sure our people don't suffer, she'd say. She'd see what was needed, then send down food, or firewood, or medicines. She wasn't one to preach or pry, just practical help. My niece Ellie, she could direct you to those who need help, having herself grown up in the village, like."

So Harriet, Susan, and Ellie the chambermaid bowled briskly out to the estate cottages, where Ellie's easy acceptance ensured a welcome for the Countess of Trevereux. Often Harriet would sit in the meagre parlours, wistfully cuddling the baby of the house. Parcels would be dispatched to the needy.

One evening, as they sat alone at the dinner table, their faces lit by the glow of the eight candles in the ornate silver candelabra that stood between them, Harriet described to Max where she had visited and what she was sending out. It was a particularly raw night, with a strong east wind cutting in icy draughts through the house. She was pleased to think of the stacks of logs she had seen delivered that afternoon, and wanted to share her satisfaction. She hoped perhaps for his approval. This chill between them froze her heart. She knew she could not have his love, but sometimes she craved his approval, even as she despised herself for doing so.

In fact Lord Trenarth knew very well what his wife was about. He did not need her half-defiant, half-anxious descriptions. He was watching with a confused and angry pride as she settled into her life at the Abbey. He began to hear glowing reports of her wherever he went, from neighbours, from his own staff, or out on the estates. It sometimes seemed that with her slight figure, so deceptively fragile, and her wide, earnest gaze, she was set to charm everyone ex-

cept himself. So now he merely looked at her, his eyes
half-hooded, and gave a slight shrug.

"How very fitting for your role, *Lady* Trenarth, to
act the Lady Bountiful. I am sure you enjoy yourself."

Harriet glared at him, furious. Furious at him for
his sarcasm, furious at herself for leaving herself vulnerable to it. She had been genuinely distressed at the
plight of many of the families she visited, and had
given much thought, and much discussion with Mrs.
Wellow, to the improvement of their conditions. She
was almost goaded into a passionate outburst, but she
stopped herself, tossed her head, and gave an answering, indifferent, shrug.

"Naturally I intend to enjoy playing the role my new
title gives me. It is my half of the bargain, after all. I
shall enjoy it to the full."

"I'm sure you will, Harriet. There is so much of
your life you are enjoying at present, is there not?"

There was that hint of angry menace in the words
that made Harriet's thoughts fly instinctively to the
times she'd spent with Austin. She knew she was
blushing as she stared back at her husband's unreadable dark eyes. She raised her chin higher and her expression became haughtier.

"Yes," she said, and forced herself to smile. "I am
finding a great deal to enjoy in my life, thank you,
sir." Her thoughts flew now to Charlotte Coningsby,
and her expression hardened. "As, I am sure, are
you," she concluded, pointedly.

Max's dark brows snapped together in a frown. He
had no idea to what, or whom, she might be refer-
ring. He leaned forward towards her, intent upon
asking. It suddenly seemed important to know.

"And precisely what are you implying by that, Lady
Trenarth?"

Harriet's bravado evaporated. She jumped up, pushing back her chair. "I will leave you now, my lord. Shall I ring for Cornwell to bring you the port?"

"Harriet, stay! I want to talk to you." His imperious tone angered her further.

"There is nothing to be said, sir. We both understand our situation. I am merely doing as you instructed me, and learning to live with it. Goodnight, my lord."

She turned and almost ran from the room, leaving Max angrily frustrated. He flung back his chair to run after her, but dropped back into it at once, aware of the pointlessness of his action. She would only fob him off as she always did. He thought nostalgically of tempestuous opera singers of his acquaintance, and half toyed with the idea of a trip back to Town, only to dismiss the thought, angry at himself. He was short-tempered with Cornwell, and drank heavily of the port.

Christmas had always been a family time at Trevereux Abbey through the Earl's childhood, and he set some store by reviving this tradition. Curtly informing Harriet that she would be required in her role of hostess, he told her that he had invited his cousin Anna with her husband George, and his sister Lady Adeline with her husband Mr. Peter Lowdham, and their various children. Harriet merely nodded when he told her.

"Of course, my lord. I am sure Mrs. Wellow and I can arrange everything to your satisfaction."

She was quietly proud to know that now she spoke the truth.

They all arrived the week before Christmas, along with the first heavy snows of the year. Harriet's days became filled with noisy chatter, exhilarating rides across snowy fields, brisk walks in the park, decking the house with holly and ivy and mistletoe. There were visits daily, from all Lady Adeline's friends and aquaintances. After the initial awkwardness all the family appeared to accept Harriet, and to her surprise she discovered she was enjoying their company. In the safety of their numbers she even relaxed enough to tease and laugh a little with Max. The Coningsbys were away at friends' until the New Year.

It was Mrs. Wellow who remembered the other Christmas tradition that had lapsed since the earl's childhood—the Trevereux Twelfth Night Feast. She sat with Harriet, reminiscing of her early days as a parlour-maid at the Abbey, when every Twelfth Night the small barn behind the house was cleared for dancing, and the vast servants' hall was crammed full of tables, and every tenant from all over the Trevereux estate came to celebrate the end of the Yuletide season with feasting and dancing at his lordship's expense.

"The highlight of the year, it was, m'lady. Far better than the harvest feasting, coming as it did in the coldest part of the year. And everyone there, from oldest to youngest, eating and drinking till they could take no more. Then the dancing..." She smiled, her face softened with memories. "Of course, the earl and countess would start the dancing, leading the way for everyone to follow... and that's his lordship's grandfather I'm thinking of now!"

Harriet laughed.

"We'll do it again," she said. "I will ask my husband. But think of the work for you and Mrs. Ganby."

Mrs. Wellow laughed then, excited at the prospect.

"Think of the fun, though, m'lady. Why, it'll be just like the old days."

"Oh, what fun!?" Anna cried, when Harriet mentioned the idea at dinner that night. "Of course you must do it, Max. Isn't it splendid that Harriet cares

about these old traditions? We shall all go to start the
dancing. Think how pleased your grandfather would
have been!''

"She's right, Max," Adeline joined in. "And it will
be a fine way for everyone on the estates to share in
celebrating the year of your wedding."

"Ah, yes," Max said. He paused, his eyes on Harriet. "There has not been much celebration of the
wedding."

"Then you must do it!" Adeline was brisk and decisive. "With a grand toast to you both. We can all
lend a hand. Maybe invite a few of our friends round,
don't you think, Max? Whatever shall you feed them
all, Harriet?"

Harriet responded mechanically, talking confidently now of the Abbey's supplies, and what must be
brought in. But she was aware all the time of her husband's eyes upon her, and the erratic way her heart
beat when she caught his sombre gaze.

Memories filled her mind, distracting her, of the feel
of his hands on her waist, steadying her as she stood
on a chair, stretched up on tiptoes, to push holly behind the great gilt mirror that hung above the mantelpiece in the Chinese Room. The others had been
laughing, teasing them. The grip of his hands had increased until she could feel the pressure of each individual fingertip. She had had no option but to turn
and jump down into his arms, held close against him
for a brief moment, before he turned away. She
pushed the thoughts angrily out of her mind.

"I shall talk over all the plans with Mrs. Ganby,"
she said, smiling at Adeline. "She is a cook who can
create a feast from less than nothing, I sometimes believe."

"My dear—you don't know how lucky you are!
What a treasure! Have I ever told you about the

dreadful little Frenchman who was with us for six
months?''

Harriet joined in talk of terrible servants, nodding
and laughing, until it was time to lead the ladies from
the table. She even recounted her favourite tale from
her days at Miss Gordon's Seminary, originally told
her as she sat shivering under the thin blankets of her
bed, darkness pressing round her and the sharp smell
of newly extinguished candles in the air. They had all
giggled hysterically then, as Julia Fotherstone told her
story of her father's butler. He was prone to funny
turns, and when afflicted would welcome all callers,
from dukes to coal-heavers, bowing deeply and taking their hats. Solemnly escorting them into the drawing-room, there he would formally present them to a
bronze statue of one of the muses, which stood in the
corner of the room, scantily clad in no more than a
veil. The butler introduced her, in tones of rigid disapproval, as Mrs. Jordan, the long-established mistress of the Duke of Clarence, and primly enquired
whether she and the visitor would care to take tea.

The laughter was warm and appreciative. Harriet
knew that Max's family, whatever they might have
thought of his marriage at first, had learned to like
her. But as for Max, she knew that his eyes were fixed
on her face as she stood to leave the room, and she
deliberately avoided his gaze.

CHAPTER SIX

"HARRIET, YOU ARE SO lucky. That dress is beautiful!"

Harriet turned to where Anna stood at her bedroom door, watching Susan put the finishing touches to her hair.

"Do you truly think so? At the last dance we gave I felt hideously overdressed."

She could chat easily to Anna now, considering her a friend, although Anna, who had always worshipped her handsome cousin Max, had no inkling that their marriage was anything but perfect. She smoothed down the dress, turning this way and that before the long mirror. In deep pink silk, the dress was deceptively simple. Hanging straight from a high waist, the fine cloth clung against her as she turned. The paler pink sash fell as long streamers down her back. Tiny puffed sleeves hung off her shoulders, the line of the dress swooping low and round over her breasts. Her skin was creamy white in the candlelight.

"Stay still, do, miss," muttered Susan, tweaking the end of pink ribbon through the tumbled pile of curls that topped Harriet's head. "There, now, that should do."

"It's perfect," Anna said. "I think you chose it specially to show off Max's pearls, you sly thing. Put them on now, and let me see."

Harriet flushed a little. Max had given her two things to celebrate Christmas. One was a horse of her own, a beautiful dapple-grey mare named Whisper who had already stolen Harriet's heart, filling her with reluctant gratitude. The other was a set of pearls, necklace, pendant earrings, bracelets and rings. They were family jewels that had originally been set into a heavy and unfashionable necklace and tiara. Max had sent them to Town to be reset in delicate filigree gold, and had given them to her on Christmas morning. She had not worn them.

"I had thought to wear rubies tonight," she said.

"Ooh, you liar, Harriet. I swear you have just been waiting for the occasion to wear those pearls. Where are they? I'll help you put them on. How I wish George had a few heirlooms like those."

With a curious reluctance Harriet reached for the box that held the pearls, and opened it. They were beautiful. And set exactly as she might have chosen, lighter and more delicate than the imposing pieces her father had always favoured in his lavish gifts to her. She idly twirled the bracelet through her fingers as Anna and Susan fitted necklace and earrings. She put on the bracelet, and the ring. Anna was right, of course. She might have chosen the dress especially to complement them. She frowned suddenly, but it was too late to change.

The distant noise of feasting in the kitchen had been evident for some time as doors, swung open, released a blast of sound and rich scents of roasted meat.

Earlier, from her bedroom window, Harriet had seen trails of dark figures plodding stolidly through the snow, and traps and carts of every shape, age and size struggling heavy-laden down the long drive. It was bitterly cold, freezing hard. Birds hunched disconsolately on the trees near the house, not bothering to stir as people trudged beneath, and down on the lake ducks were standing perplexed on the ice. As she had watched a group of boys ran on the ice and began

sliding, their whoops and calls thin and high in the
cold air. She had shivered, and pulled the window
shut.

Their own friends would be arriving now, to share
the cold collation laid out for them by a frantic Mrs.
Ganby. Later they would lead out the dancing in the
barn.

Harriet had asked Adeline to invite whom she
wished, thinking she would like another chance to
meet old friends. In her turn thinking how much
Harriet must need young companionship, Adeline had
kindly invited the younger people of the neighbourhood, including Miles and Elizabeth Frampton, and
Charlotte and Austin Coningsby, newly returned from
a stay in Cambridgeshire. Harriet glanced one last
time in the mirror. She wanted to look her best. For
whom she was unsure.

It was a couple of hours later that Cornwell knocked
discreetly on the door of the Music Room. With his
face unaccustomedly flushed, and a rare smile hovering on his lips, he murmured to the air beside the earl's
ear that his lordship's people were all assembled in the
barn, and eager for the dancing to commence. Lord
Trenarth looked across the room to his wife.

She was sitting on a low *chaise longue*. A bracket of
candles on the wall above threw a glowing circle of
light about her, and on to the face of Austin Coningsby, who was leaning towards her confidentially,
casually stroking the ivory struts of her fan between
his fingers. Max's face hardened. The pleasure he had
felt when she had chosen to wear his pearls had long
been dispelled. Austin had monopolised Harriet
throughout the supper, and Max had noticed Adeline
watching them with a perturbed frown.

"Harriet!" Max's voice was not loud, but it cut
across the conversation. His wife looked up, and
Austin leaned against the back of the *chaise longue*,

one arm stretched out along the seat behind her, and regarded Max from under insolently drooped eyelids.

Harriet had drunk a great deal more wine than usual. Her heart had lurched as she had seen the softening of Max's face as she came down the stairs wearing the pearls he had given her, and she had not flinched from his quick, approving kiss. She had almost admitted to herself that she enjoyed it, and especially the added spice of knowing that Austin and Charlotte had seen them. She had smiled pointedly at the Coningsbys, and clung for a moment to Max's side.

There was no doubt that Max was the most attractive man there tonight, Harriet thought, looking across at him. In his milk-white breeches and jacket of a blue so dark it seemed black, he stood slim, stark and austere, only the diamond pin that held the folds of his cravat catching the light. Yet he had a contained strength that was unmistakable. It was more than the hard muscle beneath the clean cut of the jacket, more than the cool, arrogant stare which could so daunt those who did not know him. Everything about him spoke of quiet authority. Harriet caught back her thoughts, disconcerted, and looked elsewhere.

Austin, by contrast, was all colour, his coat a rich puce, and his breeches sage green, an ostentatious emerald in his cravat, and fobs and rings glinting. He was more attentive than Harriet wanted now, unsure as she was, but his persistence was difficult to deter. And Charlotte was looking provokingly alluring. Her dress was dramatic pure white, and cut very, very low.

"Poor Max, how embarrassing for him," Anna had whispered to Harriet earlier, giggling as they helped themselves to food. "If Miss Coningsby leans any farther towards him I swear she will fall straight out of that dress and into that jelly she is toying with!"

"I expect he is loving every moment," Harriet retorted, betraying her anger. Anna looked at her swiftly.

"Oh, no," she began, and would have said more. But Harriet had turned away, and was talking to Miles Frampton and Austin Coningsby.

Harriet had drunk because she was confused, and disturbed. Even she had noticed that Max had not in fact looked pleased at the attentions of Charlotte, and she had been aware of his eyes upon her, watching as she laughed up at Austin. It was almost with relief that she heard his summons, and now, without a backward look at Austin, she stood up and walked over to him. His gaze seemed to draw her closer and she could not look away.

He laid his hands lightly on her shoulders. They were cool and smooth on the softness of her skin.

"We must go across to start the dancing," he said.

"Yes," she said, staring up into his dark, shadowed eyes.

Adeline, watching in some relief, jumped up from where she had been playing quietly for them on the piano.

"Come on, everybody. Off to the dance! You will need your shawls, ladies. We have to cross a yard at the back to reach the barn."

"My dear, how quaintly rustic!" Anna overheard Austin murmuring to his sister. "Shall we enjoy a romp with the peasants, do you think?"

The scene in the barn was certainly rustic. A generous profusion of cheap candles, swinging lanterns and tallow dips lit the room, their smoke already tainting the air, along with the mingled scents of lingering roasted meats, traces of the hay that until recently had been stored there, and, over all, hot, sweating excited bodies, jostling and laughing around the edge of the barn. Swathes of evergreens decorated every beam, the moving leafy shadows giving the curious feeling that the expectant gathering was in a dark forest clearing, some ancient, primitive celebration.

As the party from the house entered, the babble of talk and laughter quieted, and changed to a subdued mumble of approval. An ancient man, white-haired and bearded, stepped forward on to the clear swept floor, raising in one knotted hand a battered pewter tankard. He had run the home farm for fifty years, and still kept a beadily critical eye on the work of his sons and grandsons. He glared round the barn now.

"I'll thank'ee all for a bit o' hush."

"Hush for Gaffer Jowett," a younger man called out, and the crowd fell good-naturedly silent.

"As one who's known this earl, and his father, and his grandfather before that, 'tis a fine thing for me to thank you, m'lord, for our Twelfth-Night Supper. Very good it was." He paused, glared round his audience as if daring them to contradict, and drank deeply from his tankard. A baby began to grizzle, and near to Harriet someone hiccupped persistently. She began to feel a terrible urge to giggle.

"So I would like to call a toast," Gaffer Jowett began again, "to his lordship, and his new lady..."

Whatever more he might have said was lost as everyone sensed a fine excuse for noise and drinking.

"Three cheers for his lordship," someone shouted, and a chorus ran raggedly round the barn as everyone drank and cheered and stamped their feet in approval.

Leading Harriet, Max walked forward into the centre of the barn floor. There was a wheezing squeak from a fiddle, hastily quietened.

"Thank you, Gaffer Jowett, and thank you all. But I won't delay you further. The fiddlers are ready, and there's another barrel to be tapped! Let the dancing begin!"

The cheers broke out again, and among them a bolder voice called out.

"A kiss for the bride, m'lord, under the mistletoe!"

Those who had started moving towards the great barrel on the trestle-table at the end of the barn stopped to look. Harriet and Max both glanced upward. They were indeed standing beneath a huge bunch of mistletoe, its waxy white berries glinting in the dim light. Max looked down at Harriet and smiled. Sensing his approval, the cry was taken up round the room.

"A kiss for the bride! A kiss for the bride!"

Shaking his head with pretended reluctance, Max turned Harriet towards him. She was laughing a little breathlessly, swept up in a haze of wine and the eager encouragement of all those watching. Cupping her face between his hands, Max paused for a moment, looking down at her, while the cries of avid anticipation grew louder and more raucous. Harriet shivered. Giving one straight look over the top of Harriet's jauntily ribbonned curls at Austin Coningsby, the earl bent his head, and kissed her.

His lips were hot and demanding, crushing down on hers. Harriet forgot that she had ever needed to flinch away. Inflamed by the wine and the urgent approval all around her, she returned his kiss, swept abruptly into a dark yearning need for him, the need that for so long she had hidden and denied. His hands had slipped down from her face, over her shoulders, and clasped her tightly against him. She could feel the thudding beat of his heart, or was it her own? Dazed, Harriet could barely stand as her husband gently loosed his grip, dropped a protective kiss upon her forehead, and stood with her in the circle of his arms, looking down at her, his dark eyes blazing. All around were cheers and claps, and with much screeching three

fiddles and an ancient wheezing set of bagpipes struck
up a noise with a cheerful rhythm.

"Just follow my lead," Max murmured into Harriet's hair. "We have some traditional dances of some
antiquity here in Trevereux. They tend to be energetic, and become more vulgar as the evening wears
on!"

He stepped back, and began cheerfully lining up
other couples behind them, Adeline with George
Woodthorpe, Miles with Charlotte, and on down the
line through all their friends. Beside them other lines
were forming, nearby farmers, tenants Harriet knew
from her drives and visits, all jostling and shoving for
places, grinning at her approvingly when they caught
her eye. Harriet blushed, watching Max. His face
alight, laughing off the jocular comments, he imposed a semblance of order on the lines of dancers.
Then, with a wave of his arm, he urged the musicians
into the dance.

Harriet never was sure of the steps. A great deal of
stamping was involved, and twirling round on your
partner's arm, and galloping down the ranks, and
back up under arched arms, a lot of whoops, claps and
buffeting. By the time the music discorded to a halt
she was aching and breathless with laughter. When
Gaffer Jowett presented both her and Max with a
tankard of frothing beer, pale blue eyes twinkling
wickedly and a vast grin over his toothless gums, she
accepted, and drank gratefully. She was conscious of
Max's arm resting lightly across her shoulders, and
suddenly she was glad of it, glad and proud in the glow
of so much approval. She smiled up at him, licking a
moustache of froth from her lips, and his answering
look made her heart turn over.

Charlotte, standing by her brother, her pretty face
bored and sulky, watched the couple, petulant. She
spoke contemptuously to Austin before turning away.

He regarded Harriet speculatively for a few moments, then turned back to Charlotte with a comment and a knowing laugh. Taking her arm, he pushed a way for them through the throng and out, back to the house.

Later, when all the house party had reassembled in the drawing-room, there was an air of restlessness. The young people milled about, eager for excitement. The jolly dances Adeline was jigging out on the piano were a poor, polite substitute for the stamping, sweating urgency they had left behind in the shadowy barn. They had all sampled Gaffer Jowett's beer, and the trays of wine and lemonade seemed a tame alternative.

"What shall we *do*?" Anna stood at the window, gazing out across the snow-covered lawns. "The moon is full, and it is midnight. A mad and witching hour. Let's do something mad and witching!"

The others were all listening now, watching her with mixed excitement and apprehension. She stood with her hands clasped at her chest, eyes and smile growing with a new idea.

"I know! The very thing. We shall go out into the Abbey ruins, and discover the mournful monks, the ghosts of Trevereux!"

"Oh, Anna, how absurd! Think of the snow!" But Adeline's prosaic objections were lost in the enthusiasm of the others.

"Ghosts! The very thing. I am shivering already!"

"They will be swinging their phantom censers and chanting spectral dirges! Wonderful!"

"I shall be petrified! Will some kind gentleman revive me if I succumb to the hysterics at first glimpse of a skeletal abbot?"

A clamour of willing voices offered generous assistance in all possible emergencies that might entail the reviving of swooning ladies, and more practical voices asked for boots, pattens, cloaks and shawls.

Max caught Harriet's eye, smiled, and gave an acquiesing shrug.

"The staff are all dancing," he said. "If you can provide the cloaks and shawls, George and I can dig out boots and pattens. I suppose we had better accompany them all. Anna will undoubtedly be the first with the hysterics, and leave the others to the mercy of the spirits!"

Harriet laughed. Her face was alive with all the animation that had first caught his heart among the bored London beauties, her smile filled once again with mischievous promise. With a sudden urgent certainty, Max wished all his guests to the devil. He wanted to be alone with his wife.

What he could only sense was that, for the first time, she felt she truly belonged at Trevereux. Accepted as belonging to the house and lands, a partner to her husband. And surely, her heart was singing, surely the emotions behind that kiss had not been faked. He cared. However unbelievable it might be. She could not be wrong. His eyes were always upon her. The Charlotte of so many nightmares was there in the room with them, but she might not exist. Perhaps it was the effect of Gaffer Jowett's ale, but she felt wonderful. She was certain he cared.

"Of course," she said. "We'll go out together."

And he bent and lightly kissed her forehead, before resignedly organising the hunt for boots.

CHAPTER SEVEN

IT WAS BITTERLY COLD outside. The air clung motionless over the snow, and seemed to bite at the lungs with each breath. The light of the moon was a harsh brightness, silver-blue, the shadows black voids. The moon itself hung above them, its huge bland face smiling down, whispering secrets of madness, and the ancient howling of wolves. The snow crunched brittlely at each step as they walked round to the gaping Abbey door, and Harriet shivered. Max put an arm about her shoulders.

"In this light, in such a place," she murmured, moving closer against him, "I feel we are like characters from a Mrs. Radcliffe novel, and anything might happen, however grotesque or bizarre. Could Anna be right? Will the monks be gliding through the moonlight?"

"Why, I sincerely hope so," Max replied, laughing quietly. "Your reputation as a hostess will soar!"

He carried a lantern and candles, as yet unneeded. Anna insisted that everyone must return through the old passages, for if the monks were not at prayer perhaps the old refectory or dorter would reveal them. Even now shrieks of shocked laughter came from the group of girls just ahead of Harriet, as they anticipated the hopeful vision of assorted tonsured gentlemen in bed.

They gathered at the foot of the steps leading up to the doorway, and a sudden fearful silence quelled the chatter of the girls. The moonlight fell stark onto the high ruined wall, and within it cast a long inky pool of fear.

"You must lead us in, Max," Anna called, her voice quivering. "You are the only one who will know where it is safe to walk. There are fallen boulders."

"Such a faint heart!" he teased. But with a quick squeeze of Harriet's arm he released her, and walked forward to where Anna waited.

"Are you certain you are for this ready, ladies? Quite ready?" Max laughed at their eager faces, his own face mischievous in the moonlight. "After all, who knows what we may see? It is not only the monks who come back to walk at midnight." He dropped his voice till it was low, sinister, conspiratorial. "There is the grey lady, who, despairing, flung herself down to be dashed in a dreadful death from the ruined roof-top there above us. She landed where you now stand."

There was some agitated shuffling of feet, and small shocked squeaks.

"Her wailing cries can still be heard." Max continued remorselessly. "As can the thudding hoofbeats of the headless horseman who gallops up these very steps and into the Abbey at desperate pace, again and again, though whether to deliver some fateful message, or to gain sanctuary from his blood-lusting pursuers, no one knows. Or the lost child, white and wan, who sits atop the wall and sobs piteously—"

"Stop it, Max! You are wicked to tease us so," Anna burst out in a gasp, half laughing, half terrified. "None of that is in the least bit true. He is inventing it all."

"But are you quite sure of that?" Max asked, in sepulchral tones, and, despite her scepticism, a tingling tremor ran down Harriet's spine.

"Now come with me—" his voice was awesome "—and enter the portals of Trevereux Abbey."

Everyone was in a fever of thrilled trepidation, the nonchalant young men only too happy to offer an arm to the girls, who clung together, breathless, palpitating, peering into shadows, and starting at whispers. Mysterious ghostly wails from the mouths of innocent gentlemen produced muffled shrieks and scuffles. The black of the shadow inside the doorway was so great that at first they could hardly see each other, and they stumbled, panicking, forward towards the moonlit centre of the ruin.

It was the clapping flurry of a couple of startled pigeons that terrified everyone. The abrupt clamour, erupting into that fearful whispered progress, brought a mêlée of shouts and gasps, and left everyone with hearts pounding, clutching at each other, breaking out into shamefaced laughter.

Harriet had been at the back of the group, still in the darkest shadow, and had grabbed blindly at the nearest human being for support. Shaking, half in laughter, half fright, she now pulled free, only to find herself being held close.

"My dear Harriet. Such a throbbing heart! Let me offer what poor comfort I can," murmured Austin Coningsby, his mouth close by her ear. "Let me be your defence against the spectral powers that Max is so rashly invoking. Come, hold my hand."

She wanted to be free of him, but he tucked her hand into his arm and led her forward into the moonlight where she must draw notice to his attentions if she tried to shake him loose. Stopping by Elizabeth Frampton, who was clutching Mlle's arm, Harriet endeavoured to ignore Austin.

"Look, what was that?" someone cried urgently, and everyone started round in turmoil, staring at shadows, eyes straining.

"A movement, over there, I am certain!"

Several people now had seen the small movement of something white in the shadows behind them. One girl began to scream thinly, others willingly buried their faces in the coat-buttons of their escorts.

Austin pulled Harriet closer.

"Do you not need a manly chest to bury your face in?" he murmured.

Looking up, Harriet saw Max standing not two paces from them, watching, his face unreadable in the moonlight.

"No, indeed, Mr. Coningsby," she replied, a little too loudly. "Max's stories don't scare me." She pulled her hand loose and moved abruptly to stand by Max's side, infuriated by Austin's knowing smile.

Max put an arm about her shoulders and turned her away. She thought he was about to speak, but there were sudden shouts as the group of intrepid young men who had ventured after the white spectre routed out a large black-and-white tomcat which skittered away across the snow, its hunting on the ruined walls spoiled.

In the abrupt anticlimax everyone suddenly felt the cold.

"Let's go back in," Harriet said, stamping her feet. Her teeth were beginning to chatter. "The monks are spurning us tonight."

They all gathered willingly at the ancient door, eager now to be out of the snow, keen for the last thrill of the eerie medieval passages before a return to the blazing fires and the wine.

"You will have to lead the way," Harriet said to Max. "No one else can remember all those turns by lamplight. I certainly can't."

"I will lead with the lantern," he agreed, "if you and Anna hand out candles to those who follow."

Fingers fumbling with the cold, Anna, Harriet and George issued candles, and one by one the couples vanished down the steps into the remains of the old monastery, following the distant glow of Max's lantern, their candle flames throwing crazy dancing shadows off the walls. Charlotte was clinging to Miles Frampton, Harriet noticed, and she almost laughed at the quick grimace he gave her as he took the lighted candle. With relief she saw Austin follow close behind them, and vanish from sight. Then everyone was in, and with a sound like the sealing of a dungeon, George slammed and bolted the door.

Harriet followed the last of the bobbing lights, shivering at the dank chill of the stone, and the stale musty air. Anna took her arm.

"When I saw that white shape... Why, I thought I would just die! Then and there! It was the crying child ghost, I swear! I could see it! My heart was pounding fit to burst. And when they chased out the cat... I don't know. Was it *only* the cat we saw?"

She was panting, hurrying along, starting when she heard screams and laughter in the darkness ahead.

"The monks have been disturbed at their slumbers, perhaps," Harriet remarked, unperturbed, "unless it is another poor cat!"

Anna chided her in mock despair. "I swear, Harriet, you have not one ounce of quivering sensibility in your body. I don't believe you were terrified once. You should be on the verge of a swoon, all this in your own house!"

They were in the main cellars now, and the passage back to the house was straightforward. One or two brave souls were exploring among the storerooms, the glow of lights and stifled laughter betraying those behind the barrels. Anna ran and took George's arm.

"Come on, we shall hide from Harriet, and see if she cares! Maybe the ghost of the abbot will catch her yet. Then we shall hear her scream!"

Anna danced ahead, teasing, her face lit by the candle she carried, and dodged out of sight around a corner, pulling George with her. Harriet smiled.

"It's you the abbot will be after, to punish for deserting me!" she called into the shadows, and she heard Anna's distant laughter. She walked on slowly, determined not to give Anna the satisfaction of seeing her scurrying out, breathless.

It was as she passed the black doorway to an old storeroom that someone reached out, grabbed her arm, and pulled her roughly out of the passage. Her heart leaping with fright, she stumbled on the slight step down, dropped her candle, plunging them into utter blackness, and found herself steadied and held in somebody's arms.

"Austin!" she exclaimed, furious, her pulse pounding as she tried to steady her breathing.

"So you *were* expecting me to wait. I thought that little show of reluctance could only be for Max's benefit. Pretty, teasing Harriet! And what more probable than that some poor stray visitor should lose his way and need the guidance of his hostess? What guidance will you give me, Harriet?"

Harriet pulled back hard, trying to escape from his hold, but he was too strong, and forced her back against him.

"You are teasing me again, Harriet," he said, reproachfully.

"Let me go," she hissed fiercely, and she felt his chest shake as he laughed softly.

Just then two couples hurried past the doorway, hands sheltering their candle flames, and in an instant were gone. Almost, Harriet called out, but shame at her situation caused her to hesitate too long, and the chance was past. The cellars around them were completely silent. All the others had left.

"You fool," Harriet exclaimed angrily, helpless and disoriented in the utter blackness. "We must make our way back at once. Whatever will everybody think?"

"Harriet, Harriet, you were not always so unfriendly. What of all those visits when you sat and teased me in the Chinese Room, those drives when my hands were always on yours, holding the reins together. You can't pretend now that you hardly know me."

He still kept one arm tightly about her, his fingers biting into her side; with his other hand he pushed aside her shawl, and stroked her neck and shoulder.

Harriet was shivering. For the first time that night she was genuinely afraid.

"I should not have been so much with you," she said flatly. "I am sorry, it was foolish of me. I can see that now. Especially if it led you to expect..." She faltered, and stopped, her head turned away from him in the darkness. She could hear his heavy breathing, and the pounding of her own heart. His breath smelled of brandy.

"Expect what, Harriet? Some of what your eyes and smile keep promising? You proved to all the neighbourhood that you don't lack passion," he said, feeling for her chin and forcing her face towards him, "and after such a display you can hardly claim to be shy. Come now, every married lady has a little extramarital excitement nowadays, and you have been asking for yours for a long time."

Tears of anger and humiliation coursed down Harriet's face as he forced her chin up and kissed her. She knew he was right. She had encouraged him. Engrossed in her own game of despising Max and Charlotte, she had encouraged Austin's flatteries, always hoping, she now realised with devastating clarity, to drive Max forcibly to claim her back as his own. And Max had told her he did not take love by force. He would wait until she came to him. How she must have hurt and shamed him. Desperate to escape, Harriet struggled against Austin, but her struggles seemed only to inflame him further, and she could not escape the punishment of his lips.

"You may leave us, Austin. Now."

Max's words crackled like shards of ice. Harriet jerked her head back, half blinded by the abrupt brightness of the lantern. Her overwhelming relief at Max's sudden appearance in the doorway drained sickeningly away as she saw his face. Austin raised his head exaggeratedly slowly, and looked at Max, his breathing still ragged, but a glance at Max's expression and the smirk died from his lips before it had begun.

Max had picked up the fallen candle. He lit it now at his lantern and held it out.

"You will leave us. I wish to speak with my wife."

"We are not to indulge in a vulgar brawl over her honour?" Austin queried, his drawl insolent.

"I am not in the habit of attacking my guests." Max's voice was if possible icier. "No matter how far they forget the courtesies expected of a gentleman."

With a shrug, and a thin attempt at his usual winning smile, Austin vanished into the passage. There was silence while the slight glow from his candle vanished from sight.

"You *are* my wife, I suppose? You must forgive me if I find it difficult to tell."

Max's voice was harsh and very bitter.

"It seems I do not understand who you are at all. When I met you and fell in love with you, so fresh and alive and different from all the other fawning girls, I was arrogant enough to think you loved me too. Then you changed, became cool and aloof, brittle and flirtatious, but still, like a fool, I loved you, and I put it down to shyness, your youth.

"Since we have been married you have treated my advances as if I disgust you, yet you have encouraged Austin Coningsby at every turn. When at last, to-night, you respond to my kisses, and I am stupid enough to believe that at last you care, instantly you prove me wrong again. Obviously tonight your kisses are free to anybody who cares to demand them.

"I have tried again and again to justify and excuse your behaviour. But now at last I think you may con-gratulate yourself. You have finally convinced me. You *are* the cold-hearted schemer you claim to be. Plainly you satisfied your grasping ambition by mar-rying my title; now you amuse yourself by playing with anyone who will flatter you.

"How many others of my friends have you shamed me with during your adventurous trip back through the cellars? Or had I better not ask? I will have to continue to be acquainted with them, after all. We cannot cease visiting half the country."

He had been gazing at her furiously as he spoke, but now he turned his face aside, as if he could no longer bear the sight of her.

Harriet had been ready to throw herself into Max's arms, desperate for comfort after Austin's assault, but she listened, stricken, to the deep and bitter hurt in his voice, and she could not move. The tears ran down her cheeks unheeded, and every word he spoke flayed her raw conscience. It was not until his last taunts that anger welled over the shame and pain.

"You have no right to speak to me so. You think you were misled? What of me, a naïve girl falling in love with you, the only man who ever touched my heart, only to learn that all you had ever said to me was lies? You only needed my fortune. Your heart had long been given to someone else. How did you expect me to feel, knowing it was someone else you dreamed of holding on your wedding night? Was I expected to relish your embrace? Can you blame me for turning for comfort to Austin Coningsby? What did you offer? What sort of husband have *you* been to me?"

"I? I have been the husband you wished me to be. The sort you assured me you schemed to catch. A cipher. A walking title holding the keys to a stately home."

"And am I supposed to be satisfied with that?"

"*That* choice, Harriet, has always been yours."

"No, *yours*. You are the one who married me when your heart was given to Charlotte Coningsby. You were the deceiver. Knowing that, why should I not turn to her brother?"

Max was staring at her, a black frown knitting his brows, his thoughts in turmoil.

Before he could reply, discreetly loud footsteps heralded an appproach, and a light flooded down the passage outside. They both turned towards the door, the lantern which still hung from Max's hand casting distorting shadows over the agitation of their faces.

Cornwell coughed just outside the door, and peered apologetically round.

"People are waiting to leave, my lord. There is the business of the shillings. It is customary..." He paused, nonplussed by the faces before him, and the earl's lack of response.

"They are waiting."

He seemed at an unaccustomed loss. Always at the end of the Yuletide feast the earl himself had distributed shillings to all the people. It was a custom well remembered, and appreciated, and both Max and Harriet had determined to revive it. The shillings were waiting in two huge blue velvet bags, one for each man, woman and child.

"You must go," Harriet said, dully, all emotion abruptly spent.

Torn by frustrated indecision, Max scowled and strode to the door.

"Please see her ladyship to her room, and make her apologies to our guests," he said tersely. "She has a headache. Lady Adeline can bid our own guests farewell."

He turned and walked rapidly away down the corridor, leaving Harriet with no choice but to follow Cornwell to her room, like a chastened schoolchild.

When Susan arrived, sent hurrying by Max because her mistress was unwell, Harriet was curled on the bed sobbing. It had taken her all this time to realise that Max had loved her, and now it was too late. She had forfeited his love by her own folly. Now he would never believe in her love, never trust her, never care. She was lost in a well of despair.

Susan undressed her, chiding and shaking her head.

"Stop this wild sobbing, do, miss. You'll make yourself ill."

But to no avail. Eventually she gave Harriet a dose of laudanum, and left her to sleep.

In a surge of fear and shame, Harriet ran from her bed after Susan had gone, and locked the door. She could face no one now, not the anxious enquiries of Anna, nor the good advice of Adeline, and, most of all, not risk the reproaches of Max.

So when he did quietly try the door, later, when every lagging person had eventually set out across the moonlit fields for home, she watched the handle move in the dying glow of the fire, and made no sound.

Max went alone to his bed, and pondered long before he slept.

CHAPTER EIGHT

HARRIET WOKE LATE, her head still aching and her eyes sore. A grudging peep over the covers showed a room lit by golden shafts of sunlight which pushed joyously through the cracks in the curtains. Harriet buried her head once more.

Not long afterwards she heard the cries of Adeline's children playing in the snow, shrill as seagulls. Then Susan knocked on the door, bringing a jug of chocolate on a tray. Harriet resigned herself to another day. How she would survive the day, and survive her next humiliating meeting with Max, she did not know.

If only, Harriet thought, as she sipped at her chocolate and half heard the snowball fight that was raging down the lawns towards the lake. If only she could turn time back and start again. How unutterably foolish she had been. She deserved all Max's bitterness. She was deeply ashamed. And now it was too late.

She began to dress slowly, ignoring Susan's chatter until the maid fell silent. It occurred to Harriet that Max would probably ask her for a separation, even a divorce, and her heart froze tight with bitter anguish at the thought.

It was as Susan brushed out her hair that Harriet, restless in misery, left her seat by the mirror and walked over to stare out of the window, Susan muttering beneath her breath as she followed. The snow-

ball fight had adjourned onto the ice of the lake, and
Harriet could see the small figures skidding and sliding, their voices now too far to be heard.

She almost missed it, had almost turned back into
the room, when young Edward fell through the ice.
Always the boldest, his long gliding slide had taken
him far out into the centre of the lake. She had lost
interest in the tiny figure with the whirling arms, had
turned away, and it was only from the corner of her
eye that Harriet saw the dark of the water as the ice
gave way. And Edward was gone.

For a fleeting moment that seemed like an eternity
she stood, transfixed by disbelief. Then, her own predicament forgotten, Harriet flung across the room to
the door, tossing orders at Susan over her shoulder.

"Alert the men! Bring ropes and ladders! Hurry!"
and then at the sight of Susan's blank face, "To the
lake, you fool! Edward has gone through the ice."

And Harriet was gone, full tilt down the main stairs
and across the hall, hauling open the main door and
pelting headlong across the snow, skirts held high, kid
boots crunching and slipping down the slopes.

It was not until she was almost there that she lifted
her eyes from the necessary business of watching her
steps, and saw that someone was before her at the
lake.

Max had woken early that morning, after a night
tormented by dreams of losing Harriet. He watched
the dawn break, and the beauty of the sunrise mocked
him. Unwilling to face his guests, he had avoided the
breakfast table, and gone direct to the stables. He had
ridden far, and was returning through the trees to the
lake, his horse's breath like dragon-smoke in the icy
air, when Edward fell.

Kicking the startled horse to a gallop between the
wintry trunks that stretched to the lakeside, Max leapt
to the ground, and started across the ice, shouting fu-

riously to the other children to get back to land, and
to run to the house for help.

They passed Harriet with frantic cries, fear sharp in
their voices, and she sent them hurrying on to the
house. She could see now that Max was on the ice,
crawling close to the black menace of icy water that
had engulfed Edward. Her heart surged with relief
that he was here. Then a new fear gripped her, almost
harder to bear. For Max. She knew he would count his
own life for nothing if he could save the child. Yet
surely, by now, their efforts would be hopeless.

Suddenly, she could see Edward's head, the pale
blur of his face bobbing helplessly. Hope surged up as
she started onto the ice. She could hear Max talking
urgently to Edward, see him stretching out an arm.
Then she heard the ominous crack of heavy ice breaking, and Edward's head disappeared. Max lay spread-
eagled, the ice rocking beneath his weight.

"Max!" she shouted despairingly, "Oh, Max!"

He was feeling desperately into the water with one
arm, edged to the very brink. She saw him grab, and
attempt to lift, saw Edward's head break the surface
again, saw the ice tilt, and Max freeze into immobil-
ity, unable to move lest they both be lost.

"Harriet?" There was no time to wonder how she
came to be there. "In the boat shed. Quickly. There
are lengths of rope hanging up. Bring the one nearest
the door."

She turned and ran back to the boathouse, giving no
thought to her own safety, even when she stumbled
and her foot plunged through the thin ice by the jetty,
throwing her forward to clutch at the little wooden
quay and scramble along it to the boathouse door,
hands and knees grazed and bleeding.

With the rope in her hands, she was running, legs
feeling leaden and slow, heart pounding so she could
scarcely breathe, pushing and stumbling through mud

and reeds until she gained the firm ice again and could speed across it to Max.

There were other figures now, running down the slope from the house, and men carrying ladders from the stables, but Harriet ignored them all. Her eyes were fixed upon where Max lay, not daring to move, and on the tiny pale shape that was Edward's face, held just clear of the icy water, and ominously still.

"Keep back!" Max's voice was urgent. "Now throw me one end of the rope."

Her hands shaking, Harriet gripped one end of the coil of rope firmly, and threw the other towards Max. It fell short. His hand grasped and reached in vain.

"Try again. Just a little harder." Max's voice was tight with strain. "But stay back, or you will fall through too."

She tried again, but still the rope fell inches short. Max closed his eyes in seeming despair.

"I can't hold Edward much longer," he said. "Already I cannot feel my arm. I shall lose him."

"I am coming nearer to you. It is the only way."

Harriet edged closer to them across the ice, and knelt down, sliding knees and hands carefully forward until she was within a few feet of the broken floe that still supported them both. There was a long warning creak, but the ice held.

"Max!" she called urgently, and as he opened his eyes and looked at her, she flung the rope. It landed across his arm.

With a sudden surge of newfound strength Max took the rope, and managed somehow to tie it around Edward's chest, reaching and fumbling beneath the water round the pathetic limp body, knotting it with a struggle of fingers and teeth. All the while Harriet could see the water sloshing across the sheet of ice on which he lay, soaking him again and again, threatening each time to tip.

"Here, behind you, Harriet. Throw the rope back to me."

She had been so absorbed in Max's struggle, she had not heard George approach. Now she saw that the bank was lined with people, and some of the grooms were sliding ladders across the ice towards them.

"I have come as far as I can. You are light. If I come nearer I will break the ice around you. Throw the other end of the rope back to me where it is safe, and we can pull Edward out."

It was a relief to hear his voice, so calm and sensible. Gathering her strength once again, Harriet flung the other end of the rope back, and George secured the end about him.

"Ready, Max?"

Max nodded.

George steadily began to pull.

Using all his remaining strength, Max reached both hands deep into the water, gripped Edward's small body, and heaved it up and out onto the ice. Now George and a helping groom could pull the child towards them. But Harriet's relief died as it was born.

At this abrupt change of weight the floe that had so reluctantly supported Max abandoned him. Tilting sideways, it sent him sliding helpless into the water even as he lifted the child, then settled back, bobbing gently, leaving the lake as empty of Max as if he had never existed.

With a despairing cry, Harriet flung herself forward to where he had been.

"Max, Max! Oh, Max!" She was chanting his name like a charm as she lay flattened on the ice as Max had done, reaching her arm into the water.

Then a hand was gripping hers, and a face splashed up from the water, Max's face, and he was alive. But she could not save him. She was sliding towards him, down, down into the black depths of the lake as the ice tipped again.

She knew then that they would die together, and she minded. Minded desperately, urgently, furiously. All those wasted weeks together, and all the things she could never tell him. All of the life they could never share. In the numbing cold she gripped his hand in a fierce defiance of death.

But suddenly ladders were stretched across beside them and strong arms were pulling them both out, and laying them across the wooden rungs. There were shouted commands, and bumps and jolts, and they were slid back to the shore, pulled up to waiting arms, and blankets. Max was trying to stand and tell everyone he was fine, and they were to attend to Edward and Harriet, when he collapsed into the snow. Adeline was sobbing, "He's alive, he's alive," and hastening an improvised stretcher up the hill to the house bearing Edward. Harriet quietly fainted.

It was evening when Harriet rebelled against Susan's fussing, and got out of bed. She was tired of listening to dire predictions of the ague, inflammation of the lung, and putrid throats, not to mention the assorted fevers known in every festering detail to Susan's grandmother, and all, it seemed, liable to strike at any moment.

The doctor had been summoned and had arrived in his gig, red-faced from the cold air. He examined them all and pronounced that, given care, warmth, fortifying hot drinks, the goodwill of the Almighty, and regular doses of the particular revivifying medicine he happened to have with him in large quantities and at not too exorbitant a cost, they should all do very well. Children, he commented sourly, were remarkably resilient to such experiences, but Edward should take the full course of the physic until the bottle was entirely empty, to guard against any mischance.

Harriet, warmed, dried, fed, congratulated, admired, and dosed with medicine, mustard baths and steaming gruel, finally demanded to get up, and to know the whereabouts of her husband.

He was in his study, sitting before a blazing fire and staring into the flames, his dose of physic spurned upon the table beside him. Harriet went in, and shut the door behind her, leaning back against it.

She meant to apologise, to explain, to try to set last night behind them and retrieve something. To make him understand. But the words she had planned deserted her.

"I thought you were dead!" she cried, and her voice cracked. "Oh, Max, I thought you were dead, and I thought my heart would break."

"I know," he said. He had got to his feet, and stood gazing across at her. "I saw your face when I came up from under the ice. I knew then. But really, my love, I had always known. Known that our love was right to build a life upon. What I never understood until last night was why you tried to deny it." He gave a rueful grin. "Then you fell in too, and I was certain we were both going to die, and all I could think was that you would die believing I had loved Charlotte Coningsby." His smile broadened, and he shook his head slowly. "It all seemed such unutterable folly!"

"And you never did love her, did you?"

She stated it flatly, for now she knew it to be so. No matter what she had overheard all those months ago.

"I can't abide the girl," Max said bluntly. "Never could. And she has flung herself at my head since she was fifteen, determined I would marry her. Telling it to her gullible confidantes for all I know, despite my best efforts to shun her. It has become a family joke. She has the inflated self-opinion of a cheap macaroni, the solid hide of a rhinoceros and the temperament of a dowager's parrot."

"Oh, Max!"

Harriet was laughing as she ran across to him, so it was odd that there were tears on her cheeks. He folded her into his arms and held her close, stroking her hair with one gentle hand.

"When I thought you were going to die," she murmured, "then I knew that nothing in the world mattered more than saving you. There would be no life for me to live without you. What a fool I was to ever believe I could stop loving you. To believe I could live with you as if I didn't care. I loved you the moment I first saw you, at Lady Buckler's ball, even before I knew who you were. Before I even knew you were an earl! But I had to think I was losing you forever before I could truly admit it."

"And I went up to Town to seek a fortune, and found that without your love all the gold you brought me was so much worthless dross. I had to watch you risk your life for me before I could look beyond my own feelings, and truly appreciate that love."

He sat down in his chair by the fire, pulling Harriet onto his lap, and she lay curled across him, her head on his shoulder, his arm protectively around her, her fingers idly twisting the buttons of his waistcoat.

"But what I do not understand is whyever did you imagine that I loved Charlotte Coningsby in the first place?"

So all the story came out, of the spiteful conversation she had overheard, and her misery, and even of Maria Vintner and her spiteful gibes, and the long determination to marry an earl. Then of the hurtful emergence of Charlotte into their life at Trevereux, the way she had seemed so intimate with Max, and Harriet's realisation that she would have to learn to live as close neighbour to the woman she believed Max to love. And how she had turned to Austin for comfort.

Throughout Max cursed himself for the blindest of idiots. How could he not have realised that something had gone so very wrong? Why had he not proved to her beyond doubt that his love was for her and for her alone? How had he never managed to look beyond his own hurt pride?

"I have been such a fool, Harriet."

She smiled up at him tenderly.

"No, it is I who have been the fool."

He shook his head.

"You are not going to start arguing with me now, are you, lady wife?"

"Why—" she paused, and chuckled "—only if you are wrong, sir!"

He laughed then.

"I shall be driven to stop your arguments," he said severely, gently tipping her face up to his, "like this."

His lips were gentle until he felt the strength of her response, then he was hotly demanding, unleashing the passion of months, sweeping her into a dream of dizzying excitements, yearnings she had not begun to understand. She was quivering when at last he drew back, his breathing deep and hard, and her eyes were dark, softened with longing.

"Lord, Harriet," he murmured. "What fools we both have been."

She smiled at him then, a slow smile, dawningly naughty.

"I think," she said, "that I shall have to be an exceedingly argumentative wife."

Upon which remark he felt it necessary to kiss her again. Severely.

Later, when she was once again aware of the study around them, and of the fire, its embers glowing hotly, Max spoke.

"Harriet?"

His hand, stroking her, would not be still, and it was hard to look away from his lips. She reached a hand up to pull his head down to hers, but he resisted, his eyes smiling.

"It is early to sleep, but I think that, after all the excitements and exertions of the day, you should be in your bed. Don't you?"

"Perhaps I should be a dutiful wife," she said, mock-solemn, her eyes beginning to smile, "and not argue with that."

"And if," Max continued, taking her hand and holding it in his own, for the way she caressed his cheek distracted him, "if I were to come to see you to your bed, your door would not be locked?"

She cocked her head to one side, appearing to consider the issue, while he tightened his grip on her hand. Eventually she slowly shook her head, her eyes teasing.

"No, my lord. Not locked."

"I shall be there," he said. "In fact, we will dispense with Susan's services altogether. I shall help you to your bed." He laughed then. "And only pray that we both get there before I succumb to the ague my valet has been promising to me all afternoon if I will not swallow the vile mess wished on me by that fool doctor."

"Are you to succumb to the ague too? Both Susan and Mrs. Wellow promised it to me if I did not stay in my bed. That or worse!"

"And you ignored them? My darling girl, the situation is urgent! I must insist upon my marital rights and blisses now, before we both give way to a fatal fever! Good God, I might be deprived forever. To bed! And no arguments!"

"No, my lord," she replied primly, stifling her laughter. She put the guard before the fire and went sedately over to the door. "After all—" she opened the door and looked back at him, demurely through her lashes "—I dare say those rights and blisses will be beneficial in driving off the chill!"

He gave a shout of laughter then, and ran to catch her up, scooping her off her feet and into his arms. He carried her through a startled household, past the open drawing-room door and a brief glimpse of open-mouthed faces, up the stairs two at a time, past Adeline on the landing, who gave a satisfied grin, and into Harriet's bedroom.

"We shall not," Max said, to an astonished Susan, "be needing you again tonight." Taking her by the shoulders, he hustled her over to the door. "And take this with you," he exclaimed, grabbing the bottle of medicine from the table and thrusting it into her hand. "We have other cures for the ague!"

And he pushed the door shut behind her, and turned the key in the lock.

"*Now* are you going to argue?" Max asked.

"Well, I might," replied Harriet, smiling at him mischievously, and pulled the ribbon from her hair.

A FEW WEEKS LATER, when even Susan had stopped her talk of agues and fevers, Max and Harriet returned to Town. It was good to be back. They visited her father, to let him see for himself how happy they were, and to insist that he visit them when they returned to Trevereux. They went shopping, to the theatre, to see friends. But invariably they were together, delighting in each other's company.

At last all the society gossips were swearing that *they* had known it was a love-match from the start. *They* had never talked of grasping at titles, fortunes gained at any expense, and certain young ladies spurned with their hearts broken, their expectations shattered. No, indeed. Surely everyone who was *anyone* knew that

Max Trenarth's courtship of Miss Ogbrook had been
the great romance of last Season.

Max's friends regarded him sourly at his club, and
remarked that if he did not change his ways the institution of matrimony might even become fashionable.
He was making it appear enjoyable, an inexcusable
state of affairs. If that notion got about, who knew
where the rot might end?

Max merely smiled.

Even a chance encounter with Maria Vintner in a
milliner's in Oxford Street could not spoil Harriet's
pleasure. Maria's face was thin and sharp now, the
years of spite ingrained in the lines about her mouth.
Her husband was a big florid man with porcine eyes
and a bullying manner. Harriet felt sorry for her.

"So you did catch an earl after all," Maria said,
running a shifty, assessing eye over Harriett's outfit,
then favouring Max with an ingratiating smile.
"Amazing what money will do."

Harriet did not care to explain that money and titles were among the least important factors in her relationship with Max. She only smiled sweetly.

"Isn't it?" she agreed, and tucked her hand happily onto Max's arm as they wandered away.

"What a poisonous woman," Max remarked.
"Who was she?"

"Poor thing," Harriet said. "She is no one important any more."

But as the days began to lengthen Harriet became
increasingly restless in Town. She longed for the space
and tranquillity of Trevereux, and at the beginning of
April Max took her home.

It was on a warm spring day that Harriet was finally sure. Sure enough to want to tell Max.

"Come outside," she said impulsively, "out into the
sunshine."

It was one of those bright spring days full of the simple colours of a child's paintbox, blue sky, green grass, white clouds, and drifts of bright yellow daffodils on the slopes down to the lake. The sound of sheep bleating to their lambs floated from the fields of the home farm, and rooks cawed in the trees beyond the Abbey ruin. The black-and-white tomcat was sunning itself on a windowsill.

They walked round to the ruins, and sat down on the steps of the great entrance. Celandines pushed like golden stars from between the stones, and Harriet picked one, twirling the stalk between her fingers. She was suddenly shy.

"What is it, little one?"

She looked up at him. His tones were gentle and serious, but his eyes smiled.

"Why..." she said, studying his face. Her eyes widened in mock accusation. "I do believe you know already."

He shook his head. The smile had reached his mouth now, and his lips twitched irrepressibly.

"Tell me."

"Well," she began, a soft flush of pink rising up her cheeks, "I believe..." she continued, with a dignity at odds with her smile "... I think I should tell you that..."

She gave up, took his hand between her own, and held it gently against her. She was still slim beneath the sprigged muslin gown, only a hint of roundness to give away her secret, but her eyes sparkled.

He leaned forward and kissed her lips gently.

"Could you be telling me," he asked, "that we shall be needing to renovate the nurseries?"

She laughed then.

"You knew! You did! You are not in the least surprised. And I thought you had not suspected a thing."

"It was only the smallest suspicion," he admitted apologetically. "Not an ounce of certainty. But even a mere husband can see when the wife he loves looks smugger than the stable cat with a cream bowl."

She smiled, closing her eyes contentedly, her face turned up to the sun. She felt smug.

"And you are pleased?" she asked, although she knew the answer.

"Nothing," he replied, "could have made me happier."

And behind them a blackbird sang by its nest in the honeysuckle.

A Singular
Elopement

Elizabeth Lowther

CHAPTER ONE

THE SKY WAS GROWING dark, and already lanterns were being lit on the buildings that fringed the quayside. A fresh wind keened through the rigging of the vessels in Weymouth harbour, rattling halyards against masts and flapping canvas. Lucinda Winterton drew her cloak more tightly about her slight figure. The shiver she gave owed more to apprehension and excitement than to the cold. How could she avoid being excited? She was eloping!

For one last time she gazed about her for any sign of Bernardo before boarding the *Rosamund*. No matter how eagerly she peered into the gathering gloom, she saw no hint of his beloved figure. He would come, though, she did not doubt it. Confidently she hurried along the gangplank.

She was just in time to see Maria, her maid, and the sailor who was carrying her box, disappearing through a door. Swiftly she followed, to find herself at the head of a steep stairway. At first she descended cautiously, then as she neared the bottom happiness and exhilaration bubbled up within her. Once Bernardo arrived they would never be apart again. As soon as they reached Florence they would be married! She was to be the wife of her dearest darling Bernardo! The thought was almost too delightful for her to bear. In a fit of exuberance she leapt down the last few steps.

It was unfortunate that a gentleman happened to be coming out of one of the cabins at the exact moment

that Lucinda took flight. Instead of landing on the
floor she found herself dangling in mid-air, held
tightly against the stranger's broad chest. Her hazel
eyes were on a direct level with cold grey ones.

"Young lady, if you feel inclined to behave in such
a hoydenish manner again, I beg you to look before
you leap." The stranger's voice was as cold as his gaze.
"Had you encountered a person more frail than myself there might have been a serious accident."

Lucinda was not pleased at being reprimanded like
an errant schoolgirl. Her school-days were safely in the
past now; she was nearly eighteen. Soon she would be
a married woman.

"Sir," she said, "noting that your cabin is at the
foot of these stairs, I suggest you make sure no one is
coming down before you shoot out in such a precipi-
tant manner." She was proud of the haughty way she
had addressed this stranger. It was a pity the dignified
effect was spoiled by her being clutched against the
man's chest, suspended like a rag doll.

Similar thoughts must have been passing through
the stranger's mind, for even as he gave a snort of annoyance at her response he set her on her feet again.

"And I suggest you go and find your governess or
whatever unfortunate female has charge of you," he
replied icily.

Indignantly Lucinda pulled herself up to her full
height. Although she was not short, this only brought
her a view of the stranger's dull nankeen waistcoat—
he really was extremely tall. Tall and middle-aged. He
must have been thirty if he was a day. "Governess!"
she exclaimed. "I put such creatures behind me long
ago."

"In that case you abandoned your education too
soon, in my opinion." The disagreeable stranger
turned and began to climb the stairs. Part way up he
stopped and looked back. "And, just to complete that

curtailed education a little, let me inform you that this is not a staircase. On board ship it is a companion-way." He carried on upwards, then, to Lucinda's satisfaction, forgot how little room he had at the top and banged his head.

Putting the encounter with the irritable gentleman out of her mind, she went in search of her own accommodation. It was an easy enough matter, for the *Rosamund* was not a large vessel. She felt suddenly weary. The journey by coach from her home in Somerset had been cold and tedious enough to make the cabin's narrow bunk look decidedly inviting. With a yawn she kicked off her shoes and lay down to rest while she awaited Bernardo.

Bernardo! She loved him so much her mind could not be free of him for long. It was incredible to remember that a scant six months ago she had not known of his existence. She could smile now remembering with what reluctance she had gone home from Miss Gordon's seminary in Bath for the summer vacation.

She had never enjoyed going back to Coombe Dean. What was there there for her except loneliness and boredom? Ever since she could remember her parents had spent their time abroad as her papa went from one diplomatic posting to another. Never had they shown any inclination to have her, their only child, with them, not even for a holiday. Of course, she was not completely abandoned. Officially, at least, she was in the care of her grandmother, but that made little difference. Lady Winterton was absorbed in her own interests and quite content to leave her charge to the indifferent mercies of the servants.

No wonder Lucinda had felt miserable as the coach drew up to the house on that hot summer day, convinced she was condemned to weeks of unutterable tediousness. Her misery had stayed with her until the next morning when, while out walking, she heard music wafting over the grassy parkland. And such music! Sung by a glorious tenor voice. Her curiosity aroused, she had investigated and found Bernardo, alone in a shrubby arbour, practising a Mozart aria. At her approach he had stopped singing.

"I did not mean to disturb you," she said. "Please go on."

"How can I continue when I do not know whose presence is gracing my secret glade?" he replied. His English was excellent, spoken with a wonderful liquid accent which betrayed his nationality.

"I am Lucinda Winterton."

"The granddaughter of my kind patroness?" With an elaborate flourish he took her hand and kissed it. "Lady Winterton did not warn me that her granddaughter would possess such beauty. When you suddenly appeared I thought I was being disturbed by a woodland nymph."

No one had ever spoken to her in such a way before. She realised he was teasing her, yet his velvety dark eyes held a gleam of genuine appreciation. This also was a new experience for Lucinda.

Shyly she drew her hand away from his. "And may I not know your name, sir?" she asked.

"I am Bernardo Arezzo, a poor mountebank, a singer of worthless songs." Again he bowed low. It was a theatrical gesture, with much flourishing, yet Lucinda thought she had never seen anything—or anyone—so dashing.

"Not worthless! Never that!" she protested. "Your singing is the most beautiful I have ever heard. Please, will you sing again?"

"How can I refuse, when such a lovely lady says things that are so kind?"

And he had serenaded her, while Lucinda listened enraptured.

In a few short minutes her life was turned upside down. Loneliness and boredom were banished. By the time Bernardo had sung the final note of his last song she was hopelessly and desperately in love.

It was typical of her grandmother not to have mentioned that her latest protégé was a young Italian opera singer, but then, Lady Winterton had had a long string of protégés over the years. Incredibly, her ladyship had noticed nothing of the growing relationship between her granddaughter and the Italian.

The summer that had promised so little became one long idyll of happiness for Lucinda. She never ceased to be amazed that Bernardo should love her, for she had always regarded herself as unlovable. With his dark good looks, his talent, and his easy charm, she could not understand what he saw in her. But time and time again he had assured her of how much he cared for her, using words so beautiful that her heart almost stopped with joy, and speaking in an accent so wonderful that she felt limp with adoration. Bernardo loved her! There was nothing else she wanted in the whole world.

The idyll had not stopped with the coming of autumn. Although Lucinda had had to go back to the seminary, somehow they'd managed to exchange letters. They had even met secretly once or twice, when Bernardo had engagements in Bath. Then the Christmas holidays had come, and Bernardo had dropped his bombshell. He had received an offer to sing at the Opera House in Florence.

"*Mia cara,* how can I turn away such an opportunity?" he said as Lucinda shed heartbroken tears.

"And how can you bear to leave me when you say you love me?" she sobbed.

"I cannot!"

His reply was pure anguish. And she wept all the more for being the cause of his suffering.

It was Bernardo who decided that they must marry.

"You will go to my grandmother for her blessing?" Lucinda was so astounded that her tears had stopped.

"What would be the use? Lady Winterton would never let a penniless vagabond marry her only granddaughter. No, we must elope."

The idea of such a romantic and exciting solution to their difficulties left her breathless. It took her a moment before she could collect herself enough to whisper, "Yes! We must elope!"

That was how, instead of returning to Miss Gordon's seminary after the Christmas holidays, as her grandmother thought, she was here on board the *Rosamund* awaiting her beloved. He would soon be here . . . he would soon be here . . . Worn out by emotion and travelling, she let her eyelids droop, and she fell asleep.

LUCINDA AWOKE with a start. The cabin, which had been steady before she had fallen asleep, was now rocking and heaving.

"Maria!" she cried in alarm. "We're moving! We must have set sail!"

The only reply from the other bunk was a stricken groan.

"Oh, Maria," Lucinda protested. "This is terrible. We have left port and Signor Arezzo is not here— You cannot be seasick now! I forbid it!"

But Maria could be and was! Much as Lucinda wanted to leave the cabin and go in search of Bernardo, she was too kind-hearted to desert her suffering maid. Not until the poor girl had fallen asleep did she creep away, and by then it was completely dark.

Buffeted by the motion of the ship, she looked along the corridor. The *Rosamund* boasted just eight cabins. Was Bernardo in one of the others? Had his sense of propriety prevented him from coming to her? Well, her sense of propriety did not prevent her from going to him. Boldly she knocked on door after door, in vain. Fortunately she remembered not to knock at the last door; it was occupied by the tiresome middle-aged gentleman and she had no wish to encounter him again.

Somewhat unsteadily, she explored further until she found a door marked "Saloon." Bravely she opened it to be greeted by a waft of tobacco smoke and the gaze from half a dozen pairs of male eyes. Swiftly she excused herself and closed the door again, a cold weight of anxiety growing within her. Bernardo was not in there. There was nothing for it, she would have to look for him on deck.

As she stepped out into the fresh air a gust of salty, damp wind caused her to gasp. The stiff breeze brought an extra colour to her delicate complexion and soon had her long honey-coloured locks blowing free of their hairpins. With difficulty she pulled up the hood on her cape, and then she began her search. It was not easy, for the deck beneath her feet refused to remain still.

Then she saw someone ahead of her on the after-deck. The figure was male, of the right height, and darkly cloaked. It had to be Bernardo.

"Bernardo!" she cried, rushing forward. In her haste she forgot about choppy seas and heaving decks and would have fallen if the figure had not turned and grabbed her in time.

"Steady there. You don't want to end up among the mermaids, do you?" The voice was very young and very English.

Lucinda recovered her balance and looked at her rescuer. In the flickering of the ship's lamps she saw a cheery schoolboy face, topped by a mass of unruly curls.

"Thank you," she shouted in the teeth of the increasing wind. "That was stupid of me."

"Came up for a breath of air, did you?" enquired her new friend.

"Yes, that is right." She could not admit her true reason for being there.

"So did I. Thought I'd have a turn or two about the deck before settling down for the night. Shall we continue together? Hold on to me, then you'll be safe enough. Whoops!" As he spoke an unexpectedly large roll of the ship nearly overbalanced him, and this time Lucinda grabbed at his arm to hold him upright.

"Who will be supporting whom?" she demanded.

"You've a point there," laughed her companion. "That was me almost gone, and I wouldn't make nearly such an effective mermaid as you. Let's support each other, eh? Isn't this splendid fun? I can't imagine why my uncle and the others are stuck in that stuffy old saloon, not when they could be out here."

Another roll of the ship would have sent him staggering but for Lucinda's hold on his arm. Together they began to progress about the deck, braving the vessel's bucking and tossing.

"Doesn't this beat everything?" demanded her new friend.

"Yes, indeed, this is the most splendid fun," she agreed.

In spite of her anxiety over Bernardo she did find it thrilling to face the elements in such a way. It was not a real storm, just a stiff breeze, and the *Rosamund* was a stout vessel. She was not afraid, though she could not hold back a shriek or two of mock fear as the waves struck the ship's bow.

When they returned to the drier confines of below deck the young man's boyish face was beaming with genuine delight. "That was marvellous!" he exclaimed. "Thank you for being such a good sport.

Most young ladies wouldn't have dared to go on deck on a night like this."

"Then they would have missed a treat," she replied.

"That they would! I say, would it be in order to introduce ourselves, seeing that we have recently risked death together?"

It was impossible not to smile at his cheery earnestness.

"Under those circumstances I am sure it would be perfectly proper," she said. "I am Lucinda Winterton."

"And I am Peter Fielding. Your servant, ma'am!" His very correct bow was ruined by a sudden roll of the ship. He cannoned into Lucinda and they finished in an undignified heap on the floor.

"Pleased to make your acquaintance, Miss Winterton," he said gravely, still sitting down.

"I am delighted to meet you, Mr. Fielding," she replied, equally formally despite her unconventional situation.

Then, laughing, they got to their feet.

"Maybe we'll have time to take another turn about the deck tomorrow," said Mr. Fielding. "We won't reach Le Havre until the afternoon, not with this head wind."

"How knowledgeable you are." Lucinda was impressed.

"Not really," he admitted with a chuckle. "I heard the captain tell my uncle. If the weather permits we'll take the air together again, eh?"

"Perhaps. If the weather permits."

Lucinda liked the boy, but she had no wish to commit herself. In spite of everything she still had a feeling that Bernardo was on board somewhere, even though she had been unable to find him.

After she had bade Mr. Fielding goodnight she entered her cabin, half expecting to find Bernardo there. But all she found was the sleeping figure of Maria, who was snoring loudly. Disconsolately she undressed, and climbed into her bunk. Her last thoughts before she went to sleep were troubled ones, filled with worries about Bernardo. Where was he? What had become of him? She had one other major anxiety. What was to happen to her when she arrived in a foreign country completely alone?

LUCINDA SLEPT ON, unaware that Bernardo had actually arrived at Weymouth Docks before her. It had been his idea for them to meet on board ship, with fewer chances for discovery and fewer people to notice them. This eagerness not to be in the public gaze led to disaster. Seeing a likely vessel the moment he arrived on the quay, and wishing to get aboard as quickly as possible, he had demanded of a passing sailor, "This ship, what is she, if you please?"

"Why, the *Rose 'Ammond,*" replied the seaman.

Coincidence, the sailor's strong Dorset accent, and the clay pipe clenched tightly between the man's teeth conspired to confuse Bernardo. If the singer had only looked astern at the vessel's name, or checked a second time, all would have been well, but he did not. Instead, he dashed aboard and demanded of the captain, "I am Signor Arezzo. You have a cabin for me, I think?"

"Indeed I have," replied the captain. In fact, he had several cabins. Few passengers cared to try their luck on his trade route at this time of year. The foreign gentleman was welcome to take his pick.

Bernardo was shown below to the largest, most well-appointed cabin the *Rose Hammond* had to offer. By the time he had settled in they were under way. Alarmed at Lucinda's non-appearance, he dashed on deck and demanded to be put ashore, but he was too late. He was forced to stay aboard and endure the miseries that January could bring to the Western Channel and the Bay of Biscay.

A STEWARD BROUGHT a laden tray to Lucinda's cabin next morning.

"The captain's compliments, miss. He thought you'd prefer to breakfast privately, sooner than be the only lady in the saloon," said the man, deftly setting down his burden.

"But I'm not the only female on the ship," protested Lucinda.

She had been counting on having breakfast in company. That way she could examine her fellow passengers to make sure Bernardo was not among them. It was idiotic, she knew. What reason could he have for hiding from her? But, having spent an anxious, restless night, she was in no shape for rational thought.

"No, miss, you aren't the only lady on board," replied the steward with a chuckle. "You're the only one who's likely to show an interest in boiled ham and a mutton chop, though."

"And what of the other passengers?" Lucinda asked in a sudden fit of inspiration. "Are they all English?"

"Yes, miss, apart from one Scottish gentleman. Is there anything else I can get you?"

"No, thank you." Lucinda dismissed him and turned her attention to her food, though eating was the last thing she wanted. It was not the heaving motion of the ship which was putting her off her breakfast, it was worry. The steward's words had forced her to accept what common sense had been telling her all along—Bernardo was definitely not on board the *Rosamund*.

The wind had strengthened considerably during the night, making it unsafe for passengers to go on deck. Lucinda had no alternative but to remain in her cabin, attending to her prostrate maid, and worrying about her own immediate future. Bernardo would not have deserted her, of that she was convinced. Her last hopes were now pinned upon their arrival at Le Havre. Surely he would be there, waiting for her at the harbour? How and why he should have crossed the Channel ahead of her she had no idea, but she had to cling to this one final straw.

SADLY THE DOCKS AT Le Havre were particularly devoid of handsome Italians. Lucinda's box was deposited on the quayside, and she took up position beside it, not certain what to do next.

"Why, hello there, Miss Winterton. We didn't get our turn about the deck after all, did we?" a cheery voice hailed her.

Looking up, she saw Peter Fielding dodging his way among the disembarking passengers.

"Good day to you, Mr. Fielding," she said quietly.

He regarded her with concern. "If you'll pardon me for saying so, you're not looking quite the thing. All that tossing and bobbing about, I dare say. Do your travelling companions know you're here? Shall I fetch them for you?"

"Thank you, that will not be necessary," she replied. "I have no travelling companions."

"No companions?" he said in astonishment. "Surely you are not travelling alone? Where are you bound?"

"Florence."

"That is a prodigious way to go unaccompanied."

"It was not my intention to travel by myself. There has been some terrible misunderstanding or mix-up..." Lucinda knew it was not wise to spread details of her predicament abroad, but she could not help herself. She felt so distressed and alone, and for all his boyishness Peter Fielding had a kind face. "I was to meet my companion at the ship, but the person did not arrive. I had hoped that when—when we reached Le Havre..."

"That when you reached Le Havre your friend might be here, eh?" completed the boy. "But there is no one, is that it?"

Lucinda nodded, holding back her tears with difficulty.

Peter Fielding gave her shoulder a friendly pat. "You have no need to worry," he assured her. "My uncle's about somewhere. He's exactly the person to sort out this muddle for you. I'll fetch him. He'll find your friend and have you on your way in no time. Wait here."

He dashed off at great speed. She watched him go, feeling her spirits lift a little. When she saw him returning those same spirits plummeted once more.

"Oh, no!" she exclaimed. "It is you again."

"My sentiments exactly," said Peter's uncle.

How unfortunate that he should turn out to be the disagreeable gentleman with whom she had collided on the ship.

"Have you two already met?" asked Peter in surprise.

"Briefly, though forcefully," replied his uncle.

"Then I can still have the pleasure of introducing you. Miss Winterton, may I present my uncle, Sir Gareth Chalfont? Uncle, this is Miss Winterton." Peter beamed happily, seemingly oblivious to the chilly atmosphere which existed between the others.

"Your servant, ma'am." Sir Gareth gave a bow. As she bobbed an answering curtsy Lucinda noted that if his gesture had been any more slight it would have been indiscernible to the naked eye. However, at his age, no doubt any unnecessary movement was to be avoided.

"As I understand it, Miss Winterton, you have got yourself into a scrape," said Sir Gareth. His tone suggested that he could have expected nothing more of her.

"No, I have not, sir," she retorted. "I followed my instructions to the letter. We were to meet on the *Rosamund*; I was there, my travelling companion was not."

"Which suggests that your travelling companion is not reliable. I am surprised that your parents did not choose someone more suitable."

"That is not the case at all, sir!" she protested angrily. "I fear there has been an accident or something to cause such a delay. And besides, my parents did not make the arrangements. I did."

She should not have said that. At once Sir Gareth's dark eyebrows rose suspiciously.

"Somewhat   unconventional,   I   would   have thought," he said.

"My—my parents are abroad. I see little of them." Lucinda tried desperately to cover her slip of the tongue.

"Has no one charge of you?" His disapproval was becoming more and more evident.

"Of course. My grandmother."

"Then surely she—"

"She considers me to be old enough to manage my own affairs." Lucinda tossed her head haughtily.

Sir Gareth was not impressed. He gave a noncommittal grunt. He regarded her for several minutes, a disconcerting stare which made her feel uncomfortable. Determined not to show her unease she glared back. Seen in a decent light he proved to be more presentable than she had first thought. His dark hair held a fleck of red, and threatened to be as curly as Peter's

if not held well in check. His face was strong, with
well-defined cheekbones and an extremely determined chin. Standing on the open quayside, he seemed
altogether more massive than he had on the ship, for
his great height was matched by a muscular build,
particularly about the shoulders.

"Since your companion failed to arrive, I am surprised you did not abandon your journey at Weymouth," he said. "One can get off a ship as easily as
one can get on."

"I know that," she retorted, then added more quietly, "but I fell asleep."

"Very well," he said abruptly. "I have no wish to be
entangled in your business, but I will make enquiries
at the Customs post in case your companion has already arrived. What name shall I give?"

Lucinda did not reply.

"Come, Miss Winterton. How can I help you if you
do not give me the man's name? I presume your intended companion is a man."

She remained mutinously silent.

"I say, you aren't eloping or anything jolly like that,
are you?" demanded Peter.

Lucinda tried to say "Of course not" but she had
never been an easy liar. Her stammered words and
flushed cheeks gave everything away.

"My word, wait until my sisters hear about this!"
Peter cried. "They'll go pea-green with—" He got no
further, silenced by a fierce look from his uncle.

"A most singular elopement indeed, with the bridegroom absent," he said sarcastically. "Is it too much
to hope that you are of age?"

"I am eighteen—nearly," she replied, stung by his
disparaging manner.

"That is what I feared."

Sir Gareth snapped his fingers at two passing porters and issued an order in terse, fluent French. The

men rushed forward and took up Lucinda's box, tipping off a dozing Maria, and began returning it to the *Rosamund* at great speed.

"Where are they—?" Lucinda began, but her words were cut short as Sir Gareth took her arm and began propelling her swiftly after her luggage. "Let go!" she protested. "Where are you taking me?"

"I am putting you back on board the ship," he said through gritted teeth. "Eloping, indeed! A chit of your age!"

"I will not go!" Lucinda was torn between wanting to protest loudly yet not make a scene. "I am eloping."

"No, you are not! You cannot elope by yourself. I am putting you in the charge of the captain, with instructions to see you get back to your grandmother."

"You cannot make me go!"

"Yes, I can. I am much bigger than you, or had it escaped your notice?"

"Sir, this is most ungentlemanly and caddish and not at all the thing," Lucinda puffed. She was getting out of breath through hurrying.

"It is, is it not?" agreed her captor.

They were almost back at the *Rosamund* now.

"Let me go this instant, or I will scream and tell everyone you are abducting me," she threatened.

"Do not be foolish," snapped Sir Gareth.

Lucinda opened her mouth and uttered an earsplitting scream. Sir Gareth muttered something barely audible under his breath and let go of her arm. All about them the busy harbourside came to a halt as everyone looked in their direction. A stout gentleman moved towards them suspiciously until Sir Gareth exclaimed hastily, "The vapours, sir! The vapours. Young girl . . . first time abroad . . ."

Lucinda was gratified to notice he had gone rather pink about the ears. She faced up to him.

"I am not going back to England!" she said decisively. "I will wait here for my fiancé."

"Fiancé! I can think of a better name for a scoundrel who would entice a young girl away from her family and friends."

"He enticed me away from remarkably little," she replied honestly. "I will await him in Le Havre."

"The next packet from Weymouth to Le Havre is not until next week. What if this chevalier of yours comes by way of Cherbourg or St. Malo? Are you convinced he will come here for you?"

This was something that had not occurred to her. She knew Bernardo had very little money. In fact, she had given him his boat fare. Would he have enough resources to wait another week or might he be forced to come by another route?

"Then I will go on to Florence. I am sure to meet up with him there," she said.

"To Florence? Alone?" He evidently did not think much of her chances.

"Yes," she replied, with much more confidence than she felt.

At that moment a hot and breathless Peter came running up. In their sparring neither his uncle nor Lucinda had noticed he was missing.

"What's been happening? Have I missed anything exciting?" he demanded.

"You missed me trying to persuade Miss Winterton how wise she would be to return home."

"And you missed me refusing!" she added.

"Perhaps you should change your mind," Peter said. "I have just been speaking to the official at the Customs. He was most obliging and went through his records for me. Signor Arezzo has not come through Le Havre."

"How did you know his name?" gasped Lucinda.

"A little bird told me." Peter gave no further clue, but she could guess.

"That little bird had better learn discretion or else she will be looking for a new situation," she snapped.

"He forced it out of me, honest he did, miss," wailed Maria.

"I am sure he did, with a half-crown, no doubt."

"She did right to tell me, otherwise I could not make the enquiries," Peter said. "Now you know he isn't here, hadn't you better go back to Weymouth?"

"No! I am going on to Florence."

"Miss Winterton." Sir Gareth had lowered his voice and sounded quite reasonable—for him. "Miss Winterton, my nephew is right. We both beg you to reconsider. If it is a question of shortage of funds I would be happy to help."

"I have plenty of money, I thank you." Her reply was icy.

"You are placing me in a very difficult position, miss." Sir Gareth's bout of reasonableness was remarkably short-lived. Already he was sounding increasingly irritable. "Normally I would feel honour bound to return to England with you or else remain here as your guardian. However, I have not the time to do either. My journey is a matter of business, not pleasure, so I must continue as swiftly as possible."

"That is all right," Lucinda said airily. "I need neither a protector nor a guardian. I can look after myself. Besides, I have already told you, I have made up my mind to go to Florence."

"Miss Winterton, has anyone ever told you you are stubborn and foolish and completely lacking in common sense?" demanded Sir Gareth angrily.

"No, sir." She smiled at him sweetly. "And if they did I would not listen!"

Sir Gareth gave vent to something between a roar and a snarl.

"Very well, cope by yourself!" he snapped. "I have tried to help you. I have tried to talk sense to you, to no avail. Go to Florence by yourself! Get into all sorts of trouble and scrapes. It is no more than you deserve!"

He turned on his heel and stalked away, his nephew hurrying after crying, "But, Uncle, we can't... Uncle, pray reconsider..."

Peter's uncle was in no mood for reconsidering. He strode through puddles in his Hessian boots, the skirts of his greatcoat swirling in the wind. Sir Gareth did not look back once, and soon he had turned the corner out of sight.

Lucinda was conscious of a feeling of desolation the moment he disappeared. The landscape suddenly seemed very empty without him. Here she was alone in a strange land, and the only two people she knew had gone. True, one of those people had been unpleasant in the extreme, but it made no difference. Here she was entirely by herself. She discounted Maria. She knew her maid far too well to expect comfort or support from her.

It took a superhuman effort for Lucinda not to sit down on her box and weep. What good would tears do? She would have to find herself somewhere to stay for the night, then find some transport for the next day, and no doubt organise a route. She knew she had to go south; apart from that, her knowledge of the geography of France was sketchy. A hundred snags and problems leapt into her head as even her attempts to find a porter to carry her box met with little response. She, who was accustomed to loneliness, had never felt more lonely in her life.

The crunch of boots on gravel made her look up. Sir Gareth was striding towards her, his face like thunder.

"I know I am all kinds of fool," he declared, "but I cannot leave you here alone. My business lies in Rome. Nevertheless, against every kind of better judgement, I am willing to escort you to Florence, though I am convinced I shall regret it."

Even if Lucinda had wanted to object she got no opportunity, for Sir Gareth had again produced a couple of porters seemingly out of thin air. They seized her box once more and set off with it. Sir Gareth strode after them, leaving her to follow as best she could.

Their destination was a carriage, against which leaned the gangling figure of Peter. He straightened up as they approached.

"You are to come with us after all, then? Splendid!" he said, preparing to hand Lucinda into the vehicle.

"One moment, if you please." She paused with her foot on the carriage step. "I am not convinced this is a wise thing to do. How do I know your intentions are honourable?"

"Of course they are," protested Peter. "I swear they are."

"No doubt. It was not your intentions I was questioning." She glared in the direction of Sir Gareth.

At once Peter was convulsed with laughter. "If that isn't a one for the books," he chortled. "My uncle Chalfont's honour being doubted. The most respected man for miles! A paragon of virtue held up to us lesser mortals as an example—"

"That is enough, thank you," snapped his uncle. "I promise you, Miss Winterton, that I have not the least design on your virtue. Rest assured, my tastes do not run to immature schoolgirls. I have never lacked for more amenable mature female company..."

"That's true," put in Peter. "Run after him in droves, they do. He's reckoned to be the best catch in the county..."

"For more mature female company," repeated his uncle ominously. "I have no need to abduct young girls, no matter what you tried to suggest back there."

"Uncle Chalfont? Accused of abduction? This gets better and better." Peter collapsed with laughter once more. "Wait until I tell Mama! She'll laugh herself silly."

"If you ever wish to see your mother again I suggest you get into the carriage," snarled Sir Gareth. "And you, miss," he added as his nephew obeyed, still chuckling. "Either get in too, or else step back and let us be on our way!"

Lucinda did not have much choice. Her box had already been strapped on. She got into the carriage.

"When is our first stop?" she asked.

"In about five minutes," Sir Gareth informed her drily. "At the Customs. If you will give me your papers I will see to everything."

"Papers?" said Lucinda. "What papers?"

"Are you telling me that you have no documents? No permission of entry? No visas to travel across France?"

"No," she said in a small voice.

"What sort of a fool have you got entangled with? First he fails to keep your rendezvous, then he neglects to ensure that you have the right documents. The man must be either a rogue or an idiot!"

"He is neither!" Lucinda cried. "He is kind and charming and wonderful."

"And rich?" asked Sir Gareth, looking pointedly at her elegant bonnet, her fine cloak with its quilted lining of rich silk, her expensive kid boots.

"That, sir, is none of your concern." She thrust her hands deep into her muff so that the gold bracelets at her wrists were no longer visible.

Sir Gareth gave one of his noncommittal grunts, then the carriage came to a halt as they reached the Customs post at the dock gates.

"I had better have your full name," he said, preparing to get down, "and your date of birth. And your maid's details."

He was back in a few minutes, looking disgruntled.

"I have got you the appropriate papers," he said. "It went much against the grain, but I had to use bribery."

Reaching for her reticule, Lucinda said, "Pray tell me, how much do I owe you?"

Sir Gareth looked affronted. "I do not accept money from women," he said. "Especially silly young ones."

"Now you've offended him," whispered Peter in her ear. Aloud he said, "Uncle, for the sake of propriety we must think up a story to explain our travelling together. I know, Miss Winterton could be your daughter."

"Certainly not!" retorted Sir Gareth. "That would make me indecently precocious, a father at the age of twelve!"

"There is the difference in surnames, too," Lucinda pointed out. "And besides, Sir Gareth is not a bit like my papa. My papa is handsome."

Sir Gareth said something she did not hear, while Peter smothered a chuckle.

"Then you must be my half-sister," he said, having got his mirth under control. "That would account for the names."

"No," said his uncle. "Miss Winterton shall be my ward. I have said as much to the Customs officials." Unexpectedly he heaved a sigh.

"You're looking glum, sir," said Peter.

"Is it any wonder?" demanded his uncle. "I left England a man of honour and integrity. I have known Miss Winterton for just a few hours, yet since making her acquaintance I have been obliged to lie, deceive and use bribery, not to mention been accused of abducting females and allied crimes. So much in such a short time! I am wondering to what depths I will have sunk by the time we reach Florence."

Lucinda scarcely heard him. Her attention had been caught by the one magic word, Florence. She was on her way to that lovely city. More than that, she was on her way to Bernardo.

CHAPTER TWO

THEY HAD SPENT the night at Le Havre, but Monsieur Colmar, the courier who was to guide them across France, had insisted they depart before it was light. Five hours of rattling through Normandy now made Lucinda very thankful for the chance to stretch her legs. The half-timbered inn that was their first real stop looked promising and the savoury smells wafting from the kitchen induced an unladylike growl from her stomach.

"Our meal will be ready in half an hour," Sir Gareth said. "Would you like to rest?"

"I would prefer to walk," said Lucinda. "I am rather stiff."

"Then I will come with you."

"There is no need. I will be quite safe. You stay here and take your ease." She was suddenly stricken in case he felt obliged to accompany her.

Unexpectedly, he smiled. She had never seen him smile before. It made the resemblance between him and Peter quite remarkable. "I think I could manage to hobble along the road a little way," he said. "If you promise not to go faster than a shuffle."

"I am sorry, I did not mean to be insulting."

"You were not," he assured her. "I fancy you were showing consideration for my great age, but after being shaken up in the carriage my bones are grateful for any respite. Shall we go?"

"Is Peter not coming?" she asked.

"A game of *boules* at the inn is more to his taste."

They strolled leisurely along the road in silence for a while. Lucinda was forced to admit that Sir Gareth's massive presence by her side was reassuring. She knew she was fortunate to have met with him and Peter. Now that they had embarked upon their journey she appreciated how badly she would have fared alone.

"I have not thanked you for agreeing to be my escort to Florence," she said suddenly. "I should have expressed my gratitude to you before now. You would have been quite justified in abandoning me at the quayside yesterday."

"No doubt. But I would have worried about your fate for the rest of my journey."

She looked up at him in surprise. "Why should that be?" she asked. "I am a stranger to you."

"It makes no difference. I could not have left you alone and unprotected. So you see, your gratitude is unnecessary. I am only saving myself from adding grey hairs to my aged and feeble condition." He looked so grave that she was not sure whether or not he was joking. His next comment was far from being funny, however. "Lucinda, you have proved you have spirit. You have enjoyed your adventure. Now please return home!"

"No, sir. I will go on to Florence," she replied mutinously.

They had agreed that, since she was supposed to be his ward, Sir Gareth should address Lucinda by her Christian name. They had both balked at her emulating Peter and calling him Uncle Chalfont!

"Nor is there any point in you continuing to try to discover my father's name or any such details, as you were doing all through dinner last evening," she went on. "I have no wish to be traced."

"Will you not have been missed by now?"

"I doubt it," she said confidently. "I sent a letter imitating my grandmother's hand to the seminary saying I would not be returning."

"How ingenious of you. Such a move shows a resourceful mind."

"The idea was not mine. All credit must go to Bern—" She stopped, realising too late that he was being sarcastic, not approving. "At any rate I will not be missed until Easter."

"What will happen when your grandmother visits you, or writes to you? Surely that will start a hue and cry?"

"Why should she visit or write?" She was surprised at his question.

"Is she infirm?"

"Certainly not. But it would never occur to her to do either."

"Your parents, then. You say they are abroad. Surely they return to England sometimes?"

"Of course, but they do not care for Bath. They prefer to stay in London."

"But they write to you?"

"Not often. Why should they?"

Sir Gareth seemed nonplussed by the question. "Why? To show their concern for you. My parents wrote to me regularly when I was at school, and visited me when they could."

"Ah, but you were a boy. Had I been a boy then of course they would have shown an interest. It is my fault I disappointed them by being a girl." Her tone was matter-of-fact, with no trace of self-pity.

"I do not see why you should consider your sex to be your fault. Nor do I see what being a girl has to do with it. My parents made no difference between my sister, Peter's mother, and myself. They paid her exactly the same amount of attention."

"Did they really?" Lucinda was amazed. "Then no doubt, unlike me, she is a great beauty."

"She is comely enough, but nothing special," he said, with brotherly candour. "Tell me, who shows any interest in your welfare?"

"Why, no one. Certainly not Miss Gordon at the seminary. She will be glad to be rid of me. I was not a model pupil." She gave a chuckle at the thought.

Sir Gareth, however, was not amused. He was positively glowering.

"Your pardon, sir, you seem displeased. Have I said something to anger you?" she asked in a small voice.

"Not you," he replied grimly. "Certainly not you." Then he came to an abrupt halt. "Our meal should be ready by now," he said. "We had best go back to the inn before Peter wolfs the lot."

Lucinda was more than ready for food. But while they were eating, and afterwards when they resumed their journey, she caught Sir Gareth giving her curious glances that were half sad, half pitying. She could not think why.

Their carriage, followed by another carrying the servants and the luggage, continued through the winter countryside. To Lucinda they seemed to be moving agonisingly slowly. Much of the time she spent in happy day-dreams of being a bride in Florence. She could imagine nothing more romantic. She would buy her bride clothes when they reached Paris, and so dazzle Bernardo with her elegance that his glorious dark eyes would glow with love and admiration to look at her. It would be like a fairy tale.

Peter had found his own pastime. He had bought himself a set of *boules*, and become very keen on the French game. Surprisingly Sir Gareth seemed to share his enthusiasm, and often, when they stopped, the pair of them would find a space to practise. Uncle and nephew shared an easy family affection which Lucinda found as incomprehensible as it was enviable. Sir Gareth's reason for travelling was equally bewildering to her. She could not imagine why he should cross Europe in midwinter simply to sort out the muddled affairs of a recently widowed relative in Rome. Why had he not sent his man of business instead?

"I suppose you are keeping your uncle company?" she asked Peter, as the carriage rumbled on.

"Yes. Uncle Chalfont hopes Italy will have a civilising effect on me."

She wondered what it would be like to have a kinsman like Sir Gareth, someone who was there when you needed him. She decided it might be quite agreeable.

The less pleasing aspects of a close relationship with Sir Gareth became only too apparent the next day. The morning's journey had gone particularly well, and they arrived at St. Germain-en-Laye in good time.

"I think we have done enough travelling for today," he announced. "I suggest we do a little sightseeing this afternoon."

Considering its magnificent setting between the forest and the River Seine, the town proved to be disappointingly modest. Lucinda wondered what there was to be seen in such a place. Peter soon provided the answer.

"Monsieur Colmar says there used to be some interesting grottoes not far away," he informed her. "I would certainly like to look for them—wouldn't you?"

"Indeed I would." Lucinda gave an excited shiver. "How romantic! Perhaps they will be all dark and ghostly." She clasped her hands in happy anticipation.

Just then Sir Gareth entered the room.

"Ah, there you both are," he said. "The carriage will be here to take us on our excursion in ten minutes."

"Can we go to the grottoes?" asked Lucinda eagerly.

"I doubt if they still exist. No, I have planned a visit to the château."

"Is it one with a dungeon where prisoners were left to rot, and a torture chamber and everything?" asked Peter hopefully.

"I doubt it," said his uncle. "I believe it was built on medieval foundations, but the palace itself is in the Renaissance style."

"Renaissance!" Lucinda groaned.

"Do not sound so disparaging. You do not know what it means."

"Yes, I do!" she retorted. "It is boring classical fifteenth-century stuff. Can we not look for the grottoes instead?"

"No!" There was uncomfortable finality in the way Sir Gareth said the word. "We are fortunate to have this opportunity. While Napoleon was our enemy English people had no chance to explore France. Now that Boney is safe on Elba we can see firsthand one of the finest cultures in Europe."

Europe's finest culture could not compare with the fun of exploring gloomy grottoes, in the estimation of Lucinda and Peter. With all the persuasiveness at their disposal they set about getting Sir Gareth to change his mind.

The château proved to be everything Lucinda had feared it would be. Handsome enough in its way, she supposed, but even the Revolution had passed it by without turning it into a respectably romantic ruin. At the end of the tour the concierge led them up a twisting corkscrew staircase and thence, surprisingly, on to a narrow rooftop walk from which they could see a magnificent panorama of rolling countryside. Clutching her bonnet, Lucinda gazed about her. For the first time she forgot about her disappointment over the ancient grottoes. This was truly beautiful.

"*Voilá, mademoiselle, messieurs,*" declared the concierge. "To the east you can see Paris."

Paris! The very name gave Lucinda a thrill.

"Is it far, *monsieur*?" she asked.

"*Non, mademoiselle.* Less than twenty kilometres."

"So close?" She turned to Sir Gareth and clutched at his arm. "Let us go on to Paris," she begged. "There is plenty of daylight left. Then I can do my shopping early tomorrow and we can continue on our way in the afternoon."

"Who said we were going through Paris?" asked Sir Gareth.

"We are, aren't we? I mean—I assumed..." She stared at him in disbelief.

"You assumed incorrectly," he said abruptly.

"But I was going to buy my bride clothes there. I had set my heart on it." Lucinda's voice was almost a wail.

"Then it is just as well we are not going," snapped Sir Gareth. "It will prevent you from spending money you can ill afford."

"I can afford it!" she protested. "I have enough to buy myself bride clothes."

"I am certain you have, but if you spend it all on Paris finery how much will be left? Enough to set up home with your Italian Romeo?"

He had a point. Lucinda had brought ample funds with her, but what would happen when her resources were at an end? How much would Bernardo earn at the Opera House? Not a great deal, she suspected. Oddly enough, they had not discussed finances. It had been a sordid subject, unworthy of their great love. Somehow it had rather been assumed that she would have enough for both of them. Sir Gareth's words had come as a timely, if unpleasant, reminder. She would not admit it, though, not when he spoke in that acid tone he reserved for Bernardo.

"I want to look beautiful on my wedding day! Is that so extraordinary?" she demanded.

Sir Gareth did not speak. By way of reply he gave one of his incomprehensible grunts.

It had scarcely been a successful day. And when they returned to the inn the *patron* informed them that he had another guest, an English milady.

Lady Alicia Monkton was already in the sitting-room when they entered. She was exactly the kind of woman Lucinda longed to be. Aged about six- or seven-and-twenty, she had a poise and an assurance the young girl was desperate to attain. Her features were strikingly beautiful, and from the top of her sleek dark head to the toes of her flat silk slippers she was elegance personified. She had with her a self-effacing married couple who sat silently in the background, well away from the fire. They had "poor relations" stamped all over them.

"Sir Gareth," Lady Alicia said, after introductions had been made, "was ever a poor female traveller more fortunate than myself? I never expected to find an English gentleman—and the epitome of English kindness and courtesy, if I may say so—here in the depths of foreign soil. I am too, too grateful to you for allowing me a share of your cosy quarters."

Lucinda thought Lady Alicia was being too, too flattering. Sir Gareth, however, seemed to see nothing amiss. He bowed over the lady's hand, positively glowing as he mumbled words that were suitably modest and manly.

"And these are your two little travelling companions," simpered Lady Alicia, turning to Lucinda and Peter. "How sweet!"

Lucinda disliked her from that moment. The way the Monkton woman made up to Sir Gareth was nothing short of indecent in her estimation. She did everything bar climb into his pocket. And the way he lapped it up! Lucinda was quite disappointed in him. It had never occurred to her that he would be susceptible to feminine wiles.

At least she was spared the irritation of having to be polite to the older woman; Lady Alicia neatly cut her out of the conversation, and kept her out throughout the evening. Lucinda did not care. She ordered working candles, and, taking out her pencils, began to sketch Peter, until the boy grew bored with sitting still and went to seek more exciting company.

Unexpectedly Lady Alicia said, "You are very quiet, my dear. What can be occupying you so completely? Do bring it to show me."

Lucinda would have preferred to keep her work to herself, but Lady Alicia was already holding out her hand for the sketching-block. With great reluctance she handed over her sketch.

"So you have been drawing," said Lady Alicia, stating the painfully obvious. Then she turned to Sir Gareth and said, "Is she not adorable?" in a coy, condescending voice which set Lucinda's teeth on edge. Her tone changed, though, when she looked at the sketch.

"Why, this is good! Is it not, Sir Gareth?"

"It is," he replied. "You have caught Peter's expression exactly, Lucinda. It is a first-rate likeness."

"What a clever girl you are!" Lady Alicia's tone of praise was not convincing. "And did your governess teach you to be so clever? Or do you attend a seminary?"

"I *used* to attend a seminary," said Lucinda with careful emphasis. "Our drawing master there was very good, and I was fortunate enough to have another tutor who was even better.''

"And who was that? Will you let me into your little secret?'' asked Lady Alicia playfully.

Lucinda was getting tired of being treated as if she were a very backward six-year-old.

"Sir Thomas Lawrence has been kind enough to give me lessons.''

"Sir Thomas Lawrence?'' There was amused disbelief in Lady Alicia's voice. "My dear, you were indeed fortunate. You do realise Sir Thomas is the foremost portrait painter of the day?''

"Of course I do!''

"Well, if you must have an alleged master I suppose it is only reasonable to choose the best.''

Lady Alicia's incredulity, along with her use of the word "alleged" stung Lucinda to the quick.

"I am telling the truth!'' she exclaimed. "How dare you not believe me?''

"Lucinda!'' Sir Gareth broke in reprovingly.

She looked at him and saw the disbelief in his eyes too.

"I am not lying,'' she cried in distress.

"Lucinda, a man as eminent as Sir Thomas does not give drawing lessons to schoolgirls,'' he said.

"Yes, he does. He has given them to me. Whenever he visits my grandmother he helps me with my drawing. He is a very kind gentleman. You still think I am lying, do you not?'' She did not care about Lady Alicia, but the distress caused by Sir Gareth's lack of trust caught her unawares.

"I am not lying,'' she insisted. "And I can prove it.''

She rushed from the room, thankful to hide the angry tears that welled unbidden to her eyes. In a few minutes she was back.

Sir Gareth was alone in the sitting-room; Lady Alicia had collected her downtrodden relatives and departed.

"She should have waited," declared Lucinda indignantly. "I can prove what I say is true."

"There is no need," said Sir Gareth.

"Yes there is! You let Lady Alicia influence you into believing I was lying!"

On the table she laid a silver picture-frame. It held two portraits in water-colour.

"There!" she exclaimed, her voice trembling. "Sir Thomas painted Papa's portrait and Mama's for the Embassy. These are two of his sketches. When he learned I had no likenesses of my parents he sent them to me. He signed them on the back. Look!" Hurriedly she began to undo the clips on the frame.

"There is no need," repeated Sir Gareth more urgently.

"Yes, there is!" she repeated, still struggling with the obstinate fastenings. "You do not believe me."

"It is not important." His large hands covered hers, stilling the frantic scrabbling of her fingers. "You do not need to prove anything to me."

He had still not said that he believed her! She kept her face lowered. He must never know how much his disapproval could hurt her...never! But her tears turned traitor and began to course down her cheeks. Her hands were still held captive; she was unable to wipe the tears away. The first sniff betrayed her.

"You are crying!" Sir Gareth sounded aghast. In an instant he had released her hands. "Please do not cry!" he begged.

Suddenly she was being rocked comfortingly in his arms, having her tears mopped with an immaculate handkerchief. Bewildered, she heard him say, "I am a wretch! To have mistrusted you! It is unthinkable! I will never do so again, I promise."

She could think of no words in reply. It was unexpectedly pleasant being cradled in his arms, her damp face pressed against the nankeen waistcoat she had so recently despised. A few moments ago she had been racked by hurt and a sense of betrayal. Now she felt safe, protected, even cherished—a swift change of emotions which stunned her senses. She would have been quite happy to stay like that for ever.

But suddenly Sir Gareth cleared his throat with startled urgency. "There, are you feeling better?" he asked, holding her away from him with arms outstretched.

"Yes, thank you," she said shakily, the distance between them making her feel oddly bereft.

"Perhaps you had better go to bed now, eh? We have to be up betimes tomorrow." He was making a valiant effort to put on his "jolly uncle" voice. He was not succeeding very well.

"Yes, you are right." She collected up the likenesses of her parents, using the activity to mask her awkwardness.

"Goodnight to you, then." His uncomfortable demeanour lasted until she reached the door, then he called to her. "Lucinda, I am so sorry about today. Not only about your drawing, but for disappointing you about Paris. I should have known you would want to do some shopping. I am afraid we do not have time to make a diversion to Paris now."

"I dare say I will find some tolerable warehouses further on," she said.

"You will look beautiful at your wedding no matter what you wear. Your Bernardo is a lucky fellow." He did not sound at all like an uncle now. Instead, his voice held a hint of something which might have been regret.

Lucinda was not sure what to say. To cover her uncertainty she bade him goodnight, and went up to bed in a state of wonderment.

The next morning Monsieur Colmar had them on the road before dawn, as usual. There was no sign of Lady Alicia.

"It's a pity we did not see Lady Alicia before we set out," remarked Peter as their small cavalcade rumbled away from the inn. "Such a handsome woman, don't you agree?"

"Yes, very handsome..." Lucinda replied. "For her age..."

"I fear you consider everyone over the age of five-and-twenty as positively antediluvian," Sir Gareth remarked.

"No, I do not!" she protested. "You are far more than five-and-twenty, yet I do not consider you to be as old as that. In fact, I do not think you are really old at all, just a little bit—" She got no further, for both of her companions burst out laughing.

"Well, if you are going to mock me..." She moved back into her corner.

"Don't worry, Uncle. I don't think you are antediluvian, either," said Peter. "More sort of prehistoric."

Lucinda was glad of the joking, even if some of it had been at her expense. She had sensed a tension between Sir Gareth and herself; she feared he might have regretted being so kind to her the night before. As she joined in the laughter it dispelled the difficult atmosphere, and to her relief relationships returned to normal.

The rain began on their way to Fontainebleau, then turned to snow. For a day or two it was no more than an inconvenience, slowing their progress. Then they reached more hilly country, a densely forested region with few villages and even fewer towns, just an occasional tiny hamlet or a farmhouse.

It was as they crossed this inhospitable region that the blizzard began. Heavy white flakes were hurled against the coach by a screaming wind, making visibility impossible. In spite of the luxury of rugs and footwarmers Lucinda had never been so cold. She felt desperately anxious for Monsieur Colmar and the driver outside, not to mention the horses who were struggling bravely through the growing drifts. Her anxiety mounted unbearably when Sir Gareth took his turn on the box, to give the courier and his companion a chance to thaw out. Their situation was perilous, she knew. Stories of travellers freezing to death through being caught in snowstorms were not mere Banbury tales.

"We will stop at the first place that can offer us any refuge," decided Sir Gareth. "Even if it is only a barn."

By some miracle they found their shelter, not in a barn, but at an inn. No one cared that it was small and far from grand. The *patronne* had taken one look at them and dragged them in front of the roaring log fire, wrapped them in dry blankets and pressed bowls of hot soup into their hands, while an ostler had dashed out to take care of the exhausted horses.

The inn's accommodation was very basic. There were no private apartments, just one large room which served as bar, parlour and kitchen.

"The sleeping arrangements aren't much, milord," said the *patronne*, twisting her apron in her hands at the thought of her inn's deficiencies. "I can manage a space in the attic for the young lady and her maid. There's just grain and such up there, so she'll be private. But the best I can offer you gentlemen is a place by the fire."

Sir Gareth listened as the fierce wind swept a storm of driven snow against the shuttered windows.

"*Madame,*" he said sincerely, "no château could offer us anything more welcome."

"Oh, milord!" The woman bobbed him a delighted curtsy.

Lucinda felt more than ready for bed. She had no qualms about her attic bedroom, though she was rather taken aback when the *patronne* thrust the inn's cat into her arms with the words, "Best take Minou, *mademoiselle*, just in case..."

Whatever Lucinda thought about the arrangement, the cat decided it was a good idea and eagerly leapt up the ladder ahead of her.

"I do not mind this place for myself or Peter," said Sir Gareth, as Lucinda prepared to follow the animal, "but I fear this accommodation is not suitable for you. I am very sorry."

"We are safe and sound," she replied. "That is all that matters. As for my bedchamber, it may be rather unconventional, but I shall be very snug among the sacks of corn. I fancy you have the worst to endure."

"Then I hope you remember the fact if you see me stiff and hobbling in the morning. Please do not make any remarks about aged bones and rheumatics... Here, you must have light." He lit a candle and handed it to her. "Lucinda," he said earnestly, "you have borne up to all the discomfort superbly. No vapours, no hysterics, not even a word of complaint. You are a young lady in a million."

Surely she had been mistaken? Could this be Sir Gareth offering her such praise and approval?

Then he bent and kissed her. It was no more than a touching of his lips on hers, yet the warmth of their brief contact shot through her.

"Goodnight, and God bless you, my dear," he said quietly.

And Lucinda, still savouring the softness of his mouth and the gentleness of his words, could barely bid him goodnight in return.

The next morning there was no wind, no driving snow, just blue sky and a bright sun shining down on a world of shimmering white.

"What a change!" declared Sir Gareth, regarding the sparkling landscape through the inn door. "Nevertheless, I think we will rest here for another night, if you can accommodate us, *madame*?"

"One more night? Mon Dieu, you'll have need to stay longer than that, milord. All roads out of the village are blocked," chortled the *patronne*.

"You mean we are cut off?" asked Lucinda in dismay. "How long for?"

The *patronne* gave a shrug. "This is in the hands of le Bon Dieu, *mademoiselle*. One week, four weeks, maybe more."

A possible delay of several weeks on their journey! It was terrible! What could she do? Then she realised there was nothing she could do. Bernardo's contract at Florence was for a whole season; he would still be there when she arrived. Annoying though it was, there was no point in fretting over something which could not be helped.

Sir Gareth apparently shared her views.

"Since we are stuck here I suggest we make the most of it by going out to explore," he said.

Seeing their surroundings properly for the first time, they found that the inn was actually on the edge of St. Pierre, a sizeable village. The inhabitants were curious about the strangers in their midst, but cheerful, friendly, and clearly in a holiday mood. The heavy drifts of snow had provided them with an impromptu respite from their usual chores.

The sound of laughter and happy voices drew them to a frozen water-meadow, where many people, young and not so young, were sliding, skating, and generally enjoying themselves. Lucinda felt envious watching them have such fun. She longed to join in, but iceskates were an item she had never anticipated needing.

"I wonder where you obtain those," said Peter eagerly, as a boy his own age skimmed speedily past.

"We could try the blacksmith," suggested Sir Gareth.

Lucinda looked at him in surprise. For some reason she had expected him to disapprove of the idea of skating. Really, there were times when he was most unpredictable.

They were lucky; the blacksmith did indeed have a basket full of skates. In no time they were back at the water-meadow, their new acquisitions strapped on to their boots with leather thongs, impatient to be skating across the ice like the others.

It did not prove so easy. Lucinda found it impossible to stand up, and Peter fell over more often than she did.

"I have no control over my feet," she protested, laughing as she crashed to the ice yet again. "They will go in opposite directions. How do people learn to skate?"

As if by way of reply she found herself being lifted up in a pair of strong arms and held securely.

"Perhaps you need a little help," said Sir Gareth's voice.

"You are skating!" she said in astonishment. She had not even noticed him purchasing skates. "How extraordinary! I did not expect you to be able to skate."

"You think it is too vigorous a sport for a man of my years?"

"No, certainly not," she replied hastily, noting the edge in his voice.

"Let me remind you, young lady, that I am not the one who has spent most of the last twenty minutes prone upon the ice. Not all your youth can keep you vertical, seemingly. Now concentrate on what you are doing, or else we will finish up in an inelegant tangle. Relax more...that is better...much better..."

Lucinda felt it was more than better, it was absolutely splendid gliding across the ice, with Sir Garreth's arms supporting her. She was not conscious of time passing, until aching muscles and a chafing skate-strap forced her to a halt.

"That was magnificent!" she panted, her hazel eyes shining, her cheeks pink with exertion and cold.

"It was indeed." His face, too, was glowing. The exercise had ruffled his hair from its normal formal neatness, and now it sprang into curls as unruly as Peter's. "Enough for the moment, though. I suggest we find that nephew of mine and go back to the inn and see what our *patronne* has to offer in the way of food."

"Is it that time already?" She was amazed.

"You really did enjoy yourself, did you not?" He looked down at her. "Good! It is time you were happy!"

Before she could ask him what he meant he had struck off across the ice to fetch Peter. She watched him go. He was an excellent skater, moving with athletic grace and considerable speed. No other man on the ice was as expert nor, she had to admit, so agreeable to the eye. She wondered how she had ever thought him plain or staid. He looked neither as he skimmed effortlessly over the ice. There was only one point upon which she could fault him—his tailoring. It was excellent enough, but dull. She wished he would wear something brighter, more youthful.

When he returned he had Peter with him, a barely recognisable Peter, well covered in snow. The boy had joined a group of local lads in a game which involved going across the ice at great speed then diving head first into a deep drift at the end.

"Marvellous sport!" he gasped breathlessly. "This is a first-rate place, it really is. How lucky we were to get stuck here."

Lucinda would never have expected being snowed up to be a pleasant experience; yet it was! Surprisingly, much of it was because of Sir Gareth's efforts. He had an unlooked-for talent for devising amusements, which varied from rides about the village on a woodsman's sleigh to organising skating competitions. That he was enjoying himself too was self-evident. She only had to look at him to see it. It was as if being cut off from the outside world had caused him to shed his cares and responsibilities to reveal someone who, at times, seemed no older than his nephew.

"I have never seen Uncle so lively," remarked Peter. "You are a good influence on him."

"Me?" declared Lucinda. "Why should it be me?"

"Who else is there?"

Who else indeed! But Lucinda was far from convinced.

Under Sir Gareth's regular instruction her skating improved. Accustomed to being left to her own devices, having his undivided attention was a great novelty to her. No one, not even Bernardo, had spent so much time with her. She wondered at a man of Sir Gareth's education and experience wanting to bother, yet in the evenings or when snow showers kept them indoors he appeared to enjoy talking to her. His beloved Homer and Virgil lay neglected as they chatted together by the fire. Not that she always gave way to his ideas. She had her own opinions and was prepared to uphold them.

"You are very familiar with our modern poets," he remarked, after they had had a heated argument over the relative merits of Mr. Shelley and Mr. Wordsworth. "Miss Gordon at your seminary must be a lady of very liberal views to allow her pupils to read so widely."

"Goodness, we were not allowed to read Mr. Shelley at Miss Gordon's!" She laughed at the idea. "One of my grandmother's friends loaned me his works. Grandmother often has literary people staying at the house."

"She encourages poets and writers, does she?"

"And artists and musicians. We did have a sculptor once, but he worked in clay and made such a mess the servants grew mutinous."

"Was that how you met your Italian?"

"Yes." Her eyes shone at the recollection. "He was ill and almost penniless when my grandmother heard of him. She had him brought to our house until he regained his strength."

"She sounds a very charitable lady, your grandmother."

"She is. She cannot learn of an artist or a musician or a poet in distress but she must help him." It was only with her own granddaughter that Lady Winterton's benevolence reached its limits. "Then, when Bernardo's health was restored, she helped him to get singing engagements by introducing him to her friends. I was at the seminary at the time; I did not meet Bernardo until the summer vacation. It was love at first sight."

"And your Bernardo repaid your grandmother for her kindness by eloping with you—or at least planning to?"

She heard the censure in his voice.

"What alternative had we?" she cried. "Bernardo was going away. We could not bear to be parted. Grandmother would never have allowed us to marry."

"Did you ask?"

"There was no point. The answer would have been a foregone conclusion."

"Could your Bernardo not have found a more honourable solution to the problem?"

"He has found an honourable solution. He is going to marry me!"

"But first he intends to trail you all the way to Florence for the privilege, with no thought of the danger to yourself and your reputation on the way!"

"What else could he have done?" she replied defensively.

"I do not know, but he could have tried," Sir Gareth exclaimed angrily. "I would never have allowed the woman I love to..." His voice faded.

Lucinda knew what he had meant to say. There would have been no furtive elopement with him, he would have gone to her grandmother openly and asked for her hand, no matter what the consequences.

Sir Gareth was looking at her, the anger gone from his face. "Your pardon," he said quietly. "I should not have spoken so. It was most impertinent of me."

"No, it was not. Since you have been kind enough to take care of me all the way from Le Havre, you are entitled to express an opinion."

He rose to his feet, towering above her.

"Kind?" he declared. "Kind? Is that what you think I am?"

She rose too, and faced him.

"Yes," she answered earnestly. "You are the kindest person I have ever met."

"Oh, Lucinda!" His reply was half laugh, half groan.

Suddenly he swept her off her feet, holding her against his chest, just as he had done when they had met on board the *Rosamund.* They were face to face now, and it seemed the most natural thing in the world to put her arms about his neck and draw him closer to her. Close enough for their lips to meet, to stay, to savour one another.

Approaching footsteps broke into their private world. With evident reluctance Gareth lowered her to the ground and slowly released her.

"I should apologise for my behaviour," he said, none too steadily. "But I am not going to, because I am not at all sorry. That is how kind I am." And he walked away.

Lucinda was totally bemused by his behaviour—and astounded by her own. She should have been affronted or indignant or distressed, but she was none of these things. She felt absurdly happy. It was very strange.

COLD, BRIGHT DAYS, interspersed with snow showers, ensured that they stayed marooned at St. Pierre. Lucinda found she did not mind. It was all so unexpectedly pleasant. One thing troubled her. For hours, even days at a time, she hardly gave Bernardo a thought, and this made her feel guilty.

It is only a passing phase, she told herself. Everything will be well when I see Bernardo again.

Gradually the harshness of the winter wind eased, and the frozen edges of the water-meadow began to crumble into pools of water. Word went through the village that most roads were open. Only the narrow mountain route to the south remained blocked.

Lucinda heard the news with a curiously heavy heart. When they returned to the inn after their morning skating session her heart sank further. There was a familiar carriage in the stable yard.

"My dear friends!" Lady Alicia rose to greet all three of them as they entered, but her eyes rested hungrily on Gareth. "How glad I am that we have met up again. You must have suffered appallingly, being snowed up in such a place, away from civilisation."

"We could have fared much worse," said Gareth heartily. "St. Pierre has many advantages."

"I cannot think what they can be." Lady Alicia gave a superior little laugh. "I am sure you are simply being terribly stoic and manly to impress me."

"Sir Gareth does not need to impress anyone!" retorted Lucinda.

Lady Alicia was taken aback by this comment. But not for long.

"What a loyal champion you have there, to be sure, Sir Gareth," she said. Then she put out a hand and stroked Lucinda's cheek. "You have become quite the little gypsy since I saw you last. Never mind, I have some Gowland's Lotion in my valise. It will soon repair the ravages of snow and cold wind."

Lucinda, who was only too aware that her skin had attained an unfashionable tan of late, hated Lady Alicia even more, especially since the older woman looked sleek and elegant, showing no signs of her recent journey.

The day went from bad to worse as the newcomer inserted herself firmly between Lucinda and Gareth at every opportunity. Lucinda bitterly resented being excluded more than ever. Of one thing she was certain; at all costs she had to prevent Lady Alicia from accompanying them when they resumed their journey south. But how?

Her opportunity came that night. There being no other chamber, Lady Alicia and her female poor relation had to have beds in the attic too.

"What fun we will have, will we not?" cooed Lady Alicia.

Lucinda smiled sweetly. She had her own ideas on the subject. As she followed Lady Alicia up the ladder she collected Minou, the cat, who had become her nightly, and very necessary companion.

"Usually Minou sleeps on my bed," she said. "But I insist upon your having him." She dropped the cat on to Lady Alicia's lap. "He is invaluable for keeping the rats and mice at bay."

"Rats! Mice!" croaked Lady Alicia in horror.

"Do not worry, they will not trouble you, not with Minou on guard," Lucinda assured her. "Putting up with his fleas is a small price to pay."

"I am expected to sleep with rats, mice and fleas?" Lady Alicia's voice was a mere whisper.

"And Minou," added Lucinda.

Minou proved the last straw—Lady Alicia's screams roused the entire inn. It took one hour and a bottle of cognac before she grew calm. When she fell asleep it was with a month's supply of candles alight and her poor relation keeping guard.

Lucinda slept well that night. Minou had deserted Lady Alicia for his usual position on her feet, one yellow eye warily open. He was intrigued by the sight of an elderly human passing the night with umbrella upraised, ready to fend off marauding vermin. To his satisfaction she did not catch a thing.

A haggard Lady Alicia departed as soon as it was light, back the way she had come, to the last village. Lucinda was happy. The greater the distance between Lady Alicia and them, the better she liked it. By noon there came news that the road south was open. Next morning they resumed their journey to Florence.

CHAPTER THREE

DEPRESSION SETTLED on Lucinda as they travelled south. It was no use trying to blame her mood on the fierce Mistral wind which followed them down the valley and made everyone irritable. She knew her gloom was because she did not want the journey to end. The closer they came to their ultimate destination the greater were her misgivings, for Florence meant Bernardo and marriage. Unaccountably the opera singer seemed to have lost some of his romantic gloss in her imagination. Less and less did she dwell upon his glorious eyes and his pretty speeches, more and more she remembered his vanity and selfishness. It was as though she were seeing him with new eyes, and what she saw made her decidedly uncomfortable.

"Lyons at last!" announced Sir Gareth, as they clattered over the cobbles. "Do not worry, I have learned my lesson. We will stay here long enough for you to do some shopping."

"Shopping?" Lucinda looked at him in puzzlement.

"For your bride clothes. Surely you have not forgotten?"

No, she had not forgotten, but her enthusiasm for the enterprise had waned.

"You should be able to make some excellent purchases here," Sir Gareth went on. "The finest silks come from Lyons. Your shopping expedition shall be our first priority."

"Thank you," she replied politely.

True to his word, Sir Gareth took her on a tour of the best silk warehouses next morning.

"You have been very frugal," he remarked, indicating her few parcels.

"They are enough," she said. "After all, it was you who advised me to be prudent with my money."

"So I did," he said. "If you are sure you have bought all you require then I think we will go sightseeing."

The youngsters groaned.

"You have bought nothing for yourself," Lucinda pointed out.

"I need nothing," Gareth replied.

"How about a new waistcoat?"

"I have plenty."

"What, those dreadful nankeen things! They are terribly dreary—and ageing. At this rate you will soon be wearing flannel waistcoats."

"No, I will not!" he cried indignantly.

"I could take you to the warehouse where I purchased mine," offered Peter.

"No, thank you. I refuse to wear anything lurid."

"It need not be gaudy," pleaded Lucinda. "Just buy one. Something up-to-the-minute."

"Oh, very well! Anything for peace and quiet. But afterwards we definitely see the sights."

Sir Gareth bought two silk waistcoats, one an elegant black-and-silver stripe, the other a burgundy brocade. He was wearing the striped one as they set out to explore the city.

"How dashing you look!" Lucinda cried approvingly.

Gareth glowered; but she was convinced that secretly he was proud of his purchases.

Their tour of Lyons proved far more interesting than she had feared, thanks to him. He explained everything so well. Such an excursion would have been much duller without him, she decided. It fact, her whole life would be dull without him. This revelation was disturbing enough to cost her a sleepless night.

Lucinda entered the hotel dining-room next morning to find Gareth and Peter there, both with mysterious smiles on their faces.

"Good morning," she greeted them. "I'm sorry if I have kept you waiting." She approached the breakfast table, then stopped. On her chair were two elegantly wrapped packages, one large, one small. "What are these?" she asked, puzzled.

"They are birthday gifts for you," said Gareth.

"Birthday gifts?" Her bewilderment was growing.

"Yes. Today is your birthday, is it not?" asked Peter.

"Yes," she said. "How did you know?"

"Your travel papers. You had to give me your date of birth for them," said Gareth.

"It was all Uncle's idea to do something about it," said Peter.

"You should not have bothered." She was disturbed at the idea of them troubling themselves over her. "I seldom celebrate it."

"Not celebrate your birthday?" Peter was aghast at the idea. "Surely your parents send you a gift?"

"Certainly," she replied defensively. "Last year they sent me a lovely ermine muff and tippet from Vienna." She forebore to mention it had arrived late and was designed for a ten-year-old.

"There you are, then!" declared Gareth. "We were determined you should not lack birthday gifts. Are you not going to open them?"

"Of course." Lucinda's hands shook a little as she undid the smaller parcel. Her lavish personal allowance ensured she never went without, but gifts were a rarity, in particular gifts which were chosen with care especially for her. Pulling off the paper she revealed a pink sash of the fine silk for which Lyons was famous.

"That's from me. Happy birthday!" Peter planted a smacking kiss on her cheek. "I was told it was very á la mode."

"It is!" cried Lucinda in delight. "How every female will envy me when I wear this! Oh, thank you." And she returned his kiss with enthusiasm.

"Now open Uncle's present," said Peter eagerly.

Obediently Lucinda undid the wrapping to reveal a length of heavy white silk embroidered all over with tiny roses the exact pink of her new sash.

"Oh!" she exclaimed. "Oh . . . !"

"You like it?" Gareth asked anxiously. "You can change it if you wish."

"No!" cried Lucinda, horrified at the idea. "It is perfect. I have never seen anything so beautiful!"

"Good." He heaved a sigh of relief.

"There, Uncle, I said it would be just right, and so did the woman at the warehouse," said Peter. Then he chuckled. "You should have seen Uncle when he was choosing it. He got quite hot under the collar and couldn't make his mind up. Buying such things for females ain't much in his line, you see."

It was difficult for Lucinda to imagine an indecisive Gareth.

"I was not sure of your tastes," he said hastily, shooting his nephew an irritated glance. "You are convinced you would not prefer some other colour?"

"No," she repeated. "I have said this is perfect, and it is. Look!" She unrolled some of the silk and held it against her.

"My word, you'll turn a few heads in that," stated Peter.

"Do you agree?" Now it was Lucinda's turn to sound anxious as she looked at Gareth for approval.

He was gazing at her, frank admiration in his eyes, and she felt her heart lift. Sir Gareth considered her to be pretty! How extraordinary! There was also something unfathomable in his expression. Before she could determine more the door opened and in came Madame Mercier, the hotel-keeper, with their coffee. At the sight of Lucinda draped in the silk she came to an abrupt halt.

"Ah, *mademoiselle*, how beautiful!" she exclaimed. "It is for your wedding gown?" She turned and beamed at Gareth. "Your bride will be truly *ravissante* when you lead her to the altar, milord."

At her words an embarrassed silence fell upon the room. Lucinda felt her cheeks flame, and Gareth seemed disconcerted.

"You misunderstand, *madame*," he said, his voice oddly curt. "Miss Winterton is my ward, not my fiancée."

"If you say so then I must believe you, milord." Madame Mercier put the coffee pot down. "But I see what I see!" And she left the room with a knowing smile.

Lucinda did not dare to look at Gareth.

Even Peter sensed the charged atmosphere. "I say!" he burst out, in an attempt to restore normality, "that's a cracking idea, you know. Why don't you forget this singer fellow, Lucinda, and marry Uncle Chalfont? That would make you my aunt and..." As he realised he was making things worse his voice faded. Then he declared more heartily, "We aren't going to let the coffee get cold, are we? I've no intention of journeying today without my breakfast, no matter what you two do!"

All through the meal Lucinda covered her embarrassment with a stream of inconsequential chatter with Peter. She noticed that Gareth did not join in, nor did he look in her direction. How successful she was at putting on a show of indifference she could not tell, but in her heart her jumbled emotions refused to be calmed.

She was dressed ready to resume the journey when she remembered something. With some trepidation she went in search of Gareth. She found him in their sitting-room, already dressed in his greatcoat. Its many shoulder-capes seemed to make him more enormous, so that he filled the room. His dominant presence did not make her feel any better.

"Ah, Lucinda," he said, as she entered. "I forgot to wish you a happy birthday. It was very remiss of me."

"You did so in all but words," she replied. "I am the one who has been remiss; I did not thank you properly for my beautiful gift. Nor for your thoughtfulness in bothering."

"It was no bother!" he exclaimed.

"I have never had such a birthday. I shall remember it all my life," she said.

Although she had not been aware of him moving she now found him very close to her.

"I am glad," he replied. "I want you to be always happy, and . . ." He seemed to run out of words, and for a while they stood there gazing into each other's eyes. "There is one omission you can rectify," he said, making an unsuccessful attempt to sound jocular. "Peter got a kiss as thanks for his gift."

"He kissed me first," she retorted, trying to joke too.

"In that case I had better take the initiative."

He bent his head to give her a formal kiss. She presented her cheek to receive it. Then it all went gloriously wrong. At the last moment he tilted her face towards him and, with a groan, pulled her close, crushing his mouth on hers. His arms enfolded her, drawing her tight against him as if he would never let her go, an exhilarating contact that totally destroyed her self-control. He had kissed her before but never in such a way. Nothing in her experience had been anything like this. The raging pulse of her heartbeat, the tingling surge of emotion that shot through her, the hungry desperation to return his kisses, they all combined in one delirious certainty. Here in Gareth's arms was where she wanted to be! Nowhere else! Her arms were about him too now, and she was returning his kisses, her fervour matching his. Gradually, very gradually, the tide of their passion ebbed, spent by the intensity of its emotion.

Slowly they released their hold on one another, and for one long moment they remained transfixed.

"Lucinda, what can I say...?" whispered Gareth at last, his voice barely audible, his face drained of colour. "This should never have happened! Never!" Then abruptly he turned on his heel and strode from the room.

She continued to stand there, as immobile as a statue, trying to comprehend the incomprehensible. Gareth had made love to her—then immediately regretted it! Her own behaviour she did not dare to reflect upon.

The entry of her maid announced the arrival of the carriage. Emotional tumult or not, their journey must continue.

Their drive was only to one of the riverside quays, for they were to bid farewell to Monsieur Colmar and travel the next stage by boat. The atmosphere between her and Gareth was still charged with a vibrant electricity, making her extremely thankful they were to have a variation in transport. To have been forced to appear cool and dispassionate towards him during a long carriage journey, when her emotions remained so turbulent, would have been torture.

As an antidote to a tense relationship the trip down the Rhône could not have been better. The river roared along at an alarming pace, causing Lucinda to pray that their pilot was sober. She had found her voyage on the *Rosamund* exhilarating, but the *Rosamund* had not been required to go through narrow gorges or shoot under medieval bridges. By the time they stopped for the night her hands were white with holding on, and there were portions of the journey she had missed because her eyes had been tightly shut.

She dreaded her first confrontation alone with Gareth. Her great fear was that things would never be the same again between them. How could it, after such an explosion of raw emotion? Even now she was not sure how or why it had happened.

She was confident of her own reasons, of course. She had behaved with such abandon because she loved Gareth. There was no longer any point in trying to deny it, even to herself. Beyond that fact she dared not think, just as she could scarcely bear to dwell upon his motives.

It was useless to hope that he cared for her. He would never fall in love with an immature girl like her. Even gentle, kindly men like Gareth had needs, she knew; it was easier to regard his behaviour as an outburst of those needs rather than torment herself with pointless hope.

The dreaded meeting took place on the stairs at the inn where they were lodging. As they passed he put out a restraining hand and almost touched her. "Can I detain you for one minute?" he asked.

"Certainly," she replied. She could tell from his face what he was going to say.

"I can think of no words strong enough to express my regret at the way I acted in Lyons," he said, staring fixedly beyond her. "I behaved abominably and dishonourably. I can say nothing in my own defence.

All I can do is to offer you my most abject and sincere apologies and beg your forgiveness."

His words had a stiff formality about them which suggested a carefully prepared speech. Lucinda mumbled something about being equally to blame.

"That is not so!" he retorted, with more animation. "You are young and inexperienced, I am not! You are in my care. And having seen more of the world than you I should have protected you, instead of—of—behaving like some depraved lecher."

"Oh, never that!" protested Lucinda, in distress. "Can we not consider it a foolish incident and forget about the whole thing?" She knew she could do neither, but she could hardly admit to him how much she loved him and what pleasure his kisses had given her.

"I do not deserve such magnanimity." He was being formal again. "However, having failed in my duty to you so abysmally, if you would prefer to travel under the protection of someone else I would quite understand. There is a most respectable English couple in the inn. I am sure that if I applied to them on your behalf they would be happy for you to accompany them. You would never see me again."

It would be a way out of her misery, a means of solving all her problems... His final words decided her. Never to see him again! It was too sudden, too final, too awful to contemplate.

"I wish to stay with you," she said.

"Are you sure?"

"Quite sure—unless you would prefer I did not," she added hesitantly.

"Naturally I am honoured that your trust in me is undiminished," he said stiffly. "I promise you upon my solemn vow that your trust will not be misplaced. Such a disgraceful incident will never happen again."

He bowed very correctly to her and went on his way, leaving Lucinda no wiser as to his motives or his feelings for her. She waited until she reached the privacy of her room, then sat down and sobbed as if her heart would break.

At Avignon their river journey ended, and they continued by coach for the final stretch to Marseilles. Under ordinary circumstances Lucinda would have loved travelling through Provence. Winter had been left behind, and mimosa flowers mingled with blossoming fruit-trees. She saw none of them, her mind was so taken up with problems. Soon they would reach Marseilles, one stage closer to Bernardo. She had given her word that she would marry him, yet how could she when she loved Gareth? Which would be worse, to marry one man while caring for another, or to break her promise? The dilemma occupied her mind as they travelled the dusty miles.

Marseilles proved to be bustling and crowded, their hotel commodious, if noisy.

Gareth went out early next morning to make enquiries about the next boat to Leghorn, the nearest port to Florence. When he came back his face was grim.

"Contrary winds are blocking the port," he told them. "I hear there are half a dozen vessels lying off the harbour mouth, waiting for a chance to enter. The harbourside inns are packed with folk wanting to leave Marseilles. Many ships' passenger lists are already full, but hopefully we will be on the fourth ship out."

"At least we are better off than those unfortunate souls stuck out at sea," said Lucinda.

She would have been content to stay in Marseilles for ever. Of all the people in the port she must have been the only one who was happy because the wind continued to blow from the wrong quarter.

The reappearance of Lady Alicia came as an unwelcome shock. She arrived during the morning, as elegant as ever, exclaiming with surprise at the sight of them, feigning astonishment that they should have chosen the same lodgings. Lucinda did not believe a word of it. It was too much of a coincidence. She was convinced that, knowing their destination to be Marseilles, the wretched woman had followed them and scoured the hotels and inns until she found them.

Gareth seemed delighted to renew Lady Alicia's acquaintance and hardly left her side during the next few days. Watching them together was like a knife turning in Lucinda's heart. But what cause have I to object? she told herself. I am promised to Bernardo. Sir Gareth must be nothing to me!

It made no difference. The sharp stabbing pain in her breast grew worse. Her anguish was not soothed by Lady Alicia's patronising her and treating her like an idiot. Nor did she miss the gloating look in the older woman's eyes as Gareth continued to be attentive.

The hotel had one advantage over all their previous lodgings: it had a pianoforte in the best parlour. Lucinda was extremely fond of playing the piano, and had missed having one during the last few weeks. With her portfolio of music under her arm she went into the parlour, hoping to find it empty. Instead she found Gareth.

"Are we to have some music?" he asked hopefully. "I would enjoy that above all things."

"I was only going to practise."

"If you do not object to an audience I promise not to notice a wrong note or two," he assured her.

"Very well. I will try not to offend your ears too much."

Smiling, Lucinda went to the piano. To start with she chose a simple piece, a country dance.

"Bravo!" cried Gareth when she had finished. "That was capital. Can I please beg for more?"

For the first time in days the atmosphere between them was amiable and relaxed. If music could achieve such a thing she was happy to play all day. Turning the pages, she found a lively rondo and had scarcely begun when the door flew open. Lady Alicia entered.

"How I dote upon music!" she exclaimed. "Nothing will please me more than to join you, dear Miss Winterton."

Before Lucinda could object she had sat herself upon the long piano stool also, taking up a surprising amount of room. Learning that Lady Alicia was not as sylphlike as she seemed did little to curb Lucinda's annoyance.

"Now what have we here?" Lady Alicia peered at the music, proving she was short-sighted, too. "Ah, a piece by Mr. Mozart. I heard you playing it so prettily as I came in. Are you going to tell us Mr. Mozart taught you?" Her voice was light, as though she were funning. Lucinda knew better.

"Oh, Lady Alicia!" she said, her eyes innocently wide. "I fear Mr. Mozart is dead. Did you not know? I hope he was not a friend of yours."

From behind them came a snort of laughter.

"Of course I know he is dead," retorted Lady Alicia. "He has been dead these four-and-twenty years, so could scarcely be an acquaintance of mine."

"Oh, I was not sure," said Lucinda, maintaining her air of innocence.

Lady Alicia gave her a covert look of intense dislike, then swiftly resumed her smiling mask.

"Have you no duets?" she demanded, rifling through the music. "Ah, yes! *Greensleeves*! How delightful! I have never come across it arranged for two players before. I shall play the difficult part. I dare say you can manage the simpler fingering. We will begin after three. One, two, three..."

Lucinda was not a brilliant pianist, but she had some talent and had been well taught. In contrast Alicia Monkton did not play well. She preferred to concentrate upon affected flourishes rather than more mundane things such as notes and timing. After two false starts they were under way, only to finish in a discordant tangle halfway down the second page.

"Child, child, you must play what is written down!" exclaimed Lady Alicia.

Already she had wrongly blamed Lucinda for both false starts, and the girl refused to continue as the scapegoat.

"I fear it was you, my lady!" she protested. "You were too quick in the second bar! Those three crotchets must be given their full value. Signor Clementi was most insistent upon it."

"Signor Clementi? Are you now trying to claim the famous pianist as your music master?" The scorn in Lady Alicia's voice added fuel to Lucinda's mounting anger.

"I am not claiming anything, your ladyship," she replied. "Signor Clementi was kind enough to arrange *Greensleeves* as a duet a year or two ago, so that I might play it with him."

"Will you listen to the naughty child?" Lady Alicia appealed to Gareth. "First she tries to claim Sir Thomas Lawrence as her drawing master, now Signor Clementi instructed her in the pianoforte."

"I do not claim that," said Lucinda firmly. She had marked the triumphant note in Lady Alicia's voice and knew the other woman was sure she had more ammunition with which to belittle her. "Merely that Signor Clementi and I played duets together when he was my grandmother's guest."

"I have never heard the like." Lady Alicia pretended to sound shocked. "Even someone of your tender years should know the difference between truth and falsehood. You are aware of what happens to little girls who ignore that difference, I trust? They have the tips of their naughty fibbing tongues snipped. In fact, I have half a mind to get my embroidery scissors.''

All through their exchange Lucinda had been conscious of snorts of indignation coming from Gareth. Now, as Alicia made to rise, he leapt to his feet.

"Really, Lady Alicia, this is too much!" he protested.

Lucinda agreed with him, but she would tackle this irritating, scheming woman by herself.

"My lady," she said, restraining the older woman so sharply that she sat down with a bump, "I have had enough of this silliness. I am past such nursery nonsense. I suggest you leave your embroidery scissors exactly where they are, unless you wish to take up crewel work. Also, I think an apology is in order. I realise that, for some reason…" and here she stressed her words significantly "…for some reason you are set upon making me out to be a liar. Once, I attempted to prove that I spoke the truth, but you were not interested. Now I would not demean myself by doing so again but for one thing. You have made the accusation in front of Sir Gareth. He must be much embarrassed at witnessing such a scene. As a courtesy to him I must ask you to read aloud what is written on the title-page of the music we have just played."

Lady Alicia stared at her in stunned amazement, making no attempt to turn over the pages.

"I think you should, my lady," said Gareth sternly. He had stepped forward and put one hand reassuringly upon Lucinda's shoulder. "I cannot have my ward spoken to in such a manner."

Lady Alicia muttered something about poor light and indistinct writing.

"Then, allow me." Gareth leaned forward, his grip on Lucinda's shoulder tightening slightly as he did so. He read, " 'To my charming young friend Miss Winterton, with happy memories of a delightful sojourn at Coombe Dean. Felicitations from your humble servant and admirer, Muzio Clementi.' "

He turned to Alicia Monkton, but she did not wait to see his reaction. She fled from the room.

"You stood up to a difficult situation splendidly, Lucinda," said Gareth. "I am very proud of you."

"Are you?" she asked in happy surprise.

Hopefully she looked into his face, to find his expression strangely inscrutable. Then she was overwhelmed by remorse.

"Would you like me to go and beg Lady Alicia's pardon?" she asked.

"Whatever for?"

"Why, because I let my dislike of her cloud everything else. I should have taken your feelings into consideration. You seem to have grown fond of her company of late, and—and perhaps you have formed a permanent attachment for her. I—I would not have my behaviour spoil your happiness in any way." She stared unseeingly at the sheet music.

"Your behaviour has spoiled nothing. You have no reason to reproach yourself." Now he had two hands on her shoulders. She was very conscious of the warmth of his touch, and of his presence towering above her. "No, all regret is mine. I have been wondering how on earth to apologise to you yet again. Goodness knows, I get plenty of practice! I seem to do nothing else."

"Apologise?" Even in her astonishment she did not feel capable of facing him. She was convinced her love for him must be written clearly on her face.

"Because I allowed that awful Monkton female to patronise you and criticise you. I should have put an end to it long since."

That awful Monkton female! Was that how he thought of her? Lucinda's spirits rose. "You are very kind, but I really am capable of fighting my own battles, you know," she said.

"So you have demonstrated very successfully. All the same, it should not have been necessary."

"I quite enjoyed the skirmish," she admitted.

"I rather thought you did." Gareth gave a chuckle.

For a brief second she felt his hands tighten on her shoulders before letting go, then something touched the top of her hair so lightly that it might have been the brush of a bird's wing or a falling leaf. Or a kiss! She swung round, to see the door closing behind Gareth. He had gone, leaving her alone.

Late that night news came that at last the wind had changed quarter. Their ship would be leaving in the morning.

"Here we've been, waiting about for days, then suddenly all is hurry and scurry," observed Peter. "I am thankful we are on our way at last."

The three of them had taken refuge in the best parlour, fully cloaked and greatcoated, out of the way of the porters moving their luggage.

"So am I," agreed his uncle. "And though it is unchivalrous to say so I am doubly pleased that Lady Alicia is not coming too. At one time I feared she might."

"You say that, yet I got the impression the lady had quite taken your fancy," Peter said, with a cheeky grin.

"Nothing of the sort," retorted Gareth. "One must observe the courtesies, particular to a lady travelling alone."

"She left very early, I believe," said Peter.

"What, left the hotel?" Lucinda was surprised.

"Yes, and without paying her bill, if the noise below stairs was anything to go by," said Peter. "Escaping from her creditors, that one, at a guess."

"Lady Alicia in debt?" She could not believe her ears.

"Certainly. Could you not tell from the way she battened on to Uncle? I was quite bothered at one time, for I did not fancy her as an aunt, handsome though she is."

"That will do!" Gareth admonished the boy sharply.

Lucinda wondered if he was remembering the occasion when Peter had suggested her as a suitable bride for him. The memory made her uncomfortable.

"On the subject of weddings, I suppose you will be getting married as soon as we reach Florence?" said Peter, unconsciously compounding the pain he had already caused.

"Yes," she replied briefly.

She had made up her mind at last, after long and painful deliberation. Gareth was the man she loved, a hopeless unrequited love she could not quench, but Bernardo was the man she had promised to wed. No matter what it cost her she felt bound to honour that pledge.

"Will we be able to stay for the celebrations?" Peter enquired.

"Certainly not!" Gareth snapped. "Have you forgotten we are expected in Rome? There have been delays enough already."

Peter looked surprised by his uncle's sharp reply.

"I suppose you are right. It is a pity. I cannot say I go much for weddings but the feasting might have been fun," he said.

"I doubt if there will be much feasting. It will be a very quiet affair," said Lucinda. It took all of her self-control not to sound miserable at the prospect.

"Well, at least with your Lyons silk you are assured of a splendid wedding-gown," Peter said.

"Indeed I am," she replied, though she knew it would not be so. The silk was far too precious. It was a gift from Gareth. She would never use it.

After the long delay the voyage from Marseilles to Leghorn was smooth and uneventful. From Lucinda's point of view it passed much too quickly, and few people could have stepped ashore at the Tuscan port with greater reluctance. Gareth, too, was taciturn and short tempered.

"Uncle's very snappish at the moment," remarked Peter, after having been rebuked unusually harshly for making too much noise. "No doubt this Mediterranean food is making him liverish."

"I think you are right," agreed Lucinda. What other reason could there be?

It was a strangely subdued trio who set off for Florence. They were to stay at Schneiderf's Hotel, overlooking the River Arno. When they arrived Lucinda regarded the elegance of their apartments with reservation.

"This must be the most expensive place in the city," she protested. "Can we not go to somewhere more modest? Or else will you not let me pay my own bills?"

"No, we will not move!" retorted Gareth irritably. "And no, I will not agree to you paying your share!"

"In France you did not allow me to contribute one sou."

"Peter and I were travelling through France anyway. One person more made little difference."

"You did not intend to come to Florence, though. I have taken you much out of your way, and it is not right that I should be a financial burden in addition."

"You are not a burden, finanacial or otherwise!"

Angrily Gareth thumped the table in front of him. "I will listen to such talk no more, do you hear? Surely you can put up with me for a day or two longer? During that time the present arrangements will stand!"

She was taken aback by his anger. "I did not mean to make you cross," she said. "Nor did I intend to imply that I find your company intolerable. It is simply that I am anxious not to be a further nuisance." She braced herself for another furious outburst.

It did not come. Instead, he took a deep breath, as if to compose himself and replied quietly, "You could never be a nuisance. I did not mean to sound cross. I was trying to say that presently you will be reunited with your opera singer, and until then it would please me if you would continue under my protection exactly as before."

"If that is what you want." She was not happy, though. She was all too well aware that soon she must bid goodbye to him. It was something she could scarcely bear to think about.

"After breakfast in the morning I will go to the Opera House to enquire about Signor Arezzo." His voice roused her from her miserable thoughts.

"Enquire about Bernardo? Surely that is my task?"

"That would not be proper, not a young lady alone."

"Then may I come with you?"

He hesitated. "Certainly you may," he replied. "I was forgetting how eager you must be to see your beloved again. Lovers cannot bear to be separated for one second longer than necessary, can they?" There was an oddly bitter note in his voice.

Lucinda did not reply. It had not been eagerness to see Bernardo which had prompted her request, it had been a desperation to remain with Gareth for as long as possible.

That evening an air of gloom pervaded their apartments. Only Peter maintained his normal cheerfulness. Lucinda was so miserable at the prospect of the morrow that she could scarcely bring herself to be civil. As for Gareth, for some reason he seemed equally morose. His contribution to the conversation was restricted to monosyllabic grunts. It was a relief to everyone when it was time for bed.

As they approached the Opera House next morning Lucinda was conscious of a tight knot of apprehension in her stomach. She could hardly bear it as Gareth knocked at the stage door and said in fluent Italian, "We wish to see Signor Arezzo. Where can we find him, if you please?"

"Signor Arezzo?" The doorman scratched his head thoughtfully. "Oh, yes, he's the fellow coming from England, isn't he? He's not got here yet, *signore*. Been expected this last month or more, but not turned up."

Relief made Lucinda quite giddy for a moment.

"Your Bernardo will get here safely, never fear." Gareth patted her hand comfortingly, misinterpreting the reasons for her emotion. "We will call again tomorrow morning."

Suddenly Lucinda felt light-headed and light-hearted. She had feared that this would be the end of her time with Gareth and now she was reprieved. She had at least one more whole day in his company.

"What shall we do? Would you like to return to the hotel to rest?" he asked solicitously.

"No, thank you. I would like to explore the city, to see all the great and wonderful treasures that Florence has to offer."

"I thought such places and sights did not amuse you."

"I am growing to appreciate them and would like to learn to comprehend them more," she replied.

Her answer brought a smile of pleasure to his face, just as she had hoped it would. She had chosen to go sightseeing because she knew it was something he would enjoy above all things. It was important to her that this last day together should be very pleasurable. After they parted, when she would never see him again, she wanted to remember his face as being happy, just as all her memories of him would be happy.

"Poor Peter, he is not going to be overjoyed." Already Gareth was smiling. He had suddenly become extremely cheerful—no doubt at the prospect of exploring his beloved Florence.

"Then he will be outnumbered two to one, and so must endure it." She tucked her arm through his. "Though I dare say we will find lots of things to amuse him too."

"I am sure we will. Let us go and fetch him, then I suggest we begin at the Baptistry, where all Florentine babies have been baptised for centuries. The bronze doors there are among the greatest artistic marvels of the world..."

From then on, for Lucinda, every day which followed began with a feeling of tension until they had gone to the Opera House to ask about Bernardo. Only when the doorman had greeted them with a friendly, "Sorry, *signore, signorina*, your friend has still not arrived," did she relax and start to enjoy herself. Then they would go about the city, to the great campanile or bell tower, to the Ponte Vecchio with its little shops and houses where craftsmen still worked exactly as they had done since the Middle Ages, or to one of the many other treasures which Florence had to offer.

Rather to their surprise Peter did not grumble much at the sightseeing expeditions, and only occasionally gave vent to the faintest of bored sighs. He did, however, regularly slip away by himself. It was suspected that he found the pretty flower seller in the Piazza del Duomo rather more attractive than the architectural delights of the city.

"I suppose one could not expect him to be interested in *boules* for ever," remarked his uncle philosophically.

Lucinda had no inclination to slip away by herself. She enjoyed every minute they spent exploring Florence because it was what made Gareth happy. At least, that was how she felt at first. Gradually, however, the beauty and splendour about her began to appeal for its own sake. Set among rolling green countryside and with its many lovely gardens, Florence well deserved its title of "City of Flowers," particularly in the warm spring sunshine. In the early evenings, as they joined the fashionable Florentines and strolled about the shady walks of the Cascina, admiring the superb views, she felt that no place could have provided a more glorious background for her love for Gareth. It became interwoven with her happiness.

Often she longed for Gareth to take her in his arms and kiss her passionately as he had done at Lyons, though she knew such a thing would never happen. Even if he had had the inclination his sense of honour would have prevented it. He had sworn never to behave like that again, and she knew him too well to expect him to break his word. He was extremely kind and thoughtful, he was courteous, yet he was distant. It was as if he had put an invisible shield between himself and her.

The days slipped into one week, two, then three, and still there was no sign of Bernardo.

"What of your business in Rome?" asked Lucinda anxiously. "Why do you not go on? I can manage very well alone."

"Certainly not!" Gareth declared. "There is an excellent lawyer I know of in Rome. Already I have sent ahead to have him take charge of my kinswoman's affairs until I get there. Besides, your singer cannot be much longer. We will wait with you."

It was the answer she had hoped he would give, and she was happy—for the moment.

CHAPTER FOUR

ONE MORNING they went to the Opera House as usual, but upon this occasion things were different: the door-keeper was looking out for them.

"There you are, *signore* and *signorina*! At last I have news for you!" he cried. "Here is a message from Signor Arezzo. It came yesterday evening."

Lucinda took a deep breath and clutched at Gareth's arm. She felt him grow tense.

"A message, you say?" Gareth repeated in a strained voice.

"Yes, *signore*. It seems the poor soul's had a hard journey of it from England. What with severe storms and his ship being damaged and coming close to being wrecked. That's what comes of travelling by sea in winter—"

"Why should he come by sea?" demanded Lucinda, perplexed.

"That's what I say, *signorina*! You wouldn't catch me going to sea at this time of year. But Signor Arezzo fancied to come all the way by ship, and a long time it's taken him. Anyway, he has landed at Leghorn and should be on his way here. Your friend will be in Florence at any time."

Lucinda took a deep breath. The moment she dreaded had almost arrived. Soon she would see Bernardo again. Her mouth went dry with apprehension.

"Someone else has been enquiring about Signor Arezzo," the door-keeper informed them. "Here she comes now."

A young woman was coming towards them, with two small children clinging to her skirts. She was pretty, although she looked careworn.

"Ah, *signora*," cried the doorman as she approached. "I was just telling the English *signore* and *signorina* the good news. Signor Arezzo is here in Tuscany. He should arrive in Florence before long."

"The Blessed Virgin be praised!" exclaimed the woman. "My husband is coming home! I feared I would never see him again."

"Your what?" Lucinda stopped in her tracks.

Gareth, too, pulled up short and gave an angry exclamation.

"My husband, Bernardo Arezzo. He is an opera singer. He went to England two years ago and I have not heard from him since."

"Bernardo is your husband?" Lucinda repeated numbly. "He cannot be your husband! It is not possible!"

"I swear to you that he is, *signorina*; and the father of my children. Why should I lie?" The young woman sounded indignant, then she looked more closely into Lucinda's face. "Do you know my Bernardo?" she demanded. "Did you meet him in England?"

Bernardo had a wife! He had children! He had promised to marry her when all the time he had a wife! Lucinda was too stunned to answer the woman.

Vaguely, from somewhere far off, she heard the door-keeper answer, "Indeed, the English *signore* and *signorina* are so eager to renew Signor Arezzo's acquaintance they have come here every day for over three weeks to enquire about him."

Gently but firmly Gareth edged their little group away from the interested ears of the door-keeper, then he replied courteously, "My ward and I understood your husband was soon to appear here in Florence, *signora*. We were eager to greet him. We admire his voice and wish to hear him sing again."

Signora Arezzo was too sharp to be taken in by Gareth's diplomatic response. "You called at the Opera House every day for over three weeks simply because you admire Bernardo's voice?" she demanded. "And the *signorina*, she went as white as a sheet when I mentioned the word 'husband.' Why should she do that?"

Lucinda was still incapable of speech, so it was left to Gareth to think of an explanation. He had barely opened his mouth when Signora Arezzo dismissed him with an eloquent gesture. She turned to Lucinda.

"*Signorina*," she said with unexpected gentleness, "You are distressed to discover that Bernardo is married. Do not try to deny it, it is written on your face. I know my husband only too well, more's the pity. You are young, and pretty, and rich too, I think. Just the sort to attract the wretch. It has happened before, I am afraid. You didn't go through any ceremony with him, I hope? You don't imagine you are married to him already?"

Lucinda could only shake her head and whisper, "I hoped to meet him here, in Florence."

"The saints be praised for that!" Signora Arezzo gave a sigh of relief. "I suppose the rogue lured you here with promises of marriage?" When Lucinda nodded Signora Arezzo suddenly let forth with a voluble stream of Italian. Few of the words were comprehensible to Lucinda, but Bernado's name was mentioned several times, along with some very intriguing adjectives. Then the *signora* suddenly turned upon Gareth. "As for you, *signore*, you should be ashamed of yourself! What sort of a guardian can you be? I understand how the *signorina* was taken in by

Bernardo's silver tongue, she is young and innocent, but you…! How could you bring her here? How could a man of your years have believed Bernardo—?"

"It was not his fault!" interrupted Lucinda, getting her voice back at last. "Do not blame him. It was all my stupidity. I ran away to be with Bernardo before I met Sir Gareth."

"You did? Then why is he not with you now? What happened?"

"I do not know. We were to have met on the ship but we missed one another. Sir Gareth has been kind enough to escort me here."

"Oh, he has, has he?" Signora Arezzo shot Gareth a suspicious glance. Clearly she mistrusted men in general and those who "adopted" young girls in particular. "Well, you've no need to rely on him any more if you don't want to, *signorina*. You can come with me."

"But you know nothing about me," said Lucinda in amazement.

"I know Bernardo."

"You are very kind." Lucinda replied hesitantly. "You should be angry with me, and resentful, yet you are kind."

"Why should I be angry with you, *signorina*? Or resentful? I have gone through this before, and with women who were much more worldly-wise than you. They still fell for Bernardo and his beautiful voice and his lies." Signora Arezzo gave a bitter little smile. "I confess I envy you, though. You are free of him. You do not know what a lucky escape you have had." Here Bernardo's wife suddenly looked fierce and glared at Gareth. "But if there's someone else you want to escape from, *signorina*, my lodgings aren't much, but you're welcome to share."

"Thank you, that is most kind of you." Lucinda was moved by such generosity. "I am all right, though. I am perfectly safe with Sir Gareth."

Signora Arezzo looked far from convinced. She continued to glare at Gareth. Then unexpectedly she smiled. "That is a pity. Bernardo's face would have been quite a sight if he had found us together waiting for him."

"What will you and your childern do?" asked Lucinda.

"First, I am planning a welcome home Bernardo won't forget." The *signora*'s attractive face looked very grim as she added, "He will wish he was back in England before I am finished with him."

"And then?"

"If Bernardo mends his ways I will stay with him. If not I will go home to my parents—they farm up in the hills. Either way, he will support his children. I have four brothers to see that he does. For now, I intend to wait here at the Opera House for him. He is sure to come here first. Will you wait here too, *signorina*?"

"No, I think not," said Lucinda quietly. "I would prefer to return to the hotel, if you please."

She looked up at Gareth, and he nodded in agreement.

"I will send for a carriage," he said.

But Lucinda preferred to walk. "I think it would do me good to take the air," she said.

In truth, she wanted time to calm the great agitation that was stirring inside her, and to gain some sort of control over her bewildered thoughts. She feared it would take far longer than the brief interval between the Opera House and the hotel. They set off, after having bade farewell to Signora Arezzo. Gareth's expression was grim as they walked, and he said little. Although she protested that she was not at all faint,

Lucinda was grateful for the solid support of his arm, for she felt shaky and cold. She was also grateful for his silence. She could not have coped with conversation just then.

Only when they were back at the hotel, in the privacy of their apartments, did he turn to her.

"My dear Lucinda, what can I say?" he began, but she held up a hand to silence him. His voice was too gentle, his eyes too kind. She could not bear it. He would have been quite justified in telling her what a silly immature fool she had been. Learning that Bernardo was already married could only have proved his first impressions of her—that she was a stupid empty-headed schoolgirl who was not fit to have left the seminary. To have him being considerate and sympathetic made her distress harder to bear.

"Please!" she begged. "I would like to be by myself for a little while."

He looked at her with concern. "If you are sure..." he said uncertainly. "Shall I send for your maid?"

She shook her head.

"Very well, I shall leave you in peace." He took her hand and gave it a gentle squeeze, then he left the room.

Lucinda sank on to the nearest chair, too numb for the release of tears. What an idiot she had been, to have believed Bernardo so implicitly. Looking back she could see a dozen instances during their courtship when he had proved his untrustworthiness. In fact, recently she had been harbouring a growing suspicion that he was not really a very pleasant character at all. He had taken money from her, betrayed her grandmother, enocuraged her to be deceitful and much more. Discovering that he was already married had been the final proof that he was a rogue and a ne'er-do-well. If only she had met Gareth first! Then she would have had someone against whom to measure him. Someone of character and integrity... Here she stopped herself. It made no difference. She had been a credulous fool and it was no use trying to think up excuses for her own behaviour.

At least her heart was whole, that was one good thing! Her pride had suffered the most damage. The humiliation of having been so gullible. How Bernardo must have laughed at her behind her back! But his mockery faded into insignificance beside another problem which loomed large. What was she going to do now...? She was ruined! Her reputation was irretrievably lost, thrown away in a madcap elopement that had come to naught. There was no point in going home. Now that she had kicked over the traces her family was unlikely to have her back. How was she to survive? The money she had with her was not enough to support her indefinitely. She would have to find work. But who would employ her without a character?

There was one person who would come to her aid, of course—Gareth! Even though he must despise her he would still help her; he was that sort of person. But how could she accept his charity when she loved him so much? No matter how desperate things became she was determined not to do that. Already she had disrupted his plans enough. The best thing she could do was to get out of his life completely.

Before she could explore this idea further there was a tap at the door and Peter came in, his face pink with emotion.

"Uncle has just told me!" he declared angrily. "The rogue was married! Treating you in such a way! He deserves to be horse-whipped! I've half a mind to go out and tackle him myself."

"Thank you for being so concerned on my behalf," said Lucinda dully. "But pray do not exert yourself. He is not worth the effort."

"The deceit of the man! The lies he told you!" Peter seemed amazed that any one could behave so dishonourably.

But then, observed Lucinda to herself, he has had Gareth as his pattern all his life. How could he think otherwise?

"What are you going to do now?" Peter dropped into a chair opposite to her, and regarded her keenly.

"I was just making plans for my future as you came in." She hoped she sounded optimistic. She certainly was not feeling it.

"I fear your reputation's gone now you cannot marry that Bernardo fellow," he said frankly. "That's bound to make things pretty difficult." Then his face lit up. "I know! You can marry me!"

"What!" She stared at him incredulously.

"Do not look like that! It's not such a bad idea. My parents might cut up a bit at first because I am so young, but they would soon get used to the idea. I can usually talk Mama round, and, as for Papa, you would have him eating out of your hand in no time. We deal well enough together, do we not? Well then, why should we not get married?"

"Oh, Peter!" Lucinda did not know whether to laugh or cry. For a dreadful moment she feared she might do both at once. He was such a dear boy! Only six months separated their birthdays, but at that moment she felt the elder by a good hundred years.

"I thank you for such a wonderful thought," she said gently. "The idea of you sacrificing yourself to help me touches me to the heart. However, I must decline your offer. As you yourself say, you are rather young to be the head of a household. And, though we are great friends, we are not the slightest bit in love with one another, are we? No, when you do marry I hope it will be to someone a deal more sensible than me!"

"Hey! Do not put yourself down so!" he protested, though beneath the protestations Lucinda detected relief.

Fond as she was of Peter, and moved by his proposal of marriage, she was none the less glad when he went away and left her alone. She had her future to think out, and a half-formed plan to finalise. She could not stay here, that was definite. Gareth was certain to insist she accept his help, unaware of the terrible pain that would cause her. The only solution was for her to leave as secretly as possible.

After all, running away is something at which I am experienced, she told herself bitterly.

She only hoped this attempt would be more successful than her previous one. That very evening would be the best time. She would persuade Gareth and Peter to go for their evening stroll at the Cascina alone. Neither of them would think it odd if she claimed to be suffering from a megrim, not after the events of the day. While they were gone she would leave the hotel, make her way back to Leghorn and take the first available boat to... To where? It did not matter, just so long as she was far away from Gareth. With luck she would not be missed until the next day's breakfast. She was debating whether she should take her maid with her or leave the girl money to get home when Peter returned. He was bubbling over with excitement.

"I never thought to see the day!" he cried. "Uncle Chalfont nearly got arrested. Wait until Mama hears—"

"He did what?" exclaimed Lucinda in horror.

"He nearly got arrested. For causing a breach of the peace. If Signora Arezzo had not intervened—"

"Signora Arezzo? Breach of the peace? Peter, for pity's sake start at the beginning before I go mad! Only, tell me first, is your uncle all right?"

"Fit as a flea. Your opera singer was no match for him. Uncle will be here directly. Start at the beginning, you say. Well, after leaving you I decided I would go to the Opera House and have a sharp word with that Bernardo character after all. But, bless me, Uncle Chalfont had got there before me, and a rare set-to they had been having, by all accounts. I was just in time to see Uncle floor the swine with the sweetest upper-cut I have ever seen. I tell you, I did not think he had it in him. I mean, you know Uncle Chalfont, always so staid and correct—"

"I fear my character has recently taken a distinct turn for the worse," Gareth interrupted him. He was standing in the doorway, dishevelled, his hair in disarray, his usually immaculate coat covered in dust and with one sleeve torn. In addition, his previously spotless neckcloth was spattered with blood from a cut on the side of his chin.

"You are hurt," cried Lucinda, with concern. "That wretched boy assured me you were all right!"

"It is nothing." Gareth felt his chin experimentally. "My manservant will have to be careful when he shaves me tomorrow, that is all."

"But Peter said you were almost arrested."

"True... The management at the Opera House took exception to the confrontation I had with Arezzo. You look surprised. Surely you realised I would go and give him the thrashing he deserved? I showed him you were not alone and unprotected. By the ferocity with which he retaliated I would say it was not the first time he has tried to avoid such a hiding. That was when the Opera House manager called in the local guardians of the peace."

"You did such a thing for me?" Lucinda could scarcely believe it.

"It was nothing... At one time my life was calm and well-ordered. Then I met you. After that, being arrested for brawling was almost inevitable."

"Were you actually arrested?" she cried, appalled.

"A pair of very large Italian hands grasped hold of my collar. Fortunately Signora Arezzo arrived in the nick of time. According to her I was more of an avenging angel than a hooligan, so they let me go. They surrendered her husband into her custody." Gareth flinched at the memory. "Now, I suggest we forget about fisticuffs and concentrate upon you. I presume you will want to return to England?"

"No, thank you," said Lucinda firmly. This was a conversation she had been dreading. He was bound to offer her his charity, and she knew she had to remain strong to refuse it.

To her surprise he nodded. "Perhaps you are right," he said. "In that case, what do you intend to do?"

"I shall remain here in Tuscany," she replied, saying the first thing that entered her head. "I—I intend to open a shop."

"What sort of a shop?"

She gazed about her for inspiration. Her bonnet lay on the sofa where she had flung it.

"A milliner's shop. I shall make bonnets."

He gave a hoot of laughter. "My dear Lucinda, I have seen your sewing. You would have to pay people to take your bonnets away."

"I do not intend to do the sewing," she said haughtily. "I will employ women to do that. I shall devise the bonnets, and choose the trimmings. I have a dozen schemes . . ."

To her surprise he stopped laughing, and, taking her hands in his, gazed down at her with a tender expression in his grey eyes.

"I am sure you have," he said softly. "And I am sure that if you did start a milliner's shop it would be all the rage in no time. But I have a better idea."

"Oh, no!" she cried, trying to pull away.

"You have not heard what it is yet," he protested.

"You are going to insist upon helping me!"

"Well, yes, in a way. I was going to ask you to marry me."

"You are only saying that out of charity!" she cried.

"Charity?" He sounded startled. "I dare say I am as open-handed as the next man, but to marry you out of charity—that would be going too far. I can think of plenty of far less desperate ways of helping you in your distress."

"Name one!"

"I could wait until your shop is established and buy some of your ridiculous bonnets!"

"You are making fun of me!" she protested. "I would have thought you could at least be serious."

"You should not blame me for funning; you were the one who taught me to take life lightly." The laughter faded from his face, and the tender look in his eyes made her heart suddenly begin to pound. "But I am serious about one thing. I want you to be my wife very much indeed. I love you to distraction! I! Who have never before been distracted in my life! I know you consider me to be ancient, and a dull old stick, but—"

"I do not!" she cried. "That was only at first. I have tried and tried to tell you that I have changed my mind about you. Why do you never listen?"

"I am listening now. The word I want to hear is 'yes.' Say you will be my wife, because if you do not the rest of my life will be meaningless. It was so before I met you, but then I did not know any better. I knew little of love and laughter and fancy waistcoats.

You could not be so cruel as to take all that joy and beauty away from me.''

"You really want to marry me?'' She could not believe it.

"More than anything I have ever wanted in my entire life.''

"Oh . . . !'' Words failed her. All she could do was raise her face for his kisses.

"Gareth, my darling, I do love you,'' she whispered.

Briefly he held her away from him, gazing at her as if he too could not believe what was happening. Then with a cry of joy he pulled her close to him again, and this time their kisses were warm with passion and with happiness.

Suddenly he broke away from her. "Peter!'' he exclaimed aghast. "I had forgotten the lad!''

They looked about them only to discover that they were alone.

"The boy is learning discretion,'' said his uncle with satisfaction. "It is his Chalfont blood.''

"To think that I shall be a Chalfont.'' Lucinda nestled her head comfortably against the expanse of his burgundy silk waistcoat. "When will we be married, I wonder?''

"How would you like to be married here in Florence?''

"So soon?'' She looked up at him in amazement.

"Why not? I have already applied for the licence. We only wait upon your father getting here to give his permission.''

"My father?'' Now she really was amazed. "I never told you his name or anything. How did you know?''

"My love!'' He kissed her on the nose. "During these last weeks you have given away clues in plenty about your identity. Your grandmother the well-known patroness of the arts—yes, my sweet, I know

Lady Winterton's reputation well enough. I also know that her son is Sir John Winterton, the diplomat. You told me yourself he was in Vienna. I wrote to him from Lyons to inform him that you were safe, and sent the letter by special messenger. He should be here soon."

"He will not bother coming," said Lucinda with conviction.

"He will come!" Gareth was grimly certain. "I told him if he did not I would fetch him, by force if necessary, diplomat or no diplomat."

"You wrote that to my father?" She looked at him in awe.

"Yes. It is scarcely the proper way to address one's prospective father-in-law, is it? I must try to be more civil when I ask him for your hand. I really am getting to be the most terrible bully. You must take me in hand immediately and change my ways again."

"I absolutely refuse." She snuggled against him once more, savouring the joy of being close to him, the security of his presence. "I love you exactly as you are. But what if my father does not give his consent?"

"Then we will elope!"

"What, again?" she cried.

"It is only again for you, my love. I must remind you that I have yet to elope for a first time. But I promise you one thing. When I elope I intend to do the job properly, with no snags or mistakes. There will be no journeying in separate directions. This time it will be an elopement for two!"

His arms enfolded her once more and his mouth claimed hers, sending her into happy oblivion.

"You know, you promised once never to make love to me again," she said dreamily, when at last their lips parted.

"Why, so I did!" He sounded quite surprised at the recollection. "My word! A brawler, an abductor of young girls, a deceiver and now a man who breaks his word! What a desperate character I have become. I need the love of a good woman to redeem me, that is what I need."

"In that case, I volunteer for the task," she said happily. And she slid her arms about his neck to kiss him...then to kiss him again...and again...and again...

Pride House

Gwyneth Moore

CHAPTER ONE

England
Spring, 1813

"A RARE HANDFUL, eh, Mr. Lewiston?" Stretching his bowed and middle-aged legs, the groom ran across the stable-yard and watched admiringly as the rider dismounted with an easy swing and tossed the reins to him.

The splendid grey stallion snorted and danced. The groom held the reins tight and short, then danced himself, to avoid a kick.

Donald Lewiston laughed, but stepped quickly out of range of those flying hoofs. "Have a care, Joseph. He's a handful. But a goer."

"Ar. Well, anyone can see that, sir. And just what a young gent with spirit would want." He eyed the young man's elegance dubiously. "Will I turn him out, or do you just bring a message for Lady Pride, p'raps?"

Lewiston took off his high-crowned hat and ran a restoring hand through the flattened curls that the afternoon sunlight awoke to a fiery blaze. "I didn't come to see Lady Pride."

Joseph's leathery features contorted in a grin, even as he cursed the stallion under his breath. "Fancy that, now. And you lookin' fine as fivepence, if I may say so, sir."

The attempt at innocence was belied by that impudent grin, and Lewiston said rather ruefully, "You rogue. I looked well enough when I left home, but it's so confounded windy this afternoon." He touched his shirt points investigatively and was relieved to find them properly stiff. Glancing over the fence at the gardens that spread colourful palettes of daffodils, tulips, and hyacinths between the stables and the many-gabled house, he asked with studied nonchalance, "Any other callers, Joseph?"

"Not yet, sir. And Miss Elfreda be up at Pride House."

"Is she, by Jove?" Lewiston brightened, took back the reins and mounted up again, calling a hasty farewell to Joseph and then cursing the grey, which decided to waltz on the return trip across the stable-yard.

Joseph stood looking after him for a minute, his shrewd eyes speculative. Come a'courtin', had the young buck, by the look of that new blue coat. Fit him like a second skin, it did. Almost as tight as the breeches. A fine-lookin' gent, Mr. Lewiston, and manly, for all that he wasn't quite one and twenty. Not good enough for Miss Elfreda, 'course. A Duke, or a Prince even wouldn't be good enough 'less they was rare coves into the bargain. And rich. Not that the Prides was pockets to let, but Miss Elfreda deserved the best on the market. Mr. Lewiston might set easy in a lady's eyes with his red curls and his eyes as green as grass; he was put together nice, too, and he'd got a good chin on him. He had a temper to match that chin, which might not be such a bad thing in a young man. But the Squire was only the Squire. Not much more 'n a comfortable fortune, nor no title higher 'n a Baronet to pass on to his heir. And both would be a long time coming, since Sir Culver Lewiston was not a day older than forty-five. What was more...

"Hum," muttered Joseph, and, retreating from the sun, went into the dimness of the barn to share his misgivings with the coachman.

The object of his mental appraisal soon reached the lane leading to the Home Farm. Donald Lewiston was relieved to have found that Elfreda was at Pride House rather than at the two-centuries-old home they called the New House. He would thus be spared an encounter with either Martha or her mother, and would not have to endure a long, polite and boring conversation before he could hope to snatch a few words in private with his love.

Only five miles separated their properties, and Donald had run tame at Pride since he was breeched. He'd thought of the Prides as extensions of his own large family, and had been genuinely grieved two years ago when Sir Eustace Pride had been called so unexpectedly early to his reward. Clifford Pride, the eldest son, had been Donald's best friend before he'd gone off to become Lieutenant Pride and fight in a line regiment on the Peninsula. For two other members of the household Lewiston felt somewhat less fondness: Miss Veronica Kelton, Lady Pride's spinster sister, had taken him in dislike for some reason. He never betrayed his awareness of this phenomenon, which annoyed but did not deeply concern him. Miss Kelton was old, even older than Lady Pride, and was a poor relation, so she didn't matter. Martha Pride, the youngest child, was, in his estimation, far too opinionated for her fifteen years, apt to make dreadfully gauche remarks, and was headed for the dubious distinction of being named a bluestocking. A pretty enough girl, but argumentative and with the uncomfortable habit of winning her point. Then there was Elfreda . . . He sighed dreamily.

When they'd all played at pirates on the lake, or had hunted dragons in the woods, Elfreda had been no

more than a nondescript girl who was also a jolly good
sport. He'd never dreamed then that the unruly mop
of brown hair could magically change into the softest
light brown curls touched with golden highlights. That
the mischievous brown eyes would become so alluring, or the chubby figure become so tantalisingly cur-
vaceous. He'd not realised how much he loved her
until the garden party and fête his father had hosted
last summer, when he'd overheard that clod Terence
Brownley telling Elfreda how "glorious' she was. A
fine shock that had been. Like a thunderbolt, in fact!

He skirted the farmhouse. McCaffrey was at work
with a plough in the north field. Lewiston returned his
wave, but did not stop, following the lane for another
mile until he was approaching the hill crowned by the
crumbling mansion that was the original Pride House.
He scarcely saw the sweep of the house that was so rich
in history and now so sadly decayed. His every
thought was of his lovely Elfreda. Not that she was
precisely what one might designate a Beauty. Her eyes
were dark and thickly lashed but lacked the demure
shyness that was so desirable in a well-bred young
lady. Her mouth was adorable, but it was in no sense
a rosebud, being actually rather wide. She was too
short, and still a little too plump—though he considered that a good feature, especially since it had resulted in such an enticingly bountiful bosom. Like all
the Prides, she had a stubborn streak, which he admitted was a major fault. But her eyes held a rare
sparkle; her heart was kind, her generally amiable
disposition enhanced by a merry sense of humour.
And there was that about her musical little laugh, the
way her head would tilt up at him, the petal-like quality of the fair-skinned heart-shaped face that made his
pulses quicken with longing for her.

His pulses were quickening now, and, scanning the
weedy gardens, he was disappointed not to see his

love. It would have been romantic to offer her his heart in the rickety old summer-house. Six weeks ago he'd proposed in the conservatory at New House, and she'd said politely that she was very grateful but that they would not suit. Not suit, indeed! The withdraw-ing-room had proved no more salubrious a choice, and in the chaise when he'd let the horse run away... Well, that was best forgotten. Elfreda loved this old ruin, and with luck she would be alone, but the wretched great house was falling to pieces and full of dust, and he didn't want to soil his finery.

He dismounted and tied the grey to a branch of the oak that lightning had killed forty years ago. Tread-ing gingerly up the sagging steps, he nudged the front door open and took off his hat. The dusty old hall was deserted. The outside smells of spring blossoms and newly scythed grass were here replaced by the musty aromas of dankness and mould. He walked across the hall, taking care not to brush against any of the few remaining sticks of furniture. He was wearing the new blue coat—Elfreda liked him in blue—and the white breeches, and he wanted to look his best this time. He was confident that she would not again refuse him. It was quite logical for a lady to wish to be pursued, but Elfreda would not be so foolish as to risk causing him to lose interest. He smiled faintly. There was no sign of her, but she had undoubtedly seen him approach and prepared herself so as to look pretty and caught unawares, in the way females had of staging such scenes.

He walked into what had once been the main din-ing-room, and halted abruptly.

The girl who sat on the chimney seat had clearly made no preparation to impress a gentleman caller. Elfreda Pride wore a woollen shawl over a muslin gown of pale pink that was marred here and there by dirt and a few leaves, almost as though she had been crawling about the floor. Her head was bowed low, the fair curls rumpled and untidy, and her bonnet lay on the hearth beside her. She was murmuring softly, absorbed by something she held in her hands.

"What on earth...?" said Lewiston, crossing to her side.

She gave a yelp, dropped a small glove, and flung up her head to reveal a pale face and brown eyes wide with shock. "Good gracious," she gasped. "How you startled me, Donald. I almost dropped him! And I did drop the bottle. Some of it has leaked out. Oh, it is too bad of you!"

Not an encouraging reception. Lewiston picked up the glove, only to have it send a stream of something squirting over his immaculately clad leg. "Ugh!" he said in disgust, flinging the offending article down and dragging out his handkerchief. "If that ain't the outside of enough! Here I've tried to—" He broke off. "What the deuce *is* that beastly stuff?"

"It is—or *was*—warm milk, watered down, of course." Without the slightest concern for her beau's violated breeches, Elfreda snatched up the glove and gathered it together so that one finger was extended. "There's not much, poor mite." She bent over her cupped left hand. "But you may be able to find a little. Here, sweet Col. Come, come."

"If you refer to me, madam," snorted Lewiston, ruffled, "my name ain't Cole. And I thank you for the ecstatic welcome!"

"I do not refer to you," replied Elfreda impatiently. "Further, his name is not 'Cole.' And had you not scared me out of my wits you might have been welcomed. Though what you are doing here, I cannot guess." Her head jerked up. She exclaimed in sudden alarm, "Heavens! It is not bad news from my brother?"

"No." Lewiston stepped closer and peered at her hand. "He came unscathed through the Battle of Salamanca last summer, and I fancy he bears a charmed life, as he always has. At all events, his lordship seems more intent upon charming the ladies of Spain than on getting himself another victory."

Predictably, Elfreda fired up at once. "How can you say such things?" she demanded, her eyes flashing. "Lord Wellington has fought splendidly against that Corsican monster! Sooner or later there must be other battles, and dear Clifford seems always to be in the fiercest fighting."

"Whereby he will doubtless be a General at the least by the time Old Boney is routed. Now stop your crossgrained fidgets and show me what it is that you have got there. Good God!" He jerked back. "It is a filthy rat!"

Her lip curled with scorn. "It is not a rat. How silly you are, Donald. A fox killed Mrs. McCaffrey's kitchen cat just after she had had six kittens, and this poor little darling thing is the only survivor. I mean to save it."

"Stuff! That 'poor little darling thing' will die whatever you do. You should know by now that you cannot wean anything that small, Elf. Why, it's scarce bigger than my thumb. It cannot even lap."

Elfreda peered tenderly at the miniature and unlovely scrap of life in her palm. "It can suck, I promise you! Indeed, I wonder the glove is not in shreds! Ah, it is asleep, dear little soul. Take this, if you please."

Lewiston received the glove between finger and thumb, and deposited it, as instructed, on the mantelpiece. Elfreda wrapped her tiny charge in a square of flannel and laid it in a straw-filled box on the hearth.

"What are you going to do with it?" asked Lewiston. "Take it home?" He grinned. "Your dear aunt will be overjoyed; she don't like cats above half!"

This was very true, and Elfreda sighed as she stood and straightened her skirt. "It is not that Aunt Veronica doesn't like them, but that they make her nervous. Even so, he must have constant care. I believe one has to feed them as often as the mother would do, which is about every three hours, no?"

He shrugged. "Lord, I don't know. Seems to me that mother cats never get a moment's peace. You'd best take it back to Mrs. McCaffrey at the farm."

"And let the dogs devour him, I suppose! I shall do no such thing!" She bent over the box, frowning. "Though I suppose I must leave him there at night. But you may be sure I shall bring you up here every day, little Col."

Curious, Lewiston asked, "What is it you call him?"

"Col. Short for Colossus." Eyeing his hilarity without pleasure, she said defiantly, "I thought it might encourage him. Oh, do be quiet! You'll frighten him to death!"

Lewiston clapped a hand over his mouth. His eyes danced at her, and with muffled snorts he extended an arm. Smiling despite herself, she allowed him to lead her on to the front terrace.

Reminded of his mission, Lewiston sobered, and spread his clean handkerchief on a cracked step.

With an appreciative smile, Elfreda prepared to sit down.

"Hey!" he protested. "That's for me!"

She stared at him. Despite his rather careless approach to life, Donald was well bred, and such a lack of gallantry surprised her.

He dropped to one knee.

"Oh, no!" she groaned, dampingly. "Not again!"

"Well, if that don't beat the Dutch!" he exclaimed, affronted. "Here I am, properly dressed, which you said I wasn't last time—had these unmentionables made just for today—kneeling at your feet, which is the bang-up way to do the thing and dashed embarrassing if you want to know it, ready to offer you my all, and you're kinder to a blasted little scrap of a moggy than you are to me!"

"No, no!" His comely face was hurt as well as indignant, and Elfreda was really very fond of him. She touched his bright hair gently, then sat beside him. "Dearest Donald, I am indeed honoured, but— Oh, you know my feelings. You are not in sympathy with my vow, and—"

"No more would your papa have been," he said smoulderingly, twisting round to sit on the step and forgetting the neatly spread handkerchief. "Is *that* why you've been refusing me? Of all the rubbishing stuff!"

Her little chin lifted. "It is *not* rubbishing stuff! It was dear Papa's dream, and—"

"Yes, and a dream is *just* what it was! Besides being the height of folly! Time to have done with such childish fustian, my girl, or you'd as well prepare yourself to reject all your hundreds of suitors! The blockhead ain't yet born who'd hand over his fortune only for the privilege of making you his bride!"

Mortified, she sprang to her feet. "Oh! You are horrid, Donald Lewiston! I may not have 'hundreds of suitors,' but, when I make my début next Season, you just may discover I am not wholly undesirable to other gentlemen!"

It was his ever-constant dread, for she was such a taking little thing. She would have been brought out this year save for the fact that it was only ten months since the death of her great-uncle, and Lady Pride had thought it best to delay her come-out until the following Season. She seemed to Lewiston to become prettier every day, and, despite his jeering words, it was the fear that some wealthy old dodderer *might* come up to scratch that had driven him to make his flurry of offers for her hand.

Standing, he said sullenly, "I suppose that if I were a rich man you'd not treat me so shabbily."

To see him look so miserable wrung Elfreda's sympathetic heart. She said gently, "Donald, I am truly sorry. I do not mean to be unkind, and you must know how fond I am of you, but—"

"Are you?" He seized both her hands and held them fast. "My dearest girl, I *love* you. Won't you forget all this foolish ambition and marry me?" He pulled her closer, a flush glowing in his cheeks. She was so soft and warm, and a sweet scent of violets hung about her. Desire gleamed in his green eyes. His arms swept about her, and, despite her struggles, he kissed her on the lips—hard.

With a squeal of rage she broke free. "Oh! How dare you? You see how it is when I try to be kind?"

"Kind?" He knew that he had behaved disgracefully, but, driven by passion and disappointment, raged, "Is that how you respond when a decent gentleman offers? I think my fortune is not contemptible, but it's not sufficient to buy the noble Miss Pride, I apprehend! She prefers to sell herself to some rich old cit, even does she shrink from his wrinkled hands!"

White with wrath, Elfreda drew herself to her full fifty-eight inches. "Were I so weak-spined as to give up my plans—which I am not!—it would not be for an ill-mannered boy who mauls and insults me! Good day to you, sir!" Turning regally from that splendid setdown, she spoiled it. A curricle was racing at speed along the lane towards the New House. "Oh," she murmured, diverted. "I wonder who that can be?"

As flushed as his lady was pale, Lewiston said acidly, "You had best run, Miss Pride. That's a spanking turn-out if ever I saw one. And a jolly fine pair. Cost a pretty penny, I'll warrant. Likely you will find two or three rich old roués awaiting you, fairly panting to be reduced to paupers!"

Two disdainful eyes flashed fire at him from under haughtily upraised brows. With a flirt of her petticoats, Miss Elfreda whirled about, collected her bonnet, and swept past her glowering beau.

Watching her graceful, swinging walk, the proud carriage of her little head, Donald Lewiston's heart was heavy indeed. He obeyed her frigid request that he shut the door, and followed her. "Elfreda..." he pleaded, mounting up and walking his horse along beside her. "I'm sorry. I didn't mean it. Say you forgive me, do."

The little nose lifted an inch higher, and his repeated plea fell on deaf ears.

"Very well," he snarled. "But I won't let you sell yourself to some dirty old moneybags, my girl! Be warned!" And, driving home his spurs, he was away down the hill at a thundering gallop.

Elfreda walked briskly along the lane, watching with disapproval the headlong retreat of her rejected suitor.

"Fiddlesticks!" she said.

CHAPTER TWO

VICTORIA, LADY PRIDE, was not an indolent woman, but on the afternoons when they did not entertain company there was nothing she enjoyed more than to retire with her needlework to the *chaise longue* in her charming withdrawing-room. Once comfortably disposed, she would take up her embroidery frame, set two stitches and put it down again. She would then look around at the display cabinets with their dainty pieces of porcelain and fine crystal; the beautifully framed paintings on the walls; the gracious furnishings and Turkish rugs; and, beyond the wide bays of the windows, the bright flower-beds and emerald lawns that dear Sir Eustace had so loved. And she would know with a deep sense of gratitude that, despite her sad loss, she still managed to keep family and home together, and that she was a very fortunate and blessed woman.

She had, in point of fact, much to disturb her peace of mind. Clifford, her beloved and dashing son, was in the thick of the fighting in Spain, and one could not quite see why he must go off and buy a pair of colours in the first place. Elfreda, the dearest child any mother could have wished for, was a romantic dreamer with a tendency to dwell too much on the past glories of the Prides. Her Bath sojourn at Miss Gordon's Seminary for Young Ladies had neither cured her of an unfortunate stubborn streak, nor dispelled some of the queer notions she harboured, which were best forgotten. Martha, the youngest, was already, at fifteen, showing signs of being another of Pride's long line of really spectacular beauties, but she was bookish and so forthright and outspoken as to turn her mother's hair snow-white. And, although they were not likely to want for the price of a pound of tea, or be driven to using tallow candles in the downstairs rooms, they were not so plump in the pockets as to be perfectly easy. Still, dear Sir Eustace had always held worry to be a sinful waste of energy, and so Lady Pride shrugged her well-padded shoulders, put her trust in her guardian angel and decided that everything would work out nicely in the long run.

Most of the "working out" of things fell to the lot of her elder spinster sister. Miss Veronica Kelton had served as a sort of unpaid major-domo for ten years. She was as thin as Lady Pride was plump, and, although the sisters shared the same colouring, Miss Veronica's pale blue eyes were far from drowsily complacent, and her mousy brown locks, instead of being coaxed into the crimped ringlets affected by Victoria, were drawn into thick plaits, coiled behind each ear. Being of a bustling and energetic nature, Miss Veronica was impatient with Lady Pride's claim that she liked to work at her embroidery in the quiet of the afternoons. "Surprising how much one can get done when one is fast asleep," she would say drily. But Lady Pride would smile in her vague way and off she would go with her bag of silks, and be fast asleep within the quarter-hour.

For all her disparaging remarks, Miss Veronica was fond of her sister. She was grateful to be allowed to live in so comfortable a house, and to be a useful part of a loving family. She seldom disturbed Victoria during her "embroidery siestas," which added to the shock that lady suffered when the door burst open on this bright but windy afternoon and Veronica all but sprinted to peep out of the window.

Starting up in bewilderment, Lady Pride gasped, "Oh, my! Whatever is it? Never say that horrid Bonaparte is here already?"

"Don't be a widgeon, Lady P," said Veronica in her terse fashion. "What a splendid equipage! There's lettuce a'plenty in this young man's dish, whoever he may be. Do you suppose he has come to call upon our Elfreda?"

Despite her dislike of her sister's use of cant terms, these magical words propelled Lady Pride from the *chaise longue*, and she crossed to the window at record speed. A spirited team was slowing before the steps, and a neatly clad groom tossed the reins to the galloping stable-boy, and began to assist his employer from the vehicle.

Lady Pride put up her lorgnette fan and scanned a tall young man, who mounted the steps haltingly, leaning on the arm of his servant. His hair was very dark under the beaver hat, and his eyes were sunk in the pallid face that seemed all bones and tight-stretched skin.

"Good God," she gasped. "It's Stephen Jeffreys!"

"It *cannot* be!" Miss Veronica snatched the fan and scrunched up one eye as she peered with the other. "It is! Oh, my goodness! And he was such a handsome boy! He must have been very ill."

"I wonder if he might have been in Spain," mused her ladyship. "It would explain why he did not come to my dear husband's obsequies. I have judged him harshly for that, considering his father and Eustace were *such* friends."

Veronica nodded thoughtfully. "And Sir Eustace went to Mr. Jeffreys's funeral, although he was ill at the time. Well, the young man is here now. Probably to apologise. Shall you receive him, Lady P?"

"Of course," said Victoria. "We must have him shown to the morning-room, dear, while I change my cap."

Thus it was that Stephen Jeffreys found himself, some ten minutes later, making his bow to a gently smiling lady clad in a flowing robe of mauve silk, who seemed to him not to have changed at all in the five years since last he had seen her. He observed as much after they had shaken hands and he had been waved to a chair.

Lady Pride blushed and disclaimed, but did not feel obliged to return the compliment. It seemed to her that, although his black hair was brushed into a most attractively tumbled style, and his grey eyes were as handsome as ever, in every other way he had aged ten years rather than five, and looked rather alarmingly frail. "It is kind of you to pay a call, Mr. Jeffreys," she said, noticing how carefully he lowered himself into the chair.

"I would have come directly I arrived home, ma'am," he said with a wry smile, "but I fancy Clifford has told you the reason for the delay."

She tensed at once. "You have seen my dear son? Ah! Then you *were* a soldier! Were you in his regiment, perhaps?"

"No, ma'am. I was with Colonel Ponsonby's Heavy Dragoons, but after I was hit Cliff sometimes came and read me your letters. I cannot tell you..." his voice shredded a little "...how much I enjoyed all your news of home."

He came to his feet as Miss Veronica entered, followed by a maid carrying the tea-tray. Veronica had always had a soft spot in her heart for this tall young fellow, and a closer view of his emaciated frame and haggard face wrung her heart. When the courtesies had been exchanged and they were all seated again she passed him a cup and saw the thin hand shake. "Poor boy," she said in a gentle and seldom-heard voice. "I did not even know you were in Spain."

He said hesitantly, "Er—well, it was a . . . a sudden decision. High Golden without my father was…rather empty."

Aware of the deep affection which had existed between Charles Jeffreys and his son, the sisters exchanged glances. Lady Pride said quickly, "You may have enjoyed my letters, sir, but Clifford must be the world's worst correspondent. His rare letters are full of questions, yet he tells me nothing. Were you very badly wounded? I had wondered why—" She stopped.

"Why I did not come to your husband's last rites, ma'am?" He shook his dark head regretfully. "You cannot know how sorry I was to hear of your loss. I had meant to write to you. Indeed, I began a letter several times, but—alas—never had the chance to finish it. Sir Eustace was a wonderful gentleman, and I have lost a good friend." He saw tears come into her eyes, and went on hurriedly, "But you will be wanting to hear about Cliff. I am sure you know he was in the action at Salamanca, and came through unscathed, thank heaven."

"Yes, indeed. But—you did not, I think?"

For an instant his eyes were shadowed by a hunted look. He said quietly, "No." Then he went on, "One thing you need not worry for, ma'am, is your son's comfort. His man is the biggest thief in the army, and Cliff wants for nothing, I promise you."

Miss Veronica said with a smile, "Trust my nephew. You must have spent many months in hospital, Mr. Jeffreys. How long have you been home?"

"A week, ma'am. And have brought—"

He was interrupted when Elfreda wandered into the room. She was dazzled by the dimness of the interior after the bright glare outside, and she put off her bonnet, complaining that the wind was "positively fierce!"

Jeffreys stood, managing to conceal his increasing weariness.

With an inward groan for her daughter's unruly curls, soiled gown, and unbecomingly flushed cheeks, Lady Pride said in a faintly scolding voice, "As you see, we have company, Elfreda."

The tone implied that she should know this "company." Peering at him uncertainly, Elfreda said, "I beg your pardon. How do you do, sir?"

Amused by the frankly puzzled scrutiny being levelled at him by a pair of very pretty brown eyes, Jeffreys teased, "I think you do not remember me, Miss Elfreda."

Lady Pride looked appalled, and searched helplessly for the right thing to say.

"Of course she remembers you, Mr. Jeffreys," said Miss Veronica, stepping into the breach. "Your papa never forgot her birthday, did he, Elfreda?"

Before Elfreda could recover from her stupefaction another voice was heard.

"Good gracious!" exclaimed Martha Pride, hurrying into the room. "Are you Stephen Jeffreys, then? I would never have—"

Coming close to her aunt at this point, the tactless fifteen-year-old received the benefit of a sharp pinch and gasped into silence.

"Perhaps," said Lady Pride, for once displeased by one of her children, "you will remember your manners, Martha."

Red as fire, Martha curtsied and mumbled an apology.

"No, no," said Jeffreys with a disarming grin. "I'd not have recognised you either, Martha. How pretty you are grown." He turned to shake hands with Elfreda, and for an instant was unable to relinquish her sticky palm. His smile did not waver, but a twinkle crept into his grey eyes.

"Oh, dear," she said, all mischief as she smiled up at him. "It was the bottle for Colossus, I'm afraid. I am so sorry, Mr. Jeffreys. Mama, may I be excused? I really must wash my hands."

"At the least," murmured Miss Veronica tartly.

Elfreda fled, and Lady Pride rang for the maid and told Martha to sit beside her.

"Yes, Mama." Seething with excitement, Martha burst out, "Did you know there are—?"

"And be quiet as a mouse," added Lady Pride repressively.

Martha acquired a mulish look, but obeyed.

Wondering who Colossus might be, Jeffreys settled back on to his chair.

"How have you found High Golden?" enquired Lady Pride. "Such a beautiful estate. My dear husband admired it excessively."

"We were always glad to welcome him, ma'am. In fact, I mean to urge you to visit me. It is a delight to be home, of course, and my cousin has kept the estate in good order."

"Did you leave Adrian Jeffreys in charge, then?" asked Miss Veronica, adding in her blunt way, "I'd not have thought him steady enough to be entrusted with such a task."

Amused, Jeffreys said, "No? Do you judge him a fribble, ma'am?"

"An excessive handsome one," contributed Martha, forgetting her mama's stricture, and earning another pinch.

Jeffreys laughed. "Oh, excessive, I grant you. But, for all his looks, he's a good man, Miss Veronica, and has done splendidly."

They chatted easily about his cousin's management of the estate until Elfreda returned, wearing a gown of cream muslin with a wide sash of yellow satin, her fair curls threaded with a matching ribbon. "No, please do not get up again," she said as he started to rise. "You will be too late, you see, because I am already sitting down." She slipped into a chair next to her aunt, a dimple flickering beside her mouth.

Martha was unable to restrain her curiosity for another instant. "There are boxes on the hall table," she burst out, and fixed their caller with an excited and hopeful stare.

Lady Pride groaned, and Elfreda muttered, "Martha!"

"I thank you for reminding me." Jeffreys turned to the maid, who had arrived with a pot of hot water. "Could you oblige me by bringing them in, if you please?"

Eluding her mama's clutching hand, Martha sprang up. "I'll help!" she squealed, and danced out.

"Oh, lud!" sighed Miss Veronica. "That child!"

"No, she is charming." Jeffreys glanced at Elfreda. "Indeed, your young ladies have quite grown up during my absence. I fancy you have many admirers, Miss Elfreda. I trust I may be permitted to join their ranks?"

Elfreda looked startled. "But I had understood you were betrothed."

Bluntness, he thought numbly, ran in the family. Before he could gather his wits Martha said from behind a pile of gaily wrapped parcels, "Miss Bellington has jilted him, Elf. She's going to marry old Lord Mildendean. Didn't you—?"

"That will *do*!" cried Miss Veronica, aghast. "I think you must apologise, Miss Pride! And as for you, Martha—go to your room at once!"

Pink with embarrassment, Elfreda stammered an apology.

Martha tumbled her burdens on to the sofa and turned a stricken gaze on her parent. "I didn't mean to be rude. Truly, I didn't! These are all for *us*! Must I go, Mama? *Must* I?"

Paler than ever, Jeffreys rose again. "Please allow her to stay, ma'am. I am very sure she meant no harm. Besides, she did but . . . but speak the truth. I am well and truly—jilted, and . . ." He swayed and reached rather blindly for the chair arm.

With a little scream, Miss Veronica flew up to throw an arm about him and guided him back into the chair. "The poor dear soul is still very weak!" she exclaimed in distress. "Brandy, Elfreda! Hurry!"

Frightened, Elfreda ran to pour a glass of brandy. Jeffreys accepted it gratefully. After a minute a trace of colour came back into his cheeks, and he blinked rather bemusedly into the circle of anxious feminine faces. "What a fellow I am to . . . alarm you so. I do beg your pardon. But . . . you must humour the poor wounded soldier, ma'am, and allow Martha to stay. One of the gifts Cliff sent home is for her, you see."

Martha fairly vibrated with anguished excitement. Lady Pride muttered unhappily, "But . . . *whatever* must you think of us?"

Elfreda pleaded, "Do *pray* forgive her, sir. She truly has a dreadful tongue, but she does not mean it, and she is very young. I promise you she will say nothing outlandish for the rest of the afternoon."

Amused by her air of senior intercessor, and touched by her earnestness, he said smilingly, "There is nothing to forgive."

She beamed at him. "You are so kind. Indeed I cannot fathom how that cold stick of a girl could have preferred that crotchety old man!"

"No, indeed," agreed Martha, so disastrously eager to make amends that she did not notice the frozen expressions of her aunt and her mama. "I expect she only wanted his title!"

Five minutes later Stephen Jeffreys escaped the débâcle by murmuring his farewells and making his uncertain way back to the curricle. Once out of sight of the house, he put back his head and laughed helplessly.

"I HAVE FAILED," wept Lady Pride, her nose buried in the tiny square of cambric and lace that served as a handkerchief. "That nice young man went away in . . . the deepest shock. And . . . and heaven only knows what he will spr-spread about my daughters! Oh, was I *ever* so mortified?"

"Oh, don't be such a watering pot," said Miss Veronica, admiring the intricately worked lace shawl Jeffreys had brought. "I suspect he thoroughly enjoyed himself. I shall wear this on Sunday, I think."

Drying her tears, Lady Pride sniffed, "He could not even . . . bring himself to *look* at me! He must think I have bred up a family of hobbledehoys, and am the worst mother ever born."

"If he did not look at you it was likely because he could scarce keep from laughing." Miss Veronica picked up her sister's gift. "Such a lovely comb Clifford sent you, my dear. If he did . . ."

Her attention diverted, Lady Pride lowered the handkerchief. She was most taken with the high Spanish comb, and asked anxiously, "Do you think Jeffreys mixed them up, then?"

Being under no illusions as to her nephew's somewhat haphazard notions of filial responsibility, Miss Veronica suspected he'd had no hand in sending gifts home. She started to reply, then paused as the door opened.

Elfreda peeped in at them and asked timidly, "May I come in now, dear Mama? I should like to apologise for being so clumsy."

"The word," said Lady Pride with a little gulp, "is 'vulgar.' I can understand such behaviour from Martha, for she has not yet learned when to hold her tongue. But *you*, Elfreda! *Whatever* possessed you?"

Taking this as encouragement, Elfreda crept in and edged towards her afflicted parent. "I do not know what got into my head, Mama." She wrinkled her brow. "Save that Mr. Jeffreys looked so dreadfully, and I was angry to think he must come home from fighting for his country, with his health ruined and his looks quite gone, only to find that wretched girl had jilted him. His life is over, poor thing!"

"There, you see, Lady P," said Miss Veronica soothingly, "the child meant well. However, I cannot think he is in such bad case as you suppose, Elfreda. Not so long ago he was a handsome fellow, and when he has rested and recovered his health he will surely find someone else."

"Small doubt of that," agreed Lady Pride. "Stephen Jeffreys is a rare catch, and I fancy there will be many a handkerchief dropped for him before summer is done."

Elfreda slipped into a chair, and said, awed, "You *do*, Mama? But—he is so frail. And he must be... thirty years of age, at least!"

Miss Veronica laughed heartily.

Lady Pride, however, gave an exclamation of impatience. "He is not a day over nine and twenty. He cannot be, for I invited them to your brother's christening, and I remember distinctly that poor Amelia could not come because it was the same afternoon as Stephen's fourth birthday party. And only because you are scarce out of the nursery, Elfreda, you must not think a man of twenty-nine has one foot in the grave.''

"Even if Stephen Jeffreys did have one foot in the grave, there would be very many mamas eager to marry their daughters to him,'' said Miss Veronica rather acidly. "Speaking of which, I was surprised to see you come home alone, Elfreda. I had understood Donald Lewiston called on you, looking a regular Bond Street beau.''

"He did look rather nice.'' Elfreda sighed.

Lady Pride paled and said falteringly, "She is only eighteen, Veronica.''

"Almost nineteen, Lady P. And could have been betrothed any time this two years. Still, Lewiston is a rascal if he seeks to fix his attentions without having first asked your permission.''

"Indeed, he is!'' Anxious now, Lady Pride reached out, and Elfreda ran to take her hand and sink to her knees beside the sofa. "Dearest,'' said her mother, "has Donald—er—?''

"He asked if he might speak to you, Mama.''

Miss Veronica asked, "And—*have* you a tendre for him, Niece?''

Elfreda stroked her mother's white hand and for a moment did not reply. Then she said very softly, "I am extreme fond of Donald.''

The eyes of the sisters met.

"Oh, dear,'' murmured Lady Pride, blinking rapidly.

Miss Veronica said thoughtfully, "She could do a deal worse, Lady P. The Squire is a fine gentleman. Donald will inherit the estate and the title someday. And he is an honourable and upright young fellow.''

"Besides which, we have known them forever,'' admitted Lady Pride in a resigned voice. "I cannot pretend to be too surprised. I suppose I shall have to give my consent, Elfreda. But I do think Donald should apply to me. And he must write to Clifford."

Elfreda lifted her downbent head. Her face was grave. She said, "I think that will not be necessary, Mama. I shall not marry Donald Lewiston."

Lady Pride threw up her hands. "Oh, Veronica! It is the vow again!"

CHAPTER THREE

SUNDAY MORNING was fair and warm. The ladies wore their new finery, and when they set out for church Elfreda carried the parasol her brother had sent. It was a dainty confection of pale pink silk, edged with Brussels lace. The flounce of her off-white gown was adorned with tiny pink rosettes, the ribbons of her bonnet were pink velvet, and the poke was a foam of white lace. She had already ascertained that the little parasol framed her face quite charmingly, and she was well aware that Donald Lewiston stared at her as they walked up the sunlit path to the church, and continued to stare at her all through the sermon. He looked romantically grim and brooding when they met outside, and, although Elfreda chatted easily with his family, she avoided a direct exchange with him. She could not but feel sorry, for they had been friends since childhood, and she would have been perfectly willing to wed him and try to be a good wife—if he met her requirements. He did not.

Lewiston had formed the habit of escorting the Pride party home after church, and his absence cast a small shadow over their walk. The two elder ladies rather pointedly avoided discussing the matter, but after a while Martha, who secretly admired Donald, gave it as her opinion that Elfreda had a heart of stone. "You will meet a dreadful fate," she declared awfully. "They always do!"

"Who always do, dear?" enquired Lady Pride, intrigued.

"The beautiful young damsels in books," replied Martha. "They spurn the handsome and devoted hero for the love of rank, or gold, or some such stupid thing, and he rides off to a dreadful foreign place to die. Then the beautiful damsel is sorry, but it is too late, and she lives a life of heartbreak and regret."

"You have been reading those silly romances again," said Miss Veronica severely. "You will curdle your brains, Martha, if you fill your head with such rubbish."

"And, at all events, it will not happen to me," said Elfreda, who had been rather shaken by her sister's gloomy prognosis. "For I doubt if Donald Lewiston has the remotest notion of going anywhere to die. And, besides, I am not a beautiful damsel."

"Well, that's true enough," agreed Martha, much to her sister's indignation.

They were invited to dine with old friends that evening, but a light luncheon had been set out on the rear terrace. They were still sitting at table when one of the maids came to present the blue jade salver with a calling card which read, "Stephen C. Jeffreys."

When he had been conducted to the terrace his apologies for intruding on their luncheon were brushed aside and he was pressed to join them. By comparison with many of the splendidly turned-out fashionables who had attended services this morning, he was very simply attired. Yet, in some odd way, the plain but beautifully tailored coat of olive superfine, the neatly if not extravagantly tied neckcloth, and the sleek cream pantaloons seemed to Elfreda the very epitome of elegance.

Refusing an offer of luncheon, he accepted lemonade, and said with his engaging smile, "What a charming Easter picture you make. I wish I had brought my cousin so he might have made a sketch for me."

His remark was sincere, for the bright gardens and lush green of the lawns provided a perfect setting for the ladies; Elfreda demure in white and pink, her sister wearing primrose, Lady Pride in a flowing robe of lavender, and Miss Veronica clad in dove-grey.

"How pleasant it is," said Miss Veronica, "to have the company of a gentleman again."

"The pleasure is mine, ma'am," he responded.

Elfreda said merrily, "It would have been a pleasure deferred had you been wearing your red coat, sir. You would have clashed with Mama's gown, and Aunt Veronica could not have borne it. She has a remarkable eye for colour."

Amused, he said, "How true it is that there are two sides to everything. Only think—were it not for the fact that my uniform does not fit too well at the moment I might be banished from such delightful company!"

"In which case," said Elfreda, "we must all hope that you will very soon be banishable again."

His lips twitched. "I think I am not quite sure of how to interpret that remark, ma'am."

"Not surprising," snorted Veronica. "Seeing that there's no such word!"

"There is now," said Elfreda pertly, "for I just made it up. And you may know your dictionary, Aunt, but you must own that new words are being invented every day."

"Most of which we would do very well without," retorted her aunt.

"Aha," said Jeffreys. "We have a purist among us! Tell me, Miss Kelton, am I correct in deducing that you have also a flair for art?"

Veronica coloured up and mumbled gruffly that she could sketch a little.

"My sister is too modest," said Lady Pride. "She has done some lovely things."

"In that case, you will like to see my cousin's work, Miss Veronica."

"Ah, yes!" exclaimed Lady Pride. "I recollect that I was impressed by Adrian's talent when he was—now, let me see . . . he must have been only about sixteen years of age, for it was just before you came to us, Veronica. Has he continued to paint, Mr. Jeff—? Oh, my! How remiss I am. I suppose I should properly address you by your rank? Is it . . . Captain Jeffreys?"

"No, ma'am. A lowly lieutenant, I fear. So that you were perfectly correct in naming me 'Mr.' But I should like it so much better if you would instead call me Stephen. After all, you have known me since I was in short coats. As for my cousin, Adrian had little time for art while I was on the Peninsula, but his gift is, as you say, considerable. You must come and see his paintings. In fact, that's why I am here—to attempt to lure you all into Somerset. My aunt Hildegarde plays hostess for me, and would be delighted to receive you."

Lady Pride had not gone about much since her husband's death, but she was well aware that any guest at High Golden was assured of pleasant company, luxurious accommodations, and a superb table. Further, there was always the chance that her daughters might meet eligible young bachelors, and certainly any friends of Stephen Jeffreys and his rather formidable aunt would be above reproach. She was pleased to accept, and it was arranged that they should journey into Somerset a week Tuesday, when Mr. Jeffreys would bring coaches to convey them.

This prospect added to Martha's delight, and when Jeffreys rose to say his farewells she begged permission to leave so as to relate the delicious details to her best friend.

Elfreda said, "But I thought you were going to walk with me to the Home Farm? You wanted to see Colossus."

Already dancing away, Martha called that she would go with her sister tomorrow.

Jeffreys at once offered to take Elfreda up with him, since he would be driving past the farm. "It is rather a warm afternoon for such a long walk," he added. "Do say you will ride with me, ma'am. If your mama has no objections, of course."

Lady Pride did not at all object, for, as she later told her sister, she had the utmost confidence in Stephen Jeffreys's behaving as a perfect gentleman. "Not that I need to be concerned at all events," she said regretfully. "The poor fellow is so frail that I vow a puff of wind might push him over, much less a spirited young lady! Indeed, I only hope... You *do* think he will get better, don't you? It is a melancholy thought that such a fine man could be condemned to the life of an invalid."

"HOW NICE THIS IS," exclaimed Elfreda, looking about her as the coachman guided the stylish high-perch phaeton along the lane at a merry pace. "So much more exciting than driving in Mama's landaulet. Landaulets are dull. I had feared our Easter was to be dull also, but now you have come and cheered us up enormously." Before he could respond she added in her bright fashion, "Spring is such a marvellous time, is it not? Everything so clean and shiny and new."

"Yes, indeed. I think you've an eye for beauty, Miss Elfreda. It's a great gift."

"A gift my father taught me. He loved the countryside. The trees, especially. He used to say they were chatterboxes, even as I am."

He listened to the soft hushing sounds of the leaves, and said with his whimsical smile, "They certainly have a good deal to say."

She nodded. "I sometimes think, you know, that they really do have a mystical language. I wonder what they are saying now."

The lacy fringe of the new parasol cast a dappled shade across her face. Watching the swiftly changing expressions—the animation of a few seconds ago, the dreaming look that replaced it—he asked, "Do you mean what they say to us? Or to each other?"

"To each other. Or to the wild creatures. I had never thought they might be trying to tell *us* something. What a lovely idea! I expect they would say, 'Why do you humans take the beautiful world God has given you and turn it into ugliness with your slums and filth and crowded cities? Why must you make war on your own kind, and your men delight in killing each other so merciles—'" She broke off, and turned to him with a gasp of dismay. "Oh, dear! There I go again—another *faux pas*, to say such a thing to a soldier! You will think me a very silly creature."

"To the contrary. You are so bright and gay that you make me feel like a grandfather!"

"Oh, no! You are not *that* old! Oh! I mean—"

His grey eyes were alight with laughter. "I fear I know exactly what you mean, but, despite the great disparity in our ages, Miss Elfreda, I have not enjoyed myself so much since—" He broke off, and finished more soberly, "For a long, long time."

She thought, His eyes are really quite beautiful. They did not take that from him, at least. And she asked, "Was the war very terrible, Mr. Jeffreys? You do not mean to rejoin your regiment, do you?"

He hesitated, then said slowly, "All wars are terrible, ma'am. But Bonaparte must be stopped or assuredly we will be his next victims. As for my plans—I had intended to return to active duty, but..." Another pause, then he added with a smile, "And I asked that you call me Stephen."

"*Au contraire*, sir. You asked my *mama*, which would be quite convenable. But I do not think it would be proper for *me* to address you by your Christian name."

"Why? Because I am such an extreme elderly person?"

She glanced at him. He was adept at hiding his feelings, and it was difficult to guess whether he was in earnest. She said carefully, "Certainly not. But, after all, I only met you a few days ago."

"Nonsense. Our families have been friends forever. In fact, I know all about you."

The dimple beside her lips quivered mischievously. She tossed her curls and said, "I dispute that, sir—er—Stephen. Perhaps you will be so good as to instruct me in the subject."

"Very well. You are eighteen—"

"Almost nineteen."

"Oh. *Quite* elderly, then."

"How dreadly gauche of you, Mr. Jeffreys, to speak of a lady's age! If you cannot be more circumspect you had best cease."

With a chuckle, he said, "And I am demoted to Mr. Jeffreys again, whereas a moment ago I was knighted? I shall risk continuing, but it is clear that I must proceed with caution. Let me think... Ah, yes. You had measles very badly when you were five, so that your brother said you were one great spot, and—"

"And called me Spot for years, the horrid brute!" Her brown eyes sparkled, and she urged merrily, "Pray go on. But you are not doing very much better, and so I warn you!"

He said in mock terror, "Heaven protect me! What dare I list? Hmm... You are devoted to your family

and made a great fuss when you were sent off to the
Seminary. Very soon, however, you were so surrounded by friends that you often could not come
home for the holidays, but were whisked off to stay at
some great estate or other. You excel at the harp, can
speak and read Latin adequately, and have written
some nice poems. But your headmistress gave you
poor marks because you chattered too much and were
always dreaming."

"Which only proves how contradictory was the
lady," said Elfreda with a decisive nod. "Because one
cannot do both at the same time, now, can one? And
I think, sir, that you *have* been gossiping about me
with Clifford, who has betrayed my guilty secrets!"

"But not all of them," he argued. "For I still do not
know who Colossus may be."

The phaeton had turned off the lane on to a dirt
road and was approaching a picturesque whitewashed
and half-timbered farmhouse with a thatched roof and
a rose vine climbing a trellis by the front door.

Elfreda said, "Are you brave enough to find out,
Mr. Stephen?" And at once added, "Oh, but how
thoughtless I am. You will be tired. If your coachman
would just take me to the top of that hill I shall say
goodbye."

He glanced in some surprise from the neat farm,
which he had supposed was their destination, to the
distant hilltop, on which stood what appeared to be a
very large and abandoned mansion. "Is that where
Colossus lives?" he asked apprehensively. "What a
gloomy ruin. Surely he would not attack a sick old
gentleman?"

He had spoken in jest, and was rather taken aback
to see that she looked concerned. Gad! How ancient
did he appear to her?

"Colossus would not harm a fly," she said. "But I
really think you should not come inside today."

He was feeling tired again, but his blood was up now, and he said doggedly, "I must. Else I shall be too consumed by curiosity to get a wink of sleep tonight. This bridge looks to be of the same vintage as the house. Is it safe?"

She said, "Yes," and made him laugh by adding as they rattled over the wooden structure, "It has not fallen down for a month, at least."

Ten minutes later he peered at the minuscule creature in the palm of Elfreda's hand, and exclaimed disbelievingly, "*That* is Colossus?"

"Yes. And you must not laugh or you will frighten the poor mite." Picking up the makeshift glove "bottle," which Mrs. McCaffrey had left beside a pan of milk, Elfreda said, "Oh, dear. I am rather late, but the milk is still lukewarm, thank goodness. Hold him for me, if you please."

Jeffreys drew back in alarm. "Lord, no! I might crush him."

She was firm, however, and, albeit with great reluctance, he accepted the tiny kitten. Elfreda filled her "bottle" and turned to find Jeffreys holding his burden at arm's length and watching it as though it might at any minute explode.

She giggled, retrieved Colossus and poked the milk-swollen finger at the tiny mouth. The kitten immediately started to move its head about in a weak flopping until it found the source of sustenance.

"Jupiter!" whispered Jeffreys. "A tiger *veritable*!"

Her eyes lifted to him eagerly. "Do you think he will survive? Donald says he cannot, and that I should have let him die in peace. I am not being unkind, am I, Mr. Stephen?"

How anxious she looked, and how tender she was with that wisp of life. "One should never say die, ma'am. Unless life becomes—er—unbearably grim, perhaps. For how long have you been trying to wean your great beast?''

''A week! And only see how strong he is growing. Surely if he has managed to—'' She broke off, glancing to the door as the sound of hoofs could be heard outside.

A moment later Donald Lewiston marched in. He shot a resentful glare from Elfreda to the tall man who, despite his gaunt face and figure, somehow achieved an air of poised elegance. ''I saw that bang-up phaeton,'' he said, the words clipped and harsh. ''Found your moneybags, have you, Elfreda?''

Jeffreys stiffened. One eyebrow lifted, and he said coolly, ''I think you forget your manners, sir. You are, I presume, old enough to have been taught some.''

His instinctive antagonism deepening, Lewiston snarled, ''Perhaps you would care to teach me some more?''

Donald was in an ugly mood, thought Elfreda, and, although he could be charming, his fierce temper was well-known. Poor Mr. Jeffreys looked even more frail beside the robust good health of the younger man, and Donald was sufficiently enraged to ignore the obvious fact that Jeffreys was in no condition to defend himself. Alarmed, she said, ''Donald, this is our old friend Mr.—''

''Spare me,'' interrupted Lewiston rudely. ''I've no interest in the fellow. I want a word with you, Elfreda.''

''I judge from that flaming poll that you are one of the Lewistons,'' drawled Jeffreys. ''If your vocabulary is as crude as your behaviour I would advise the lady to have none of it.''

His face brick-red, Lewiston stamped forward.

''No, no!'' squeaked Elfreda, running between the two men. ''Donald! Do you forget this is Sunday?'' Lewiston showed no sign of remorse, and she pushed him back with one hand and said apologetically, "Donald is inclined to be hasty, but he does not mean it, sir." She thrust Colossus at Jeffreys. "Please feed him for me. I shall be back directly."

"We'll see about that," grated Lewiston. The expression of dismayed revulsion on the other man's face as kitten and "bottle" were bestowed on him was so comical, however, that Lewiston accompanied Elfreda outside with no further display of ferocity.

Jeffreys called pleadingly, "He will not take it from me, Miss Pride!"

Walking across the terrace, she said over her shoulder, "Perhaps he senses that you don't like him. You must talk to him kindly."

Lewiston gave a snort of laughter.

Jeffreys regarded the creature on his palm. "Talk to him kindly?" he muttered. "Be damned t'you, cat. Eat this filthy stuff!" He nudged the "bottle" against the miniature jaw, and to his astonishment it opened and the tiny tongue curled around the finger of the glove again. "Like a blasted limpet!" whispered Jeffreys with an awed sense of great accomplishment.

He concentrated on his task, but kept his ears tuned to the proceedings outside. Elfreda must have taken her fiery swain some distance off, but his voice could still be heard. After a while it became irate. Jeffreys frowned and started to the door, but at that moment the girl ran back inside, and he caught a glimpse of Lewiston flinging himself into the saddle and galloping away at a great rate of speed.

Elfreda's cheeks were pink, and Jeffreys said, "I think I should not have allowed you to go off with that hot-at-hand young sprig. I hope I may not receive a scold from your mama."

"Oh, no." She tried to speak calmly, although her breathing was rather tumultuous. She despised quarrels and she had been obliged to speak quite sternly to

Donald. "Mama likes him very much, for he is not disagreeable as a rule. In fact, I believe she hopes that he—that I—"

"That you will make a match of it?"

"Yes." She went to him and reached out. "I'll take him now."

"No such thing." Jeffreys swung his hands away. "He is doing quite nicely, thank you." She gave a little laugh, and he grinned, and added, "If you are promised to Lewiston he had some right to be annoyed, and I should not have given him such a set-down."

"He deserved a set-down. Besides, we are not betrothed."

The joy and exuberance that had been so marked earlier faded away. Longing to banish her troubled look, he probed, "But he was fairly maddened to find me here. He is surely in love with you?"

She stared at the dusty floorboards. "He says he is."

"Is it, then, that you do not care for him?"

"I care for him. Very much indeed."

"Oh, I see. It is just a lovers' quarrel, eh?" He said bracingly, "May I hope to be invited to the nuptials?"

"There will be no nuptials. Not between Donald and me, at least. We live in a modern age, Mr. Jeffreys. And to marry for love is—is not the thing."

Fascinated, he said, "It isn't? Then what *shall* you marry for, Miss Elfreda?"

She looked up and met his eyes squarely.

"Money," she said.

CHAPTER FOUR

"I HAD FORGOTTEN how many acacia trees there are,"
said Elfreda, looking ahead as the curricle followed
the long drivepath.

Stephen Jeffreys had delegated his cousin Adrian to
escort the Prides on their journey into Somerset, a
development that Martha thought exciting, but one
that Elfreda found disquieting on several counts. Most
ladies would have been proud to drive out beside Adrian Jeffreys, who had the reputation of being something of a nonpareil. As tall and dark as his military
cousin, whose heir he was, he possessed an adequate
if not large income, was a fine athlete, and of a lin-
eage none could fault. Certainly, he was better looking than Stephen, and far more sure of himself. Mr.
Adrian's lazy drawl and casual manner did not charm
Elfreda, however. She judged him affected and found
she could not be quite at ease in his company. From
the moment of his arrival at Pride House she had
thought he watched her with just a hint of contempt
in his cold grey eyes and she could not but wonder
what Stephen had told him, and, more to the point,
why Stephen had not come himself, as he'd promised.

When asked that question by Aunt Veronica, Adrian had shrugged his broad shoulders and said that
Stephen had been jaunting about too much of late,
and was properly knocked up. "I serve as a sort of
unpaid major-domo for the poor fellow," he'd added
with a faintly sardonic smile. "And I promise you I

have been given strictest instructions to drive with care and guard my precious charges with my life.''

Everyone had laughed dutifully. Everyone except Elfreda, who had read both mockery and some hidden meaning into his remarks. He had perhaps sensed her reaction, for he'd turned his handsome head in her direction and given her look for look, a boldness in his glance which further irritated her.

She had not wished to ride in the curricle, but Lady Pride had not been slow to note the admiration in her younger daughter's dazzled eyes. Having long been aware of her late husband's opinion that Mr. Adrian Jeffreys was as dangerous as he was handsome, and an overly proud care-for-nobody, she intended to keep her baby as far from him as possible. Not that any well-bred gentleman would flirt with a fifteen-year-old girl, but Martha was too impressionable by half, and it would be most undesirable if she should fall into an infatuation for so suave a young man about town. Besides which, lurking always in the back of her mother's mind was the knowledge that Martha, for all her outspoken candour and sometimes downright gauche behaviour, was already distractingly pretty. Thus the more level-headed Elfreda had been designated to ride in the curricle, while the rest of the family followed in the luxurious coach Stephen Jeffreys had sent for them.

Adrian had conversed politely, and apparently idly. But Elfreda was on guard and had kept her replies brief and bland. Now he reminded her that the hill towards which they were riding had given the estate its name. ''Have you never visited us when the acacias are in bloom, Miss Pride?''

''It seems to me that we came for Easter once, but it rained the entire time. And another visit was paid at Christmas, when it snowed.''

"Good gracious," he said laughingly. "What a dreadful opinion you must have formed. We shall have to exert ourselves to please, for it would be sad indeed if you should carry away a dislike of Stephen's home."

Again she thought to detect a sneer, but before she could comment he added, "Ah, here comes my indomitable cousin. And— Deuce take it!" He muttered something under his breath, and, glancing at him, she saw that his brows were down-drawn, his jaw tight with anger.

Stephen Jeffreys came at the gallop, mounted on a big bay horse that pranced about and tossed its head impatiently when he reined up.

"Welcome," said Stephen, raising his hat and essaying a slight bow.

Returning his smile as she leaned to shake hands, Elfreda decided that he looked much more like his old self in riding dress.

Of a different frame of mind, Adrian growled, "You stupid block. You know blasted well the doctor said—"

"A fig for doctors." Stephen grinned at Elfreda and rode back to call a welcome into the window of the carriage.

He rode with the easy grace of the cavalryman, and Elfreda asked, "Is he not supposed to ride, Mr. Jeffreys?"

He scowled, and replied curtly, "Not that particular horse, certainly. But it is a waste of time to try to protect the idiot!"

A little flushed and his eyes very bright, Stephen joined them again and stayed beside the curricle as they moved on. He thought the light beige travelling gown with its gold silk trim, and the bonnet with gold ruffles in the poke, became Elfreda admirably, and he said with undisguised admiration, "How glad I am

that you could come, ma'am. I hope you will forgive
my not calling for you myself, but I—er—had pressing matters to attend to."

Adrian gave a scornful snort. "Your absence did
not throw the lady into the dismals. We have gone
along famously, although Miss Pride would find your
estate more acceptable were the trees in bloom, eh,
ma'am?"

Resenting his choice of words, Elfreda refused to be
thrown into confusion, as she suspected he'd intended. She said brightly, "I have never found it disagreeable. But I'll own I'd not realised how beautiful
it must be in summertime."

"Then you must come to us in August, and I shall
order my acacias to outdo themselves in your honour,
ma'am. They listen to me, you see."

"Do they, indeed?" said Elfreda with a sparkling
look. "How nice. But I was not fishing for another
invitation when I have scarce begun to enjoy this one.
And you must tell me, please—how is my kitten?"

Up went his brows. All innocence, he said, "I think
I do not know of such a creature."

"You certainly do! I mean Colossus, whom you
stole away from me and have likely slain with your
great strong hands!"

Adrian slanted a sardonic glance at her, but Stephen laughed, not displeased by the remark.

"Your Colossus is the reason why he would not
come and fetch you," drawled Adrian. "He will trust
no one else to feed the little rat, and I doubt has had a
decent night's sleep since he brought it here."

Stephen looked irritated. "Rubbish! I enjoy caring
for the creature. You will be surprised, ma'am. He has
improved vastly while under my roof, and is a regular
king among kittens."

Amused, she said, "What—in one week?"

"You see, I have been talking to him. As instructed."

She was beginning to know the way he had of keeping his lips perfectly solemn, even as his eyes gleamed with laughter. She said with equal solemnity, "You must have chatted a great deal."

"Actually, I read to him. Every cat should have an informed mind, do you not agree?"

"Oh, absolutely. Of what did you inform him? Homer, perhaps?"

"And Virgil."

"He thoroughly enjoyed the *Aeneid*," put in Adrian, entering their banter.

"Is that so? Which book?"

Stephen said, "Why—all of them, of course."

Elfreda laughed gaily and said she wondered he was not hoarse.

"Only *on* one," he responded, turning in the saddle to watch her merry face. Adrian looked from one to the other of them, shook his head, and whipped up the team.

High Golden was a magnificent estate, and Elfreda was almost sorry when their small cavalcade had wound up the hill and left the groves of trees. The vehicles halted before the terraced front of the great house. The doors were already opened. The butler, flanked by footmen, waited to receive the guests, and no sooner had Stephen ushered them up the steps than Hildegarde Stratton was bearing down upon them.

This very large *grande dame* was the relict of Mr. Edgar Stratton, brother to Stephen's long-dead mother. She was an eccentric lady, and, being slightly deaf—which she indignantly denied—spoke in a consistently loud and high-pitched voice. She was most fond of both her nephews and made Stephen an excellent hostess. No effort had been spared to ensure the comfort of the guests, and after the briefest of formalities they were shown to luxurious suites, where maids were waiting to attend to their every need. Mrs. Stratton decreed that they must rest after their long journey and would not be expected downstairs until they were perfectly restored. "Dinner," she added resonantly, "will be served at six o'clock. Sharp."

Stephen caught Elfreda's eye and winked, and she stifled a giggle as she went upstairs to wash, change her dress, and "rest," all in forty minutes.

Repairing to the library, Stephen found his cousin sprawled in a chair with his booted feet propped on a leather-topped table and a glass of Madeira loosely held in one muscular hand.

"Well?" asked Stephen, lifting Adrian's feet and sliding a copy of the *Morning Herald* under his spurs.

His cousin looked at him enigmatically. "She ain't all that beautiful, my tulip."

Mildly surprised, Stephen said, "Did you not think so? I found her delightful. I'll wager you never saw a more unaffected little creature. And did you mark how swiftly she can be brought from the most sober contemplation to that enchantingly mischievous laugh?"

Adrian sipped his wine. "The most sober contemplation of your fortune?"

"They all do that." Perching on the arm of a sofa, Stephen shrugged. "I've not much else to offer at present, Lord knows."

Adrian uttered one explicit and vulgar word.

Stephen chuckled. "Will you own that at least this one is honest about it? There'll be no pretence from her."

"Nor love... Well, never look so steely, coz. You yourself said she cared for another."

His lips tight, Stephen stood. "I must go and feed my cat."

Standing also, Adrian said, "Instead of flying into a dudgeon you might better use your head, you block.

Half the mamas in town have set their daughters embroidering their prettiest handkerchiefs to drop at your feet. There is no call to opt for a mercenary little fortune-hunter when you may select from the fairest flowers among the ton. If you would but take the time to glance at the current crop you might..."

Stephen had started away, but at this he turned back and looked at his cousin steadily.

Adrian scowled. "Oh, go and feed that stupid cat, then."

With a rather grim smile, Stephen continued to the door.

"You know very well he cannot live," grumbled his cousin.

Stephen said quietly, "I choose not to accept such gloomy diagnoses, heir apparent. We may both surprise you."

Adrian watched the door close. His habitual air of boredom replaced by an unwontedly bleak look, he kicked the footstool, and swore.

Dinner was a pleasant meal, enlivened by the fact that, since Mrs. Stratton often misheard the soft voices of the Pride ladies, she returned such odd answers to their remarks as to throw her irreverent nephews into muffled whoops. She said indulgently that they were "silly creatures," and apologised because covers were not set out for other guests.

"Stephen," she explained, "wanted you to have a quiet family dinner, but I promise that tomorrow we shall have some company to entertain you. I fancy the young people will wish to ride in the morning, my dear Lady Pride, but, for myself, I prefer to keep to my room until twelve. You and Miss Kelton may do exactly as you please, of course. You may like to walk into the village, and I am sure you will wish to see the Italian garden. Stephen thought to get up a party to drive to Bath Abbey one afternoon, and our annual fair visits the village green day after tomorrow. We all are invited to a ball at Dering Court, and..." She was still enumerating the delights to be enjoyed during their visit when she rose and led the ladies into the hall.

Once they were all comfortably disposed in the large and richly appointed withdrawing-room, however, Mrs. Stratton started to bemoan Stephen's continued indifferent health, and begged that they would pardon him should he retire early. "The poor dear boy's recovery has not been as rapid as we had hoped," she said mournfully.

Elfreda was conscious of a brief irritation. The way they all coddled Stephen Jeffreys, one might have supposed him to hover at death's door. It was almost a year since Salamanca, and he had obviously endured a horrid time, but he was now up and about, and unfailingly light-hearted and cheerful.

Less sanguine than her daughter, Lady Pride looked troubled, and murmured, "Perhaps we should not have come."

"The hot sun has nothing to say to the matter," trumpeted Hildegarde. "Stephen became quite accustomed to it in Spain. The problem is that he is of a most stubborn nature and refuses to follow the advice of those who know what is best for him. Will you take a cup of tea, Miss Kelton?"

The gentlemen joined them quite soon, and Elfreda was pleased to find Stephen still among them. When he eventually gravitated to her side she asked if she might now be allowed to see her cat.

"By all means, Miss Elfreda, if I have your mama's permission to take you into the wilds of my conservatory."

Overhearing, Martha said eagerly, "Oh, may I—"

"It is past time for you to be laid down upon your bed, child," interpolated Miss Veronica in her brisk way.

Martha's lower lip jutted, but, before she could protest, Adrian saved the day by suggesting that the ladies might like to see the long gallery and some of his own paintings before they retired, and he led the little party up the main staircase.

Lady Pride, a trifle disconcerted by her sister's demeanour, whispered, "Veronica...? You surely cannot think...?"

"Thinking, Lady P," muttered her sister with a firm nod, "is good for the brain."

"Yes, indeed! Are they not the most odoriferous articles?" boomed Mrs. Stratton, turning to them. "We have had a dreadful time with ours, and to find a plumber able to get them to flow smoothly—hopeless! Whatever England is coming to I honestly do not know!"

While this small misunderstanding was taking place Stephen was conducting Elfreda through the conservatory. This high and spacious area adjoined the morning-room, and was walled and roofed with glass. The air was warm and moist, and the neatly assembled plants and shrubs appeared to thrive. So, too, did Colossus. A cosy nest had been provided for him, and Elfreda gave a chuckle to discover the tiny creature curled up on a velvet cushion set in a deep basket, and with a soft shawl over him.

"You see," said Stephen, tugging on the bell-pull, "he *is* still alive."

At first glance Elfreda thought that the kitten looked not very different from the last time she had seen him, but when Stephen lifted him his eyes blinked open. His ears, she noted, were more pointed, his fur had taken on a ginger hue, and he covered a larger portion of Stephen's hand.

"Oh!" she exclaimed joyously. "He is really beginning to bear some resemblance to a cat!"

A footman hurried in, carrying a scent bottle which contained warm milk and had the end portion of a glove's finger tied tightly over the opening.

Stephen deferred to Elfreda the honour of feeding his tiny protégé, and she sat down in the chair he pulled over for her, and accepted Colossus eagerly. "He moves his head with much less wobbling about," she said. "And only see how strongly he pulls. You have done so well with him!"

Stephen touched the kitten with one gentle finger. "He will be a huge brute in no time. Only wait and see."

She scanned his face. "That would be splendid. But I did not expect that you might lose sleep over him."

"I've lost very little, I promise you." Still, she looked troubled, and he said, "You are most kind, but pray do not fret over me."

"No, I won't. You need no more of that." She saw his lips quiver, and knew she had spoken too impulsively. "That is to say," she amended, "I have noticed that, although you go along so well, your family seems determined to wrap you in cotton wool. Er—with the very best of intentions, I am sure."

"The very best. But tiresome at times. And, speaking of intentions, Miss Elfreda, when last we met you told me you intended to marry for money, and—"

"And you were shocked," she said with a roguish glance at him. "You did not know what to say, so very politely changed the subject. I quite thought you would withdraw your invitation, since I was so outrageous."

"Say—honest, rather. After all, do not most young ladies hope to marry a gentleman of fortune who will establish them in a nice home, with a position in Society, the luxuries of life, and—?"

"Pooh, I have no interest in all that," she said with breezy indifference. "Your pet is asleep again, sir."

They restored Colossus to his box, and returned to the wide hall.

"I think," said Stephen as they strolled together, "I do not understand. Have you changed your mind about marrying for money?"

"Oh, no. But I did not phrase it properly. What I *should* have said was that I will only marry a gentleman willing and able to restore Pride House."

Stunned, he halted and stared at her.

Elfreda read his expression correctly. "Yes, I know it is a trifle run-down at present—"

A trifle run-down... he thought dazedly. Good God!

"—but it is the ancestral home of my family. May we go outside?"

He opened a glass door and they went on to the terrace. The scents of hyacinths and wallflowers permeated the cool evening air, but the light was fading fast, heavy clouds bringing an early dusk. Stephen offered his arm, and they paced slowly along. "There is so much of history in the dear old place," said Elfreda. "The land was awarded to Sir Arthur Pride by King Edward III, in the fourteenth century, as a reward for valour during the French campaign. Down through the years, Prides have served in many great battles, and served well, for our name has never known dishonour. Men of the house of Pride fought for Henry Tudor in the Wars of the Roses; two sons of Sir John Pride sailed with Drake against the Spanish Armada; Sir Neville Pride was slain fighting to protect King Charles in 1646; Sir Charles Pride fought against Monmouth; my father's elder brother died of wounds received during the War of the Spanish Succession. Now Clifford carries on the tradition by serving with our great Lord Wellington. And all those brave men were born in Pride House, and loved and guarded it, and went out from it to fight for their country. Until now."

Her voice rang with enthusiasm; her eyes were glowing. Watching her, Stephen thought she was well-named, and said, "Pride House means a great deal to you."

"Yes. And to England. It should be restored and lived in again, poor old thing. It should know warmth and laughter and the happy voices of little children." Her small chin set and she said vehemently, "It is a *crime* that so splendid a heritage should be allowed to rot away and fall to pieces! If nobody else cares about it, *I* will not let it happen! I suppose," her voice became rather less militant, "you think that foolish, since I am almost nineteen and not over-burdened with admirers."

He smiled. "The gentlemen hereabouts must all be blind. Even so, I'll not believe you have received no offers besides the one from Lewiston."

"Thank you for that kindness, sir. Actually, I've not yet made my come-out, but several gentlemen have been good enough to be interested in me, and I really thought . . ." She sighed disconsolately.

"You liked one or two?"

"Oh, they were all quite nice. But—not one of them was willing to restore Pride House, and live in it."

"*Live* in it? Do you say you actually mean to make it your home?"

"But of course. Whatever did you think?"

He decided it was better not to voice what he thought, and said cautiously, "But, surely, most gentlemen already own homes?"

"True, but many gentlemen own more than one home. It would not hurt, surely, to use Pride House in the summertime? You must own that one could scarce find a more beautiful setting."

They wandered past the withdrawing-room windows and were touched by the warm glow of candlelight. Moved by the wistful look that softened Elfreda's piquant face, he asked gently, "And what shall you do if you cannot find a gentleman of means who is willing to meet your terms? Marry Lewiston?"

"Good gracious, no! Why should I do so?"

"I thought perhaps, if you could not achieve your goal, you might be content to—er—marry for love."

Her chin tilted up again. "Grandmama used to say that a carefully selected mate is far more likely to guarantee future happiness than one chosen during the temporary insanity engendered by the tender emotion."

Stephen threw back his head and laughed heartily.

"Besides," said Elfreda with a defiant toss of her curls, "I am fond of Donald Lewiston. Probably as fond as I shall ever be of any gentleman. But I think Grandmama was right. Love is greatly overrated!"

Sobering, he said, "Do you know, I believe you are correct? And, after all, what right-minded person could rate insanity over common sense?"

It sounded very cut and dried, and she looked at him doubtfully. They had passed the lighted windows and it was darker, and difficult to read his expression. He was so kind, however, that she decided he must be sincere.

Her good impression of him deepened during the days that followed. He was always eager to keep his guests amused, and entered into their pursuits with enthusiasm. Suspecting often that he hid fatigue, she fell into the way of being as protective of him as was his family. If she saw even a hint of the tell-tale whitening of the skin about his mouth or under his eyes she would contrive to guide him into a less strenuous activity. In so doing, she inevitably spent much time in his company, which she did not grudge in the slightest.

When the time came to leave High Golden she experienced a very odd depression of the spirits, and on the way home found herself thinking most uncharitably of Gertrude Bellington, who must, she decided, be the silliest widgeon of all time.

CHAPTER FIVE

NEW HOUSE SEEMED quiet when the ladies returned, and, as they all gathered in the withdrawing-room and put off their bonnets and shawls, the room itself appeared smaller and rather shabby in comparison to the glories of High Golden. "But," said Miss Veronica briskly, "we had a lovely time. And this is still home."

Leafing through the pile of correspondence that had accumulated during their four-day absence, Lady Pride said, "And only look, there is a letter from dear Clifford! Now, everyone be seated while I read it."

They were only too glad to do so, for the fear that he might join the many hundreds who had been wounded was a shadow that haunted them all.

Lieutenant Sir Clifford Pride was, however, in excellent health as, he trusted, were his ladies. Having conveyed this much information, Lady Pride read on in silence, and after a few minutes laid the closely written sheet in her lap, folded her hands, and looked around at their expectant faces. "Oh, dear," she said in a failing voice.

Martha sprang up. "What is it?" she shrieked. "Is he wounded, after all?"

"No, God be thanked. But—" Lady Pride blinked "—he wants to—to exchange into a cavalry regiment."

Martha sat down again. There was a hushed silence. Then Elfreda asked in a rather thready voice, "Can we afford it, Mama?"

"It will be..." Lady Pride wrung her hands. "It will be expensive, of course. But it is a truly splendid opportunity, and—er—what dear Papa had pr-promised."

"Four years ago," said Miss Veronica, her mouth very grim. "When prices had not gone mad, and we'd not been obliged to put on a new roof after that dreadful storm. What else does he want?"

Lady Pride threw a furtive glance at Elfreda's face and took up the letter again. "Well," she said with a little gulp, "he must have a better horse. And there will be the new uniforms, and... one or two other things. But I suppose he is perfectly right. Papa did promise... one day, if he could see his way clear."

Miss Veronica frowned from Elfreda to Martha. "What about Elfreda's Season? And Martha should make her come-out the following year."

Lady Pride began to roll the letter into a tight tube. "Yes," she said miserably. "I know. But I—I do not quite feel we...can let Clifford d-down." The strained pale faces of her daughters brought the tears very close, and, after the fashion of weak-natured people, she took refuge in anger. "We shall have to delay your presentations by another year, that is all! If *only* you had not been so particular, Elfreda! One might think your promise to Papa were carved in stone, and I am sure he never expected you to keep it. If you'd not been so adamant you might have been safely betrothed to Lindervale by now, and your sister might not have a three-year wait to be presented."

Elfreda swallowed hard. "She will not have to do so, Mama," she said bravely. "I have received some quite unexceptional offers, as you said, and Martha must have her chance. If we are careful, and sew some of her gowns ourselves, perhaps we can save enough to buy Cliff his exchange and still let my sister make her come-out next Season."

"No!" said Martha, her eyes glistening suspiciously. "You must be presented first, Elf. In three years I shall only be...as old as you are n-now, and—" Here, disappointment proved stronger than self-sacrifice, and with a muffled wail, she fled.

Lady Pride burst into tears.

ADRIAN JEFFREYS GAZED slowly from mouldering walls to rotted floors; from the cracked chimney in the withdrawing-room to the warped and sagging window-frames in the main hall. He turned his gaze on his cousin, who watched him gravely, then, shaking his head, wandered to the foot of the stairs and looked up the uneven treads. "So this is Pride House. Is this magnificent structure safe, do you suppose?"

Stephen came up with him. "We'll soon find out. Best let me go first. I'm not so hefty as you."

"If you mean I'm not a skeleton," grunted Adrian, "I'll— Look out!"

He grabbed his cousin's arm as the rotted wood cracked under Stephen's boot, and hauled him down to the lower step.

"Good God! What a débâcle! If *that* don't sink the scheme, be dashed if I know what does! The only thing I cannot fathom, Lieutenant, sir, is why in the name of all that's wonderful you dragged me all this way. You did but need to say it was sturdy as any wet house of cards, and I'd have grasped the gist of it. Let us go home."

"Oh, don't be such a pudding heart! Come on, I want to see what the upper rooms are like!"

Stephen moved to the other side of the stairs and ascended cautiously. Following, Adrian grumbled that the upper regions of this ghastly old ruin were likely even worse, and that nobody but a dicked-in-the-nob caper-wit would risk a broken neck by investigating.

"You're just jealous because you cannot have it," said Stephen, turning on to the first-floor landing.

"Cannot *have* it?" echoed his cousin, brushing a trailing cobweb from his ear. "You could not *pay* me enough to be drawn into such a mare's nest, were the lady the reincarnation of Venus de Milo and—" He checked, tilting his head. "What was that?"

"A cow, I suppose."

Adrian peered uneasily about the long and gloomy corridor. "Didn't sound like any cow to me. Ye gods! Is this pretty palace a rendezvous for ghosts and goblins?"

"Beyond doubting. And this is their conference chamber." Stephen wrenched at a reluctant door latch, gave a shove, then jumped back as the door fell from its rusted hinges to land with a crash, sending up a cloud of dust.

Adrian yelped, and recoiled instinctively. Stephen waited for the dust to settle, then walked inside. The bedchamber was vast, and still contained an enormous canopied bed and a worm-eaten chest of drawers.

Following with reluctance, Adrian wrinkled his nose. "Place smells like toadstools!"

"It does, rather." Stephen crossed to draw back window hangings that fell from the rod at his touch. Slanting a wry look at his cousin's mirth, he said, "I'll—er—open the window." His attempt was doomed. The casement, apparently the only well-preserved object in the room, defied his efforts.

"Never mind, dear boy." Adrian strolled to join him. "I've a faster way to bring air into this charming chamber." He poked his cane at the wall. He had thought he was being amusing, and was stunned when the cane, with very little effort, did indeed make a small hole in the wall.

"Oh, dear," murmured Stephen.

"Oh, dear, my aunt's garter! 'Abandon hope, all ye who enter here' is a jolly sight more like it!"

"Hmm."

"No, Stephen, you cannot be too besotted to acknowledge this ruin is no more than a festering pile of dry rot."

Stephen sighed. "I fear you are perfectly right, Coz."

"No one but an unmitigated lunatic would spend one single night in the place, much less expend a fortune to restore it! You'd have to raze the blasted monstrosity and begin all over again."

"Oh . . . I'd not say that, exactly."

They walked to the door together, keeping wary eyes on the creaking floorboards.

"It wouldn't amount to much less," argued Adrian. "Your little lady shall have to find another pullet for plucking. One can but hope it don't plunge her into a decline when she finds *you* ain't going to be humbugged."

"I don't believe she ever considered me."

"You're too modest by half, my pippin. For four days the two of you were all but inseparable. It was fairly laughable to watch her do all in her power to ensnare you."

"A misapprehension on your part, Coz. I believe it was just her natural kindness to someone she thought to be ailing."

"Kind indeed, when she was so unselfish as to saunter sedately with you while the rest of us were up and down and round about Bath Abbey. More than kind when she sat at the side and chatted with you instead of dancing every dance at the Dering ball, as she might have done. Downright noble when she would not return with us to the fair after dinner, but said she would prefer to stay and play cards with you." Adrian gave a snort of derisive laughter. "She played her cards exceeding well. Damme, but she did! And, having done so, she likely has the wedding gown already ordered!''

''They were happy days for me,'' said Stephen with his slow smile. ''Though her kindness must have made it a sad bore for her.'' He threw up one hand to silence his cousin's attempt to respond. ''No, Adrian. I refuse to believe that Miss Elfreda has judged me to be worthy of ensnaring. If she thinks of me at all she likely views me only as a rather pathetic semi-invalid, to be catered to and pitied. Certainly not as a candidate for her hand.''

Before Adrian could comment, a lady ran across the lower hall and, weeping, vanished into the dining-room.

''Be damned,'' murmured Adrian, at his most cynical. ''Miss Pride appears to have plunged into a decline after all. But how very well-timed.''

Huddled on the chimney seat in the dining-room, Elfreda was thinking miserably that nothing could have been more ill-timed. She had pinned all her hopes on her London Season. Sadly she touched the worn bricks beside her. How she longed to give life back to this dear old house. How she dreamed of restoring it, just as Papa had yearned to do. As Cliff had promised to do. Papa had smiled and thanked him for that promise. But when they were alone together he'd said with resignation in his fine face, ''He won't, you know, Elfreda. He'll never have the funds. And, if he had, he would spend them on something more practical. Clifford's a good boy, but he has not the feeling for this dear old place that you and I share.''

That was when she had taken her father's frail hand and made her own vow. ''*I* will, Papa. I promise you faithfully that someday, somehow, if it is humanly possible, I'll rebuild Pride House, and make it as glorious as ever it was!'' And it *had* been glorious. Papa had loved to tell them, as Grandpapa had told him, of the balls that had taken place here, when the Prides were at the height of their fame and fortune and their name a power throughout the south country. Of the banquets, the garden parties, the carriages rolling up with their cargoes of grand ladies in farthingales and ruffs and jewels, and dashing gentlemen in hose and doublet, with swords at their sides and *l'amour* in their hearts. It was said that Queen Elizabeth herself had attended a gala here. She might have flirted with Essex in this very room... Pride House held so much history, so much of the past that it always seemed to Elfreda as if those who had dwelt here before still occupied the house. That someday she'd close her eyes for a moment, and when she opened them she would be looking into the laughing eyes of a gallant cavalier.

Unaccountably she found herself thinking of Stephen Jeffreys. He had laughing eyes. Sometimes. Sometimes they were veiled and quite impossible to read. And once or twice she had caught them watching her with an almost fond expression. But that was just her silly imagination, of course. His cousin had told them that Stephen was still breaking his heart for the girl who had jilted him. Elfreda scowled and wiped tears away. That stupid Gertrude Bellington, who was as brainless, vain, and cruel as she was beautiful.

None of which had anything to say to the matter. The horrible reality was that her dreams were ashes. Clifford must have his exchange. He was off risking his dear life for England, and they could deny him nothing, of course, for heaven knew what might lie ahead. Aunt Veronica and poor Mama had sympathised with her disappointment, and Martha was quite crushed, but none of them really knew how deeply she had loved her gentle father, or how intensely she longed to fulfil her vow. How many nights she had lain awake, making plans, dreaming of how Pride House would look when the work was done; of how wonderful it would be to live here, and feel that somehow Papa would know, and be so happy.

She bowed her head into her hands.

"Please don't cry, little lady."

Elfreda jumped, and looked up. A pale thin face was bent above her. Two darkly lashed grey eyes met her own in kindness and concern. She gave a gasp of shock and dragged the heel of her hand across her wet cheeks. "Stephen!"

He sat beside her and took up one hand. "Whatever has happened to grieve you so? Is there anything I can do to help?"

"How...how very...kind you are," she gulped, so flustered that she forgot her manners and groped about in her bodice for the handkerchief she had tucked there.

Jeffreys watched this procedure with no little interest, then gave her his own handkerchief. "Is it, perhaps, that someone has offered? Some evil old man you purely detest, but who is rich, and willing to meet your terms?"

His eyes twinkled. He was trying to cheer her up, of course. She managed a quivering smile, and blew her nose. "No. And nobody will—now."

"I think you underestimate your charm."

She said wryly, "To the contrary, I fear I have overestimated it, for I really did hope, you know. Papa used to say that, although I wasn't beautiful, I had taking ways, and that a gentleman might be willing to make do with those."

His lips quirked. "I agree. To an extent."

She sniffed and scanned his face anxiously. "Do you? Really? I mean, you are a man of the world, and would know."

"Then you may take your papa's words as gospel truth, ma'am. Save that I think he erred in one respect; you *are* beautiful."

She stifled a sigh, and patted his hand in an endearingly impulsive gesture. "Thank you. It's nice of you to say so, at all events. You came just when I needed cheering up."

"Then tell me what has happened to throw you into the dismals."

"Oh, it is that poor Mama has—er—has suffered an unexpected reversal. It means I cannot have a Season, as I'd hoped. So..." Her lips trembling, her voice shredded and she shrugged helplessly.

"So you have given up your plans for the old place?"

She nodded. "For a year or two."

Startled, he exclaimed, "Jove! For how long do you mean to keep trying?"

"Forever, if need be," she said proudly. "Now, why do you look so shocked? Did you think I meant to give up altogether? Good gracious, but you must fancy me a proper faint-heart!"

"I only thought— That is— Well, time is passing and you—"

"Are getting old?" She frowned with a ferocity he thought enchanting. "That is very true. In less than two years I will be twenty! But if I pamper my skin and do not eat cakes and pastries and jellies—which, alas, I love—I may still have a chance."

"But—surely, there must be other—"

Her chin tossed higher. "No buts! I am not one to surrender only because fate has thrown up a barrier."

Sitting there, with tear-stained cheeks and one curl trailing down over her temple, she looked much too young and innocent to be burdened by the vow she had taken upon herself. Jeffreys experienced a rush of tenderness for her, and a following surge of anger. He said, "I do not mean to pry, but surely Clifford should come home and support your mama?"

Elfreda sighed. "Mama told him that my uncle Stanley is managing things, but his wife is in poor health and says she will not leave her own home, so we very seldom see him."

"If ever I heard of such a thing! If Cliff knew that, he *would* come."

"Yes. And hate it, poor dear. He has always loathed the thought of managing the estate, and wanted only to be a soldier. Aunt Veronica is marvellously shrewd, and the Squire—Donald's papa, you know—is a great help to Mama. If we practise stringent economies we will probably go along well enough. Only I simply must keep my promise to Papa, and now I just...just don't quite see..." She bit her lip and couldn't finish the sentence.

"My dear little lady," he said. "Is it really so important? To throw your youth away, to sacrifice yourself in so foolish a cause, seems—"

"Foolish!" She sprang to her feet and faced him, her woebegone look vanished, and her eyes bright with wrath. "Is that how you view the history of our land? As something *foolish*?"

"Why—no, but—"

"I thought you understood, but you are just like all the rest! They let our great houses rot, our ancient castles crumble into dust, and all they care about is that everything be new. *New!*" She fairly spat out the word.

Jeffreys blinked in the face of such zeal, but argued mildly, "There is something to be said for comfort, I think. And—"

"And nothing to be said for tradition, I suppose!" She stuck her small nose under his chin. "Well, you may laugh, Mr. Stephen Jeffreys, but—"

"No, really—" he protested, retreating from her impassioned advance.

"You may mock and jeer and revile me," she went on, warming to her theme.

"Thank you. But I shall do nothing of the sort. In fact, I have been thinking that—"

"But I shall fight on," she proclaimed, very much in the way she fancied Jeanne d'Arc might have spoken. "No matter what obstacles I must over—"

"—that I would very much like to be your rich old man," interpolated Jeffreys in a rush.

"—come. So there is not a bit of use—" Elfreda's mouth fell open, and she stared at him. "What...did you...say?"

"I know I am eleven years your senior, and—er— far from being a dashing and heroic type. But—it would make me very happy if you would allow me to speak to your mama, Elfreda."

Astounded, she gasped faintly, "Wh-why...?"

"To ask for your hand, of course."

"I mean—why would you want to marry me?"

He smiled. "Because I think you are pretty, and kind, and delightful, and I admire your ideals, and your spirit. And because I believe that we might—er— deal very nicely."

For the first time Elfreda faced the fact that she had built up a vague picture in her mind of a very elderly gentleman, who would offer for her only because she was so young. A kindly old fellow of whom she would become very fond—in a granddaughterly way—and who would expect nothing more of her than that she keep him company and be a credit to him. Stephen Jeffreys had obviously come very near to death, and was still thin and ill-looking. But she had a sudden picture of him as he'd been before he'd gone off to war. He had seemed to her schoolgirl eyes very good-looking. Quite the dashing Corinthian, in fact. When he recovered his health it was doubtful that he would ever again become a dashing Corinthian. But he might. In which case he would expect her to... And she, of course, would be obliged to... And he was deep in love with another lady!

"Oh," she said.

It was far from the answer Jeffreys had hoped for. He stepped closer, took her hand again and pressed a kiss upon it. "Don't you want me, little Elfreda?"

He looked so wistful. And she did like him. In fact, she liked him very much.

"I *am* quite rich," he tempted.

"True. So you qualify," she muttered, so shaken that, much to his delight, she spoke her thoughts aloud. "And you have been kind to Colossus." She said in a less shaken voice, "And you would be willing to restore this house?"

He took a breath. "Yes."

"And—to live here. For part of the year, at least?"

Oh, Lord! he thought. But he nodded, and, having a shrewd notion of why she looked so terrified, added, "I'm afraid, however, that I might not be a very—er—effective husband. In one respect, little Elfreda. My present health... I mean, I'd likely not trouble you often—for a while. At—er—night, that is." In view of her youth and innocence, he had chosen his words with care. Glancing at her, expecting to encounter downcast eyes and shy blushes, he instead met a beaming smile.

"Oh. Well, in that case, do by all means speak to Mama, Stephen." She recollected her manners, and added hastily, "And—thank you very much. It is most obliging of you."

He smiled rather ruefully. Her relief was so obvious. Sweet innocent, she was willing to sell herself to him so as to realise her ambitions, but there would be little of love there. She had said in her funny, judicial way that she considered love to be "greatly over-rated." Even so, he ventured to ask, "May I kiss my future bride?"

She nodded and lifted her face, and he bent and kissed her very gently.

The only other man to kiss her, apart from family members, had been Donald Lewiston, who had seized her like any bear and all but crushed her lips to a pulp. This kiss, so soft, so tenderly, tantalisingly different, was rather nice. In fact, it made her feel quite tingly, and she wouldn't at all mind if he—

"What a charming scene! Seduction among the ruins!"

The bitter voice caused Elfreda to jerk away with a shocked gasp.

Lewiston stood in the doorway, looking ready to do bloody murder.

Jeffreys thought, He really loves her, poor fellow. He said coolly, "I think there was no call for such a remark. You should know that Miss Pride has just given me leave to speak to her mother."

"And I suppose you are proud of your conquest, eh?" Paling, Lewiston growled, "In point of fact, Jeffreys, you've small cause for congratulation. I could have bought her, had I your fortune! Any man could have!"

Elfreda said furiously, "How dare you be so crude, Donald? I never—"

He glared at her from under frowning brows. "You and I have been as good as betrothed this five years and more, as well you know!"

"I saw no such advertisement," said Jeffreys. "If your betrothal was official I am very sure that Lady Pride would have informed me of it."

"What, and lose all your lovely gold?" Scourged by hurt and rage, Lewiston snarled, "You poor dupe, you've been properly gulled!"

"And you, my lad, want for manners. I apprehend that you are mortified. But you must learn to take disappointments like a gentleman, not like a sulky brat."

As red as he had been pale, Lewiston hurled his heavy riding crop into Jeffreys's face, and sprang forward, large and formidable against the invalid's frailty.

Elfreda gave a shriek of terror as Jeffreys staggered. What happened next was so fast that it seemed to blur and she had no clear impression of it, but somehow Donald was being marched to the door with one arm twisted up behind him, while he howled words that made her clap her hands over her ears.

Releasing him, Jeffreys said in a voice of steel, "That will do, sir! You forget there is a lady present!"

Shaking with pain and thwarted fury, Lewiston ignored Elfreda, and howled, "You've dislocated my shoulder! You'll answer to me for this, damn you!"

"Do try not to be so absurd. Go home and get that shoulder looked at. And next time you—"

"Blast your conniving hide, I *struck* you! I *demand* that you name your friends!" All but weeping with humiliation, as Jeffreys regarded him pityingly, Lewiston shouted, "Or are you afraid?"

"Terrified." Jeffreys gave him a shove, and turned to Elfreda. "Come, my dear. I think we must—"

"*Stephen*!" she screamed.

Her horrified face confirmed his surmise. He stepped nimbly to one side. Lewiston could not halt his maddened charge, and shot past, collided violently with the mantelpiece and sank into the littered hearth.

Stephen extended his arm. "Do you suppose your mama might allow me to stay for lunch?" he enquired chattily.

"Go...on," wheezed Lewiston. "*Go* with him... *Have* your old ruin!" He appended savagely, "*Both* of 'em!"

Ignoring him, Jeffreys led his lady on to the steps. "I think this touch of exercise has done me the world of good. I feel quite hungry."

His calm words helped settle Elfreda's nerves, but her smile was rather wobbly, and she said nothing as they walked towards the phaeton that Adrian was driving back up the hill.

Jeffreys glanced down shrewdly at the troubled face of his chosen bride. "My dear, did you think I was too harsh with him?"

"Harsh? Certainly not! He behaved like a boor. In fact, my brother would have—" She bit her lip, then said staunchly, "You handled it very well, Mr.—er—Stephen."

"But you think I should have accepted his challenge? He was quite distraught, poor fellow. And he is only a schoolboy."

"You are not so very much older. Donald has an exceedingly ugly temper, and I only hope—" She forced a smile. "You did just as a sensible gentleman should. I despise duelling, and so does Mama."

He said he was glad to hear it, and handed her up into the phaeton. But, climbing in beside her, he knew she thought he was afraid.

CHAPTER SIX

MR. STEPHEN JEFFREYS'S offer for the hand of Miss Elfreda Pride was received by her family with jubilation. Lady Pride viewed Jeffreys in the light of a heavenly gift; Miss Veronica, who had always liked him, thought him "a much better catch than that wild Lewiston boy"; and Martha, having transferred her secret admiration from Lewiston to Adrian Jeffreys, was overjoyed.

Almost at once the household was plunged into a whirlwind of preparations. Mrs. Stratton sent notices to the newspapers, whereupon both establishments involved in the happy occasion were deluged with callers and well-wishers. There was much to be done, since the engagement was to be brief. Mrs. Stratton gave a spring ball at High Golden to present the prospective bride to the groom's family, friends, and neighbours. The following week Lady Pride gave a tea for the purpose of introducing the groom to the bride's family, friends, and neighbours. It was necessary that various elderly and venerated members of both families receive a personal visit from the bridal pair. Wedding invitations must be written and sent out; the banns were called at the quaint old village church in which Elfreda's parents and grandparents had been wed; and Adrian Jeffreys spent many hours with Lady Pride's solicitor, arranging the marriage settlements, the terms of which sent the good lady into raptures.

"Stephen has been truly generous," she told her sister tearfully. "I vow, he is the very best of men. Dear little Elfreda will want for nothing."

"If," said Veronica with a boding look, "he doesn't ruin himself on the ruins!"

Elfreda found that being engaged to be married offered many pleasant benefits. Quite apart from all the parties and visitations, the marriage settlements had removed much of the financial burden from Lady Pride's shoulders, and Elfreda was able to shop for her bride clothes without the need for careful economies or feelings of guilt. The ladies went into town several times, and twice Jeffreys accompanied them on these jaunts, cheering them with his humorous comments, and deriving a great deal of amusement from all the excitements.

Elfreda was becoming quite fond of her prospective spouse, and was genuinely terrified when he collapsed suddenly during a visit to his favourite great-aunt's home in Bath. He soon came to himself, but much to his chagrin a physician was summoned. Dr. Bartley, a stout and pompous individual, gave it as his opinion that the gentleman's constitution was still too weakened for him to be "frippering about like this," and that he must remember he was extreme fortunate to have survived his wounds. Jeffreys made light of the incident, but Elfreda had been touched by the cold hand of fear. She delighted both her affianced and his great-aunt by becoming suddenly militant and insisting that he accept an invitation to rest and overnight in Bath, and not return home until the following day.

She herself was driven back to High Golden, where she explained matters to Mrs. Stratton with sufficient calm common sense as to prevent that fond creature from falling into flat despair. Going next in search of Adrian Jeffreys, Elfreda found him in the conservatory, trailing a wisp of string for a wisp of cat. Colossus had survived thus far, but was very thin and undersized, and Elfreda had begun to give up hope that he would ever reach maturity. She still was not at ease with Adrian, and she was very conscious of his steady stare while she told him what had transpired. Refusing to be intimidated by that silently judicial manner, she tightened her lips, then asked firmly, "Shall you be able to drive to Bath in the morning, Mr. Jeffreys?"

He replied in his bored drawl, "I have no doubt of my ability to do so, ma'am, but question the need. It was my understanding I was to escort you back to Hampshire. My cousin does not care to be maudled over, and you need entertain no fears as to his safety on the journey home."

"Thank you. Since you are reluctant to incur his displeasure, however, I will go to Bath with his man first thing in the morning. I'd not put it past Stephen to ignore the doctor's recommendation and decide to ride here."

It occurred to Adrian that this small female had more than her share of gumption. Petite she might be, but she faced him with her firm chin held high and the light of battle in her dusky eyes. Small wonder, he thought cynically, and said with a mirthless smile, "Such commendable devotion. I bow to your wisdom, Miss Elfreda, and will ride with all speed to the rescue of my kinsman."

It was a pity, decided Elfreda, that the string he held was neither long enough, nor strong enough to be used for the purpose of strangling the horrid creature. She informed him in glacial accents that he was "too obliging," and turned to the door.

His mocking drawl followed her. "A near-run thing, was it? You must have suffered a severe fright, ma'am."

Her hand tightened around the door handle. Seething, she achieved a creditable little laugh, and said airily, "Oh, I scarce think my fiancé will expire."

He made no attempt to open the door for her. Glancing back, she saw that he was again playing with Colossus, but she sensed that from under those thick lashes he was watching her. Not looking up, he said with an enigmatic smile, "You are a brave woman, Miss Pride."

She went out without further comment, and marched briskly along the hall. It was very clear that Mr. Adrian Jeffreys not only judged her to be a fortune-hunter—which she had freely admitted—but that he saw in her a threat to his hopes. If she should have a son his own days of being heir to the Jeffreys fortune were done! She blushed, and thought, Not that there is much likelihood of my presenting Stephen with a son...

Starting up the stairs, she mulled over Adrian's final remark. It had sounded uncomfortably sinister. She found it all too easy to cast him in the role of creeping treachery, but, if he fancied Elfreda Pride one to be easily frightened from her course, he was vastly mistaken.

None the less, that night she locked her bedroom door and pulled a chair in front of it. She did not sleep well, and awoke at dawn from a nightmare in which Adrian had tied her hand and foot and was preparing to bury her under one of the golden acacia trees, while screeching, "You are a brave woman..."

THE WEDDING TOOK PLACE late in May, at the Church of St. Francis. Much happier than she had expected to be, Elfreda was radiant. Her gown, with its long train, was of cream satin, and both the gown and her billowing veil were embroidered with seed-pearls. Jeffreys wore regimental dress uniform, which had been tailored to his present measurements. He looked proud, and Elfreda thought him surprisingly dashing and a good deal more like his old self.

The cool spring relented and gave them a glorious day, and the reception was held in the grounds of New House. The flowers seemed to be even more brilliant than usual, and the sticky buds of the chestnut trees were sending out delicate yellow-green fans. The colourful gowns of the ladies, the elegance of the gentlemen, the sprinkling of military uniforms, combined to create a charming and unforgettable picture that was marred for Elfreda by only one detail. Sir Culver Lewiston, besides being the Squire, was a kindly gentleman and a friend of long standing, and to refrain from sending him an invitation was unthinkable. Rumour had it that Donald had angered his sire and been sent to Ireland to select some horses. Believing him to be safely in the Emerald Isle, Elfreda was shocked to see the glow of his red head beside Lady Lewiston. He managed to avoid the reception line and hovered in the background, his sombre gaze seldom shifting from the bridal couple. She did not mention his presence to Stephen, but when they stood side by side to cut the wedding cake with his sabre, he murmured in her ear, "I see your volatile ex-suitor is among us. I only hope I may not be slain before we escape."

She shared his hopes, and could not fail to be relieved when, at dusk, they were seated in the closed coach, rolling along the country lanes on the start of their honeymoon.

Jeffreys pulled her into his arms and kissed her. She had come to enjoy his gentle caresses, and was a little startled when his arms closed about her with more force than usual. His mouth was hard and insistent, awaking a reaction in her that set her shivering. Releasing her, he smiled into her wide eyes, and ran his long fingers gently down her cheek, which made her shiver even more. "Was I too rough, my love?" he asked huskily. "My apologies. You look much too adorable in that gown, and now you are all mine at last. My own captivating little Mrs. Jeffreys."

She had never seen that ardent expression in his grey eyes, or heard that note in his deep voice, and a thrill that was half eagerness, half fright quivered through her. She said, "You have been so very kind, Stephen." But when he pulled her close once again her own voice trembled with nervousness as she added, "Do we go to High Golden?"

His lips quirked, and he leaned back, but kept his arms about her. "Your family go there, but I have another destination in mind for us."

"My family?" she echoed, puzzled. "Why on earth...?"

"Partly because I knew how they would miss you, and I thought a change of scene might be apropos for a month or two. Your mama has wanted her withdrawing-room and saloons repainted, which can be done while they are away. And partly because my aunt Hildegarde will be desolate with only Adrian to maudle over, and she enjoys your family."

"How thoughtful you are. I see that you even had a picnic packed for us."

He chuckled, leaned forward and opened the lid of the hamper. A tiny mew sounded.

"Colossus?" exclaimed Elfreda. "He is to accompany us—on our *honeymoon*? But—but, if we have a long journey, whatever shall we—?"

"Now do not be in a taking for my sake, sweetheart. Colossus is rather like me in that he is of a retiring disposition and... undemanding." Having said which, he yawned, put back his dark head and appeared to fall asleep.

Elfreda glanced from her new and somnolent husband to the tiny and somnolent kitten. Perhaps they

were alike, at that. She felt ashamed of the thought at
once. Stephen had been the soul of kindness and generosity. And besides, although he was still not very
strong and tired easily, his life was not in jeopardy as
was that of poor Colossus. The kitten had survived
thus far, and was an affectionate little creature with
dark orange fur prettily marked with white. He was
sadly undersized, however, and showed only traces of
the playfulness of his kind, spending most of the time
sleeping.

It was getting dark, and, peering out of the window, Elfreda could see only trees and fields. She had
been sure they would honeymoon at High Golden.
Paris was not available—and, at all events, her bridegroom could probably not have sustained such a trip.
There was Brighton, of course. It would not be
crowded, with the Season at its peak, and since the
Regent had built his great pavilion the town had grown
so that there were any number of fine houses Stephen
might have been able to hire.

The coach, which had been labouring uphill, was
slowing.

Jeffreys stirred, and yawned. "Here we are," he
said. "I hope they will have dinner ready for us."

Astonished, Elfreda was able to detect the outline
of a large house. Lights gleamed from the windows,
which looked rather dirty. In fact—

She gave a gasp. "*Pride House*?"

Jeffreys opened the carriage door. The pleasant
weather seemed to have departed with the setting sun,
and a chill gust of wind blew in. He climbed out and
handed his bride down.

"Yes, my love, Pride House." He said trium-
phantly, "I knew that of all places in the world you
would be happiest here."

Oh, my God! she thought. But he had meant so
well, and she had the teeniest suspicion that he did not

much care for Pride House. Thank heaven he had not noticed her dismay. She said bravely, "You are the most kind and unselfish individual I ever have met. And you are quite right. I should like of all things to start my married life in the dear old house. No!" her voice rose to a squeak as he swung her into his arms. "You must not! You are not strong enough!"

"Nonsense," he gasped, teetering up the steps. "A man must carry his . . . his bride across the threshold. I am . . . quite capable . . ."

But he wasn't, and the servants came hurrying to help them up.

When they were safely inside, and brandy had been brought to restore the master, Elfreda was able to take the time to glance about. The hall floor had been swept and scrubbed, new draperies hung at the windows, and boards were nailed over the missing panes. She could detect the gleam of a fire on the dining-room hearth, and had taken a cautious step in that direction when Jeffreys came to her side again.

"Poor sweet. You think me a sorry excuse for a bridegroom, I dare swear. Are you hurt?"

Her hip felt decidedly bruised, but she said gamely, "No, of course not. And it was truly a romantical thought. How—er—nice your people have made the house for us."

"They are not *my* people, Mrs. Jeffreys. Martin Coachman is the only one of my servants whom I have brought here. They are *our* people. And I have kept the staff to an absolute minimum, so that we might enjoy some privacy." He saw her widening eyes and confirmed with satisfaction, "Ah, I thought that would please you. Yes, we shall stay here until the renovations are complete."

She said in a failing voice, "But—I had thought perhaps . . . Cousin Adrian would handle all that?"

"Adrian is a good man, but inclined to be careless. You will be able to ensure that the workmen do exactly as you wish, for I will not have my wife dwell in any home that does not please."

THOSE WORDS CAME BACK to Elfreda when she awoke during the night. It had been an eventful night in more ways than one. Wilkins, the thin and very starched-up butler, had enquired in a decidedly pained fashion if Mr. and Mrs. Jeffreys desired to go up to their suites *before* dinner. Stephen's haughtily raised brows had won a more respectful attitude, but it seemed that Cook had "done her best." Wilkins coughed, and added ominously, "In...the *circumstances*." Elfreda would very much have liked to see their "suites" but Stephen had reverted to his meek way and suggested that they not upset Cook. They sat down to dine at a magnificent new table, which somehow made the room seem even more shabby. The chimney smoked, the fumes becoming more and more acrid. Squinting through the hazy air as the maids carried in the second remove, the butler remarked that Cook had experienced some difficulties with the stove. Another cough prefaced a second ominous remark, "Being accustomed to more *modern* conveniences." Elfreda expected her new husband to apply a firm set-down to such impertinence, but Stephen only sighed and said that the cutlets didn't look "too bad" and he was sure Cook had tried.

After they had hacked their way through the cinders, they were rewarded with a presentable if plebeian custard pudding, and some excellent cheeses. Elfreda then left her husband alone. He joined her shortly in the even more smoky withdrawing-room. The wind was rising, the air had become quite chill, and tea was a long time in arriving. Elfreda prolonged her enjoyment of it until the smoke defeated her, and she followed the decidedly bracket-faced cook up the shaky staircase to her "suite." This large chamber had been brightened by the addition of red velvet draperies and an enormous four-poster bed with red velvet curtains. A depressed-looking, colourless young woman was in attendance. Her name, she announced in an adenoidal voice, was Sylvia, and she wasn't really an upstairs or lady's maid, but the kitchen maid. This became very obvious when she did nothing until she was told, and then required to be instructed how to do it. Elfreda dismissed her as soon as possible, finished her toilette herself, and waited in stark terror for Stephen's arrival.

He had come in at last, carrying a candle, and wearing a nightshirt that looked four sizes too large. She had been won to a giggle when he had grinned and spread his arms, revealing the true enormity of this garment, and bemoaning the fact that his man must have packed the wrong nightshirt. He had looked at her then in such a way that she had realised that the moment of truth was at hand. His lovemaking had been tender, and he had dealt very gently with her— until one leg of the bed had gone through the floorboards. Between nervousness and the shock of being abruptly precipitated to the floor, she had succumbed to squeals of hysterical laughter. For an odd few seconds she'd had an impression of silent fury, but then Stephen had joined in her mirth and invited her to come to his own chamber for the rest of the night. She had declined, however, and had fallen into a deep sleep, to be woken now by some unfamiliar sound.

Lying there, thinking drowsily, she was comparatively comfortable, for, although her mattress was upon the floor, it was a thick feather bed. But it *was* on the floor, as she discovered when a large spider skipped across her arm.

With a shriek she leapt from the bed and turned up the wick on the oil lamp. She was brushing frantically at her nightgown when Jeffreys stumbled in, carrying an enormous horse-pistol and looking rumpled and sleepy.

"Get it off!" she sobbed. "Oh, please get it off!"

He hurried to her side. "Get—*what* off?"

"A *huge* spider! It was—"

The sound that had awoken her recurred, and her words were cut off, the spider forgotten. In a very fast involuntary movement she was in Stephen's arms, clinging to the mighty nightshirt with frantic hands. "What was that?"

He kissed her forehead. "Just the wind in the dry rot, m'dear."

"It d-didn't sound like the wind. It sounded like—like a groan."

"A possibility. You would be the authority on the resident ghosts, but, since they are doubtless all Prides, I think you've nothing to fear." He disentangled her gently. "To bed, Mrs. Jeffreys. You need your sleep."

When he reached the door however, Elfreda was close behind him, clinging once more to his nightshirt. He chuckled, put the candlestick aside, and took her by the shoulders. "What's all this? Is my resolute small person actually afraid of spectres and goblins and such?"

She nodded, her eyes huge and imploring.

Jeffreys chuckled again and swept her into his arms. "Might you feel more at ease were you to—er—share your husband's bed for the rest of the night?" His eyes twinkled at her. "Only, however, if you promise to behave with propriety, and not tease a poor old man."

She would. And she did. And, since Jeffreys had made some promises of his own, she did get her sleep.

CHAPTER SEVEN

ELFREDA WOKE before her husband. She was shocked
for an instant to realise that someone shared her bed,
then, blinking at the unfamiliar bed-curtains, she remembered. She turned cautiously on to one elbow,
and looked at this man she had married. Stephen lay
on his back, relaxed and unexpectedly youthful in
sleep. His black hair was tumbled, his brows and
lashes dark bars against his face. It was a very nice
face, she decided, and would be nicer when the hol-
lows that still remained around the eyes and under the
cheek-bones had filled in. Studying the straight nose,
the strong chin and humorous mouth, she thought
that Mama was right: Stephen might have had his pick
of many ladies. Why, then, had he offered for her,
knowing she would marry him only for his money?
The thought made her cringe a little. But, regardless
of why he had chosen her, the deed was done. Her life
as Miss Elfreda Pride was a closed chapter. She was
Mrs. Stephen Jeffreys now, and forever. She blushed,
and suddenly felt guilty and ashamed. Touching his
outflung hand very lightly, she whispered another
vow: a fervent promise to try and make him happy, to
be a good and loving wife. Then she crept from the
bed, tiptoed to the door, and went back to her own
room.

She looked with a faint smile at the collapsed bed,
and then wondered whatever the servants would think.
Her desperate tugs at the end post achieved nothing;

the bed was much too heavy for her to move, and with a fatalistic shrug she gave up and rang the bell.

The maid, Sylvia, carried in a tray, and bobbed a curtsy. When her pale blue eyes alighted upon the bed her drooping jaw sagged even lower and she fixed Elfreda with a look of awe. Elfreda murmured something airily about the rotted floorboards, and, once the girl had departed, giggled to herself.

She felt refreshed after drinking her chocolate, and better able to cope with the day. The wind was stronger this morning, and the temperature had plunged. She breakfasted in the dining-room, since the breakfast parlour had not yet been cleared of cobwebs and debris, and told the butler that it appeared they were to have more cold weather, and the first thing that must be done was to send for a chimney-sweep. He cleared his throat and informed the ceiling that there were "matters" that must be spoken of, including the "*strange sounds*" which had been heard during the night.

Elfreda felt her cheeks become hot. "Oh, it was just the wind," she said, trying to sound nonchalant.

"Mrs. Wilkins was alarmed," he persisted woodenly.

"Nothing to be alarmed about." Jeffreys wandered into the room. He was dressed in riding clothes and carried a hat from inside which Colossus peeped with mild curiosity. Starting towards his bride, and noting her pink cheeks, he asked, "Should you care to go for a ride, my love?"

"And there are rats in the cellar," said Wilkins with marked disapproval.

Elfreda, who had never ventured into the cellars, shuddered.

"Are there, by Jupiter?" Jeffreys looked thoughtfully at the occupant of his hat. "Then we must set the cat to work."

Wilkins gave him a hard stare.

Elfreda laughed. "No, really, sir. A rat would make short work of him. We had best get a ratter. The coachman must be sent into the village to hire Bert Driver and his hound."

"You see, m'dear," said Jeffreys, bending to press a kiss on her brow. "Already you are setting things to rights."

He looked proud, and, touched, she clasped his hand. "By the way, Mr. Jeffreys, how many maids have we?"

He glanced at Wilkins.

The butler gave a thin smile. "None, sir."

"The devil you say! I thought you'd taken on three?"

"They left first thing this morning, sir. Two did, at all events. They said they were unwilling to work in a haunted house." His cold eyes turned to Elfreda. "The third left after she took the mistress up her hot chocolate. She was a very strait-laced girl."

Again Elfreda's face was hot with embarrassment.

In a voice of ice Jeffreys said, "If you wish to continue to work for me, Wilkins, you had better—"

"There is nothing we wish less, Mr. Jeffreys," announced Cook, coming to stand in the doorway with her arms akimbo and her narrow face flushed and belligerent. "If ever I saw such a disgraceful establishment I do not know when! Wilkins and me are used to homes of the quality. Not to a run-down rats' nest what is *haunted* on top of all else!" She shrilled on, enumerating the faults of the old building and the indignities she and her spouse had suffered during their three days here. "Pride House, indeed," she said with an indignant sniff. "*Poor* House, more like! Wilkins and me—"

Jeffreys, who had listened politely to her tirade, now lifted one hand to halt it, and pointed out that his cousin had explained when the Wilkinses were taken on that the house needed to be redecorated.

"*Redecorated*," snorted Cook. "What it needs is—"

"More efficient servants," he overrode blandly. "My coachman will take you to the nearest coaching station, and— But I must not interfere in Mrs. Jeffreys's domain." Turning from spluttering servants to aghast bride, he said, "I do apologise, my love. I shall leave you to turn off these people. Provided, of course," he added, "you see fit." And he wandered from the arena, conversing amiably with Colossus and showing not the slightest interest in the ensuing uproar.

It was, as Elfreda informed him an hour later, typical male treachery. Ushering her to the phaeton, which had just returned from removing the Wilkinses from their lives, Jeffreys looked pained. "You thoroughly enraged them," she said, "and then slunk off like ... like a coward, and left me to face their wrath all alone!"

"But you dealt with them in fine style, my love," he declared, handing her into the vehicle. "Now where shall you go to hire more servants?"

She whirled on him with a dismayed gasp. "Where shall *I* go? Do you not accompany me?"

"But with the greatest pleasure, if you wish it." He hesitated, then said with a wry smile, "Only ... for some foolish reason I seem to be rather tired today, and I would so dislike to embarrass you again."

Sufficiently embarrassed, Elfreda insisted that he remain at home and rest. Martin Coachman drove out, carrying a quiet lady who was wondering if her husband's remark had been as much a *double entendre* as she'd thought, or if she had a vulgar mind.

She had hoped to persuade Mama to let her borrow some of their servants, at least while the family was at

High Golden, but when the phaeton reached New House it was deserted save for Mr. McCaffrey, who was consulting with the workmen about the new paint. Lady Pride had left early this morning, he explained, giving the servants a holiday, and leaving him in charge until her return. Disappointed, Elfreda instructed Martin Coachman to proceed to Horsham. In that lovely old market town was a registry office, where Aunt Veronica was well-known, and Elfreda experienced no difficulty in hiring a buxom cook, a pleasant and agreeable butler, and two cheerful maids. She returned to Pride House, weary but triumphant, armed with assurances that the new servants would arrive on tomorrow's midday coach.

Walking up the front steps, she was greeted by sounds of dispute. She hurried inside, only to halt abruptly. The hall floor was black and gritty. Treading gingerly across it, she paused in the doorway of the withdrawing-room. Two blackened men turned from the fireplace to face her across a sea of soot. One of them said in a tired and hollow voice, "Hello, my love. I'm afraid the chimney-sweep has had a little difficulty..."

By seven o'clock, with the aid of the chimney-sweep, Martin Coachman and the cowman from the Home Farm, some semblance of order had been restored to the withdrawing-room and hall. The bricks, which had fallen when the sweep had thrust his brushes up the chimney, had made the withdrawing-room fireplace unusable until suitable repairs were made. Elfreda had managed to re-light the fire in the kitchen stove, which had been allowed to go out, and had heated sufficient water to enable Martin Coachman to assist her exhausted husband to bathe. She had then ordered Stephen to his bed, and had the cowman driven home with a request for dinner to be sent up. It did not arrive until a quarter past eight o'clock, when

Martin Coachman, with a kindly light in his blue eyes, told the bride that he would prepare the tray and carry it up to her and the master so they might enjoy their dinner together.

Thunder rumbled as Elfreda gratefully climbed the stairs. The vast bedchamber was cold, and Jeffreys, wrapped in his dressing-gown, was in bed reading the *Gazette* by the light of a candelabrum, with Colossus curled up beside his pillows.

"My poor little bride," he said, tossing the paper aside and reaching out to her. "What a miserable day you have had!"

He had every right to greet her with reproach, and the sight of his eager and welcoming smile banished tiredness and her persistent and quite unwarranted sense of ill-usage. At all events, it was not his fault that, in his trying to please her, their honeymoon had been ruined. She hurried to take his hand, and, sitting on the bed, touched his cheek rather diffidently. "It has been no less horrid for you, Stephen."

He said with a twinkle, "It has had its moments, dear wife."

"Yes," she murmured, then blushed as he laughed and hugged her. "But," she went on, "you would be perfectly justified did you scold me. Still, I am not quite a hopeless case, for I have managed to find some servants, and your splendid coachman is going to fetch us our dinner. I think we should ask him to start a fire in here, also."

"McCaffrey's cowman tried to do so, but unhappily the chimney will not draw, and he thinks there must be a nest in it. Never mind. Only think how cosy we will be together. Just you and I, like two lovebirds."

Elfreda smiled shyly, and went away to wash in the frigid water from her washstand pitcher, and to tidy her hair. The bed had been moved to another spot, and made up neatly. Stephen must have enlisted the cowman to help him with it. She was too tired to change her gown, but wrapped a warm shawl about her shoulders before going back to her husband's cold room.

Martin Coachman brought up the tray, and the newlyweds enjoyed their unorthodox dinner, Jeffreys's ready sense of humour turning what might have been a dismal evening into a funny adventure to be stored in memory. When Elfreda left him to change into her night-rail he called cheerfully, "Do you know, my love? I think we have weathered the storm, and—" he paused, chuckling, as thunder rumbled louder and rain began to patter at the windows "—and we are over the worst of it," he finished.

His optimism, alas, was unwarranted.

A builder was summoned first thing in the morning. Mr. Morleigh was mournful of aspect and disposition, and said with a shake of his head, "That there bridge o' yours ain't none too steady, Mist' Jeffreys. We get much more o' this here rain it won't be there come mornin', I doubt."

Jeffreys sneezed, and apologised. "Dear me," he said from the depths of his handkerchief. "Now—about the roof . . ."

Mr. Morleigh's thin lips puckered into a ghoulish grin. "What roof?"

His inspection of the house seemed to lift his spirits considerably. There was, he allowed, "a tidy bit o' work" to be done, and he would get his "lads" on it right away. "If," he added, plunged into gloom once more, "that there bridge stays up."

By the time he left Jeffreys had sneezed three times. Although he declared staunchly that he felt "perfectly fit," Elfreda worried that his weakened constitution had not benefitted from the leaking ceiling above his bed.

The builder brought his "lads" at ten o''clock, and they at once began an extremely noisy assault upon the house. The noise was augmented by their raucous remarks and occasional bursts of stifled laughter, which Elfreda judged to be ominous. They seemed to share a fondness for one particular comment, which began to annoy her, this being a low-voiced, "Look at this 'ere!" invariably followed by sounds of hilarity.

At half-past twelve the new servants arrived. The glances they exchanged as they threaded their way through the welter of ladders, buckets, miscellaneous building materials and grinning workmen did not, thought Elfreda, bode well. Fortunately Martin Coachman had also brought a good supply of food, and the buxom cook, perhaps to ensure her continued buxomness, soon had the kitchen stove functioning fairly effectively. The builders no sooner covered one hole in the roof than another was found. By mid-afternoon it was clear that Jeffreys had taken a feverish cold, and, fearing a second night of dripping ceilings, Elfreda instituted a search for a more weatherproof bedchamber. After three birds' nests, a deceased seagull, an old hat, and a quantity of branches were cleared from its chimney, the morning-room was found to have the most promising hearth, and a fire was lighted and found to smoke not too devastatingly. Jeffreys's bedroom furniture was hauled downstairs, and Elfreda and one of the maids spent the afternoon drying bedding and attempting to make the room habitable.

Soon after four o'clock Mr. Morleigh came to report to the bridegroom. The roof, he said with a mournful sniff, would have to be replaced, which they couldn't do until the walls was rid of all the dry rot. Also, the foundations weren't too reliable, seein' as they'd "sunk a bit. Here and there."

"Here and there?" echoed Jeffreys hoarsely.

"And everywhere," supplied Morleigh, a glint of humour lighting his eyes. "Furthermore," he continued, "the mortar's rotted from 'twixt the chimney bricks and they'll have to be rebuilt." He sniffed loudly. "The marvel is the whole perishin' lot hasn't fell in on yer."

Elfreda enquired as to the state of the main staircase.

Mr. Morleigh turned his pale gaze on her, and sniffed again. "Hazardous, marm. If I was you, I'd not go up nor down without grabbing hold o' the rail and treadin' careful. Most careful."

Watching his bride, Jeffreys asked gravely, "What do you think we should do first, Morleigh?"

The builder blinked from bride to groom, and back again, sniffed, and made a reluctant surrender to conscience. "Tear it dahn, sir. It won't take much doin'. And we can build yer a nice new house on yer hill."

Perhaps because she was so tired and cold and dispirited, Elfreda was unable to protest with the resentment she felt. Instead, a lump rose in her throat, and her eyes filled with tears.

"No such thing," said Jeffreys staunchly. "My wife is not one to give up so easily." He paused for an explosive sneeze. "Are you, my love? If you do not want the commission, Morleigh, I'm sure there are plenty of builders who'd be glad of it."

"Woods is full of 'em," agreed Mr. Morleigh, the glint in his eyes becoming a full-fledged gleam. "It'll be expensive, mind yer. But we'll be only too *happy* ter do whatever we can fer you, sir. Only too *happy*!"

Jeffreys told him to take on some more "lads," and Morleigh nodded and took himself off. Staring after him wearily, Elfreda heard him talking to his workmen in a low voice, his remarks followed by a burst of muffled giggling, and a barely audible comment about milking pigeons.

Jeffreys's arm slipped around her. It would be easier to bear, she thought, if he looked at her with anger or resentment, instead of with such sympathetic understanding. She buried her face in his cravat, and offered them—*him*—an escape. "Perhaps," she gulped, "we should move out until they finish the work?"

He did not at once reply. Then, "That might not be wise," he said. "I believe you will be obliged to keep a close eye on Morleigh. His fellows seem a rather frivolous lot to me, and you must ensure he does just as you desire. This is your dream, my dear, and I'll not break my promise to you."

Elfreda sighed, and said, more forlornly than she guessed, that he was very good.

It continuing to hold true that one man's meat was another man's poison, the dream of Elfreda was nightmare to others. The two maids were notably less cheerful after a night during which a series of odd bumps and wails convinced them that Pride House was literally crawling with spectres. Jeffreys's calm explanation that the house was old and settling didn't seem to reassure them. Later in the day Elfreda overheard one of them remark bitterly that the house was very likely going to settle right into the ground and carry them all with it to an early grave. The pleasant and agreeable butler became noticeably less pleasant after he inadvertently put his foot through a stair and dropped the flask he had been smuggling up to his room. The eyes of the buxom cook took on a smouldering resentment when her attempt to open a casement window resulted in its falling out. This incident, which caused her to suffer a spasm, had a similar effect on the workmen, whom she apostrophised as "a lot of ignorant gowks."

The days crept past and the disasters mounted inexorably. Morning after morning dawned with leaden skies and pouring rain. Jeffreys's cold worsened, and he took to his bed, leaving Elfreda to cope with Morleigh and his noisy and flippant workmen. The builder seemed determined to argue with her every suggestion, and his obvious belief that she was a feather-witted female did little to improve her state of mind. Cook was becoming less and less amiable, and the two maids spent a good deal of time whispering together and casting fearful looks over their shoulders.

Elfreda had never been more uncomfortable. She knew she would only have to say one word to Stephen and they would be gone from this misery, but she fought against bowing to defeat. One damp and dreary mid-afternoon, tired, cold, and cross, she tried to appear cheerful as she went into the morning-room cum bedchamber. Jeffreys was up, and hunting for Colossus. A search of the room convinced them that he must have wandered out of the door unnoticed. He had been not in the least affected by the trials which had beset his humans, and Elfreda was now quite optimistic about his survival, but he was as trusting as he was small, and for him to venture forth among whom Elfreda privately designated "galumphing" workmen and irate servants was perilous. She embarked on a desperate search for the little creature. He was not discovered upstairs or down, and she was beginning to despair when a chorus of shrieks and shouts sent her running to the kitchen. She entered a chaotic scene. One of the maids was peering inside a large plucked turkey arranged in a pan on the table. Her cohort was ministering to Cook, who had fallen into strong hysterics. Two workmen, who had apparently dropped in for a cup of tea, were also in hysterics, and Jeffreys, holding Colossus, stood leaning against the wall, weak with laughter.

Gradually the tale unfolded. Colossus, it appeared, had wandered into the kitchen, and managed to scramble on to the table, where he had encountered what had probably seemed to him to be an enticingly aromatic cave. He had lost no time in entering. When poor Cook had deposited a handful of stuffing in the turkey her efforts had resulted in a raucous protest, and her terror had been compounded when, as she had persisted in shrieking that she had been "bit by a dead bird!", Jeffreys had arrived to find Colossus sitting in the turkey pan, adorned with pieces of stuffing, and blinking at the strange antics of humans.

The tears of the workmen did nothing to assuage Cook's outrage. Ghosts and ruins, she declared, was one thing, but cats lurking inside of dead turkeys was more than she could be expected to endure.

In vain did Jeffreys remind her of Jonah and the whale. In vain did Elfreda attempt to bribe her. Within the hour Cook, butler and maids had gone the way of their predecessors.

CHAPTER EIGHT

NEXT MORNING Martin Coachman was despatched to Brighton, to hire some servants. By half-past eleven o'clock the workmen had not appeared, and Elfreda was engaged in a rather unnerving battle with the kitchen stove, when she heard the pealing of church bells. The bell-ringers must be practising, she thought. Some time later a boy came to the house with a message from Mr. Morleigh. Everyone was having a holiday, he wrote, because of the wonderful news that had come from the war: Wellington had crossed the river Esla and was moving northward at speed, the French, under that noddicock King Joseph, flying before him.

Elfreda was, of course, pleased by such tidings, but her heart was too heavy for her to feel cheered for very long. Her attempt to prepare dinner last evening had not been a great success. The turkey had been overcooked and tough, the potatoes lumpy and the gravy a disaster. When she'd carried the tray in to Stephen she had thought he looked worn, but his ready smile never failed her and he'd uttered not a word of complaint. The poor soul had fared no better this morning. It had taken forever to heat the water, and the fire that Martin Coachman had lighted in the morning-room before he had left had commenced to send out puffs of smoke again.

She'd managed the eggs and bacon quite well, but when she had carried in Stephen's tray she'd tripped on a loose board, and the contents had showered into his lap. The coffee, which for some reason was full of horrid grounds, had scalded his hand, and for just an instant she had once again had the impression of barely suppressed rage. He had been silent briefly, almost as though holding his breath, then he had told her with really saintly forbearance that she was "doing splendidly" and that he was proud of her fortitude. "Someday," he'd asserted, spreading butter on his reddened wrist, "we will look at what we have achieved with this grand old house and be glad we persisted. However many years it took."

Elfreda sighed miserably. The poor dear man, how he must yearn for his own luxurious and well-run home. What a wretched bargain he had made! She could well imagine Adrian Jeffreys's behaviour had he been forced to endure one tenth of what his cousin had borne so patiently; that sarcastic tongue of his would have cut her to ribbons, and he would have dragged her off to Town or to Brighton after one day in this ghastly old— That was to say, in this unfortunate house. She pulled back her shoulders. Stephen was truly the dearest husband any girl could wish for, and he deserved the best—instead of the scheming little wretch he had married. But perhaps this good news would cheer him, at least.

She carried Morleigh's note to the morning-room. Stephen was seated at the dressing-table, adjusting a neckcloth that would, she realised, have reduced Donald Lewiston to speechless awe. When he saw her in the mirror he stood at once. "I have been a slugabed far too long," he declared. "My most unromantical cold is much better today, and I mean to be of whatever assistance I may."

The cheerful words, the smile in his clear grey eyes, caused her throat to tighten up and her lips to tremble. Speechless, she handed him Morleigh's note.

He read it, and uttered a shout of triumph. "How splendid! *North*! The man's a magician! Who would guess he'd turn north? That block King Joseph will be properly hornswoggled, and I'll wager this will mark the beginning of the end for Boney! Hurrah!" He seized Elfreda and whirled her around, his eyes brilliant with excitement, his cheeks a little flushed. In that moment she thought he looked almost his old self again, but ineffably more dear. He gave her a smacking kiss, and set her down, exclaiming, "Oh, if we were but in Town, little wife! I'll warrant there will be many parties to celebrate this grand achievement. Gad, how I wish I'd been with my men!" He checked, and said in a different voice, "But then, of course, I would not have been here with you."

And suddenly it was too much. She managed to mumble something appropriate, and fled back to the kitchen. The stove was smoking. The breakfast dishes stood in water floating with grease. The room was chill, and permeated as usual by the smells of mould and dust, in addition to the aroma of burned toast. Unable to endure it for a minute longer, Elfreda rushed across the withdrawing-room and hall. The front door stuck, and with a squeal of fury she kicked it, and tore it open.

Outside the wind tugged at her skirts and a thin drizzle fell from low-hanging, leaden clouds. She leaned back against the wall, bowed her face into her hands, and wept. "How I wish I'd been with my men..." Of course he wished that, poor darling! Why should he wish to be with her, after the way she'd treated him? By this time that horrid cat Gertrude Bellington must seem to him as an angel from heaven! His earlier remark returned to scourge her: "...we will look at what we have achieved with this grand old house and be glad we persisted. However many years it took..." *Years*? Years, trapped in this perfectly frightful old ruin? "No!" she sobbed. "Oh, no! Papa, I...I *cannot*!"

"Well, well! So the mercenary bride is already reduced to tears!"

Elfreda's head shot up. Donald Lewiston stood at the foot of the steps, running the thong of his riding crop through one gloved hand and watching her with gloating satisfaction. She dragged a hand across her wet cheeks and said irritably, "What on earth are... are you doing here?"

"Is an old friend not permitted to visit the bridal couple?" His smile held only mockery. "I came to see how you went on in your...slavery."

Elfreda stood straighter. "I am not a slave. And we go along very well, thank you."

"Yes, I can see you do." He laughed unpleasantly. "When you sold yourself I fancy you thought you'd have but a short wait to become a rich widow. How will you endure him if he—?"

Her small fists clenching, Elfreda felt seared by wrath. "How *dare* you say such a wicked thing?" she said shrilly. "My husband is—"

"Is doomed. As well you knew, else you'd never have tolerated the stupid clod."

She became paper-white and stared at him, great-eyed. "You lie!" she whispered. "He—he would have—"

"Told you of it?" He gave a snort of malicious laughter. "You think you properly gulled him, don't you? Well, he gulled you also, sweeting. He wanted to leave a proper heir behind him, to cut out his precious cousin Adrian. When the Bellington threw him over he knew his time was running out, so he decided you'd do for a brood—"

"Do you know, Lewiston," drawled Jeffreys, strolling on to the terrace, "you have a singularly un-

pleasant mouth? I think—no, really I do—that I must
teach you when not to open it.''

His eyes bright with unholy joy, Lewiston said, ''We
may be private in the back meadow. And we'll not wait
for seconds.''

Jeffreys nodded, and followed him down the steps.

''No!'' With a shriek of terror, Elfreda flew to seize
Lewiston's arm. ''You *must* not! He is very ill. You
said yourself—''

''My love,'' protested Jeffreys, firmly removing her
clasp from Lewiston's coat, ''you must not listen to
what others say. Especially,'' he added, with the smile
that never failed to clutch at her heart, ''to what doctors and discarded suitors—'' He swung Elfreda aside,
and Lewiston's flying fist barely missed his jaw.

''Damn you! I'm no discarded suitor,'' snarled
Lewiston.

''You are a hot-headed young fool! You might have
struck my wife, and if you had—''

''Your wife! Your purchase, more like! She don't
give a button for anything but your money, and can
scarce wait for you to make her a rich widow!''

Jeffreys's lips tightened, and a flame appeared in his
usually calm eyes. ''Which you mean to ensure,'' he
said softly. ''Is that it?''

''That's it!''

''*No*! No!'' cried Elfreda, wrenching at Lewiston's
arm. ''For the love of God! Be sensible! You—''

Jeffreys's mouth was set in a grim line. His voice,
cold and steely, knifed through Elfreda's pleas.
''Enough! Go back in the house, Mrs. Jeffreys! At
once!''

She had never heard that note to his voice, never
seen such a deadly blaze in his eyes, and she fled.

Inside the house, she ran to the morning-room.
Donald had, she knew, really cared for her, and had
likely been brooding over her marriage. His temper,

never very predictable, was now completely out of
control, and when Donald lost his temper there was no
telling what he might do.

Frantic, she tore open Stephen's valise and rum-
maged through the contents. Certainly there must be
a pistol. He would have carried one, if only to protect
her. She blinked away scalding tears. She had brought
him so much misery, and if, as she suspected, he had
begun to look at her with fondness, Donald's blight-
ing words must have caused him more pain. She would
not now stand idly by and let him be hurt by that great
strong oaf...!

But there was no pistol. Frenzied, she ran outside
again, and collided on the steps with a man she would
never have dreamed she'd be glad to see.

"Cousin Adrian!" she panted. "Oh—thank God!
Donald Lewiston is...is killing Stephen!"

He stared at her, his lip curling slightly. "Is he,
now...?"

"Yes! I tell you—*yes!*" She pounded her fists
against his chest. "Oh, why do you *stand* there like a
block? Do you *want* him to be slain? You must *stop*
them! Quickly."

He looked amused. "But I really think—"

She saw his tall black horse tethered to a post, and
with a furious exclamation she pushed Adrian aside
and was down the steps in a flash. The saddle holster,
as she'd expected, held a long-barrelled pistol. She
wrenched it forth, swung around and sped to the side
of the house and the back meadow.

Even as she ran, she saw that the antagonists had
shed their coats and, horrifyingly, Lewiston was
brandishing a pistol although Jeffreys appeared un-
armed.

"Hey!" Adrian roared, pounding up behind her.
"That's a Boutet duelling pistol, you madcap! And it
has a hair trigger! Put it *down!*"

She didn't even hear him. She was aware only of Stephen, wrenching Lewiston's gun from his hand, then reeling back as Lewiston's fist caught him squarely. Panic lent her wings and she fairly flew across the meadow. Sobbing for breath, she halted and levelled the heavy pistol with both hands. Strong fingers grabbed her wrist. Adrian panted, "A moment, if...y'please. Which one d'you...mean to shoot, ma'am?"

"*Lewiston*, of course! What did you expect, you *horrid* creature?" She clawed at his fingers. "Let *go*!"

His grip tightened.

"My God!" she gasped. "I think you *do* want him dead!"

"Madam, if you would but—" he began.

Strengthened by terror, she tugged madly.

There was a deafening explosion; a stunning jolt.

The smoking pistol fell from Elfreda's numbed fingers. From the corner of her eye she saw Lewiston soar backwards and sprawl on the grass.

"Oh—heavens!" she whispered. "I have killed him!"

Adrian gasped, "Devil you have."

Jeffreys came sprinting up. There was a darkening bruise beside his mouth, but he seemed otherwise unhurt. He stared at Adrian, who had sat down heavily and was clutching his right leg.

"Why...ever," panted Jeffreys, "have you shot my cousin, ma'am?"

Elfreda saw that blood was welling through a rip in Adrian's right boot. Conscience-stricken, she cried, "Oh, no! Good gracious! Have I?"

"You may believe...you have," groaned Adrian.

Jeffreys knelt beside him and managed to remove the boot. "Let's have a look here, old fellow."

Lewiston was struggling to his feet, a handkerchief pressed to his bloody nose. He staggered over and looked curiously at Adrian, who was making unkind remarks about women and pistols. "Made a pest of himself, did he?" asked Lewiston. "Don't blame you a bit, Elfreda."

Distraught, she said, "I meant to shoot *you*!"

Jeffreys was winding his handkerchief tightly about Adrian's calf, but he paused at this, and slanted a sparkling look at her.

"*Me*?" echoed Lewiston. "Well, if that don't beat the Dutch! After all the years we've been friends, I'd think—"

"I thought," she gulped, her voice beginning to tremble, "that you were going to kill my husband."

Dabbing at his nose, Lewiston boasted rather thickly, "So I would have if he'd had the decency to face me in a duel, like a gentleman of honour!"

Adrian grumbled that he was being neglected. "You can stare at your wife for the rest of your days, Stephen. As for you, Lewiston, you . . . may be thankful that my cousin *is* a gentleman of honour and . . . and took pity on a blasted young cloth-head. If you'd ever set foot outside your home county you might have learned that Stephen Jeffreys is the . . . the finest shot in his regiment, and there's scarce . . . a man in Town would dare go out with him."

Lewiston's high colour faded, leaving him very pale. He stared, goggle-eyed, at Jeffreys, then stammered, "Never say— You're not the . . . the one they call '*Jeopardy* Jeffreys'?"

"Correct," said Adrian contemptuously, "however belated."

In an awed half-whisper Lewiston said, "By . . . Jupiter! And *I* have fought with him! Wait till my father hears this! Oh, gad, Lieutenant Jeffreys, I do beg your pardon! I've a beast of a temper, but I'd no right to hold a grudge because Elfreda chose—" He broke off, then finished buoyantly, "Your left is everything they say of it! I can vouch for that!"

Jeffreys gripped Adrian's shoulder. "It's not much more than a graze, old fellow, but we'll have the apothecary out to look at it before you return to High Golden." He stood, and said to Lewiston, "I'll accept your apology, but remember in future to curb your tongue in front of ladies. Meanwhile, I am not yet up to hauling my cousin back to the house, so, if your nose will allow you, please help him."

Lewiston went off, supporting Adrian, and Jeffreys turned to face his bride.

It had dawned on her that she'd married what Clifford would term a "top of the trees," but her mind was on weightier issues. "It—it wasn't true, was it?" she asked, searching his face with intense anxiety. "You—you're not going to—? I mean, you *are* getting better?"

He clasped his hands lightly behind him. "I'm rather afraid I am," he said gravely. "My doctor has abandoned hope of his initial gloomy findings proving correct. It looks as if you may not be an early widow, after all."

"That is a perfectly horrid thing to say," she said, blinking rapidly. "I may have w-wanted you to...to help with...with this wretched old— But I meant to be a good wife in return, and never—*never*—thought—I didn't even *dream* you m-might—"

He said very softly, "I rather hoped you didn't."

She burst into tears and stood looking up at him, and tearing her handkerchief to shreds. "If I had even *suspected* such a thing I— Oh, Stephen, *truly* I could not have borne it! You were so good, and I was so...so grateful! I had...even begun to hope—"

He stepped closer and tilted up her chin, scanning the woebegone little face narrowly. "To hope what, Mrs. Jeffreys?"

She sniffed. "To hope you might . . . begin to forget about your br-broken heart, and—"

"My—*what*? Good God! You never mean poor Gertrude? Whoever told you she had broken my heart?"

"Your cousin." Looking up at him, she said hopefully, "Is it not so?"

He laughed. "That rascal! I thought your mama might have told you the truth of it, for she knows the whole. The thing is, you see, that I am—er—of the old school in some ways. I demand that the lady I choose must be true to me. Only."

Whispers she had heard about the Bellington crowded back into her mind. She said incredulously, "Do you say that . . . *you* broke the connection?"

"No, how could I?" His eyes twinkled at her. "It would be most ungallant."

She murmured tenderly, "And, of all men, you are so very, very gallant. Indeed, I think Gertrude Bellington made a poor bargain." She sighed. "As did you also, I fear."

"Not so! I began to love you, my little schemer, from the first instant I saw you. You came like a breath of spring into my life with your unspoiled loveliness, and your unaffected ways, and kind heart."

"Oh . . . *Stephen* . . ." Ecstatic, she melted into his arms, but, even as he bent to her, she pulled back and her brow wrinkled. "Why, then, would Adrian have said such things? I know he dislikes me because I have come between him and his expectations, but—"

He gave a shout of laughter. "No, you must acquit him of that, dear one. Adrian is, and always has been, my closest friend. He is loyal to a fault and I do believe that of all things he was most distressed by the possibility that he might inherit my fortune. He is inclined to be a remorseless judge, I'll own, and he thought you were . . . well—"

"A callous adventuress," she sighed. "As I was."

"Nonsense." He tilted up her chin and smiled lovingly into her eyes. "You were enchantingly honest, that is all. Besides, I am very sure that, when you came running down here to save my life, you quite won him over."

"And sealed his regard by shooting him! Oh, Stephen!"

He chuckled. "He knows you did not mean to dispose of him. Even so, I fear I must put an end to this farce, ma'am."

"Wh-what?" she gasped, blanching.

"I have waited and watched you struggling, day after day, and I hoped you might come to me and confess it was hopeless."

"Oh. But you—promised," she said, without much force. "And you know how I...love this dear old—"

"Disaster?" he prompted.

"No! That is, I—"

He put a hand on each side of her face and said gravely, "You are beautiful and dear and dauntless, and I love you with all my heart. But we will spend not another day among the ruins, for I mean to take you at once to Town."

With an inward sigh of relief, she murmured, "Oh."

"Furthermore," he said, "I am going to tear down your dream house, my little one."

"Oh."

"There are far more important things for you to manage," he went on, drawing her closer.

Again she held him back, and demanded suspiciously, "What important things am I to manage?"

"Our children, of course."

"But...we *have* no—"

He put a stop to that remark by crushing her to him and kissing her ruthlessly. "Not today, perhaps," he said as she sank weakly against him. "But..." He bent and whispered in her ear.

She gave a shocked gasp, and pushed him away. "How *naughty*!" she exclaimed, her eyes full of laughter.

"True. I doubt any lady could find it in her heart to love such a naughty husband."

Standing on tiptoe, she kissed his chin. "If you did but know how very much this particular lady adores her dearest and best of husbands."

After a pleasant interval he murmured, "And you can forgive me for destroying your dream?"

"I forgive you, my darling. But... I shall be sorry to see the poor old house pulled down, I'll own."

"Yes, I feared you might. And it *is* full of history, so I thought it would be nice to build a smaller replica of it here. Containing memorabilia from the old days, perhaps."

She clapped her hands joyously. "What a lovely notion! A sort of museum? Mama has lots of historical items, and we could write little tracts to go with each article."

A small ginger creature dealt Jeffreys's boot a proprietorial whack as it shot past them and rocketed into the house with ears back and tail held on one side.

"Ingrate," cried Elfreda indignantly.

Jeffreys said with a grin, "Our first tract, beloved, should tell of the Colossus who was born here to a deceased turkey!"

Watching them through the kitchen window, and hearing their distant laughter, Adrian muttered, "He was right, after all. They did confound everyone, the pair of 'em..."

Lewiston asked, "What did you say, sir?"

Adrian smiled. "Nothing that is of any importance—now," he said. "Be careful with my boot—there's a mad cat in it!"

MUCH LATER THAT NIGHT, lying in a comfortable bed in a luxurious Clarendon suite, Stephen Jeffreys kissed the tumbled curls of the head pillowed on his shoulder. "How wicked I was," he confessed, "to use our honeymoon to prove to my beloved how hopeless were her schemes."

"Mmm," said Elfreda, snuggling closer.

"Tell me, Mrs. Jeffreys," he murmured, "do you still incline to the belief that love is greatly overrated?"

Elfreda smiled happily into the darkness. "For a dashing Corinthian, and a regular top of the trees," she answered, "you do ask the very silliest—"

The Eccentric
Miss Delaney

Gail Mallin

CHAPTER ONE

"OSTLER! OSTLER!" The deep voice rang round the inn yard.

Jethro came running but halted in awe as the sporting curricle came to a precision halt in the centre of the Peacock's modest yard. It had a glossy yellow body and was drawn by a high-stepping pair of match-bays. To add to his astonishment, it was being tooled by one whom even he recognised as a Nonpareil.

Nick Verlaine sighed. He should have waited until he had reached Barton Grange but the fact that this little wayside tavern lay on the outskirts of the modestly fashionable resort of Parkgate had encouraged him to hope that it might offer better service than that usually found in such places. Still, beggars could not be choosers and he had a thirst on him that would brook no further delay.

"Look lively now, lad," he encouraged the undersized youth who was still standing there, scratching his head in disbelief.

"Yes, sir." Released from his trance by the note of impatience in this unusual customer's baritone tones, Jethro leapt forward to take joyful charge of the most wonderful horses he had seen in a twelvemonth.

Lord Verlaine sprang down with an athletic grace that belied the hours he had spent on the road, and Jethro enviously noted his height. Six feet at least, aye, and broad-shouldered to match, he'd be bound, though that many-caped Benjamin made it difficult to be sure.

After giving his long limbs a stretch Nick strolled off in the direction of the taproom. To his surprise, it was impeccably clean and furnished with more comfort than the modest exterior of the building had seemed to promise. His black brows rose a further fraction of an inch when he perceived that instead of a tapster there was a dumpy middle-aged woman presiding over the tankards.

"Good afternoon, sir."

Her voice was as genteel as her dowdy dress of brown kerseymere. For an instant Nick wondered what the devil this image of respectability was doing in such queer employment, but abandoned his curiosity when she handed him the tankard of cool ale he had been craving this hour past.

"My compliments, ma'am. An excellent brew!" His first thirst slaked, Nick called for another and while it was being poured became aware of the stir his entrance had caused. Mildly amused by the covert looks directed at him by a pair of farmers in stained smocks and the more frank stare from an ancient crouched in the inglenook, he concluded that the fashionably clad were not often met with on these premises.

"Begging your pardon, sir, but perhaps you would prefer to sit in the coffee-room?" asked the woman with a quiet deference.

Curbing the impulse to retort that he had no intention of being stared out of countenance by a parcel of yokels, Nick nodded. The offer was meant well and although he did not think himself top-lofty it might grow wearisome to be the object of such abundant curiosity.

"Thank you. Where may I find it?" he asked.

"Step into the passage, sir, and it is the first door on your left. It will be empty, since all our guests are out at present."

Nick proceeded to follow these directions but as he entered the long low room he saw that the proprietress was mistaken.

"Well, now, here's a hive of industry!"

At the sound of his voice her cheerful humming abruptly ceased and the girl spun round, affording him an excellent view of her enchanting countenance, framed by untidy but glossy blue-black curls spilling from a frayed ribbon.

Nick whistled softly. Replace that shabby gown and apron with some fashionable frippery and this wench would give the beauties of Almack's a run for their money! He'd never seen eyes more blue...or a more kissable mouth.

"Don't you find it too warm a day for such work?" he enquired, abandoning his tankard upon a table and striding forward.

"Cleaning is required at all times of the year."

Neither the coolness of this curt answer nor the surprisingly cultivated tones in which it was delivered registered with Nick. His attention was far too taken up with admiring her figure. She was a little on the tall side perhaps, but so exquisitely proportioned that he wouldn't cavil at that!

One shining black ringlet had strayed across her lusciously full bosom. Nick raised his quizzing-glass. Damn it, but she'd skin like satin! So smooth and creamy white that it made his fingers fairly itch to reach out and stroke it.

A bloom of colour stained the beauty's cheeks.

"Did you require anything in particular, sir?" she enquired in a tight little voice, laying down her duster.

A mischievous smile lit Nick's eyes.

"Only this," he replied, sweeping her into his arms with a speed and efficiency born of long practice.

Before she could recover from her astonishment at being handled in such a fashion, Athena Delaney found herself being thoroughly kissed.

"Oh, how dare you behave in such a way?" she exclaimed the instant his lips left her own. Struggling to free herself from a stronger hold than she had ever known, she added hotly, "Let me go at once."

The steely arms merely tightened their grip. "Not unless you give me another kiss first," Nick laughed.

"Give!" Athena's angry voice rose in protest. "A strange notion you have, sir, of giving. I'd as lief give you the plague!"

"You little firebrand," Nick said admiringly. "Tell you what, I'll trade you a guinea for it."

If she had not been quite so crushed against his chest, Athena's bosom would have undoubtedly swelled, but a strangled shriek left Nick in no doubt of her indignation.

"Come now, am I as repulsive as all that?" he demanded with a grin.

"You, sir, are entirely repugnant," Athena spat at him, not entirely truthfully, for it had not escaped her notice even in these trying circumstances that he was a very handsome man, if one had a fancy to swarthy looks, which she did not, of course. "But that is hardly the point—"

"You're not going to tell me that other customers haven't tried to steal a kiss or two before now," he interrupted in a wondering tone.

A furious nod of her raven head answered him.

"What, never? You must be bamming me, or else they are such a set of slowtops here on the Wirral as I have never encountered before in all my life!"

Nick's expression was ludicrously droll and for an instant, insanely, Athena was tempted to smile back at him, but she had no intention of encouraging his effrontery.

Instead she said with all the severity she could muster, "Pray release me and be done with this nonsense. Or I shall be forced to scream for help."

"Ah, that does put a different complexion on it! Will you shout for that looby in the stables, I wonder? I declare I'm quaking in my boots."

"Will you be serious?" Athena squirmed wildly in his embrace, infuriated by the teasing note in his voice, a deep voice she might have found pleasingly velvet-toned in any other man.

"Oh, I am serious, my beauty." His arms tightened about her. "Hold still! I intend to have that kiss come what may."

There was a devilish light glinting in his dark eyes and Athena suppressed a shiver. He was as swarthy as a Spanish brigand with his black hair and tanned skin and instinctively she felt sure he was equally ruthless.

"You are mad, quite mad—" she began, but her protest was cut off abruptly as his lips captured hers once more.

A strange tingling filled Athena's limbs, and, although her brain was instructing her to fight him, foolishly she could not comply. Her body seemed to have acquired a will of its own and moulded itself pliantly to the hard contours of his frame. Incredibly, instead of trying to pummel his shoulders, her fists uncurled to clutch him eagerly to her. Even more horrifyingly, obeying the warm skilful pressure of his mouth, her tightly closed lips parted in invitation.

Her senses swimming, Athena was scarcely aware at first that he had finally released her until he spoke.

"Name whatever price you wish, wench," Lord Verlaine said hoarsely, still breathing hard. "By God, it will be worth it!"

"You . . . you villain!" The exclamation was ripped from Athena's throat as her hand flew up to make explosive contact with his cheek.

Ruefully rubbing his sore face, Nick reflected on the folly of relaxing one's guard before making certain of victory. "There's no need to look such daggers at me, girl. I can take a hint!"

"My virtue is not for sale." Athena spoke through clenched teeth.

"Obviously," Nick drawled, leaning back to prop his lean hips against the nearest table. He surveyed her with a faint smile as he folded his arms across his chest. "My luck must be out. I encounter the prettiest chambermaid in England, only to find she is virtuous to boot. What a curst pity!"

Athena's Celtic blue eyes widened. "You . . . you think me a chambermaid?"

He directed a silent glance over her untidy hair and faded dimity gown that spoke more eloquently than words.

Taking a deep breath, Athena strove to control her temper. "You are mistaken, sir. My name is Delaney and since my ancestors were once kings in Ireland I dare say my birth is as good as yours."

"Then what the devil do you mean by dressing up in that rig?" Nick retorted. "Good God, what did you expect me to take you for?"

"Oh, I see, you would not have molested me if you had known my quality?"

Her sarcasm brought an unaccustomed tinge of colour into his tanned cheeks. "I play by the rules, Miss Delaney," he growled.

"And chambermaids are fair game, are they not, for men of your stamp?" She sniffed disdainfully.

Nick coughed and fingered his neckcloth as if the Trône d'Amour he had tied that morning had suddenly become too tight. "What can your people be thinking of," he exclaimed gruffly, "letting you run loose in such a manner with not even a maid in attendance?"

"There is nothing in *my* behaviour to cause the least distress to anyone," Athena declared. "And I'll have you know that I do have a chaperon."

Comprehension dawned in Nick's dark eyes. "Do you mean that dowdy, bracket-faced female in the taproom?" he demanded incredulously.

"Sherry is not bracket-faced! She has a great deal of countenance," Athena fired up in passionate defence of her beloved former governess.

He grinned at her. "Doing it rather too brown, Miss Delaney."

"Your opinion, sir, does not concern me in the least!" Athena sought refuge in dignity. "What does signify, however, is that you had no business to pounce on me in that odious manner and if you were a gentleman you would apologise instantly."

His grin broadened, revealing excellent white teeth. "I haven't the least intention of apologising for something I enjoyed a great deal." He paused significantly. "What's more, unless I'm very much mistaken, you enjoyed it too. At least on the second occasion," he added fairly.

"Oh, you are . . ." Athena blushed furiously.

"Impertinent?" he supplied helpfully, as she struggled for words.

"An outrageous coxcomb!" she snapped back.

"No doubt, ma'am, but you must shoulder some blame for my behaviour. I would never have acted in such a manner if you had not been dressed like a servant—"

"Would you have me wear a ball gown to wield a duster? Pray, do not be ridiculous," Athena interrupted.

"The only absurdity, ma'am, lies in finding a lady of your quality engaged in such a menial occupation," he retorted swiftly.

Athena's beautifully shaped mouth thinned to a narrow line, a sure sign of temper, as any of her friends could have informed Lord Verlaine.

"I'm not surprised a blockhead like yourself should think such old-fashioned, fustian nonsense," she replied scornfully. "There is no shame attached to honest work, my buck! Why should I not dust this room, pray, when I own a share in the inn?"

Nick gazed at her blankly, and, taking advantage of his astonishment, Athena went on coolly, "And now I'll thank you to leave, sir. I have work to do even if you have not!"

For an instant Nick was inclined to dispute the matter but common sense, to say nothing of previous experience in dealing with females wearing just that determined expression, warned him it would not serve.

"As you wish, Miss Delaney." He bowed with exquisite grace and headed for the door, where he paused, his hand on the handle. "But I'll be back."

BARTON GRANGE LAY on the north-western extremity of the Wirral peninsula. Enclosed by lush acres of parkland, the original black and white half-timbered Tudor hall had been much enlarged and improved upon by subsequent generations of the Barton family.

The improvements included a handsome library in the west wing and it was to this apartment that the present incumbent, a stoutish, fair-haired gentleman in his mid-thirties, led his guest once Lord Verlaine had rid his person of the dust of the road.

"Try some of this Madeira," Sir George offered genially, directing his friend to the most comfortable chair with one expansive wave of his hand.

"Thank you, I will." Nick accepted the proffered glass. "I have need of it."

A wide grin split George's round face. "I know, I know. Why must I live beyond the reach of civilisation? Family obligation, dear boy. I durst not sell the place. Only think of what my mother would say!"

Nick, who had the doubtful privilege of being acquainted with the Dowager Lady Barton, acknowledged this remark with a smile, but his darkly handsome face sobered as he murmured absently, "I wasn't thinking of the journey."

"Don't leave me in suspense, dear boy," his former comrade in arms begged, as Lord Verlaine fell into a brooding silence.

Thus admonished, Nick apologised for his lapse of manners and related the events that had taken place earlier. All he left out was any mention of his second attempt to kiss the lady. For some strange reason, he could not rid himself of the marvellous feel of her, so soft and willing in his arms. He strongly suspected her wonderfully wanton response had amazed her almost as much as it had surprised him, but he did not want to talk about it, even to so good a friend as Sir George.

"I might have known there'd be a petticoat in it," George chuckled. "There always is with you!"

Nick shrugged wryly. "Ah, but this time I didn't even manage to find out the lady's given name."

"Athena," replied Sir George promptly.

"You know her?" Nick's gaze sharpened.

"Oh, everyone hereabouts knows of the eccentric Miss Delaney!" George grinned. "You're not the first to be smitten by those glorious eyes, you know. Half the fellows in the county fancy themselves in love with her, but the devil of it is that she's a confirmed man-hater."

Nick's eyebrows soared.

"It's true." George gave his fair head a solemn shake. "A great pity, but there it is. Says she won't get married. Got some crazy notion in her head of making her own fortune on the 'Change."

"Gammon." Nick snorted derisively. "Females don't speculate."

George spread his hands in a doubtful gesture. "Thought so too myself until I met Miss Delaney," he admitted, "but she's been devilishly successful according to William Taylor."

Seeing Nick's look of enquiry, he explained that this gentleman was the owner of the area's most influential banking house. "He's been advising her on her investments. Knows about the latest ships leaving Liverpool and all that sort of thing." A faint sigh escaped his lips. "Dare say he'll succeed in winning her in the end. Respectable fellow, well-blunted, just the steady sort of man females fancy."

On this depressing note he rose to pour them more wine.

"That's all very well," said Nick, impatiently dismissing the worthy Mr. Taylor. "But what in hell's name is a girl like that doing at the Peacock?"

Sir George rubbed the side of his nose with a reflective finger. "Can't rightly say. What I do know is that since she arrived at the Peacock last February with that female dragon in tow the place has changed out of all recognition."

A discreet knock at the door heralding the arrival of Sir George's butler with the announcement that dinner was served prevented Nick from making a reply. Over an excellent meal of fillets of turbot, roast duck with French beans and mushrooms, mutton chops and a Chantilly basket contrived to tempt Sir George's sweet tooth, he confined himself to safely neutral topics of conversation, but once the servants had withdrawn and they were left alone to enjoy their port he immediately returned to the fascinating subject of Miss Delaney.

"Do you think it's true that she comes from a good family as she claimed?"

"Oh, aye," George confirmed. "Her grandfather is old General Sir Patrick Delaney."

Nick whistled. This gentleman's exploits in the late war with the Colonies were well known to all military men.

"Say, do you ever regret selling out after Waterloo, Nick?" George demanded suddenly, his thoughts turning to his own recent career. "I know I do sometimes."

"Sapskull," Nick retorted affectionately. "You'd hate to serve in peacetime."

"I suppose so," his friend sighed. "But we did have some good times in the Peninsula and civilian life can be so damned boring!" He glanced slyly at Nick. "I swear that's the reason you began kicking up larks all over Town."

Nick shrugged, unwilling to consider the matter. His former life as a Major in the 5th Dragoon Guards was in sharp contrast to his present idle existence, a fact he tried hard to forget. Lack of purpose since quitting the Army had made him restless, and his efforts to solace his boredom with deep drinking, heavy gambling and a series of dazzling mistresses had earned him a dashing reputation but no inner peace.

"We ain't discussing my affairs," he said firmly, "but Miss Delaney's."

"Ho, ho, so that's how the land lies, is it?" George exclaimed. "You'll catch cold at the game, Nick. She ain't keen on rackety fellows, I warn you."

"Then how did you come to meet her?" his friend enquired sweetly.

George grinned. "Harmless as a newborn lamb, that's me," he declared.

Nick snorted rudely, but his threat to repeat several warm stories to refute this claim was averted by George hastily embarking on a recital of his first meeting with Miss Delaney at the Assembly House in Parkgate.

"She is received, then?" Nick asked in a carefully uninterested tone.

"Oh, lord, yes. Parkgate ain't one of your stuffy resorts like Worthing. She dances divinely, too." George chuckled reminiscently. "Course, some of the tabbies objected on account of her doings at the Peacock but nobody took any notice of their spite, I can tell you, least of all Athena. She don't give a fig for the gossip about her."

He paused to offer his guest a cigarillo, a habit he had acquired while in the Peninsula. Nick declined but waited politely until it was lit and George had settled himself comfortably back into his chair before resuming the conversation.

"So, in your opinion, Miss Delaney is no shrinking violet," Nick remarked thoughtfully.

George gave a shout of laughter. "Not she! Up to snuff if ever I saw one. I've seen her dampen the pretensions of more than one hopeful buck with just a haughty look."

An impish grin suddenly appeared on his cherubic countenance. "Mind you, none of them could claim your polished address. Wonder if you'd fare any better?" He began to chuckle. "Lord, I'd give a pony to see you succeed in storming that citadel!"

"Is that a challenge, George?" Nick murmured softly. For once there was a glint of something other than boredom in his dark eyes.

"Aye, damme, why not?" His host's face shone with enthusiasm. "That fascinating little witch has broken more hearts than I can count. It is time someone struck a blow for our sex. Come on, Nick, say you'll do it!"

Lord Verlaine remained silent for a moment, staring into the heart of his wine glass and remembering the scorn in those great sapphire eyes. She had dismissed him as though he was of no import and it still rankled!

Nick knew it was merely his vanity that had been hurt—he had grown too accustomed to easy conquests—but there was something irresistible about the idea of teaching Miss Delaney a lesson.

He lifted his dark head and saw that George was watching him eagerly.

"Done! A pony it is, then."

Sir George let out a crow of triumph and raised his glass. "Let's have a toast to your success," he cried. "What shall it be?"

Lord Verlaine raised his eyebrows. "To the surrender of the citadel, what else?"

"IS THE FISH NOT TO YOUR liking, my dear? You've scarcely touched a mouthful."

Athena Delaney jumped guiltily. Her mind had not been on her supper but the extraordinary event that had taken place earlier. In fact, she hadn't been able to stop thinking about it or the tall, swarthy stranger who had forced his way into her peaceful life!

She had been kissed before, of course. After all, she wasn't some green miss of seventeen; she was almost twenty-two years old and without being vain knew she was attractive to men. Their protestations of love and desire had never affected her cool judgement and it had not been in the least bit difficult to hold them off.

So what on earth had possessed her this afternoon?

He was very handsome, a little inner voice reminded her.

Yes, but I have known several men just as good-looking and never given them a second thought, so that cannot be the reason, she answered herself quickly.

This reflection did not cheer her, and, failing to solve the mystery, she turned her attention to silently scolding herself for her shameless behaviour.

Any normal, well-bred girl would have fainted or fled, but I stayed to bandy words with him!

"Athena? Is there something wrong?"

Her one-time governess's anxious voice finally penetrated her chaotic thoughts and Athena strove to put her idiocy out of her mind.

"No, I'm just a little tired, that's all, Sherry," Athena prevaricated, pushing aside her plate.

"I knew it!" Miss Sherrington exclaimed. "You have worn yourself out. I wish you had not persuaded me to let that wretched girl have leave of absence."

"But her mother is ill and you know very well that Peggy is needed at home," Athena laughingly protested.

"Perhaps, but my first duty is to you, my dear. You were not bred for this kind of work. What would your father say if he could see you now?"

Athena's lovely smile faded. "Doubtless Papa would say it served me right for not going to stay with my godmother as he wished," she answered in a brittle tone.

"I do wish you had not quarrelled with him," Sherry sighed.

"Are you sorry you came to Parkgate?" Athena asked quickly. She stretched out a hand across the scrubbed pine table and laid it gently over the work-worn fingers of her friend. "I did not mean to drag you into something you disliked."

Miss Sherrington's expression softened and she gave Athena's hand an affectionate little squeeze. "Foolish girl, for my own part I have no complaint! Indeed, I think my situation improved beyond all recognition. Trying to drum anything at all into the heads of those silly children was an impossibility, but if you had not turned up that day and suggested we set up house together I should still be teaching in that abominable school and hating every minute of it."

"I could not have managed without you," Athena replied. "Tom would have been reluctant to let me stay here on my own."

Miss Sherrington acknowledged this with a nod of her grey head. Tom Shaw, the innkeeper, was her brother-in-law. They had not kept in touch after her sister's death three years ago, but, knowing him for a warm-hearted man, if something of a rough dia-

mond, she had tentatively proposed they seek refuge
at the Peacock.

"It will be a convenient base from which we can decide on our next move," Miss Delaney had said, ac-
cepting the suggestion with alacrity.

In the event, their future had resolved itself. Appalled to find the inn in a filthy, run-down state, they
had turned their energies to restoring it to its former
glory. Shaken out of the drunken lethargy which grief
had plunged him into, Tom was so grateful for their
efforts that he had begged them to stay and help him
run the place.

It had not been Athena's original intention to remain at the Peacock, but Tom's entreaties soon persuaded her that it was an excellent idea. Renting a
house would make deep inroads into her small sum of
capital whereas living at the inn would provide them
with a roof over their heads free of charge and leave
more money available for her ambitious schemes.

However, they both knew the situation was most
irregular.

"Really, my dear, this is no life for you!" Sherry
burst out at last. "Living in a tavern! Eating in the
kitchen!" She waved an agitated hand around her. "It
may do for a middle-aged spinster but you are a young
lady of excellent family. You ought to be enjoying
yourself at parties and balls and all that the season has
to offer."

Her outburst fell on deaf ears.

Such dark eyes he had. They appeared almost black
but when you got close enough, and heavens, she
could have hardly got any closer, it could be seen that
they were really an intense moss-green, like agates!

"Athena? Athena, are you listening to me?"

Jerked abruptly from her reverie, Athena flushed
hotly.

What is the matter with me tonight? she thought crossly. I must stop thinking about that detestable man.

"I'm sorry, Sherry. What were you saying?"

Miss Sherrington, deciding her young friend was more tired than she had first thought, obligingly repeated her remarks.

"Oh, Sherry, I have done all those things and a dead bore I found it for the most part!" Athena exclaimed. "As soon as I was old enough to put up my hair Papa insisted on taking me about with him."

"But that was on the Continent, my dear. You have never enjoyed a London season."

Athena shrugged this objection aside. "I cannot see that it would be so very different. Whenever Papa was in funds he spent lavishly, you know. Heavens, when we were in Paris a couple of years ago I had more dresses than I could possibly wear even though we were out every evening!"

She stood up and began to gather together the dirty plates. "Of course, when Papa's fortunes were reversed we had to dodge his creditors while pretending that nothing was wrong." A rueful laugh shook her. "You cannot imagine how horrid a time we had of it in Italy. I was never so glad as when Papa decided to come home the year after Waterloo."

She carried the dishes over to the big stone sink, saying over her shoulder as she did so, "Unfortunately, time had not softened my grandfather's anger. He had not forgiven Papa for eloping with Maman, so our journey to Ireland was all a waste."

"I never understood why the General was so set against your mother, God rest her soul!" Miss Sherrington shook her grey head. "I know it was very wrong of Mr. Delaney to act as he did, but he was only a young man at the time, and, after all, your mother was of good birth. She was the daughter of the Comte de Montargis!"

Athena returned to the table and sat down.

"That was the trouble!" she explained. "Grandfather could not abide foreigners, you see. Papa told me once that he'd had a devil of a time persuading him to let him go on a Grand Tour in the first place. Perhaps if Maman had possessed a good dowry he might have forgiven her, but her branch of the family was a poor one."

A faint frown creased Athena's brow. "I dare say it didn't help smooth matters over that I looked like her, apart from my colouring, which I get from Papa."

Miss Sherrington smiled. "Indeed you do resemble her in many ways, my dear, but that's nothing to be ashamed of, whatever your grandfather may have told you."

"Oh, yes, I know. Maman was a dear but her memory still rankled with the General. He seemed to blame her for Papa's gambling, of all things. As if Maman could have stopped it!"

She sighed philosophically.

"In the end, of course, we came away with nothing. Not that I blame Papa in the least. After so many unpleasant things had been said, what else could he do?"

A little shiver ran through Athena. "I would not be beholden to that man for anything. He might be my grandfather but he is a miserable old curmudgeon."

Since Miss Sherrington agreed whole-heartedly with this view she did not think it incumbent upon her to reprove her young companion but strove to direct the conversation back into its former channel.

"I appreciate that you might have had a surfeit of parties, but how on earth are you to find a suitable husband if you do not go into the right sort of company?"

"Oh, Sherry, you know I don't want a husband! I prefer to rely upon my own wits, thank you."

"But your investments might fail," Sherry wailed.

Athena's eyes began to sparkle in a militant fashion.

"Then I shall survive by using my own two hands. I'm not afraid of hard work. I do not need a man to keep me. In fact, I do not see that I need a man at all!"

Detestably, the image of the tall stranger of that afternoon came flooding back once more to mock her defiant words.

"If I ever marry at all," Athena continued grimly, determined to ignore the tricks her perverse memory was playing on her, "I shall take care to choose a sensible, quiet-living man and not some charming rake like my papa!"

CHAPTER TWO

THE SUN WAS OUT the next morning, making the waters of the Dee estuary sparkle brighter than a diamond necklace. The sight lifted Athena's spirits as she let herself out of the inn and strolled down the lane.

Directly ahead of her stood the Custom House, but as it was still early there was no one about, and Athena halted for a moment, drinking in the cool breeze and relishing the peaceful view.

She had passed a disturbed night, which was unusual for her, and woken with a headache.

"Go and get a breath of fresh air while I cook breakfast," Sherry had ordered.

Meekly acquiescing, Athena had offered to make herself useful. "I can call in Swifts while I am out and leave our order. It will save time later."

Since the butcher's shop was situated not far distant, only in School Lane, Sherry approved this plan, merely admonishing Athena to wear her cloak.

"I know the weather has been astonishingly warm for October, but it cannot last and I don't want you catching a chill."

Athena had not argued but now she threw the offending garment back and, closing her eyes, lifted her face up to the gentle warmth of the sun.

"Good morning," said a deep voice.

Athena's eyes flew open and saw the tall stranger of her daydream sitting astride a handsome roan not a yard away. What was more, he was just as handsome as her memory painted him with his clear-cut features which might have been modelled by a sculptor of classical inclination.

"What are you doing here?" To her annoyance her voice came out as a squeak.

"Did I startle you? How inconsiderate of me! Do forgive me, Miss Delaney." Lord Verlaine's tone was suitably apologetic but there was nothing humble in his expression. In fact, there was a hint of laughter in his dark eyes.

"There is nothing to forgive," Athena replied tightly.

The shock of seeing him so unexpectedly was wearing off and an unworthy pang of regret that she was wearing her plainest cambric gown assailed her.

"It relieves my mind to hear you say so."

Athena glared at him, longing to ask him what the devil he was doing here in Parkgate when she had imagined him miles away by now.

"I'm staying with George Barton," Nick said, almost as if he had read her mind. "He's an old army friend of mine."

"Indeed." Athena hid her dismay with a cool indifference but she could not help thinking that Barton Grange was far too close. "Then do not let me keep you from him."

"Oh, George won't mind!" Nick said easily. "He's too idle these days to ride before breakfast but he wouldn't begrudge me the pleasure of your charming company."

The smile that accompanied this flattering remark was one of Nick's best.

"Well, I do," Athena retorted bluntly, frantically ignoring the sudden thumping of her pulse. Really, it was a very engaging smile! "I have an errand to perform and even if I hadn't I still wouldn't waste my time talking to you."

Nick winced. Well, he had been warned!

"Wait! Won't you let me accompany you?" he asked, quickly dismounting as she turned to go.

"I have not the slightest inclination for your company, sir, and you must know why." Athena spoke rapidly but her mouth felt dry.

"Then will you at least accept my apologies for yesterday?"

Illogically, Athena felt a spurt of irritation and was betrayed into exclaiming, "But you said that you enjoyed kissing me...oh!" She blushed in confusion and fell silent, mentally cursing her idiocy.

Nick concealed a flicker of triumph. So she was not as indifferent as she was pretending! "I am still of the same mind about that," he admitted. "What I do regret, however, is that I appear to have caused you distress and I am most heartily sorry for it."

Athena hesitated. It was on the tip of her tongue to tell him to go away but it seemed churlish to reject his apology.

"Please. I promise to behave myself."

His grin was infectious and Athena found herself laughing.

"You are quite absurd, sir."

"Come, if we are going to be friends, you must call me by my name." He bowed slightly. "Nick Verlaine, at your service, ma'am!"

"Considering you are holding the reins of your horse you managed that with considerable grace, Mr. Verlaine," Athena said sweetly. "I dare say you've had a lot of practice. However, I am not in the habit of bestowing my friendship at such short notice."

"Actually, it's Lord Verlaine," Nick said, falling into step beside her and ignoring this attempt to put him in his place.

"Am I to be impressed?" Athena could not resist the impulse to flash a saucy smile at him.

"Oh, I hope so," Nick murmured lazily.

Their eyes met and held for an instant before Athena looked quickly away.

"Tell me," she continued a shade too brightly, "is that coat one of Weston's? Papa always used to say he was the best tailor in London."

"I hate to contradict any relative of yours but I prefer Scott."

Recovering her poise, Athena nodded sagely. There had been something too intimate in his smile and it had thrown her. She would take care not to let it happen again.

"I have heard Scott is favoured by military men. You did say you were an army friend of Sir George's, did you not?"

Nick concurred smoothly, explaining that they had both served with Wellington in the Peninsula.

It did not surprise Athena to learn that he had been in the 5th Dragoon Guards. He had the splendid figure and erect bearing which was *de rigueur* for a cavalry officer and his seat on horseback was superb.

I wonder what he looked like in uniform? she thought curiously. He cut a handsome figure in his riding clothes but she suspected regimentals might suit him even better.

Suddenly realising that her musings were most indelicate, and entirely redundant besides, Athena hastily sought a safer topic of conversation.

Luckily, they had reached the part of the village where a sea-wall had been constructed to provide a promenade for visitors.

"This stretch is known as the Terrace," she announced thankfully. "All our fashionable visitors stroll here on fine afternoons."

"Do you do so, Miss Delaney?" Nick asked at once.

"Oh, I do not count as a visitor!" Athena shook her head at him. "I am here to earn my living."

"Yet you are hardly a chambermaid," he countered smoothly.

A tinge of colour crept into her face. "You really must not refer to that deplorable incident."

"So prim, Miss Delaney? Next you'll be telling me that I'm not to flirt with you either."

There was such a twinkle in his agate eyes that Athena could not help laughing back at him.

"Have you no shame, sir?"

"None whatsoever," he said promptly.

"Then you must be prepared to pay the penalty. No lady hereabouts will speak to you if you behave in such a scandalous manner."

"You think they might not like it?" Nick asked innocently.

Since Athena suspected that most of her acquaintance would like it only too well, she did not dare answer this!

"Not that it signifies," Nick announced. "I have no desire to pay court to any lady other than yourself."

"Indeed, sir? How very rash, for I might give you the go-by and then where should you be?"

"Surely one so fair could not be so cruel!"

It was a long time since Athena had enjoyed this kind of flirtatious sparring; her current admirers spouted ponderous compliments that bored her to tears. Without meaning to, she found herself automatically responding in kind to Nick's teasing gallantry.

"Now let me see, do the scandalous attentions of a peer of the realm count as more flattering than those of a mere commoner?"

"Oh, definitely," came the prompt answer.

"Then I must be careful you do not turn my head, must I not?"

"I could hope for no happier fate than to be allowed to try."

Athena's eyes sparkled. "I hate to cast a rub in your way but I feel I ought to point out that such hopes must be in vain. I am no green girl, you see."

Nick smiled at her. "Thank you for the warning—
you may be sure I'll bear it in mind. Of course, I cannot promise not to flirt with you. You are too entirely
beautiful for any man to resist."

Athena coloured slightly. She had meant to be
coolly distant and here she was encouraging him to
make outrageous remarks!

Sherry is always telling me I am an incurable flirt,
she thought dismally. Perhaps she is right!

A somewhat tense silence descended.

"Are those bathing machines down on the shore?"
enquired Lord Verlaine lightly. He was too experienced a campaigner not to recognise her sudden discomfort and he had no intention of spoiling this
promising beginning by rushing his fences.

Athena gladly turned her gaze to follow the direction of his. "Yes but they are meant for the use of ladies only."

"How can you tell?"

Thus prompted, Athena pointed out the modesty
hood gracing each vehicle, which was meant to keep
prying eyes at bay. "The bathing woman also ensures
that the horse has pulled the machine well into the
water before she allows her customer to descend so
that there is no chance that modesty may be offended. That would never do!"

"Have you tried this sea-water cure, Miss Delaney?"

"Only once," Athena laughed. "It was horridly
uncomfortable. You have to wear the most volumi-
nous gown made of stiff canvas and if you do not
meekly permit your bathing woman to duck you under the waves she all but drowns you in her attempts
to do so."

Nick listened to her description with lazy enjoyment and so skilfully did he draw her out that Athena
quite forgot her previous reservations and continued

to chat to him in the most natural manner as they walked along.

"Oh, here we are already!" she exclaimed in some surprise as they drew level with the shop which was her destination. "I must say goodbye now, my lord."

Rather shyly she held out her hand.

Knowing he must not offend her by going too fast, Nick did not make the mistake of raising it to his lips but shook it politely.

Athena let out the breath she did not know she had been holding. Perhaps she had misjudged him and he could be trusted to behave as a gentleman ought. And yet...

"I have enjoyed our conversation, Miss Delaney. Perhaps you will do me the honour of letting me call upon you tomorrow?"

Athena's instincts prompted caution. His behaviour this morning had been exemplary but she wasn't such a fool as to plunge headlong into intimacy with a man she strongly suspected of being a rake.

"I'm afraid my commitments at the inn do not permit visitors, sir," Athena replied demurely and noted his swift frown with a *frisson* of wicked enjoyment she could not quite suppress.

So, the little baggage was prepared to flirt with him, was she? But only on her terms, it seemed. We'll see about that, thought Nick to himself grimly.

"Then may I look forward to seeing you at the next Assembly? There is to be one on Thursday evening, I believe."

"How clever of you to have found that out so quickly," admired Miss Delaney. "But I seldom attend at the Assembly House, I'm afraid."

Keeping a tight hold on his temper, Nick tried another tack. "But you will be going to the firework display, surely?"

Athena contemplated denying it but guessed that he had already discovered that this was to be the last big public event in Parkgate's season. Everyone would attend and both Sherry and Tom would think it very odd if she cried off.

"I may do so," she murmured cautiously.

"Good." Nick smiled at her but to her surprise he did not go on to offer his escort.

Since she had fully intended to turn him down had he suggested it, Athena could not understand her sense of disappointment and she watched him remount his horse feeling distinctly piqued.

My point, Miss Delaney, thought Nick with savage satisfaction as he caught a brief glimpse of her inner turmoil before she schooled her expression to bid him a polite farewell.

Lord Verlaine rode off and Athena lingered for a moment, watching him. However, as soon as she realised what she was doing she flushed and quickly turned away.

"WELL, MISS, YOU LOOK right handsome tonight, that you do!" exclaimed the landlord of the Peacock as the fairy-tale vision that was Athena Delaney in an evening gown of sapphire silk floated into their private parlour.

"Why, thank you, Tom," Athena replied, gratified by his reaction.

It had been so long since she had occasion to wear this particular gown that her reflection in the looking-glass in her tiny attic bedroom had surprised her. She had forgotten how the low-cut Russian bodice and tiny puffed sleeves suited her.

"Good gracious, child, you're never going to wear that, are you? You'll freeze to death!"

Miss Sherrington was staring at her in consternation. Her own stout figure was sensibly clad in grey bombazine, cut high at the neck and low on the wrists.

"But it is a lovely evening, Sherry," Athena laughingly protested. "And I mean to wear my blue velvet pelisse, so you mustn't worry."

Sherry sniffed. She wasn't convinced but she knew that stubborn look of old so she contented herself with merely saying, "Watching fireworks go off is a cold business. You would do well to forgo fashion in favour of a little comfort."

Athena agreed soothingly.

The night sky was clear as they stepped out of the inn a few moments later.

"Signor Saxoni will have his work cut out to rival these stars," Sherry remarked, looking up.

"Eh, watch where you are putting your foot, sister-in-law!" Tom exclaimed as she promptly stumbled. "You'd best take my arm."

Muttering about disgraceful pot-holes, Sherry accepted his assistance.

Tom then turned to Athena and asked her if she wanted the use of his other arm. Since he was much of a height with Sherry, and twice as stout, she knew that they would present an odd sight but she accepted, not wishing to hurt his feelings. When they had first arrived at the Peacock he had treated her with awe and although that initial awkwardness had worn off Athena knew he still considered her above his touch.

Tom's girth did not incline him to walk at speed so by the time they reached the shore beneath the Terrace it was crowded. With a sinking feeling, Athena saw that most of the forms set up on the sands were already taken.

"Let's try further along and see if we can find any free seats," she suggested.

Her companions exchanged dubious glances.

"I doubt if there will be an inch of room anywhere, my dear," Sherry said doubtfully. "But we shall try it if you wish."

After a few minutes jostling, Athena realised it was hopeless. Everyone seemed determined to struggle to the fore to claim a seat.

"Bother!" she exclaimed impatiently. For herself she did not mind standing in the least but she knew that neither of her companions would enjoy the spectacle if they had to remain on their feet.

Just then, Tom spotted a crony of his, who hailed him with an offer to squeeze up and fit them in.

Encouraged by her brother-in-law, Miss Sherrington sank down thankfully, but once Tom had taken his place next to her it became clear that there simply wasn't enough room for another person on the wooden bench.

"No, Tom, please do not get up," Athena said swiftly, forestalling his attempt. "You must remain with your friends."

"Are you sure, miss?" He wavered in the face of this determination, feeling it was hardly his place to contradict her.

"Truly, I prefer to stand," she insisted.

"I don't rightly know, it don't seem right. Shall I ask Sherry—?"

"Oh, there is no need! I will see you both later," Athena murmured and slipped away before he could interrupt his sister-in-law's conversation with her neighbour on the other side.

The crowd thinned beyond the benches and Athena soon found a convenient place to watch the first rockets go up in a blaze of coloured light.

It wasn't until they had faded and the next group of fireworks were being set off that she became aware that she had acquired a considerable quantity of the beach in one dainty sandal and it was rubbing her foot.

"Sherry was right. I should have worn boots," she muttered.

Since it was clearly impossible to hop up and down on one leg while trying to remove the offending particles, she decided to move further back and steady herself against the sea-wall before attempting the task of shaking them out.

"Sand in your slipper, Cinderella?"

Athena jumped in alarm and would have fallen over if a strong arm had not instantly appeared to hold her up.

"Must you keep sneaking up on me?" she exclaimed furiously.

Light showering down on them from an exploding rocket revealed the grin on Lord Verlaine's face as he released her. "Sorry, ma'am."

Athena was so incensed at being caught at such a disadvantage when she had meant to be so cool and elegant, if they did happen to meet, that she forgot to keep her unshod foot clear of the sand.

"Let me help," he ordered. "You are only making matters worse."

Taken by surprise, Athena found it was too late to object. He had her slender foot in a firm grip and was dusting off the sand.

His hand was warm and its heat penetrated her silk stocking. The movement of his long fingers was equally disturbing. She could feel the strength in them but she knew he was trying to be gentle. In fact, his touch was almost like a caress...

Involuntarily, Athena caught her breath and the tiny sound carried to Nick's keen ears in spite of the noise all around them.

He glanced up at her quickly. "Did I hurt you?"

"No, not at all." Athena strove to sound calm.

Nick slid the sandal back into place and straightened. "There, you're done."

"Thank you." Athena tried to quell the absurd regret that flooded over her the instant he released her. Was she going insane?

Nick stared down at her, his gaze absorbing her lush beauty. He had been very tempted to sweep her into his arms and kiss her just now and only the thought that she must surely repulse him had stopped him.

He had been looking for her, of course, but he hadn't expected the crowd to be so great. The whole town must have turned out. If she hadn't been standing in this lonely spot he would never have found her.

"Surely you did not venture out here alone?" Concern suddenly sharpened his voice.

"Of course not," Athena snapped back.

He was standing very close. She had only to stretch out a hand and it would encounter the fine cloth of his coat. Giddiness swept over her as she realised that was exactly what she wanted to do. She wanted to touch him!

Heavens, but she was behaving like an idiotic fool!

"Not that it is any of your business, but I came with friends," she informed him tartly.

"Where are they? I'll take you back to them."

"Oh, no, you won't!" Athena's nerves were so on edge that she bridled instantly. "You have no authority over me, my lord. You may keep your odious masterfulness for those unfortunates in your employ. I have no intention of going anywhere with you."

Nick took a deep breath. "Look, I'm sorry if I offended you. I didn't mean to sound overbearing."

"Well, you did." Her retort sounded childish even to Athena's ears.

"Only because I'm concerned about your safety. You shouldn't be wandering around in the dark on your own," Nick protested.

"Heavens, this is Parkgate, my lord, not London. What on earth do you suppose might happen to me?"

"You can meet rogues anywhere," Nick affirmed doggedly.

"How true!" Athena's gaze raked him up and down.

Nick began to laugh. "Well, I'll not quarrel with that!"

His good-natured acceptance of her gibe made Athena realise how bad-tempered she was being.

"I beg your pardon. That remark wasn't fair," she admitted in a small voice. "You have been most kind to me this evening."

"Gammon!"

Her raven head came up with a jerk of surprise.

"Don't spout polite nonsense at me; I don't want that from you." Nick hardly knew why he felt so angry. Didn't her conciliatory tone prove he was at last getting somewhere?

"I . . . I don't understand." Athena felt bewildered by his sudden change of mood. "What do you want from me?"

"Can't you guess?" he demanded savagely. "No? Then take a look in your mirror, Miss Delaney."

"Are you trying to warn me you are a rake, my lord?" Athena asked with more composure than she felt.

"Foolish of me, ain't it?"

Nick had regained control of himself. Damn it, why had he behaved like some canting Puritan? He'd had her eating out of the palm of his hand. Now he'd blown his chance of winning George's wager for sure. Ten to one, she'd take fright and freeze him out before he could wangle an opportunity to rectify his mistake.

To his surprise, however, her lovely mouth twisted in wry amusement.

"Amazingly chivalrous, I would have said. I suppose I ought to be grateful."

Nick's frown vanished at her light tone.

"You, Miss Delaney, are a flirt," he said slowly.

"Then we are well matched, sir," she answered serenely.

Lord Verlaine gave a shout of laughter but his mirth was suddenly drowned out in a burst of clapping and cheering from the crowd.

"I fancy the display must be concluded," he said.

Athena saw people beginning to stand up and leave the benches. "You are right, sir."

"Won't you reconsider and let me escort you back to your companions?" Nick asked gently.

"I suppose I ought to hurry. Sherry will be having an apoplexy by now," Athena replied evasively.

Dared she risk his company? He was too handsome for her good and he had admitted he was a rake but as she looked up into his smiling eyes Athena came to a decision. Caution be damned, she *wanted* to get to know him better!

"Very well, my lord. I will accept your escort but on one condition."

Nick cocked his head at an enquiring angle. "Which is?"

"That you don't tell Sherry about the sand in my shoe!" Athena laughed. "Or I will never hear the end of it!"

"How goes the wooing, Nick?"

Lord Verlaine paused on the threshold of the breakfast parlour. "Good God, George, don't you know better than to ask such questions at this hour?"

"I'll admit I ain't at my best so early in the day either but damme, man, you ain't hardly ever here. How else am I to find out?" Sir George protested.

"Later, dear friend, later!"

Nick strolled over to the sideboard where a lavish array of viands had been set out. Rejecting the covered silver dishes, he selected some cold beef and took his plate back to the table.

His host poured him a cup of coffee, knowing that Nick's taste did not run to ale at breakfast, and said with heavy sarcasm, "Now are you ready to talk?"

Nick grinned at him. "You know your trouble, George? You've got no patience." Then, seeing his friend's cherubic countenance begin to purple, he relented.

"Miss Delaney has accepted me as a suitable escort. I think she finds my company amusing."

"So she should, by thunder!" George exclaimed, disappointed that Nick was not being more forthcoming. "I've never known you dance attendance on a female like this before. I've scarcely seen you since that firework display the other week."

He sounded distinctly miffed and his tone caused Nick to glance up at him in surprise.

"Blue-devilled, George?" he asked, laying down his knife and fork.

"Aye, well, but there's precious little fun to be had when you are forever off chasing that saucy little baggage."

"Forgive me, I didn't realise I was neglecting my duties as your guest." Nick's voice hardened.

"Now don't fly into a pucker, for God's sake," George begged. "Ignore my nonsense. I know very well that it was at my suggestion you started flirting with the wench so I can hardly cavil at your absence, can I?"

Nick scarcely heard this cheerful apology. He was too astounded by the wave of anger which had swept over him on hearing Athena described in such terms. For an instant he had wanted to knock George down!

It had been ten days since he had escorted Athena back to her friends and been introduced to them. Ten days and not one of them had gone by without him calling on her at the Peacock. They had strolled on the Terrace, taken a picnic on the Green and ridden together down winding country lanes. She had even stood up with him for one of the country dances at the Assembly House but most of all they had talked.

He had never known it was possible to enjoy a woman's conversation so much. Oh, he had flirted with innumerable pretty girls, relishing the cut and thrust of witty sparring and amorous innuendo. Sometimes he'd even found them capable of discussing serious matters in an intelligent way, but with Athena it was much more than that. It was as though he had known her forever and could talk to her about anything!

It was an enlightening experience. From being merely the object of his desire, she had become a friend.

"I've got an idea. Why don't I ask her to pay a visit to the Grange?" George's face lit up as he made this suggestion. "That way you won't have to go into Parkgate. Mind, we'll need a female to act as hostess. How about my mother?"

Nick raised his brows sardonically and George hastily amended his offer. "Perhaps you're right, but we could ask someone else. My widowed cousin Emily would do, or better still your sister."

"Of all the cork-brained notions, George!" Nick gave him an exasperated grin. "Verena lives in London and has three children. She won't want to come posting up here at a moment's notice just to entertain a girl she hasn't even met."

"She''d do it if you asked her. None of my relations are so devoted to my interests, let me tell you!"

Nick admitted that he was lucky. "But I won't impose on Verena's good nature in such a shabby fashion," he added firmly.

The baronet's expression became thoughtful. "Well, how about my giving a ball, then?"

"It is very kind of you, but are you sure you wish to go to such effort?" Nick was dubious. Athena had declared her distaste for formal occasions, but long acquaintance with Sir George had taught him that his friend could be very persistent.

"Aye, why not?"

Lord Verlaine's attempt at tact was wasted. Sir George had the bit between his teeth.

"Damme, it's too long since I entertained and this is as good an excuse as any to enjoy a party." He laughed heartily. "Particularly as I stand to lose a pony if you win our wager."

"Look, George, I think there is something you ought to know," Nick said abruptly, but his friend wasn't listening.

"Champagne, that's what we'll need. I'd better go and check the cellars with Butterworth. Don't want to run out halfway through the evening or people will be saying it is a shabby affair." He jumped to his feet.

"George! About that wager; I want to—"

"Oh, don't worry your head about that, Nick!" said the baronet jovially as he hurried towards the door. "I ain't bothered about the money."

"Wait a minute, will you? George! It's not the money I want to talk to you about, you mutton-head! I want to call it off!"

But Lord Verlaine's voice fell upon empty air.

"MR. TAYLOR IS HERE to see you, Miss Athena. I've put him in your private parlour."

Peggy's greeting brought a little frown of dismay to Athena's wind-flushed face. She had just spent a delightful hour driving with Nick in his curricle and somehow she had no taste for William's sober company.

It is very remiss of me, she thought to herself as she thanked the chambermaid and slowly mounted the stairs, but it is all Lombard Street to a china orange that he will lecture me on the evils of frivolity!

Athena's forebodings proved to be accurate. There was a distinctly pettish look on William's long, narrow face as she entered the room and his expression did not grow any warmer when she airily informed him she had been driving with Lord Verlaine.

"My word, Athena, I wonder at Miss Sherrington's allowing you to frequent that fellow's company."

"Sherry is not the arbiter of my conduct, William." Athena spoke quietly but there was a dangerous glitter in her Celtic eyes.

Seeing it, Mr. Taylor, who was no fool, decided to moderate his sharp tone. "I did not mean to imply any criticism of you, my dear. *Your* behaviour must always be ladylike, but I cannot trust that man. I have heard the most shocking reports of him. His reputation is a disgrace!"

"I didn't think you listened to tittle-tattle, William," Athena replied cuttingly.

"It is my business to keep an ear to the ground," Mr. Taylor protested, a rather smug little smile turning up the corners of his thin mouth. "Anyone who wishes to succeed in banking must know the weaknesses of his clients. They say Verlaine is a gamester as well as a rake. I should not like to touch his account."

"I doubt if you will get the chance," Athena retorted with poisonous sweetness.

"Athena, have I said something to upset you? I...I don't understand—"

"It is really very simple," she interrupted. "I know I have cause to be grateful to you, William, but that does not give you the right to criticise my friends."

"My dear, I have been most happy to help you with your investments! Surely, you realise I have only your well-being at heart?"

He looked so stricken that Athena's annoyance evaporated. "You are all that is kind, sir. Now, perhaps we had better change the subject if we are not to quarrel."

"Yes, yes, indeed." He accepted this olive-branch with eagerness. "I have been waiting for you to return so that I might talk to you about that copper mine you thought to invest in." He smiled at her pacifically. "It was doubly disappointing for me to find you out, you know, since I had been hoping you would visit me."

Guiltily aware that she had half promised to do so, Athena obediently banished Lord Verlaine from her thoughts.

"Please, won't you sit down, sir? We can discuss the matter now if you wish."

Folding his thin frame into a chair by the fireplace, William accepted her offer of refreshment. "Some tea would be very pleasant. There is a distinct nip in the air, I find. I shouldn't wonder if this unseasonal spell is finally drawing to a close."

"Oh, I hope not. It has been excellent for business," Athena laughed, tugging the bell-pull to summon Peggy. "I think we may even finish the year in profit."

"Ah, it would be very gratifying to see this place paying its way once more. Such a satisfactory conclusion to all your hard labours!"

Athena agreed, wishing he would get to the point, but William did not like to be disturbed when dealing with financial matters and he waited until Peggy had taken their order and left the room before opening the discussion.

"Now I've had that fellow, Davis, investigated and I must tell you that I don't think it would be a wise move to invest in this mine."

Gareth Davis had been one of their visitors earlier in the summer. Athena had liked the man and his eager desire to open his own copper mine in the Vale of Clwyd had aroused her sympathy. Seeing her interest, he had offered her the chance to throw her luck in with his.

"Why?" she enquired. "The terms he offered were advantageous. I could reap a large return on my investment."

"It is more likely that you would lose your money," William answered. He handed her a closely written sheet. "Here are the figures. Apparently, there is a problem with drainage. The engineers I have spoken to tell me that the mine is too wet to be profitable. I dare say Davis forgot to mention that little fact, eh?"

"Actually, he did tell me about it but he hopes to solve the difficulty with one of the new steam-engines."

"Huh, then the man is a fool!" William snorted impatiently. "It would be a ruinously expensive proceeding, from what I'm told. You would be well not to touch this scheme, my dear."

Athena hesitated, giving the paper in her hand a second glance. In the past William's advice had been sound, but this particular matter lay outside his expertise and Gareth Davis's jaunty optimism had struck an answering chord within her.

"Perhaps you are right, William, but I think I will stick by my arrangement with Mr. Davis," she said quietly. "Can you arrange for a transfer of funds?"

He frowned at her. "I think you are making a mistake," he warned, and for a moment Athena thought he was going to dispute her decision, but then he shrugged. "However, if that is what you wish, I will put the matter in hand."

She smiled her thanks at him, glad to avoid further argument.

Athena couldn't help wondering what had put him in such a bad mood. It wasn't like William to be so touchy. He had been a very good friend ever since she had asked him to handle her finances. Perhaps her inadvertent neglect had seemed discourteous?

A brisk knock interrupted her musing.

"Here is Peggy with our tea," she murmured.

But the door opened to reveal Lord Verlaine.

"You dropped one of your gloves," he informed her, strolling into the room with the lithe grace which was so characteristic of all his movements. "I noticed it on my way back to the Grange."

"How kind of you to return it so promptly." Athena rose to her feet, instinctively smoothing the folds of her sprigged muslin skirts. She moved into the centre of the room to meet him, holding out her hand to take the lavender kid glove.

Nick's long fingers closed over hers. A little shiver went through her at his touch. "Thank you," she murmured, tilting her head to gaze up at him. The answering smile in his dark eyes set her pulse racing and she could not look away.

A loud cough from behind her recalled Athena to reality.

Flushing, she became aware that her hand still lay in Nick's warm clasp. Quickly disengaging herself, she turned to the banker, who had risen to his feet, and said in a creditably calm voice, "I don't believe you have met Lord Verlaine, have you, William?"

He's a little older than I am, about thirty-four perhaps, Nick decided, as the introductions were performed. The banker was dressed quietly in grey, his eyes were also grey and his blond hair was fine and wispy, but there was nothing colourless in his expression.

A rival, unless I mistake my guess, Nick thought with a touch of amusement. If looks could kill!

"Do you intend to remain in Cheshire for long, my lord?"

The icy dislike in William's tone made Athena blink in astonishment.

"I haven't decided." Nick flashed a glance at Athena. "It all depends on the circumstances."

William swallowed hard. "I see," he muttered.

Anxious to dispel the tension, Athena spoke up quickly. "Lord Verlaine is staying with Sir George Barton, William. They served together in the Peninsula."

"Indeed?" Mr. Taylor's expression seemed to imply that the French had neglected their duty in overlooking this opportunity to dispatch his lordship.

"I fancy you are no admirer of the military, Mr. Taylor," Nick said smoothly.

"Most certainly not!" William glared at the taller man. "I consider most soldiers to be little better than vagabonds. The recent war was a great waste of our resources, in my opinion. We would have done better to save our money and stay at home."

A gasp of mortification escaped Athena but Nick's eyes twinkled with amusement at this vitriolic bluntness.

"I'm sure Bonaparte would have agreed with you, sir," he remarked sweetly and was rewarded by the dull flush that mottled the banker's thin cheeks.

Then, seeing Athena's embarrassment, he adroitly changed the subject. "George is giving a ball in a few weeks' time. He plans to invite half the county, I believe. Dare we hope that you might be able to attend, Miss Delaney?"

"I should be delighted to do so," Athena asserted, forgetting any reservations in a sudden burning desire to show Nick that she did not share William's ridiculous views.

"I think I had better take my leave," Mr. Taylor announced abruptly, realising she was angry with him.

"Yes, pray do so, William," Athena agreed sharply.

Watching him depart, Nick knew he had made an enemy.

Just then Peggy arrived with the tray of tea.

"Will you stay, my lord?" Athena smiled at him in invitation.

"There's nothing I'd like better," Nick replied, and promptly forgot about the banker.

CHAPTER THREE

ATHENA PAUSED at the entrance of the Peacock's empty taproom where Peggy was busy sweeping the floor with a broom.

"Could you tell Sherry that I've gone to the Marine Library if she asks for me, please?"

The chambermaid looked up from her task and nodded, leaving Athena free to set off for the circulating library, which was situated at the seaward end of Drury Lane.

When she had first arrived Athena had thought it an odd coincidence to find so many Parkgate place-names the same as those in London, until Tom had explained to her that it had been a deliberate policy to make the village seem fashionable and so attract a better class of visitor.

Thinking about this reminded Athena that their remaining guests had departed that morning. Unfortunately, William's prediction concerning the weather had proved right. The lingering warmth of the last golden days of autumn had vanished and although the bigger inns such as the Princess Royal and the Boat House, which catered for ferry passengers sailing to Flint, might still be busy, the Peacock suddenly seemed deserted.

Well, it might be grey and windy but at least it isn't raining, Athena told herself stoutly. Yet even as she tried to imagine how pleasant it would be to have some time to herself after working so hard she was uneasily aware that winter would bring marked changes to the village.

As if to confirm her gloomy forebodings, the library was almost empty. A trio of ladies were scanning fashion magazines and an elderly gentleman stood reading the latest copy of the *Chester Chronicle* but Athena did not have to queue to change her books.

She was just about to leave when Lord Verlaine appeared.

He was looking very elegant in a blue coat of Bath suiting over a cream waistcoat and pale primrose pantaloons and Athena's pulse quickened. It was an effort to appear nonchalant as she said lightly, "I did not expect to see you here, my lord."

"Marble-backed novels hot from the Minerva Press are not my favourite reading," he agreed with a teasing smile. "However, I was told I could find you here, and what more promising lure could there be?"

A rosy blush coloured Athena's cheeks at his unexpected compliment and Nick promptly took advantage of it to relieve her of her basket and shepherd her outside.

"Shall we stroll along the beach?" he enquired, tucking her arm firmly into his.

"We should be blown away," Athena laughed in protest.

"But I need a walk," he retorted, adding with mock solemnity, "Consider it an act of charity. George keeps too good a table!"

"If you desire exercise, you could try swimming."

"No, thank you!"

"What, not even in the sea-water baths?" Athena waved a hand towards a building they could see in the distance where the sea-wall ended. "They have a warm bath, you know, for the convenience of valetudinarians."

"Minx!" He grinned at her.

"Then we had better retrace our steps and essay the Cheltenham Walk if you are set on the idea of a stroll."

"Where the devil is that?"

Athena explained that this sheltered promenade had been constructed as an alternative to the Terrace when the weather was rough. "We can reach it if we go this way. It cuts across the far end of Drury Lane."

Away from the houses the road soon assumed an air of rural tranquillity.

"Don't you find it too quiet?" Nick enquired, as the silence around them grew, broken only by birdsong and rustling autumn leaves.

"It is very restful."

"So is the grave, my dear Miss Delaney!" Nick shook his head. "The more I think about it the odder it seems."

Puzzled, Athena tilted her chin enquiringly at him.

"Finding you here. You ought to be cutting a dash in Society." He gave her an intent look. "You have never told me the real reason."

"But I did! I'm here to work," she said, her expression innocent.

"Don't try to fob me off by telling me you enjoy playing innkeeper, my girl."

"I wouldn't dare," Athena replied meekly, but her eyes brimmed with laughter.

"I think you would dare anything." Nick's tone was suddenly serious. "It takes courage to defy the conventions and seek to control your own destiny."

There was genuine admiration in his agate eyes and Athena felt a spurt of pleasure. "I'm not so brave, sir," she said, trying to hide her elation. "It is merely that I did not care for the idea of being a companion or a governess and the only other respectable occupations open to women required skills I did not possess."

He looked sceptical and she hurried on. "Truly! I can sew a straight seam but I should never make a dress-maker or a milliner."

"That doesn't explain what a girl of your breeding is doing slaving away in a little country tavern."

Seeing he would not be fobbed off, Athena gave in. "It was an accident. I never meant to turn innkeeper but I saw at once that it was an occupation that would suit me. My only talent is a knack for organisation."

"From what I have heard the Peacock needed rather more than that," he interjected.

"It was in a dreadful state," she admitted. "But the money Papa had given me was sufficient to cover the necessary repairs to the roof and for fitting everything else up in style."

"*You* paid for the work to be done?"

"Naturally," Athena said crisply. "There is no need to look so astonished, my lord. How else was I to persuade Tom Shaw into a partnership? It was a good bargain. I no longer need worry about providing a home for myself and Sherry and I have enough capital left over for my investments. Not that Papa would approve of my dabblings on the 'Change. He wanted me to use the money to pay for a trip to Ireland but I hate the place and I haven't seen my godmother since I was a baby so we quarrelled, of course."

"I'm damned if I can make head or tail of this," Nick declared frankly. "You had better tell me the whole story. We can sit down over there out of the wind."

Athena surveyed the grassy bank he indicated.

"Aren't you afraid it might be damp?" she enquired with a provocative glance at his elegant attire.

"My God, she thinks me a curst dandy!" Nick raised a pained hand to his brow and a gurgle of laughter escaped Athena.

"Oh, no, sir, a dandy would never deign to be seen carrying a straw basket filled with books!"

Fortunately, the grass was dry and once they had settled themselves Nick said, "What's this about visiting your godmother? You have never mentioned it before."

Athena shrugged. "It was Papa's idea but he would not listen when I told him that nothing would induce me to live in the same neighbourhood as my grandfather—"

"The General, I assume?" Nick interrupted.

"I suppose Sir George told you I was related to him?" Athena asked, and when he nodded she continued in the same rapid voice. "He is a detestable man. Papa was prepared to overlook his shabby behaviour but I am not! Two years ago we visited him in the hope of mending an old family quarrel but it was a waste of time. Far from agreeing to heal the rift, he told Papa that he no longer considered him his son!"

Athena snorted with indignation. "I dare say Lady Fitzpatrick is all that is amiable but my grandfather is a near neighbour of hers and as her guest I would certainly meet him again. I doubt if I could be civil to him so it is better if I stay away. Imagine the scandal it would create if I snubbed him at one of her parties!"

"Aye, that would set tongues wagging!" Nick grinned for an instant at the picture she painted but then his tanned face sobered. "Why did your father want you to go to Ireland? Surely you would have been better off living under his protection."

A little sigh escaped Athena. "Not in the circumstances," she murmured.

"You needn't tell me more if it distresses you," he said gently, sensing her hesitation.

Glancing up at him, Athena saw the concern in his dark eyes. Until this moment Sherry was the only person she had ever confided in but her instincts told her that he would not be shocked.

"We have not known each other for very long but I feel that you are my friend and I do not wish to keep secrets from you," she said slowly.

A few weeks ago Nick knew this candid declaration would have sent a surge of triumph pounding through his veins. He had achieved the conquest he had set out to win but it no longer mattered. All he was conscious of was the fact that she valued his friendship enough to trust him.

Burning with a desire to chase that look of worry from her face, he said eagerly, "Perhaps I can provide a fresh insight."

"My father is an inveterate gamester," she began, strangely relieved to be able to talk about it at last. "All my life I've known he couldn't be trusted not to gamble away our last shilling. Oh, there have been times when we lived magnificently! He is a very generous person, you see, but his luck has been poor ever since we returned to England. Finally, last January, his creditors were about to pounce so he decided to flee to the Continent. He wanted me to go with him. He had this wild idea that he could open a gaming house in Vienna, but I was tired of forever travelling."

A hint of bitterness crept into her tone. "We never had a settled home. I used to watch how the worry and strain of it all made my mother ill. She died when I was twelve and Papa began to send me away to school. I suppose I was an inconvenience to him."

Nick let out a low whistle of surprise. "Don't tell me he was a rake as well as a gamester?"

She nodded, her disapproval obvious. A slight uneasiness possessed Lord Verlaine. Had she taken his warning seriously or had she imagined he was merely joking when he had told her of his own wild reputation?

"To be fair, I believe Papa was a faithful enough husband, but he maintained a string of mistresses after Maman's death," Athena continued, and Nick forced himself to concentrate. "Naturally, he was discreet, and Sherry said it was indelicate of me to take any notice, but I must admit I did resent them."

A frown creased her brow. "I have no wish to be introduced to any of Papa's light-skirts but I still think it is silly to have to pretend that I don't know that they exist just because I am unmarried."

"Society imposes some stupid rules," agreed Lord Verlaine, tactfully curbing his amusement at her frankness.

"Not that Papa let his personal life affect his choice of school for me. He took great care to select the best available. Once I even attended an expensive Bath seminary!"

"The apogee of any young lady's education, to be sure."

His dry comment brought a fleeting smile of appreciation to her lips but it vanished when she spoke again. "Of course, when his luck was bad, I'd be fetched back to his current lodgings until the next time there was any money to spare."

Nick thought it was a tribute to her intelligence that she had surmounted these difficulties but decided she would think he was bamming her if he told her so.

"Occasionally Papa hired a governess for me instead but Sherry was the only one who stayed for any length of time. Maman had employed her as my nurse when I was a baby and she always responded whenever Papa sent for her, even though he did not always pay her wages."

Athena's mouth twisted in a wry grimace.

"He is a very charming man, you see. People usually end up doing what he wants. He thought I would agree to his Viennese scheme but I resisted his persuasion. He was furious with me!" Her voice trailed away.

"So he went abroad and left you to your fate," Nick concluded for her and she nodded.

A strong desire to land the absent Mr. Delaney a facer began to possess Lord Verlaine and he could not prevent himself from saying hotly, "It was infamous of him to abandon you like that!"

"What else could he do? Debtors' prison beckoned! What's more, I am of age and he could hardly drag me on board ship by the hair." Athena flung out her hands in a telling gesture. "In fact, he delayed as long as he could in order to try and talk me into visiting my godmother if I would not go with him. It is hardly his fault that I did not wish to be beholden to her but at least he knew I would be safe with Sherry and he gave me most of the money he had salvaged, which he could ill spare."

A lock of raven hair tossed by the breeze strayed across her cheek and Athena brushed it impatiently aside.

"Most people think I am eccentric. I suppose you also consider me a fool to reject my godmother's aid in favour of this kind of life," she muttered, her fingers plucking nervously at her skirts.

"Not in the least!" Nick possessed himself of her restless hands and held them in a comforting grip.

Athena's strong affection for her wastrel of a father had touched Nick deeply. She hadn't blamed Delaney for the strange situation she found herself in but had made the best of it and come about by sheer hard work. Far from despising her, Nick's respect for her courage was increased by hearing her story. She presented a brave front to the world but now he knew that she was far more vulnerable than people supposed. Beneath her determination he sensed that she longed for security.

"Didn't we just agree that we are friends?" Nick gave her hands a slight squeeze. "And friends do not criticise each other, my dear Miss Delaney."

Unconsciously, Athena began to relax. Until he had spoken so warmly, she hadn't realised just how much she had been dreading seeing his expression freeze with scorn.

"Don't you have any other relatives you could turn to?" Nick asked, carefully releasing her after a moment.

Vaguely wishing he had not observed the proprieties, Athena shook her head. "Papa was an only child and most of Maman's family perished during the Terror. I believe there may be some cousins still living in the Loire but Papa lost contact with them years ago." She shrugged lightly. "Not that it signifies. I would not trouble strangers for help."

He was staring at her with a thoughtful frown on his handsome face.

"Come, sir, don't look so gloomy. I cannot think what possessed me to burden you with my tale of woe." She gave a rather artificial laugh. "Do forget my nonsense, I implore you."

"You ought to get married," he said abruptly, ignoring her attempt to change the subject.

A sudden flush of colour stained the skin over Athena's high cheek-bones.

"Now you sound like Sherry," she replied, oddly breathless. "She wants me to marry William Taylor."

Nick stared hard at her, a muscle flickering at the corner of his well-cut mouth. "Does she, by God?"

An imp of mischief prompted Athena to murmur, "It would be a suitable match, I suppose." She cast him an innocent glance. "He is a very respected man hereabouts."

"He is a pompous idiot!" Nick glared at her. The shaft of jealousy that tore through him was unbearable.

"William might be a little stiff-necked but you cannot accuse him of being stupid!"

Since Nick knew this protest to be justified he curbed a desire to curse, contenting himself by saying grimly, "Marry him and you'd be bored to tears within a week of the wedding."

"I *knew* you did not like him!" A peal of laughter escaped Athena but her merriment swiftly faded. "Oh, dear, I should not have teased you when you have been so very kind to me this morning. Please don't look so cross."

The tension in the pit of Lord Verlaine's stomach uncoiled. "Then you aren't serious about marrying him?"

"I have no wish to marry anyone! In my experience, matrimony does not bring happiness. I have never met a couple who were truly content with one another."

"My sister is happily married." Nick was surprised to hear himself defending an institution he had hitherto despised.

"Then she is a lucky woman," Athena retorted. "No doubt I am prejudiced, but it has always seemed to me that women lose their rights when they marry. They are expected to become mere shadows of their husbands, but I have grown to value my freedom while I have been in Parkgate. It is hard supporting oneself but at least I can make my own decisions. Marriage is too risky a business!"

Until a few weeks ago Lord Verlaine, a confirmed bachelor, would have had no hesitation in agreeing with this sensible statement. It was unsettling to realise that his sentiments were no longer so clear-cut.

"Then you don't believe in love?" he asked slowly.

"Love?" Athena's Celtic eyes blazed. "If you ask me that is a fairy-tale invented by men to dupe their victims into doing exactly as they wish. Our happy acquiescence is assured because we imagine ourselves cherished and adored whereas in reality we are nothing more than playthings to be ignored at will."

This spirited declaration made Lord Verlaine blink.

"You have a very poor opinion of my sex, ma'am," was all he could manage to utter.

The fact that she had nonplussed a gentleman renowned for his polished address seemed to afford Miss Delaney no satisfaction. She merely shrugged and avoided his gaze.

Staring hard at the ground and pretending an urge to crunch the fallen leaves beneath the heel of her crimson jean half-boot, Athena wondered what on earth had possessed her to make such an outrageous statement. In her heart of hearts she knew it wasn't true. Even if she had once thought very little of most of the men she had encountered, she was now painfully aware that it was possible to find a man who was neither boring nor a rogue. The proof sat beside her.

"Are you by any chance a devotee of Mrs. Mary Wollstonecraft?" Nick enquired, breaking the silence.

The realisation that her former beliefs had undergone a drastic change was so disturbing that Athena almost missed the point of this query.

"What? Oh, I see. Yes, I have read her book, *Vindication of the Rights of Women*, but I do not agree with all she says."

"Thank God for that!"

His wry expression brought the smile back to Athena's lips. "Nor, in case you are wondering, does my past contain an unhappy love-affair which has left me broken-hearted and embittered," she added lightly.

This solution had occurred to Lord Verlaine, but he was happy to see it demolished.

"I cannot even lay claim to a schoolgirl infatuation. Not one of the countless dancing-masters and music-teachers I encountered made the least dent in my heart," Athena continued in the same vein. "No doubt my nature must be cold."

Remembering her passionate response to his kiss, Nick raised his eyebrows in disbelief.

Possibly the same thought occurred to Miss Delaney, for she immediately hurried on, "In any event, I think Sherry is mistaken. I do not think William Taylor would wish to marry me. He is just a friend."

"There's more to it than that!"

Athena considered this remark. "I dare say you are right. We share the same interest in financial affairs but it is my travels on the Continent that intrigue him. He has never had the opportunity to go farther afield than London and he likes to hear me speak of foreign places."

Nick wondered if she was being wilfully blind. No doubt Taylor was flattered by her requests for advice and he was obviously impressed by her air of worldly sophistication but could she not see that the man was in love with her in his dry fashion?

It hadn't taken Nick above a few moments in the banker's company to realise this fact. That Athena herself was ignorant of the truth was astonishing and he could only conclude she had decided to regard Taylor as a friend and the notion was too firmly fixed in her mind to be shifted.

Pondering this revelation, Nick decided that his powers of perception regarding Miss Delaney must be heightened. She had intrigued him from the day that they had met and that initial attraction had swiftly deepened.

She fascinated him! Half worldly sophisticate, half vulnerable innocent, she was like no other woman he had ever met. She was intelligent and outspoken, and her desire for independence was almost as unusual as her methods of obtaining it. She was capable of discussing matters normally considered a male preserve and yet she remained none the less a most deliciously feminine creature.

She was an enigma! Most puzzling of all was her avowal that she wanted none of love. It's like waving a red flag at a bull, Nick thought ruefully. How could any man resist such a delicious challenge!

And yet...she trusted him! How could he abuse her faith in him by making love to her unless he was sure he meant it? And for the first time in his life he wasn't sure about anything at all except a certainty that he didn't want to hurt her.

You are a fool, Verlaine, Nick thought to himself sardonically, but, high ideals not withstanding, the urge to draw her into his embrace and kiss her non-sensical ideas into the oblivion they deserved was so strong that he had to exert every ounce of will-power to resist it.

Instead, he grasped the basket lying beside him and rose swiftly to his feet. "We shall both be stiff with rheumatism if we sit here an instant longer," he remarked easily as her surprised gaze flew to his face. "That wind's turned curst cold."

He stretched out his hand to assist Athena to her feet.

Taking it, Athena felt her safe, familiar world dissolve around her.

A moment ago he had held her hand to comfort her. His clasp had been steady. Now it trembled. She glanced up at him. He was pale beneath his tan and his eyes were glittering...

"Thank you," she murmured, hardly daring to breathe.

She had made no move to withdraw. Her lovely face was still upturned to his, her eyes smiling in shy invitation, the tender curve of her pink mouth only inches away...

Nick released her hand quickly. "Let's go and find this famous promenade of yours," he said, fighting temptation.

Athena swallowed her disappointment. "Of course."

ATHENA PLACED the hip-bath in front of the fire in her tiny bedroom, for the November evening was chilly. Filling it from a succession of brass cans of hot water, she added a liberal dash of jasmine essence.

It was two weeks since she had confided in Nick on that grassy bank in Drury Lane and although she had seen him on several occasions since they had never been private together. Luxuriating in the warm scented water, Athena's thoughts returned yet again to that day.

He wanted to kiss me, I know he did! And I wanted him to, she admitted to herself honestly. Why had he drawn back? Athena suspected that her own sharp tongue was to blame. After the way she had ruthlessly criticised the whole male sex, he probably thought she detested all men!

But Nick is different, she thought. He made every other man she knew seem insignificant. She enjoyed his company and valued the friendship which had grown between them, but there was more to it than that.

I am in love with him, she thought wonderingly, acknowledging the truth at last. A great tide of joy surged through her entire being as she allowed herself to drop her defences and admit it. How could she have not realised it before? She wanted to be with him, to share his hopes, his fears, his whole life.

The only question was whether Nick felt the same. That he desired her she did not doubt. She had seen it in his eyes, but was that all he wanted from her? She didn't know. Desire is not the same thing as love, Athena told herself sternly, but she couldn't prevent her heartbeat from quickening as she completed her preparations for the ball.

Barton Grange was brilliantly lit as Athena and Sherry stepped down from the gig loaned to them for the evening by Tom.

"You will find refreshments in the kitchens, Jethro," Athena informed him and he nodded happily.

Several damsels not blest with her looks sighed enviously as Athena appeared. Her ravishing gown of white tulle shrieked of Paris while her black curls were dressed *à la Sappho* and the glow in her eyes outshone the pretty little sapphire pendant that encircled her slim white neck.

"Damme if I've ever seen you in such looks!" her host exclaimed as she made her curtsy, and only the reproving frown of his cousin checked George's continuing flight of admiration. Recalling decorum, he introduced Athena to Mrs. Emily Brockenhurst.

After a moment they passed on into the ballroom George's grandfather had built in the East Wing to please his wife. Athena searched eagerly for Lord Verlaine but there was no sign of him. Reluctantly she allowed her dance-card to be filled, carefully saving the dance before the supper-interval.

She was taking part in a cotillion when her partner, a local farmer who was one of her most devoted admirers, said gruffly, "Do you know that fellow over there, Miss Delaney? He is staring at you."

Athena turned and saw Nick leaning against a column watching her with a slight smile on his handsome face.

"Damned—I mean, dashed rude to stare like that! Shall I call him to account?"

There was a note of uncertainty in her young swain's voice, as if he suspected the task might prove beyond him. Athena, dragging her attention from the splendid figure Lord Verlaine cut in his impeccable evening-clothes, politely pretended not to notice, saying only, "Indeed, you must not, Mr. Briscoe. That gentleman is a friend of mine."

"Oh, well, in that case!" Relief brightened her partner's expression. There was something faintly dangerous-looking about the big, tall man with the black hair. Secretly wishing that his coat sat so superbly across his shoulders and that he had the knack of tying his neckcloth so elegantly, Mr. Briscoe risked no further objection when Athena desired him to escort her to Lord Verlaine after the dance ended.

"Breaking all the local hearts, I see," Nick remarked with an amused look after the departing Mr. Briscoe's stiff back.

"He thinks my choice undeserving," Athena said severely, to hide the giddy pleasure his nearness aroused in her.

"How can I help staring when you look so lovely?"

Athena blushed. This simple compliment pleased her far more than Sir George's effusions, which she strongly suspected to be inspired by the bottle.

"George is a trifle flown," Nick remarked, confirming her theory when she mentioned that the baronet did not seem his usual self. "The relief of everything turning out as planned, I expect."

Athena chuckled. "It does look striking."

Sir George's fancy had led him to have the ballroom draped in swags of patriotic red, white and blue silk and decorated with masses of hothouse flowers all in the same hues.

The sets began to form for the next dance and out of the corner of his eye Nick saw Athena's partner approaching.

"No doubt I am too late but will you dance with me?" he said quickly.

Athena pretended to consult her card. "You may have the waltz before supper."

"I shall look forward to it," Nick replied with a great deal of truth.

Athena was talking to William Taylor when the musicians Sir George had hired struck up for the waltz, but she broke off her conversation in mid-sentence as she watched Nick come towards them, her pulses quickening.

The sight of his lordship did not afford Mr. Taylor the same gratification.

"I wish you would reconsider, my dear. The waltz is still frowned upon by older persons as improper—"

"Fiddlesticks!" Athena interrupted briskly. "I have danced it in the best houses in Europe."

"Not with Verlaine as your partner," William continued heavily. "His reputation is none so sweet. You cannot wish people to think you favour him. They will say you are fast."

Athena's eyes flashed dangerously. "Thank you for your concern, William, but I believe it misplaced on this occasion. My credit will surely survive one dance with his lordship."

He sighed. "If you are set on waltzing, won't you accept me as your partner instead?"

"But I have already taken part in a quadrille with you and two dances would occasion the kind of gossip you seem so anxious for me to avoid," Athena retorted.

Since this was undeniable, William was at a loss.

"'Servant, Taylor," said Lord Verlaine, reaching them. He bowed elegantly to Athena. "Miss Delaney. I believe this is my dance."

There was a hint of amusement in Nick's greeting, for he had discerned the banker's annoyance and guessed its cause. "Have I cut you out, sir? Never mind, better luck next time."

For an instant it looked as if William would forget his inherent caution and give vent to his injured feelings, before he shook his head and said coldly, "It pleases you to jest, my lord, but my friendship with Miss Delaney does not rest upon such trivialities."

"Excuse us, the dance is starting," Athena intervened, laying her gloved hand upon Lord Verlaine's arm.

Nick led her out on to the floor and Athena immediately forgot about William's absurd homily. Nick's arm clasped her lightly to him and she surrendered to bliss as he whirled her round in perfect time to the music.

Their steps matched as if they had danced together a thousand times. "You dance divinely," Nick murmured in her ear. "You are as light as a fairy."

Breathlessly, Athena laughed. "What nonsense, sir!" She felt as if she had been drinking vast quantities of champagne instead of just one glass.

Looking up into his face, she saw that he was smiling at her with such an expression of warmth that her heart thundered against her ribs.

His arm tightened around her waist. "You know what I would like to do now?"

"Dare I ask?" she murmured irrepressibly.

He grinned. "Well, of course I would like to kiss you, but not here! No, I'd like to take you to see George's lake. There is a beautiful moon. Wouldn't you like to escape from this crowd, sweetheart?"

Athena was sorely tempted by this improper suggestion.

"I cannot think Sherry would approve," she said with a little catch of longing in her voice.

"You think me incapable of turning her up sweet?" Nick enquired with a wicked chuckle.

"I'm sure you could!" Athena shook her head reprovingly at him. "You must know you are a favourite with her in spite of your—" She broke off abruptly.

"In spite of my disgraceful reputation," he finished for her, the smile vanishing from his face.

Athena coloured, wishing she had not allowed her tongue to run away with her.

Silence descended and while Athena was desperately casting around for some means of letting him know that there was nothing she would like better than to be alone with him in the moonlight Nick was thinking hard.

He was not accustomed to putting the needs of others before his own desires. Generously indulging any mistress to the top of her bent, he'd dismissed them the instant he tired of their company. It hadn't occurred to him until now that his behaviour had been self-centred but as he gazed down into Miss Delaney's flower-like countenance he knew that he didn't want to hazard any romp which would risk her reputation.

"Forgive me, I should not have suggested such a thing. It would do you no good to be seen with me in such improper circumstances."

His rueful apology tore Athena's remaining composure to shreds. "Oh, don't, Nick! I don't care what people might say; I want to be with you!"

The moment this impetuous confession left her lips Athena blushed, realising how forward she must sound.

"That's the first time you've used my name," Nick said, tactfully pretending he hadn't heard the rest of her speech.

"Ah, but you called me sweetheart," Athena pointed out lightly, recovering her poise by sheer willpower.

"So I did," Nick agreed and they both burst out laughing.

Across the room William Taylor watched them, his expression blank. He did not hear his name being spoken until it was repeated a second time.

"George." He turned reluctantly to greet the speaker.

"Hope you are enjoying my little party."

"Of course," William said politely, but he couldn't prevent his gaze from returning to the couple leaving the floor.

"You've met Verlaine? One of my oldest friends. Known him even longer than I've known you." Sir George grinned jovially at the banker.

William forced a smile. They had been neighbours for many years.

"They make a handsome couple, don't they?" George chuckled. "If I didn't know better, I might think Nick in danger of marching to the altar before he was much older."

William's attention was caught.

"My dear George, whatever can you mean?" he asked smoothly, scenting a mystery that might, with any luck, discredit his rival.

George coughed and looked sheepish. "Don't think I ought to say," he muttered.

William chuckled. "Oh, come now, surely you can tell me!"

Foggily George considered this request and concluded that there was no harm in sharing their little joke with another man of the world.

Meanwhile, Nick had taken Athena in to supper. She was far too excited to eat but sat happily sipping the champagne he had procured for her.

She had eyes for no one else. It was as if they were wrapped around by an enchanted bubble which excluded the rest of the world.

"I suppose we had better return to the ballroom," she sighed when the informal meal was over.

"Your next partner will be waiting," Nick agreed.

"I know," Athena nodded dolefully.

"In fact, your dance-card is crowded," he added, trying to ignore the hammer of his pulse.

Casting him a mischievous glance, Athena impulsively tore the little card in two.

"There, now I am free!" she laughed.

"Then I suggest we find a quiet spot to enjoy our freedom before we are besieged by a host of your angry admirers." Nick's tone was light, giving no hint of the fierce emotions raging in him. His desire to be alone with her was so strong that it robbed him of his good intentions and he forgot that he had resolved not to jeopardise her reputation.

Without knowing quite how he accomplished it so neatly, Athena found herself swiftly whisked through the crowd. A maze of corridors led them to a small parlour, dimly lit by a few candles and a banked-down fire in the hearth.

"It is probably too cold to view the lake now but I think we should be safe from interruption here," Nick announced.

Athena's hand abruptly released his arm and, looking down at her, Nick saw that she had turned pale.

"What's the matter, sweetheart?"

The silence was intense and Athena thought he must hear the thudding of her heart.

"Perhaps we should not have...that is..." She hardly knew how to frame her sudden unease. Until they had reached this lonely room their escape had seemed a game but their solitude abruptly brought home to her the gross impropriety of her conduct.

Lord Verlaine raised his brows. "I see, you have had second thoughts."

Athena hung her head. What must he think of her?

"Don't worry, I shall return you to Sherry if that is what you wish. But I wasn't planning to seduce you on the hearthrug, you know," he reassured her in a tight voice.

The frightened mist cleared from Athena's brain. "Oh, Nick, I'm sorry for being so missish! I did not mean to imply that you would behave in an ungentlemanly way."

Her frank admission wiped the frown from his face.

"It is my fault; I should not have encouraged you," she continued dolefully.

"I'm all for such delightful encouragement," he murmured with a little chuckle. "Oh, sweetheart, if we are to indulge in confessions, then I must admit I hoped for this,'' he went on, taking her in his arms.

Miss Delaney made no move to pull away.

"And this," he added softly, bending his head to hers.

His lips were warm and gently persuasive, coaxing a response until Athena forgot her fears and kissed him back, her mouth parting beneath his as their embrace became more passionate.

Desire coursed through Athena's veins and her arms came up to lock themselves behind his neck, one slim hand burying itself in the thick hair that clustered on his nape. Eagerly, she obeyed the prompting of her dazzled senses and pressed herself against the lean length of him.

Nick stifled a groan. He wanted her very much but she wasn't one of his practised flirts. For all her abandoned surrender, he was aware of her innocence, and he wasn't so steeped in dissipation that he would take advantage of it.

"Sweetheart, we had better go." Reluctantly he disengaged her clinging arms and stepped back.

Athena's gaze was cloudy with passion as she stared up at him in bewilderment. "Go?" she echoed blankly.

"If we linger here any longer, I'm afraid you'll make a liar of me," he said gruffly.

Comprehension dawned on Athena and she blushed, looking so adorably confused that he instantly exclaimed, "Oh, my darling girl!" and drew her back into the circle of his arms.

When at last he lifted his dark head again Lord Verlaine said thickly, "Now we really must return before they send out search-parties to look for you."

Athena giggled at the wry expression he pulled. "Let them," she murmured happily, as she laid her head against his shoulder with a voluptuous sigh of content.

"Minx!" Nick brushed his lips against the dark cloud of her hair. "If we are to avoid gossip, I had best give you a wide berth for the rest of this evening but may I call upon you in the morning? There is something I must tell you."

Athena quickly tilted her face up to his. Suddenly she thought she knew what it was that he wanted to say and elation made her smile even more bewitching as she replied, "Of course you may."

THE SOUND OF breaking crockery assaulted Lord Verlaine's ears as he handed over his horse into Jethro's enthusiastic care a little before noon the next day. The noise was even louder when he stepped inside the Peacock and to add to his surprise he saw William Taylor descending the stairs.

The banker was looking a trifle pale but his expression became triumphant when he noticed Nick. "Good morning, my lord."

"What the devil is going on?" Impatiently Nick ignored this greeting.

"You must discover that for yourself, sir."

It puzzled Nick why the banker should sound so smug, but he had no time to waste on the fellow and with a murmured farewell took the stairs several at a time.

As he had suspected, the noise was coming from Athena's private parlour. He rapped on the door smartly and walked in.

"Oh, it's you!" Miss Delaney ejaculated in accents of loathing. A vase was in her hand and to Nick's astonishment she hurled it at his head.

Thanks to his swift reactions the ornament did not strike him but smashed against the wall. Surveying the fragments Nick exclaimed, "Good God, Athena, have you run mad?"

This demand did nothing to soothe Miss Delaney's outrage. Her bosom heaved beneath its covering of jonquil muslin as she spat at him, "Get out, you...you snake!"

Understandably bewildered, Lord Verlaine stared at her. "Did Taylor say something to upset you?"

"William?" Athena emitted an unladylike snort. "I might have known you would try to pin the blame on William when all he did was tell me the truth."

A sinking sensation assailed Nick's stomach.

"The truth?" he murmured weakly.

"Oh, stop pretending! George told William all about your odious wager."

"Ah! Actually, I was going to tell you about it myself," he began, but she flung out a warning hand to silence him.

"Don't! There is no point in spinning me any more of your lies. Oh, how could I have been such a fool?" Tears of humiliation sparkled in Athena's eyes. She had behaved like a wanton hussy and now she was paying for it.

"Sweetheart, I know it looks bad, but believe me it isn't quite how it seems." Nick took a step towards her, holding out his hands, but she backed away, a look of disgust on her face.

"Is there nothing you will not stoop to?" she exclaimed bitterly, wondering how she could have really believed that he cared for her when all the while he had been skilfully playing on her emotions to satisfy his own vanity. "How can you pretend that you give a straw for my feelings when thanks to you I am made an object of mockery for the whole town to laugh at?"

"If that is what Taylor told you then he is a damned liar!" Nick exclaimed heatedly. "My wager with George was a private one. I don't know how Taylor managed to persuade George to speak of it but I can assure you that I have never done so."

Athena took a deep breath, trying in vain to compose herself. Did he expect her to be grateful for this forbearance?

"Listen to me." Nick grasped her hands, ignoring her squeak of outrage. "I should never have agreed to that idiotic wager. It was only a jest—"

"A jest!" Athena interrupted, her eyes blazing with fresh fury. "You may think it amusing—I do not!"

Nick winced, cursing his unfortunate choice of words. God, he was handling this badly! Desperately he tried again. "I only agreed out of pique. You seemed so indifferent that I wanted to teach you a lesson but I swear to you that I had forgotten my original motives long before the first week of our acquaintance was out."

Athena tugged her hands free. "I don't believe you," she said flatly.

Anger began to stir in his lordship.

"Good God, girl, if I had intended to seduce you do you think I would have missed last night's opportunity?"

The angry flush faded from Miss Delaney's cheeks and, seeing how she trembled, Nick regretted his blunt remark. "Oh, damn!" he muttered. "I should not have said that."

Athena bit her lower lip. "There are very many things you should not have said to me, my lord," she declared unsteadily.

She could have forgiven him the wager. Men possessed such odious habits, as she knew only too well, but he had done more than exercise his charm. He had pretended to be her friend and, remembering how she had confided in him, she wanted to weep.

"I should have told you earlier but I knew you would be angry so I delayed." Nick smiled at her ruefully. "Now Taylor has beat me to it and I am well served for my cowardice but I give you my word of honour that I never meant to hurt you."

Athena stared at him. He looked so earnest that for an instant she was almost tempted to believe him but then she shook her head. She had made the mistake of trusting him once already and it had brought her only heartbreak.

"Your word of honour is worthless. Men of your stamp will say anything to achieve their aims," she stated coldly, concealing her despair. "Your apology is as false as your friendship and I want none of it. Now please go; there is nothing more to be said."

"There you are mistaken, you little termagant!"

Nick seized her by the shoulders and shook her roughly. "By God, how dare you accuse me of trifling with you when I came here this morning intending to apologise? I was even going to ask you to marry me!"

Since it was this romantic expectation that had sent Miss Delaney off to bed on a cloud of blissful hope, her reaction was all the more fierce. "Oh, how dare you make a mock of me?" she gasped, struggling to free herself.

Guessing her intention was to box his ears, Lord Verlaine kept a tight hold on her and ploughed on.

"Perhaps I should not have spoken just yet but I assure you my sentiments are sincere. I would consider it a great honour if you would accept my hand in marriage."

It never occurred to Athena that he might be feeling so shaken that his customary address had deserted him, leaving him as self-conscious as a callow youth. She had never seen him lose mastery over himself and thought his exaggerated formality was just another mocking jest.

If she had been pale before, it was as nothing compared to the deathly pallor that now robbed her of every last vestige of colour. For an instant Nick was worried that she might swoon before she recovered her breath enough to speak.

"You must think me very green not to know that you are laughing at me—"

"Laughing at you!" exclaimed his lordship, thunderstruck. "You little idiot, I love you!"

"How very obliging of you, but I fear I cannot return your affection, sir," Athena retorted bitingly.

Her sarcasm made Nick flinch and release her as if he had been burnt. "My God, you really believe that I asked you just to insult you," he said slowly.

"I believe that you are a rake and the sort of man I despise," Athena declared in a shaking voice. "I doubt if you even know the meaning of the word love. It is merely that you are not used to being rebuffed and you are so piqued that you are willing to go to any lengths to avoid being bested."

"If that is what you truly think then I see it is useless for me to seek to persuade you otherwise," Nick said stiffly.

"Just go," said Athena tragically, her last lingering hope that he would deny her accusations fading. Oh, why hadn't he sought harder to convince her of his feelings? Surely he would have at least tried to kiss her if he really loved her, instead of standing there like a statue?

"Gladly, ma'am." Lord Verlaine executed a graceful bow, and, turning on his heel, left the room.

His departure, far from pleasing her, prompted Miss Delaney to burst into tears, the first she had shed since she was twelve years old.

CHAPTER FOUR

"MY DEAR, won't you come and sit by the fire? These February evenings can be so treacherous and I do not want you to catch a chill after your long journey. There now, are you quite comfortable?" Lady Fitzpatrick beamed upon her guest and rattled on without giving Athena time to answer. "I hope you found your room to your satisfaction. My daughter Cathleen helped me choose the curtains for it, you know. The ones we found hanging were so shabby, a fault, I'm afraid, of hired houses. Not that I expected such a thing in Cavendish Square, which I was told was a superior address."

She paused for a moment to hand Athena a cup of tea.

"I have told them to take a tray up to Miss Sherrington. The poor woman looked quite done in! Unlike my son, who rushed off to Tattersall's the minute we arrived from Ireland!" She laughed merrily. "You shall meet them both at dinner, my dear. Cathleen was wild with excitement when she heard you were coming to pay us a visit but unfortunately she was promised to Lady Hetherbridge this afternoon and could not stay to greet you."

"I am looking forward to meeting your children, ma'am," Athena murmured, feeling somewhat dazed by this flood of information.

Her godmother beamed upon her and immediately launched into a eulogy concerning her offspring, giving Athena time to take discreet stock of her surroundings.

The drawing-room in which they sat was elegant. Furnished in the latest style, the walls were hung in pale green silk, which served as an admirable foil for her hostess's auburn hair.

Lady Fitzpatrick's appearance was, in fact, much as Athena had imagined from her father's description. She was a dashing widow in her early forties; her figure had lost its youthful slenderness but her face still retained charm. What did surprise Athena was her propensity to worldly chatter. Listening to the rambling monologue, she decided that her godmother was kind but rather shallow.

"To think that the last time I saw you was at your christening, my dear. You have grown into a beauty like your mama." Lady Fitzpatrick sighed sentimentally. "I was so pleased when Miss Sherrington wrote to me."

Athena bit her lip, wondering how to answer her.

Prompted by the grey despair which had engulfed her young friend since Lord Verlaine's departure for his hunting-box near Grantham, Sherry had eventually written to Lady Fitzpatrick without Athena's knowledge. When the answering letter had come at the end of January bearing an invitation to visit her godmother, now residing in Cavendish Square, Athena had been angry and refused to go.

"Why not, might I ask?" Sherry had demanded. "There is nothing to keep us here and a change of scene could only benefit your spirits."

Knowing that she had been poor company in spite of all her efforts to hide her misery, Athena took refuge in saying that Tom needed them, but Sherry quickly dismissed this excuse.

"Now that the festive season is over Tom can manage very well on his own. Your godmother has written a very pretty letter, pointing out it is time you renewed your acquaintance with her, and since she is over here to give her family a taste of London life it will be no trouble to include you in her plans. Now, are you going to take advantage of her offer, which as you very well know was what your papa intended for you, or are you going to sit here nursing a broken heart forever?'' she had added craftily.

This spurred Athena to action as she had hoped it might and before she could change her mind Sherry had booked places for them on the stage from Chester. To travel post was a luxury they could not afford and any objections Athena might have had were swiftly dispelled by William Taylor's protests when he arrived on his customary weekly visit.

"My dear Athena, you cannot travel on the common stage!'' he stated, wagging one finger at her as if she were a wayward child. "If you must go to London, and I own it sounds an excellent scheme, though I shall miss you sorely, then let me arrange a post-chaise for you.''

She stared at him and shook her head. "I cannot allow you to frank me, William.''

"It would give me the greatest pleasure, but it won't be necessary.'' He smiled at her. "You see, I have something very important to tell you.''

Unease stirred in Athena. For almost a year she had persisted in thinking him merely a friend but lately it had been borne in on her that she was mistaken. Sherry had always prophesied he would make her an offer and even Nick had insisted that William was in love with her.

She bit her lip at the memory, unable to bear thinking about his lordship. His perfidy had wrecked their golden autumn idyll but she missed him more than she had dreamt it was possible to miss anyone, and his absence had reduced her existence to a grey waste-land.

Slowly she became aware that William was still speaking.

"I beg your pardon; what did you say about the Vale of Clwyd mine?"

William laughed heartily. "Ah, my dear, I'm not surprised that you are wool-gathering at the thought of such riches coming your way."

Urgently she requested him to repeat his explanation and then to his astonishment she burst out laughing.

"An income of eight thousand a year, you say? That makes me as rich as an heiress!" she choked, her mirth becoming slightly hysterical.

"My dear, shall I procure you a glass of hartshorn and water?" William asked uneasily, wishing that Miss Sherrington was not out marketing.

Athena coughed and forced down her unseemly amusement. "I'm sorry, William. It was a shock, you see."

"Well, it is rare that I can give a client such excellent news," he conceded with as much satisfaction as if he had suggested the investment in Davis's mine, rather than opposed it. "Now all that remains for us to do is decide how to re-invest this windfall. Of course there is no need for you to economise on travelling to London and no doubt you will wish to buy a few new gowns when you are there, but you must put the rest of the money to work. I'm sure you will be guided by my advice this time for such a wonderful stroke of luck is not likely to befall you again."

His complacency caused Athena to lift her brows a little. Rather angrily she remembered that it was his interference that had provoked the disastrous quarrel with Nick. William intended nothing but good but his attitude rankled.

"You must not make it a habit to try and run my life for me, William," she said coolly.

"Ah, but I hope that you will give me permission to do so in the near future, my dear."

To Athena's dismay he then proceeded to go down on one knee and launch into an elaborate marriage proposal.

"Pray do get up," she begged him. "I am very obliged to you, but really we should not suit."

William threw her an indignant look, since he hadn't finished. His feelings were further lacerated when she continued to refuse his gracious offer. It had never occurred to him that she might do so and he was deeply offended.

"I declare, Athena, if you think this money will bring suitors flocking then you are a fool," he said heatedly. "Your odd behaviour in Parkgate must offend any gentleman of quality."

"Really?" Athena's feeling of guilt vanished. "Then I wonder why you bothered to ask me to marry you, William." She gave him a long cool look. "I assume it is because my company has become a habit with you, since I do not wish to insult you by supposing it is my windfall that made me suddenly acceptable."

He had the grace to colour, for, in fact, it was the success of her investment that had tipped the scales. He was very fond of her but it was not part of his plans to marry a penniless girl.

"My affection is genuine," he began to protest, but Athena flung up her hand to cut him off.

"I do not doubt you think so, but it would not survive the rigours of marriage, sir. My taste for independence would drive you wild!" She did not add that he would soon bore her to distraction, but smiled at him sympathetically. "Come, please do not spoil our friendship. Let us at least part on a civilised note and then perhaps when next we meet we can pretend this never happened."

Reluctantly he had accepted this olive-branch, but, remembering that awkward scene as she listened to her godmother outlining the list of sights she intended to show her, Athena restrained a sigh.

She had come to London to please Sherry and because she couldn't think of anything else to do in spite of acquiring all that money. William's proposal had brought home how silly she had been to think that happiness depended on being secure from poverty. She had achieved the fortune she had set out to win but she had never been more miserable in her life!

No, happiness couldn't be found in material things. It didn't even depend on marrying a safe, solid man as she had once imagined it might. William was both those things but she had turned down the settled home he offered.

I don't want security, she admitted to herself sadly, I want Nick! It doesn't matter that he is a rake; he is the only man for me because I love him and that's more important than anything else!

"My dear, is there something wrong?" Her goddaughter's continuing silence at last penetrated Lady Fitzpatrick's self-absorption.

"Only that I am more of my father's daughter than I thought," Athena murmured ruefully, coming to the depressing conclusion that she should have been more careful in what she wished for. A kind fairy had granted her longing for security but it had proved to be Dead Sea fruit! The only eligible husband for her was a rake, but, unfortunately, she had learnt this lesson too late!

ATHENA AND CATHLEEN were sitting looking at the latest fashion magazines when Connor Fitzpatrick came bounding into the morning-room, a wide grin on his freckled face.

"I say, Athena, what's this I hear about you setting up as a London innkeeper? Mama's as mad as fire!"

"Do try for a little more conduct, Connor!" his sister scolded, making a hasty dive to rescue her property as he plumped down on to the sofa next to her. "You know you should not ask embarrassing questions."

Athena hid a smile. Connor reminded her of an overgrown puppy, sweet-natured but decidedly clumsy.

"Don't worry, Cathleen, I'm not offended," she said. "Nor am I ashamed of my plans. I intend to buy a small tavern called the White Bear in Bloomsbury. It is quite respectable and I have hopes of turning it into a hotel for visitors to London who cannot afford more fashionable hostelries. In fact, the agent handling the sale assures me that my idea is just what the area needs."

Two identical pairs of hazel eyes stared at her in amazement before Cathleen exclaimed, "But Athena, no one will ever receive you again if you dare do such a thing!"

Athena laughed. "So your mama told me! She was nearly as vehement on the subject as Sherry, but really I don't care a fig."

Connor let out a whistle of approval. He wished he dared scorn Society's opinion but there was still another year of his minority to go and his mother controlled the purse-strings. "Well, I think it is a bang-up scheme," he announced. "Much more fun than hanging around drawing-rooms doing the pretty to a parcel of old dowagers!"

"Oh, how can you say so?" Cathleen rounded on him with a reproachful frown.

Just turned eighteen, she was enjoying her first taste of fashionable life and could not understand why anyone failed to find the whirl of parties, concerts, balls, plays and other similar amusements utterly enthralling.

Athena smiled at her. She was a pretty damsel, petite and slightly plump with her mother's auburn hair and pale skin, thankfully free of the freckles that afflicted her brother.

"You forget that such entertainments are not new to me, Cathleen. To please your mama and Sherry I have attended every function they suggested this last month or so but I have no taste to continue. Spring is upon us and it is high time I set up my own establishment."

Recently, while the other ladies in the household rested to recruit their energies for the evening entertainments ahead, Athena had spent several afternoons being shown around likely inns by eager property-agents. The task had been more daunting than she was prepared to admit but she was determined to stick to her plans.

Spring had arrived and the blooming new growth all around her was a poignant reminder that life was slipping pointlessly by. Perhaps if she could keep busy to the point of exhaustion—and surely running a hotel would tax all her energies—she would not have time to feel so unhappy. In all the hustle and bustle she might be able to forget the man she loved and if she could not then at least it ought to help ease her ever present sense of desolation.

The idea of returning to Parkgate was one she could not bear to contemplate. Every inch was imbued with memories of Nick and she knew that it would be hopeless to think she could escape her unhappiness there. London offered her the best chance of making a fresh start on her own terms. It was going to be very expensive but the money from Gareth Davis's copper mine would enable her to ignore what the *ton* might say.

Money was the subject also exercising young Mr. Fitzpatrick's mind as he listened to his sister pelting Athena with questions about the White Bear. Uneas-

ily, he thought of the multitude of unpaid bills se-
creted in the top drawer of his dressing-table. He had
been convinced of his luck on the turf but his losses
had been heavy and when added to the sums he had
spent playing billiards at the Royal Saloon or drinking at the Daffy Club the amount was worrying.

Every penny of the generous allowance his mother
had made him on their arrival in London had been
spent. But, fortunately, only that very morning a
friend of his, Mr. Barnabas Crutchley, had given him
the name and direction of one of the more honest
money-lenders. The slip of paper was in his pocket and
he fingered it gratefully while forcing himself to pay
attention to the conversation.

"Your grand announcement has thrown my little
snippet of news into the shade," Cathleen was saying
plaintively.

She dimpled happily as Athena obligingly asked her
what she meant. "Well, you see, I met an acquaintance of yours last night at the opera. He asked after
you most particularly! Mama said it was a pity that
you had not elected to come with us for it seems he is
a very eligible gentleman. And a very handsome one
too!"

A languishing sigh accompanied this last remark
and the blood ran cold down Athena's spine. "His
name?" she snapped in a tone that caused Cathleen's
eyes to open very wide.

"Lord ... Lord Verlaine," she stammered.

The beat of her pulse thundered in Athena's ears.
Her throat was suddenly too dry for her to speak and
she was grateful when Connor broke the silence.

"Verlaine?" He cocked his red head on one side in
thought. "Tall, big-shouldered fellow with black
hair?"

Cathleen affirmed it.

"Saw him t'other day at Jackson's. You know, the
boxing school in Bond Street." Connor tried to look

suitably casual, although he had been honoured by a word of praise from the great man himself after his bout with one of the ex-champion's assistants. "Barney told me his name. Appears he's been in Devon, just inherited a fortune there. Some great-uncle stuck his spoon in the wall and left him everything. Lucky devil!" Connor sighed enviously.

Athena struggled to retain her composure. Nick had never mentioned a word of this possibility to her. In fact, now she came to think of it, he had never spoken of his own financial circumstances. She had assumed he lived on the edge of insolvency like so many retired army officers with expensive tastes and tactfully avoided any questions that might have embarrassed him.

"Mama has invited him to dine with us on Saturday evening," Cathleen announced.

Athena leapt to her feet. "Excuse me, I have something I must do."

Connor and Cathleen stared in amazement as she rushed from the room. They would have been equally surprised if they could have overheard her conversation an hour later with the property-agent to whom she had fled.

"This is absurd, sir. I come here willing to meet your client's price and now you tell me that a new buyer is bidding against me."

Mr. Brown met her angry gaze apologetically. "I'm sorry, Miss Delaney, but business is business and Lord Verlaine has offered a higher—"

"Verlaine! Did you say Verlaine?" Athena exploded.

She left the agent's office in a rage. Too angry to return to Cavendish Square, she tried to walk off the worst of her fury in the Green Park, but all she could think of was Nick's despicable treachery.

He must have heard of her scheme from Lady Fitzpatrick, who was an incurable rattle. No doubt he had pretended concern, as an old friend of Athena's, and she had poured out her woes into his willing ears. Not that it really mattered how he found out; it was his spiteful interference that was so devastating.

He must be doing it for revenge! I wounded his pride and now he is extracting payment, Athena thought miserably. He must really hate me.

The idea hurt so much that she could hardly bear it but pride came to her rescue. The devil if she would sit tamely by and let him worst her! She was going to buy the White Bear if it killed her!

Where am I going to raise the extra money to outbid him at such short notice? she pondered, turning her footsteps for home.

This question was still vexing her when she descended to the dining-room and it robbed her of any appetite for her luncheon. Luckily, Lady Fitzpatrick did not notice in her concern for Connor, who also picked uninterestedly at his food, contrary to his usual custom.

"I'm all right, Mama," he answered, brushing aside her enquiries.

They were leaving the table when he asked Athena in a whisper if he might have a word. Correctly interpreting that he wished the assignation to be kept secret, she nodded silently and went upstairs to wait for him in her room. A few moments later he tapped quietly on the door.

"Hate to bother you like this, Athena, but I don't suppose you could see your way to lending me a little blunt, could you?"

The notion of borrowing off his mama's rich guest had suddenly struck him during luncheon, but, meeting Athena's astonished gaze, Connor blushed.

"Sorry. Stupid idea," he muttered, preparing to slide out of the room.

"Wait! Are you in debt, Connor?"

"Can't discuss it with a lady," he protested, but Athena responded with such sympathy that he found himself telling her all about it.

"Don't look so worried. You aren't the first young man to have gone wild when set loose on the town and I dare say you won't be the last."

"No," Connor replied heavily. "But if you can't lend me the ready then it'll have to be the money-lenders for I cannot face Mama." He pulled out the scrap of paper from his pocket and handed it to her.

Athena's delicate brows rose.

"I think I had better keep this," she murmured, trying to quell the sudden thudding of her heart. "You won't need it. I shall settle your debts for you if you will but be patient."

Connor's expressions of gratitude were prolonged but at last Athena managed to get rid of him.

She stared at the paper in her hand. Here was the solution to her dilemma if only she had the courage to take it. Papa had always decried the cent-per-cent bloodsuckers but her case was different. She *did* have money but not immediately to hand!

The image of Nick's darkly handsome face rose to taunt her and Athena's lovely mouth thinned. Mr. Mendoza it was. She would not be beaten!

ATHENA DRESSED for dinner on Saturday evening as if for war. Her skilfully arranged locks, the clinging sapphire silk dress, her alluring perfume were her armour. Nick Verlaine was the man competing against her and she was determined to show no weakness.

The first sight of his tall figure clad in his dark evening-clothes melted her resolve. Involuntarily, she moved towards him, her lovely smile lighting up her face. "Nick!"

"Miss Delaney." His voice was as cool as his bow.

Athena felt as if he had slapped her and her dismay increased when he turned to greet Cathleen with one of his engaging smiles.

Her godmother had arranged the table so that they were seated next to one another but Nick took no advantage of this privilege. Without being openly discourteous, he made it clear that he had no interest in her.

Despair destroyed what little remained of Athena's appetite. She toyed with her food, praying that the evening would come to an end.

Lady Fitzpatrick had arranged a visit to the Argyll Rooms to entertain her guests, but when the time came to leave Athena cried off, pleading a headache.

I cannot endure another minute of this torture, she thought, while assuring her godmother that she would be perfectly well again if she had a good night's sleep.

Athena was horribly conscious of Nick's eyes watching her. Did he know she was shamming it? Perhaps, but it hardly seemed to matter. Her last hope that their quarrel might be mended if only they could meet once more had been destroyed this evening.

"He doesn't love me any longer," she whispered to herself as she made her way to her room.

The words echoed in her head as the maid she shared with Cathleen helped her undress and get ready for bed. She couldn't seem to think of anything else. It was as if she was moving in a fog of numbness. Nothing seemed quite real.

"Goodnight, miss."

The maid left the room and Athena picked up the book that lay on her bedside table, knowing that she could not settle to sleep. As she opened it a piece of paper fluttered out.

It was the address Connor had given her, which she had placed there for safety. Staring at it, Athena remembered her vow, and a spark of anger pierced her despair. Deliberately, she let it rekindle into flame, welcoming the rush of fury which blotted out the pain of Nick's rejection.

Athena flung back her bedclothes. Selecting a plain round gown, she began to get dressed again, her expression grim.

So, his lordship thought he could wreck her plans and then just dismiss her, did he? Well, she would teach him that he was wrong!

"WHAT DO YOU MEAN, man? Where can she have gone at this hour? It is nearly eleven."

The young footman stared nervously at Lord Verlaine.

"I can't rightly say, sir," he mumbled. "Miss Delaney just asked me to call a hackney and said I was to give this note to milady if they returned before she got back."

"Give me that note," Nick demanded.

"Sir! It's addressed to Lady Fitzpatrick," the footman protested unhappily.

"Damn you for a fool, do you think her ladyship will object?" Nick growled, holding on to his temper by sheer effort. "I shall take any blame but I must know where Miss Delaney has gone if I am to go after her. God knows what harm she might come to!"

Since the footman privately agreed it was shocking for a young lady, especially such a pretty young lady, to disappear into the night, he decided to obey his lordship's imperious request.

Scanning the single sheet, Nick let out a groan of incredulity. An alley off Tavistock Street! He restrained the impulse to tear at his black locks and confined himself to a few terse instructions.

He left the footman still nodding as he strode out to where his tilbury was waiting.

"I shan't need you any further tonight, Beech," he told his groom.

Giving the spanking grey between the shafts the office to start, Nick drove off. He maintained a fast pace even when he reached Covent Garden, which was as usual crowded with strollers of all descriptions. Beyond the piazza, his surroundings became less salubrious, and his anxious frown deepened.

If Lord Verlaine could have but known it, Athena shared the same apprehension as her hackney threaded its way through the narrow, twisty streets. The entire area seemed composed of decaying hovels interspersed with mean little taverns. The darkness was lit here and there by flares and the light coming from the buildings, and she could see that the inhabitants were mostly ill-clad.

"I should not have come," she whispered in dismay as the hackney turned into a narrow alley.

It drew to a halt before the only prosperous-looking house.

"Here we are, miss." Disapproval was evident in the jarvey's voice.

Athena remained seated, her fingers nervously pleating her skirts. Dared she go in there alone? If she had known that the money-lender lived in such squalid surroundings she would have waited until she could have persuaded Connor to escort her.

"Are you getting out or what, miss? I can't wait here all night."

His impatience acted as a spur, curing Athena's hesitation. "Perhaps not, but you can at least wait until I have concluded my business," she retorted briskly, jumping down. She flipped him a coin. "Here, take this on account and don't worry—I shall pay you handsomely for your trouble."

He grunted, but Athena ignored him and rapped smartly upon the door. After a long interval it was opened a crack by an old dame dressed in black.

"I wish to see Mr. Mendoza," Athena said with a calmness she was far from feeling. "Here is my card."

The sharp eyes surveyed her, taking in her plain but obviously expensive apparel. "Come in." Grudgingly the woman opened the door a further few inches, allowing Athena to pass inside.

"He don't like to do business 'cepting for special clients," the old woman grumbled.

Athena slipped a coin into her hand. "Please!"

"Wait here. I'll go and ask if he will see you."

The hallway was bare and chilly and Athena's nervousness increased. She had the sensation that she was being watched, although she could see no one, and the minutes stretched out endlessly before the servant returned.

"He says you must come back tomorrow," she announced.

The old woman moved to open the door and Athena's flicker of amusement vanished.

"Wait! My business is urgent. I must see Mr. Mendoza tonight."

"Tomorrow," said the custodian inexorably.

"But I shall not be able to get away!"

"Suit yourself." She shrugged indifferently and began to bundle Athena out of the door.

It slammed shut in Athena's face, leaving her gasping with indignation.

Her indignation turned to dismay when she realised that her hackney had disappeared. She looked quickly up and down the length of the street but there was no sign of it.

Gritting her teeth, she began to walk rapidly, hoping that she could remember the way out of this maze of back streets. Hopefully she would be able to find another vehicle once she got nearer to Covent Garden.

She hadn't gone a hundred yards when she realised that she was being followed. Her heart began to pound and she quickened her steps.

"Hey, not so fast, little lady. Me and Tom here would like to talk to you."

Athena swallowed hard. There were two of them, both scrawny and dressed in dirty rags with mufflers round their necks. She thought that they were probably rather younger than she was herself, but they looked tough, particularly the speaker, a blue-jowled individual with greasy hair.

"Get out of my way," she snapped.

"Hoity-toity, ain't she, Tom?" An unpleasant smile twisted his mouth. "C'mon, hand over your purse."

"No!" Furiously, Athena knocked aside his searching hand. "Leave me alone, you little rat."

"You'll be sorry for that," her assailant muttered, trying to grab her.

Athena screamed at the top of her lungs. At the same time she kicked him hard in the shins.

Her determined resistance startled them and for an instant they hung back.

Athena seized the chance and took to her heels.

"After her!"

Knowing she could not lose them on their home ground, Athena did not try to dodge and hide in one of the alleyways but ran straight on. She cast a glance over her shoulder. They were gaining on her. Hampered by her skirts, she couldn't outrun them.

A sob of fright escaped her as her foot slipped on a piece of decaying cabbage. Her balance lost, she tumbled to her knees.

"Got you!"

There was a hissing sound and the bully's cry of triumph was abruptly cut off.

Gasping for breath, Athena watched him lift a dazed hand to his cheek and bring it away covered in blood.

The horsewhip sang swiftly through the air again, a deadly black snake in the hand of the tall man surveying them through narrowed eyes. It landed with a

malevolent hiss, slicing open the second thief's bare
arm. He gave a yell of pain and jumped backwards.

"C'mon!" He grabbed his friend, who was still
standing in a stunned daze, and they turned tail.

The sound of their running feet faded and Athena
looked up. So deep was her terror that she hadn't even
heard the carriage draw up but now she recognised her
rescuer as he leapt down to haul her ungently to her
feet.

"Nick!"

He ignored her whisper of amazement and threw
her up into the tilbury. "That pretty pair might have
friends," he said tersely as he sprang up after her and
set the grey in motion.

Soon the dingy streets were left behind and, her fear
receding, Athena became aware of what a sight she
must look. She had lost her bonnet and her pelisse was
streaked with filth. Her hands shook as she lifted them
to tidy her disordered hair and she saw that they were
dirty too.

"This isn't the way back to Cavendish Square.
Where are you taking me?" she asked a moment later,
breaking the silence.

"To my sister's." He glanced at her and smiled
suddenly. "Don't look so worried. Verena is never
shocked."

Athena's spirits soared. At last he was the man she
had known in Parkgate and not some distant stranger.

Mrs. Gresham lived in a pretty little house in Strat-
on Street. To Nick's relief all the lights were shining
when they arrived.

He handed Athena the reins. "Let me have a quick
word with her before I take you in," he said.

The grey was too well schooled to require Athena's
attention and her imagination ran riot during the few
moments Nick was absent but she tried to appear calm
as she allowed him to hand her down.

"My poor dear!" Verena Gresham's sympathetic smile enfolded her. "Would you like to come with me and wash your hands while they make you some tea? I have ordered it to be served in the front parlour. Nick can wait for you there."

Athena nodded shyly. She followed her hostess, who was amazingly like her brother with the same dark hair and eyes, up the narrow staircase to what was obviously a spare bedroom.

Mrs. Gresham intercepted the ewer of hot water at the door and Athena was grateful for her tact.

"There is not much we can do about your pelisse, I'm afraid, but at least your dress is only stained about the hem," she remarked as Athena removed the offending mantle. "Now, would you like me to help you with your hair?"

Athena accepted gratefully. Her hands were still unsteady.

Verena Gresham's dark eyes brimmed with curiosity, but, mindful of her brother's request, she restrained the questions that were burning her tongue as she rearranged Athena's curls into a semblance of order.

"There, I think you'll do," she said in an encouraging tone. "We had better go down before Nick frets himself to flinders."

At the door to the parlour Mrs. Gresham halted. "I won't come in with you. I'm sure you will wish to discuss matters with my brother in private."

Feeling rather like a Christian martyr about to be thrown to the lions, Athena walked into the parlour.

Nick was standing staring into the fire but he turned swiftly at her entrance. A few quick strides and he had crossed the room to her side.

"You little fool!" he said thickly, taking her into his arms.

Athena clung to him. "Oh, Nick! Nick!"

Her lips parted as his mouth caressed hers with searing passion. Their breath mingled and as their tongues touched Athena felt a flame of pleasure igniting that strange liquid heat in the pit of her stomach. It was the same dizzying flood of desire that had swept over her the very first time he had taken her in his arms and she knew she never wanted to let him go.

"I like it when you kiss me," she whispered huskily when at last he lifted his dark head.

"Good, because I intend to do so frequently, you adorable minx!" Nick replied, his dark eyes lighting with tender laughter.

She blushed and he tightened his arms around her.

"Oh, sweetheart, what a fright you gave me! What on earth possessed you to go to such a disreputable place?"

His question restored Athena to sanity. She pulled away from him. "How did you know where I had gone?" she countered warily.

Nick shrugged. "I ordered Lady Fitzpatrick's footman to hand over your letter."

Athena gasped but before she could say a word he calmly swung her up into his arms and carried her over to the sofa by the fire, where he sat down, keeping her firmly on his knee.

"Now listen to me, you beautiful goose, I had to follow you. How else was I to apologise?"

Deciding it would be undignified to struggle, Athena sat still but she eyed him dubiously. "Apologise?"

"For my ridiculous behaviour during dinner." Nick shook his head and sighed. "You'll never know how difficult it was to ignore you but I was determined to show you that I no longer cared. The moment I saw you again I knew it was no use but my curst pride wouldn't allow me to admit it."

He fell silent, remembering how his conscience had smote him at the sight of her little wan face as she had made her excuses to the company before saying good night. She had tried so hard to appear composed but her eyes had betrayed her.

Their stricken expression had haunted him, making him cut short his entertainment and return to Cavendish Square, intending to have it out with her once and for all. But she had vanished and the circumstances in which he had next found her had driven every thought of recrimination out of his head. She could have been seriously hurt, killed!

The shock had brought home to him just how much he needed her. Their disastrous quarrel no longer mattered. Nothing mattered except the fact that he loved her.

Nick swallowed hard, trying to summon the courage to risk putting his fate to the touch. Did her wonderfully responsive kiss mean what he hoped or would she spurn him once more?

Before he could decide Athena said softly, "I thought you might be going to apologise for trying to stop me buying the White Bear."

It was very strange but somehow it no longer seemed important—still, she was curious. "Was it revenge, Nick?"

"Of course not!" His indignant glare faded. "I was trying to stop you making a social outcast of yourself. It seemed to me that you would be unhappy once the novelty had worn off but by then it would be too late."

"Why should you care if I ruined my life?" Athena whispered, unable to meet his gaze.

"Because I love you," he said simply. "I told you once before and you would not believe me, but it is true. I have tried to forget you but I can't."

How could he explain that she had given his life new meaning? When he was with her his restlessness dissolved and he was happier than he had been in years.

His arms tightened around her waist. "You are a fever in my blood and I shall never be cured, my darling, unless you marry me."

Athena threw her arms around his neck and hugged him fiercely. Her throat felt suddenly tight and for an instant she thought she might cry. "Oh, Nick, you don't know how I have longed to hear you say you still cared," she murmured.

She gazed wonderingly into his eyes and saw her own love reflected there.

"My beautiful girl." Nick traced his forefinger gently down her cheek to touch her mouth with a butterfly lightness but when he would have kissed her Athena drew back.

"First, you deserve to know the truth," she said, steeling herself. "I went to that dreadful place intending to borrow money so that I could outbid your offer."

"Did I make you that angry?"

To her relief he was gazing at her with a rueful smile.

"You aren't disgusted by my behaviour?"

"Sweetheart, if I wanted some conventional little ninny ready to agree with my every word, then I should settle for someone like your pretty Cathleen."

For an instant, jealousy darkened Athena's sapphire eyes but it faded as he continued. "But I don't. want you. You, my love, with your funny notions of independence and outrageous ideas. Just you, that's all I need to make me happy."

"I don't think I do want to be independent any more," Athena admitted candidly, her hand sliding of its own volition to twine itself into his hair. "Not if it is at the cost of love. I've learnt that lesson at least."

Nick grinned. He wondered how long this mood of humility would last. Not that he cared. Marriage with Athena might bring its own problems, but it would never be boring!

"You haven't answered my other question, you know," he reminded her. "Will you marry me, my dear Miss Delaney?"

"I should be honoured, my lord," she replied gravely, but her eyes sparkled with laughter.

"I adore you!"

His lips took passionate possession of hers and Athena's laughter died. Her heart raced and she felt a surge of overwhelming desire tingling in every nerve. Pressing herself even closer to him, she kissed him back with a wanton fervour that left them both breathless.

"I didn't know it was possible to feel so happy," she murmured when the long intoxicating kiss was over.

He smiled at her but before he could speak the ormolu clock on Mrs. Gresham's marble mantelpiece chimed the hour.

Athena started up in alarm. "Nick, look at the time! What will they be thinking in Cavendish Square?"

Lord Verlaine pulled her firmly back down on to his lap.

"If they have returned, which I beg leave to doubt, I hope your godmother's footman will have the sense to relay the message I left for her."

"She might not feel so anxious if she knows I am with you," Athena admitted.

"Your godmother is a woman of the world. I mentioned that I hoped to start a new life on my country estate and she thinks you will make me an admirable chatelaine."

This remark made Athena survey him narrowly. "Why did you not tell me that you were a rich man?"

"I wasn't until my uncle died," he answered mildly.

"But you had sufficient for your needs?" she persisted.

"It seemed tactless to mention it."

"So I let my prejudice trick me into thinking you must be penniless," she said ruefully, and then suddenly realised something else. "You told my aunt that you wanted to marry me?"

"I did hint at it," he confessed. "It seemed a good way to enlist her aid." He grinned at her. "She's right, you know, sweetheart. I can't imagine any one more suited to restoring old Uncle Nathan's property to order."

"I see. You are marrying me for my housekeeping skills," Athena retorted.

He shook his head. "Actually, I had your other talents in mind."

She eyed him quizzically. "Such as?"

"This...and this, my love," he whispered tenderly, drawing her close to him.

Athena surrendered willingly to his kiss, a deep joy filling her.

Life with Nick might not be easy but together they would weather the storms. He was the calm beyond the reef, the safe haven she had always longed for. She had come home.

WHO SAYS THE PAST IS OLD NEWS?

Harlequin Regency Romance is bringing the past to life with six exciting new books!

June marks the publication of our 100th title and an all-new concept. The REGENCY QUARTET brings you a collection of stories by well-known British authors, offering you hours of big-book enjoyment. And you'll be sure to fall in love with a simply divine comedy, A MATCH MADE IN HEAVEN, by reader favorite Jeanne Carmichael. And don't miss the latest from popular author Barbara Neil—GENTLEMAN ROGUE.

Feel the heat in July and August with sizzling Regency romances by Barbara Neil, Elizabeth Michaels, Winifred Witton and Brenda Hiatt.

Join us this summer and find out what's new!

Look for Harlequin Regency Romance wherever Harlequin books are sold.

RGF

Harlequin is proud to present our
best authors and their best books.
Always the best for your reading
pleasure!

Throughout 1993, Harlequin will bring you
exciting books by some of the top names in
contemporary romance!

In July
look for
The Ties That Bind by

Shannon wanted him seven days a week. . . .

Dark, compelling, mysterious Garth Sheridan was no
mere boy next door—even if he did rent the cottage
beside Shannon Raine's.

She was intrigued by the hard-nosed exec, but for
Shannon it was all or nothing. Either break the
undeniable bonds between them . . . or tear down the
barriers surrounding Garth and discover the truth.

Don't miss THE TIES THAT BIND . . .
wherever Harlequin books are sold.

BOB3

Relive the romance...
Harlequin and Silhouette are proud to present

by *Request*™

A program of collections of three complete novels by the most requested authors with the most requested themes. Be sure to look for one volume each month with three complete novels by top name authors.

In June: **NINE MONTHS** Penny Jordan
Stella Cameron
Janice Kaiser

Three women pregnant and alone. But a lot can happen in nine months!

In July: **DADDY'S HOME** Kristin James
Naomi Horton
Mary Lynn Baxter

Daddy's Home ... and his presence is long overdue!

In August: **FORGOTTEN PAST** Barbara Kaye
Pamela Browning
Nancy Martin

Do you dare to create a future if you've forgotten the past?

Available at your favorite retail outlet.